les

Mike

ANGEL'S RAINBOW

MICHAEL HALEY

First Published in Great Britain 2017 by Mirador Publishing

First edition: 2017

Any reference to real names and places are purely fictional and are constructs of the author. Any offence the references produce is unintentional and in no way reflects the reality of any locations or people involved.

A copy of this work is available through the British Library.

ISBN: 978-1-912192-44-1

Mirador Publishing
10 Greenbrook Terrace
Taunton
Somerset
TA1 1UT
UK

Angel's Rainbow

It's about Life and Death

It's about Heaven and Earth

It's about Time and Space

It's about Truth and Faith

It's about Tragedy and Salvation

It's about Reality and Magic

It's about the Beginning and the End

It's about History and the Here and Now

It's about the Past, the Present, and the Future

It's about Ordinary people and Famous people

It's about Rights and Wrongs

It's about You and Me

It's about Angels

It's not about Religion

Angel's Rainbow

"Take a deep breath.
Look around you.
It's a beautiful world if you let it be."

"Take your time. Live your life at a stroll not a sprint."

"Look! Listen! Learn!"

"So let's just walk a way together while we can,
and not head off to our separate heavens never holding hands."

"On a wing and a prayer; searching here, searching there,
Turning over, turning over, only turning over stones."

"The horizon is not at the end of your nose,
Or the tips of your fingers, or tips of your toes,
The horizon is set at the end of a rainbow. "

"It's only one small step, just another grain of sand,
From Once upon a Time, to Never-Never Land."

"Each life is just another song,
A rhythm and a melody, some words you sing in harmony."

"Night fell so heavily.
It fell for me like it had never fallen before.
One second I was reaching for something in my pocket,
and the next all there was around me was darkness."

"Tell me more about this beautiful graceful naivety."

"Well, the easiest way to look at it is by regarding yourself as a beginner.

A beginner is just starting to learn how to do something.

If we use the letters of the word "begin" to remind us, we get:

B for beautiful, E for enlightened, G for graceful, I for intelligent, and N for naivety.

Keep that in mind, and you will begin to understand."

"Why isn't it obvious, Michael?

You are stardust, the essence of the Universe

that fills the void and gives meaning to all life."

"Time does not work in the same way here in Heaven

as it does in the Earthly Realm."

"Here in Heaven we have time without end

and we have no time at all."

Foreword

I owe the existence of this novel to my very good friends, past and present, at the White Horse Writing Group and the Maldon Writer's Group. These groups are follow-ons from 2 separate Creative Writing Courses. I attended an adult education course which finished in April, 2012 and some of the attendees then formed the White Horse Writing Group. We meet once a month at the White Horse public house in Mundon, near Maldon, Essex.

Sometime later, I joined the Maldon Writer's Group which meets once a month at the Blue Boar Hotel in Maldon.

At both the meetings, we read pieces we have written; usually stories or poems, and occasionally I play guitar and sing new songs that I or other members of the group have written the lyrics for.

The raison d'être of both the groups is to listen, critique positively and then encourage each other to produce good writing.

The seeds of an idea for writing "Angel's Rainbow" were sown at these meetings and were then nurtured during a period of time lasting nearly 5 years. You could therefore say that the novel is living proof that from small acorns mighty oaks do grow.

Here is how it came together.

On 3rd December, 2012 I wrote a short story called "Angel's Holiday" after the homework from a November meeting had been set to write something called "Holiday".

Similarly, when homework was set in November, 2014 to write something with a Christmas theme, I wrote another story between 24th December, 2014 and 5th January, 2015 called "Angel's Mission".

Homework for January 2015 asked for a story titled "A Star in my Pocket", and I then wrote a piece between 31st January, 2015 and 23rd February, 2016.

I had no inkling when these 3 short stories were written that they would all eventually be part of the same novel.

"Angel's Holiday" and "Angel's Mission" bore some similarities in terms of the characters involved and the essence of the stories. The plot for "A Star in my Pocket" had elements of something mystical and philosophical, and a possible link to aspects of heavenly beings.

It took a while for the penny to drop.

When the concept of a novel finally fell into my lap probably in March 2016, I decided to write the project in 3 discrete books.

Book 1 would be in the 3rd person and would illustrate the life of someone called Michael Hartson, a financial whiz kid living in London in the present time. The Short story, "A Star in my Pocket" became Chapter 1 of this book, which eventually grew to 11 chapters.

Book 2 would be in the 1st person seen from Michael's point of view after his arrival in Heaven. In the fullness of time "Angel's Holiday" became Chapter 4, and "Angel's Mission" became Chapter 7 of this book. The finished book has 9 chapters.

Book 3 would revert to the 3rd person to provide a satisfying conclusion in one chapter by describing a heavenly celebration of Michael's achievements.

I set myself a task to finish the first drafts of each chapter by December 2016, and I almost succeeded with this by setting myself monthly deadlines.

Then I brought the chapters and books together for series of massive editing sessions lasting 5 months. That is where, hopefully, I weeded out spelling, context and punctuation problems, before attacking consistency and continuity issues. I am indebted to Nicole Gay for her invaluable help in proof reading and correcting my often inconsistent punctuation.

So here is "Angel's Rainbow", a novel with many differences to a standard approach and a story well worth reading…

Although there is plentiful mention of religious themes, perhaps with more than a fleeting Christian slant, I think the story may be irreligious, in that there is little adherence to established theological doctrines. Perhaps the tale I am telling just illustrates another alternative way of addressing important questions of life and death. In the final analysis, I would most of all like you to read carefully and leave the book having experienced a feel good factor.

Throughout the novel, I make great contextual usage of poems and lyrics to songs that I have written. The lyrics are assembled in an appendix, and the songs have been recorded, and are available on a compilation CD album also called "Angel's Rainbow".

If you like what you read in "Angel's Rainbow", then you can find out more about me, my poems, songs and other novels I have written by having a browse through my website, "redberryash.co.uk".

You can also contact me at my email address: info@redberryash.co.uk

Book One

The Earthly Realm

The Time is Now

Chapter 1

Opportunity too good to miss

The maze of busy city streets groaned under the late May sunshine, laying like the oppressive weight of an electric blanket over the City. At the up and down extremities, dizzy high perfect blue skies were complemented by oven ready pavements like hotplates in a burger bar. The plate glass frontages of the tall buildings stood like huge radiators. Car bonnets were near blistering in temperatures hot enough to fry rump steaks. The metropolis was a turmoil of sweat and toil, noise and bravado; angry streets full of people too busy and too hot to focus on anything but themselves. On this uncomfortably hot late May day, nobody wanted to walk on the sunny side of the street.

Mike Hartson meandered back homewards from his office at Connor, Hartson and Bromberger Futures in the City's financial heartland. His apartment was 2 tube stops away, but today of all days he wanted to avoid the black hole of Calcutta that was the London Underground. He could have hailed a cab, but for the third time in a year one of the utility companies was busy digging up a section of roads around the area where he lived. He didn't care if it was water, gas, electricity or fibre-optics; it was just another bloody inconvenience.

In the late afternoon there had been no let up in the heat, and as he arrived back at his 7th floor luxury apartment he was relieved at having successfully scurried back to his own air-conditioned, protected bolthole. Here it was spacious, open, cool and comfortable. This was his territory, Hartson country; untouched by the parasitic toxins of external influences. It was just the way he wanted it - ultra-modern, all hard, clinically clean surfaces, top of the range furniture and fittings, no frills, no ornaments to gather dust; his world, impregnable and sterile. Every weekday his "daily", the super-efficient Audrey Bairstow, made sure of that when she cleaned and sterilised the place from top to bottom.

He flicked the Bose sound bar on, selected Mahler's 5th symphony, and quickly discarded his sweat and work stained clothing into Friday's dry cleaning bag, ready for collection by Audrey in the morning. He enjoyed a quick shower with the temperature set just on the edge of cool, washing away the discomfort of the walk home, and the mental stresses of the working day. Refreshed, he dressed light and casually in a Hollister t-shirt and Armani chinos adorned by his favourite designer labels, and made coffee. Blue Mountain Arabica coffee beans from Jamaica were his elixir of the day, just as Ramey 2008 Chardonnay was his evening ambrosia. Mike didn't comprehend how the world could function without a quality coffee to stimulate the brain cells and a fine wine to titillate and excite the taste buds.

He liked to separate his life into boxes. To him, there was company-time and me-time. Now he was on me-time. While at work, he focussed totally on his business with no distractions, and as a result he was efficient, successful and sometimes bordering on the edge of utterly ruthless. When he came home he could flick a switch and deal with his personal life completely separately. If anything was going to change that, even temporarily, it would have to be a seismic shift, something world shatteringly important. He attended to his mail, his email, and his mobile messages as Mahler's 3rd movement, Scherzo in D-major, wafted out of the hi-fi system. Then the financial pirate enjoyed the prawn and avocado sourdough club sandwich Audrey had left for him in the fridge.

The iPhone rang and he picked it up with a smile knowing who it would be without looking at the screen.

"Hi, Taylor, how's it going you old untouchable?"

"Great, Mike. Fucking hot, isn't it?"

"Yes it is for the plebs outside, but I'm sitting here in my cool threads with the air-con on full blast, and all the cares of the day washed away. Where are you?"

"Still at work finishing off some last minute jobs. It's been a hell of a day in the financial markets. We've made a few major killings today."

"Christ, mate, you need a better work/life balance. I knocked it on the head over an hour ago, and I bet we made more than you today."

"That may be so, but you don't have a wife that thinks that Harvey Nicholls is her personal boutique, and three fast growing juvenile delinquent sprogs at private schools to accommodate."

"Too busy looking after number one, that's me all over." Mike chuckled.

Taylor Brandon and Mike were old friends; had worked together a few years ago, and sometimes they met on Friday evenings to talk football and women and old times. The Untouchables was the nickname Mike gave to the company that Taylor worked for, because as financial rivals they always seemed to make bigger killings than any other firm in the market. There was always the suspicion of a potentially shady element to some of their dealings. But Mike had always attempted to remain squeaky clean, and avoid controversial transactions. Where there were big bucks to be made he couldn't say that sometimes he hadn't been tempted.

"Anyway, mate," Taylor continued, "I was talking to Sir Eric McClintock earlier. You know him, don't you?"

Mike hesitated. Sir Eric was the senior partner in Taylor's firm, nicknamed Maverick Mack in the trade, and everybody knew two things about him. Number one was that if there was shady deal going down, Eric would be somehow involved in it. Number two was that he was head untouchable, the big cheese who never, ever got caught red-handed. A more slippery sod never graced the city dealing platforms, but when it came to filling coffers full of loot, there was no equal.

"Yeah!" said Mike, after his pause for thought, "He's an old school super brat, but knows how to broker a good deal. What about it?"

"Well, we've got some business we could put your way. It's top secret and only just this side of legal. Could make a magic mountain of gold for both of our outfits. It involves the Iraqis and Saudis in a major oil deal. Interested?"

Mike needed a fleeting second thought, the temptation was too much, and this time, just this once, the lure of a lucrative business arrangement turned him on. "Are you kidding?" he answered, "Course I am."

"Only one problem, mate; we've got to act quickly to set this up and cash in on the deal. It's like; now or never. Can you meet me and Eric at the Captain's Table in Churchill Avenue at 7 sharp?"

"Shit! That's cutting it a bit fine, but if it's going to be big I'd be daft to turn down the opportunity. Tell me, mate, why is it in the Captain's, and not at the office?"

"Ah, well, it's like I said, just this side of legal. You know how Eric likes to cover his arse. Going off piste is his way to avoid suspicions."

Mike laughed, "Maverick Mack didn't get where he was by not bending the rules a little here and there."

"It's up to you, mate. Be there on the dot at 7 and we'll be meeting 2 bigwigs from the States lined up to discuss the ins and outs. Be 2 minutes late and you've maybe missed the boat. It's going to be Eric's way or no way. Hate to see you dropping a clanger."

"OK, I'm on my way. But I'm dressed casual; is that alright?"

"Sure thing, mate, good cover, just be there."

Mike grabbed his wallet and keys, put the iPhone in his pocket, and made swiftly for the door. As he moved to the lift shaft, his mobile rang again. It was Courtney, his very latest and for him uncharacteristically long term squeeze.

"Shit! She's coming over at 9." he thought.

He didn't know if he would be back home by then, but after a few moments deliberation he decided to risk it and not to answer the call.

Courtney left a text message, "Hi Mike, have the wine nicely chilled and me nicely warmed up later. x C"

There were just 25 minutes to get to the meeting, and he didn't reply. He had itchy feet waiting for the lift to arrive, and when at last it swept into view, for some annoying reason it went up rather than down. Two minutes later he marched impatiently and with focussed determination across the entrance hall only to be confronted by Charlie Evans shaking his walking stick as if he was waving Mike down. Charlie was the very correct and always polite chairperson of the apartment block's management company.

"Mr Hartson, how are you?"

Charlie's grey wrinkled features displayed a man prematurely aged by city living, pollution, stress and solitary existence.

"OK, Mr Evans."

"Can I remind you that we have a meeting with the freeholders next Thursday to discuss the annual maintenance and cleaning contract?"

"Yes. I got the note you put through the door. I will be there Mr Evans."

"I'm glad to hear that Mr Hartson, but can I just run something past you?"

"I'm sorry, but I'm in a bit of a hurry. Can it wait 'til Thursday?"

The wheels turned excruciatingly slowly as Charlie deliberated, and then he smiled and answered politely, "I suppose so; sorry to delay you Mr Hartson."

Mike smiled, gave a cursory wave and stepped out into the sweltering evening air. He moved thankfully onto the shady pavement and attempted to hail a taxi. He glanced at his TAG Heuer Aquaracer watch and thought, "That's already 5 minutes wasted."

It was the third attempt at attracting a cabbie's attention that brought the desired result. The passenger climbed in saying "Captain's Table, Churchill Avenue, quickly please!"

"Do me very best guv'nor." said the cabbie.

The black cab weaved this way and that through the maze of streets with their flow disrupted by the road works for the water company. Then progress was abruptly halted by a temporary traffic light which seemed to stay on red for far too long. It took 4 sequences of light changes before the cab moved again with any purpose. Three, four, five, six more changes of direction left and right, and then progress again ground to a full stop.

"There's been an accident up ahead I think," said the driver," I'd turn around, but we're in a one way street. Just have to sit it out. Sorry!"

Mike quickly glanced out of the window and recognised where they were. He jumped out, threw the cabbie a tenner, and began to run. Twenty yards away was the entrance to the City oasis of Blenheim Circus Park, and he knew that if he jogged swiftly through from one end to the other, he'd be just around the corner from his destination.

He glanced at his watch again and muttered, "9 minutes. I can still get there!"

He raced through the black wrought iron gates at the entrance to the park, pounding along the terracotta coloured tarmac, fringed by the early summer flowerbeds, blooming luxuriously with peonies, primula and clematis in neatly arranged bursts of a myriad of colours. The agitated jogger didn't see them. He didn't see the splendid display of huge blue and pink blooms on the azalea and rhododendron shrubs. He didn't see the happy couples strolling in the shady boughs making for the bandstand. He didn't hear Dave Wilson's Dixieland Warblers improvising their way through another jazz classic. Then he realised he had a lace undone on his Dolce and Gabbana trainers. He flopped quickly down on a park bench to do up the lace, not noticing at first that he had sat next to what looked like pile of dirty clothes. A weather-beaten and grimy face stared at him, showing yellow teeth in a slimy smile.

"Spare us a couple of quid for a cup of tea, guv'nor?" pleaded the vagrant.

Mike got up quickly, and as he resumed his jog he hurled back, "Fuck off, you idle, dirty bastard!"

The semi-circle path through the park continued, passing the beautifully constructed duck pond where the inhabitants were quacking their way through the evening in delighted playful reverie. Soon the ice-cream van was in his sight, and he knew that just after it, around the back of a small parade of lime trees, the path met the other black wrought iron gate that would be his exit to Churchill Avenue and a well earned cold beer in the Captain's Table tavern. The cool shade of the limes was most welcome, as was the relief from the brightness of the light. But what was this?

"Oh No! No! No!" he screamed out loud, "The fucking gate's been locked."

He rattled the bars of his imprisonment in exasperation as if it would do some good, and seriously considered climbing over the top. The barrier to his quest was fringed all around the edge of the park by a metal fence; 7 feet tall and topped with arrow-like spikes. There was no way he could get through or over without the risk of injury. His heart sank as he turned around and jogged back, faster, more furiously. He had 5 minutes to get there, and there was no chance. He would have to make an alternative route through the streets.

Many questions filled his thoughts, "Would it matter if I was a little late? How late would I be if I went back to the entrance and followed the road around the park? Can I make it by 10 past? Would Eric and Taylor wait?"

Chapter 2

A Star in my Pocket

Michael was back through the limes, past the ice-cream van, and alongside the duck pond in Usain Bolt record breaking time. After the jazz band struck up with "Meet me in St Louis", and before he had noticed his trainer lace was undone again, he tripped up and fell heavily to the floor, grazing his right knee and bumping his head on an inconveniently placed rubbish bin.

"Fuck! Fuck! Fuck!" he squealed. He had ripped the knee of his best Armani chinos and the errant trainer had flown off into a flower bed. He sat for a moment and collected his breath. Another look at the watch revealed it was now almost 7 o'clock.

On the adjacent bench, there was a repeat appearance of the yellow toothed, grinning vagrant, seeming to ridicule the jogger's obvious plight. Mike picked himself up, retrieved the trainer, retied the lace, and resumed his jog while shouting back "What the fuck are you laughing at, you useless, ugly, idle lump of shite?"

He reached the entrance gate puffing hard, and as he turned back on to the roadside, something told him to check his pockets. A cold sweat ran over him from brow to knees as he realised his Alexander McQueen wallet was missing.

"Oh shit! That's it!" he thought, knowing he'd have to turn back and look for it, "Now I'm truly fucked up. That's the chance of the big deal gone up in smoke. I give up!"

His shoulders dropped. He sighed, and suddenly realised just how exhausted he had managed to make himself. His mind still raced as his heart rate slowed while he mentally retraced his steps. He needed time to gather his thoughts. When he began to think more lucidly, he quickly came to the conclusion that he must have dropped his wallet when he tripped over his laces. He turned on his heels, walking briskly, checking the edges of the path as he went, and soon he was back next to the rubbish bin where he had fallen over and banged his head. He scanned around with a heavy heart, but his search was fruitless. He sat down on the nearby bench, holding his head low in both hands; his distress preventing him from noticing that the tramp he had abused twice in the previous 15 minutes, was still there.

Dave Wilson's jazz band was in full swing with a rendition of "Sweet Georgia Brown", and the happy bustle of activity with people streaming through the park continued as if he didn't matter because he didn't exist.

"It's a lovely evening." said the tramp gazing upwards at the sky.

Mike ignored him, thinking that he didn't want to talk to the lowlife.

"Look at the perfect blue heavens." the vagrant persisted.

Still there was no response.

"This park is surely a beautiful place, look at the flowers, the colours, the couples holding hands and smiling. There is so much joy here."

The whiz kid at the opposite end of the bench was too exhausted to move, too enmeshed in his own distress to want to respond, too good to converse with the heap of shit for a man sitting uncomfortably too close to him.

"The jazz band are really excellent, uplifting, makes you feel good to be alive." said the tramp smiling.

Then there was a response, "Why don't you shut your fucking dirty, ugly, mouth? You utterly useless pile of dog's vomit!"

Unphased by the abuse, the tramp turned towards Mike showing his old and all knowing brown eyes, set deep in a worn and wrinkled face, beneath a weather stained cap. He stared at Mike in a long, sustained smile of broken teeth and cracked lips.

Mike turned slowly, reluctantly; ready to hurl more abuse in response to the invasive insistence of his park bench neighbour. He lifted his head as he turned, seeming to clamber his way out of his turmoil, but ready to generate more anger. Now he focussed on his antagonist. There was a strange, imperceptible aura about him; a kind of dim, but at the same time exceeding bright light surrounding his dishevelled and dirty appearance. A black light!

The smile persisted as the City that surrounded the two men seemed to stop and take a deep breath. Eyes met across the bench as Father Time took that breather, and then a leathery, wizened hand was extended with the words "Is this what you are looking for, my friend?"

There in the ancient hand was the expensive wallet. Mike grabbed it quickly, and with the first thought, "You stole that, you dirty, thieving bastard."

It was only a thought, but as if by some kind of magic there was a soft reply, not spoken, but directly in his brainwaves, "If had stolen your wallet, my friend, then why would I be giving it back to you now?"

The recipient checked the contents of the wallet. Nothing missing, everything in its place. A tsunami of relief washed over him. For the first time in a long stream of tense minutes, he relaxed and felt totally at ease. There was a protracted silence from both men, as the happy hubbub of city and park life continued around them.

After many minutes Mike said "Thank You!" to the tramp, and offered a £10 note. There was that now familiar smile as the delighted vagrant accepted the gift. Then the donor got up to go.

A quiet request followed, "Don't go yet, my friend. I'd like to have a little chat with you."

He was in two minds, but something pulled Mike back down to the bench. He felt a gentle, persuasive compulsion to stay put. Then the tramp spoke slowly, and with deliberation, in short sentences in a soft, velvet smooth, enchanting voice.

"Take a deep breath.
Look around you.
It's a beautiful world if you let it be.
Enjoy the warm sunshine.
Drink in the blue sky.
Smell the flowers.
Delight in their colours.
See the happiness of people together.
Listen to the birds singing and the ducks quacking.
Hear the music.
Feel the satisfaction in the blend of music and words.
Take your time.
Live your life at a stroll not a sprint. "

It was haunting. There was no need to respond. He remained silent as if he were being supplied with something very important. After a minute or two the orator continued.

"You have been in a hurry, not just this evening, but all of your life.
Learn a lesson today.
You thought you needed to be somewhere at 7 o'clock, and you failed to get there in time. Am I right?"

Nods of agreement were exchanged. A pause followed.

"You will be glad that you failed, my friend.
Sometimes life tells you that you shouldn't go somewhere or do something.
Instinct, a 6th sense, whatever it is, intervenes, and it is seldom wrong.
Sometimes life tells you to go somewhere, or do something, and you don't listen to that little voice. That's when you might get it wrong.
Life is a vast learning curve."

Mike took a deep breath, and thought carefully about the lesson he was receiving. It was simple, it was obvious, but it sounded like a gospel-like lesson.

"How could this dirty, old tramp be so wise, and so eloquent, and so engaging, and so right." he questioned himself.

Another pause followed, and then the subject changed.

"Those trainers; expensive aren't they?"

Mike nodded, "Yes, they are Dolce and Gabbana; they cost me £315.00."

"Hmmm! Look good don't they? But," the tramp took a long breath, "Looking good, and being designed for the purpose of running are not necessarily compatible here, and that's why your laces kept coming undone."

There was another pearl of wisdom coming, and Mike continued to want to listen.

"Appearances are often deceptive.
What looks good may not actually be good."

Two seemingly incompatible men on a Blenheim Circus park bench on a fine May evening exchanged eye to eye looks, and face to face smiles, as somewhat ironically, Dave Wilson's jazz band began to play another classic.

"Summertime and the living is easy....."

Mike laid back, felt the sun on his face, and enjoyed the music.

Sometime later he asked his new comrade, "What's your name?"

The reply came with a confident grin, and the teacher's hand was offered in friendship, "I'm George O'Donnell." The gesture was reciprocated. The pupil noticed that the grip was surprisingly strong for a feeble old man.

"Thank you, my friend." said Mike, getting up to go, and in that moment he realised how much his knee hurt, and his head was thumping from his accident tripping over the laces of his expensive trainers.

"Yes! Go home now, I can smell rain. There's a storm in the air." concluded George.

On the way back to his apartment, Mike sent a text to Courtney, "I'm sorry, sweetheart. I've got a monster of a headache. Can I put you on hold 'til tomorrow lunchtime? See you here at 11, OK? x Mike"

Then he tried to contact Taylor, but there was no reply from his mobile. He left a voicemail apologising for not making the meeting.

Back in the apartment he took another shower, put a bandage around his grazed knee, and went straight to bed exhausted. It was still hot enough for him to want to sleep in the buff, and he was asleep the moment his bruised head landed on the soft pillow.

The rain that George had predicted arrived with a bang at 3 in the morning, rattling the windows, and dropping the temperature enough for Mike to be woken up and to go in search of his Calvin Klein silk pyjamas in the brilliant white lightning flashes. The storm oscillated to and fro overhead for more than an hour, keeping him awake, thinking about where George may have been taking shelter, and then gradually fizzled out into a retreating low and remote rumble at about 5 am.

When finally he woke from his slumbers at about 8 am, he followed his weekend morning routine by switching on the large TV on the wall opposite his bed in order to catch up with the latest news. He caught the tail end of a news item, as a reporter stood glum faced outside the Captain's Table in Churchill Avenue saying, "The 10 hour siege was thankfully brought to an end about 3 hours ago when the SAS moved in and eliminated the Al-Qaeda terrorists. Since just after 7 pm yesterday evening, the Captain's Table patrons have been systematically executed at hourly intervals by 5 Jihadists demanding the release of a selected list of prisoners from Guantanamo Bay, 10 million U.S. dollars, and a safe passage to Afghanistan. Exact details have not yet been ascertained, but what we do know is that at least 20 people have been killed, including the well known financial wizard Sir Eric McClintock, several of his senior staff, and 2 American businessmen. There are also many critical injuries. A government spokesman who asked not be identified said that the tavern was targeted by the terrorists because it was a favourite haunt of many City financial experts. The policy of non negotiation was enforced, but eventually the SAS were sanctioned to enter the tavern to prevent further loss of life."

Mike gulped, truly shaken by the news. His face was ashen white, his hands were trembling, and he felt sick. He wanted to dive back under the duvet and pretend he was having a nightmare. But it was real; the atrocity had really happened!

For the first time in his life since his father had died 5 years ago, he cried. He cried like a child who had been separated from his favourite teddy bear. It was over an hour later when he composed himself sufficiently, and got up out of the refuge of his bed, red-eyed and tear stained. A realisation came over him that he would need to pull himself together because Audrey would be arriving around 10 am. After a bathroom visit and a frugal breakfast, he dressed and sat in front of BBC World News listening over and over again to the coverage of what was by now being labelled the Captain's Table massacre. As he sat there, his mind replayed the events of the previous evening; the phone call from Taylor; the frantic rush to get to his destination; the mounting catalogue of obstacles that prevented him getting there on time, and then the soothing words that he had learned from a dirty, ragged tramp called George.

Wise words echoed continuously in his brain.

"Take your time. Live your life at a stroll not a sprint."
"You have been in a hurry, not just this evening, but all of your life.
Learn a lesson today."
"You thought you needed to be somewhere at 7 o'clock, and you failed to get there in time. You will be glad that you failed, my friend."
"Appearances are often deceptive.
What looks good may not actually be good."

He patted the throbbing lump on the side of his head, picked up his wallet from the coffee table, and had the compulsive need to inspect it as if he had never seen it before. It looked and felt somehow different. He opened it and examined the contents.

£100 in cash, his 2 credit cards, and the current account debit card, his driving licence, a small photo of Courtney; it was all there. But, there was something in the zip portion of the wallet that he hadn't seen before. It was a small purple velvety piece of fabric in the shape of a 6-pointed star upon which was written in gold script "Look! Listen! Learn!" with the initials "G O'D" underneath. He placed the star on the coffee table and just stared at it.

There was that echo again.

"You thought you needed to be somewhere at 7 o'clock, and you failed to get there in time. You will be glad that you failed, my friend."

Michael shuddered. His blood ran cold. How? How was it possible?

Time seemed to stand still, and then he heard Audrey coming in through the door with her usual cheery, "Good morning Michael. How are you today?"

But as she entered the room, her countenance changed completely.

"My God! Have you heard the news?"

Chapter 3

Devils in disguise

Sophie squeezed her way along the ancient grey brick wall, between the solid wooden garden tables shaded by huge red Fuller's Pride parasols, apologising to the gaggle of early evening drinkers. She was attending to her pride and joy; her hanging baskets. This was her important watering routine for around 7 o'clock on summer evenings at the Captain's Table, and she always stuck to it religiously.

Job done, she stood back admiring her beer garden. She was the landlady, the boss, and this was her territory. She could feel an immense satisfaction in the way the regular pattern of greying bricks and discoloured yellowing mortar of the wall contrasted perfectly with the natural cascading of the myriad of colours falling from the huge hanging baskets. The luscious colours of pink, red and blue fuchsia and begonia fell in their transient delicacy; a blaze of passionate embrace against the steadfast solidarity of the 8 foot high 300 year old brick wall. The wall, allegedly built soon after the Great Fire of London, always gave Sophie a comforting sense of security.

The exceptional late May blistering hot weather would bring in a flood of extra imbibers ready to rinse away their dehydration, cancel out the trials of the working day, and refresh their taste buds with something more pleasant than traffic fumes. In the distance there were faint reverberations of an orchestra of intermittent road drills, and the much sweeter sounds of Dave Wilson's jazz band in full swing with "Sweet Georgia Brown".

Sophie folded her bingo wing arms and then brushed imaginary petals from her floral print white and blue dress in pride at a job well done. She smiled through her pink lipstick, adjusted the hairpins holding in place the large bun in her bleached blonde hair. Then she checked the fastenings on her gold hooped earrings, took a deep breath, and carried on. Pub landladies have a lot to think about, and keeping all the punters happy came easily to her.

"Good evening, Sir Eric. It's good to see you again. Are you well?" she asked.

"All the better for seeing you, sweetheart", he oozed greasy charm.

"You haven't got any drinks. Can I help?"

"No, it's alright Sophie, Taylor's at the bar seeing to our wishes, thanks for asking. But could you bring me a pack of my cigars when you've got a minute?"

"Certainly, Sir Eric." she replied while ambling back to the bar slightly bemused by Eric's pals.

Sir Eric McClintock had enjoyed an immensely successful day at work, and now he was about to sew up a mega-deal with his two new drinking companions. He was very comfortable in his own skin, and smartly attired in his standard light grey Jasper Littman, Savile Row business suit, a made to measure Egyptian light blue cotton shirt, and a handmade Berg and Berg dark blue wool tie. His shoes were black Burberry leather.

Standing out like 2 rejects from a vegetarian barbecue, his strange bedfellows wore buff shorts, brown sandals with long white socks, Nike golf shirts and orange and white Texas Longhorns baseball caps.

Taylor Brandon was inside the building in the process of ordering, and soon he arrived in the beer garden with a tray laden with four pints. He looked like a younger version of his expensively attired boss. The only differences were his pink silk tie and his Jeffery West brown shoes.

"Now, gentlemen," smiled Sir Eric, handing out the glasses. "As this is your first visit to little Olde Englande you just have to try our bitter beer. This is a tricky tasty potion called Kilminster's Krackpot, our guest ale. It's a 6.1% abv dark bitter with the bollocks of a charging bull elephant."

The 2 American businessmen, tough Texas millionaire oil baron rednecks, looked worried. Carlos (Chuck) Monteverde and Clint Westerbrook drew quick mental comparisons with their perceptions of what a beer should look like. "Killie's" bore no resemblance at all to Texas Lone Star or even to Budweiser or Coors. They sipped Yankie style while Eric and Taylor quaffed John Bull style, and as the four men slaked their collective thirsts in their individual fashions, they began to discuss a lucrative financial proposition for dealing in Iraqi oil.

Sir Eric and his business associates, in common with the 20 or so other patrons in the beer garden, didn't notice the huge oak door, 7 feet tall and 5 inches thick, swing open. They paid no attention to the five men in dark blue overalls entering the door from Blenheim Close. Five men, who were carrying large black bags positioned themselves over the manhole cover at the rear of the garden and began muttering to each other. There had been an intermittent bit of a whiff coming from the drains. Wally, the pub landlord, had reported it, and when Sophie returned with Sir Eric's cigars, she felt safe in the assumption that the 5 workmen were sanitary engineers inspecting the drains.

Sophie was approached by one of the men. She noticed how tall, slim and handsome he was and how he carried his dark complexion with a super confident air. But most of all she fixed on his perfect white teeth and acid blue eyes. He was boss of a motley crew. He may have been tall and handsome, but among the other four were a short very fat one, a muscular ugly one, and a set of relatively ordinary looking twins. All had dark features and olive skin.

"We have problem reported with a smell coming from sewer." the good looking one smiled. London was full of people who spoke broken English, but the landlady couldn't place the accent, Polish perhaps, although it was clear that didn't fit with the man's appearance.

"Yes, I reported it yesterday. Comes up every now and again, probably because it's been so hot in the last week."

The man in charge smiled again.

"Need to remove manhole cover and is not going to be pleasant. Could I ask you? Move all beer garden customer indoors!"

Sophie wasn't pleased. The bar was already packed.

"Do you have to do this now?" she asked

Blue overall man's smile dispersed as he showed a small hint of annoyance.

"Look, lady, if we don't do work now, you will put up with stink for another 2 weeks before we come back to fix."

There was a sigh of resignation, "OK!"

Sophie diligently flitted from table to table, politely requesting her guests to adjourn indoors. There were quizzical whys, but everybody obliged. The blue overall brigade stood and watched in sullen silence.

"Happy now?" jabbed Sophie without reply as she also moved inside.

Once the garden was cleared, the workmen moved quickly, lifting the manhole cover and throwing 2 stink bombs towards the pub. The boss nodded and lifted a digit.

"One minute!" he said as two of the men picked up the black bags and went back to the street. Then he threw the 3 bolts on the huge oak door in the ancient wall, before the team picked up the remaining black bags and moved towards the rear door of the saloon.

The Captain's Table was a large corner pub, built in the early 1900's stretching around a corner from Churchill Street and into Blenheim Close.

Made of top quality London bricks, rising up to 3 storeys in sections interrupted by tall sash windows, and with a smart red and black livery, it was a popular meeting place for those working in the city financial markets. The hot weather had brought in extra clientele, and there must have been close to 70 early evening revellers in the place. It was a place of good cheer, bonhomie, a proper London pub with a regular loyal following and a steady passing trade.

Wally Chandler was the affable landlord. He was old school, and had grown up in an East End pub owned by his granddad, that had been frequented by many criminal gangs including the Krays. His regulars referred to him as the grey haired jolly fat man. He loved the rumble and banter of Friday evenings, and was busy collecting glasses when 3 blue overalled men entered through the back door and stood at the bar. They seemed to be surrounded by the blue fug of an eggy stench which the bar customers couldn't fail to notice. Many made exclamations of disgust and held their noses. It was busy, and there was little chance of anyone being served quickly. The two attractive barmaids, Charlotte and Emma, Wally and Sophie's beautiful blonde haired daughters, 20 and 22, were working behind the bar, doing their best to accommodate everyone's needs. Helen, the 3rd daughter, petite with a ginger ponytail, was collecting glasses and polishing tables, when she noticed that all three entrance doors had been locked from the inside. She went to tell her dad.

It all happened so quickly. So quickly that at first hardly anybody noticed what was happening.

Suddenly both of the doors to the street were locked and guarded, as was the door to the beer garden. Then before Sophie and Wally could react, each door was blocked by a man holding a black bag. The 2 remaining "sanitary inspectors" turned towards the centre of the room.

Near the end of the bar, the grandfather clock chimed quarter past 7 and immediately someone jumped up on the bar and delivered a series of blows with a baseball bat into the glass face and mechanism.

As the chimes groaned and died, shards of glass, metal and wood splintered across the corner of the bar. There were screams and shouts, and then near silence as everybody stopped dead in their tracks. The happy chatter and vibrancy of the room dissipated to a quiet worried rumble, as all present focussed on the situation. There were tears from the ladies, and some punters cowered or crawled into the corners for safety.

Sir Eric McClintock moved forward and said "What's all this about?"

He was quickly upstaged. The grandfather clock was a family heirloom which Wally's family had treasured for 3 generations. He was incensed.

"What the fuck's going on?" shouted Wally, angrily reacting to the strange circumstances around him.

"You!" shouted the ringleader up on the bar pointing at Wally, "Come here! Quickly!"

Wally knew no habitual fear; he had been a sergeant major in the Army and a middleweight boxer. Nobody told him what to do, even if he fancied himself wielding a baseball bat. He lifted his pint to his lips, took a large slug, wiped the froth from his greying moustache and moved forward out of the throng.

"Who the fuck do you think you are, telling me what to do in my pub?" he snarled.

The antagonist sneered back, slowly withdrew a handgun from inside his overall and pointed the weapon in Wally's face..

"You are very silly little man. Have you no seen that you and all friends are trapped and at my mercy."

As he uttered those words, 3 of his gang quickly opened their black bags and each one withdrew a Kalashnikov rifle. In a frozen moment, the pub was further stunned into a shocked and complete silence. Nobody dared to breathe. The one exception was Chuck Monteverde who quietly hissed "Son of a bitch!"

"Now I have everybody attention," the head man said, "I am Mohammed, and these are my brothers, Ibrahim, Ali, Yusif and little Ishaq. Be careful my friends, Ibrahim is very bad man. You call him Big Butcher. He love blood."

Taylor surveyed the terrorists, wary of the way they had been described by their leader, and making sure not to make any eye contact. Ibrahim was a brute of a man, over 6 feet tall, weighing all of 15 stone, and the way his body bulged in his blue overall he was clearly possessed of a muscle-bound physique. He had a shock of black hair, a profuse unruly moustache and a pock-marked face with very small ears. He carried a permanent expression in his black eyes of uncontrollable rampant anger. Ali and Yusif were twins; comparatively small in stature. They could have been any Middle Eastern men in the street with short dark hair, dark brown eyes and 5 o'clock shadow beards.

Ishaq wasn't little at all. Whilst he was less than 6 foot tall, he may well have been 5 feet round, and weighed about 20 stone. His fat greasy face and massive hands made Taylor think he might be a supreme candidate in a kebab eating contest. He was dark and swarthy with a scratchy black growth of beard. He seemed very ill at ease, but greeted his captives with a nervous broken toothed yellow grin.

Wally looked around him seeing the 3 men with rifles and an unusual ripple of angst ran up his spine. This was no loudmouthed drunkard causing a little fuss and liable to be thrown out on his ear. The ex-boxer could handle that, as he had done so easily a hundred times before. Here was something very different. But this was the Captain's Table and it was one man's territory. He moved forward.

"I don't give a shit what your name is, and I've no interest in your family connections. I don't care what axes you've got to grind. Just climb down from my bar and get your ugly arses out of my pub."

"It is important nobody move. Stand still or be trouble." Mohammed instructed.

"Are you being serious?" asked the landlord approaching his quarry.

"I show you!" was the answer.

The man climbed down off the bar pulled up a barstool, sat down slowly, nodded and whispered, "Ibrahim!"

The huge brute moved towards Wally reaching inside his overalls, pulling out a pistol and quickly screwed on a silencer. The pub patrons parted in sheer terror like the Red Sea.

The ex-boxer was frozen to the spot.

Sophie screamed.

Helen whined and hugged her mum.

Chuck fumbled inside his briefcase for something.

Clint shook his head mouthing "Wait!"

Ibrahim held the pistol at Wally's left ear. He snarled.

Mohammed said, "You are disgusting man who sell heathen alcohol."

Wally shouted, "You bastards!"

They were the last words he ever said.

Big Butcher smiled and shot him in the head. Blood spurted from the head wound and peppered the drinkers standing nearby. Mine host was stone dead before his heavy set body crashed over a table, smashing glasses and spraying beer as his fall shook the ground.

Sophie went rushing forward, but in the melee her clientele were quick to crowd around her and keep her from being the next victim.

Around 70 people shuddered with disgust and fear. Tears flowed from the female's eyes. Adrenalin coursed through the men's arteries.

Clint shook his head at Chuck.

"Now we have demonstrate how serious. You will please do as I say." said the leader, revealing his Kalashnikov, and throwing another one in Ibrahim's direction.

"All men this way." he waved to his left.

"All women other side." he indicated to his right.

Slowly the drinkers separated as they were pushed into 2 unbalanced groups, 50 men, 20 women.

"All doors now locked. No way out. We hold hostage until police arrive and we get what we want. Understanding?"

There was silence.

He repeated louder, "Understanding??"

There were quiet murmurs of agreement.

"Now! Ibrahim collect all mobiles. Please put all in black bags."

The mobiles were collected. When Chuck tried to remove his mobile from his briefcase, the terrorist punched his face and wrestled the case from him. He took it across to Mohammed, who looked inside and signalled for Chuck to be removed from the crowd. He resisted but was roughly dragged forward.

"American!" smiled the head man, "Very nice gun."

A Smith and Wesson Model 41 pistol was revealed.

"Any more guns in here?"

Clint shuddered.

"If we find, we shoot with own gun."

Clint raised his hand. He was shaking.

His rucksack was thrown forward. A quick inspection revealed another gun.

"Oh, I like very much American guns. This is Smith and Wesson SW1911, 11 rounds. Yes?"

Clint nodded hesitantly.

"I like American guns." he paused for 15 seconds while he closely examined the weapon.

"But I no like Americans. They kill my people. Planes bomb my village, kill my mother and father. Make me anger, very anger."

He smiled menacingly, took a deep breath, sighed, pointed to the floor next to him and said.

"Both Americans come here."

Sir Eric McClintock had been shocked into silence up to that point, but the thought of losing out on his lucrative deal urged him into action. He moved slowly forward 2 steps and asked, "Please, my friend, may I speak with you?"

He was signalled forward.

"Whatever it is that you want, I am sure we can come to some arrangement."

"Englishman very good at arrangement."

"How can we help to resolve this situation without further trouble or bloodshed?"

"Not possible! We have list of prisoners to release from Guantanamo Bay. We want 10 million U.S. dollars, and safe passage to Afghanistan. Can you do that my friend?"

Sir Eric shook his head. He was waved derisorily back into the crowd.

Mohammed spoke again.

"Ladies and gentlemen, or better I say dirty whores and cheating slimy infidel, let me full and undivide attention get from you. We taking over these filthy depraved whorehouse until police arrive and we give demands. We tell police that we kill 2 people every hour until demands met. Now, we have good work to do. Ibrahim, check cellar."

The butcher lost his angry expression and looked worried.

The instruction was repeated more assertively, "Ibrahim, check cellar."

With some reluctance the main man's brother came behind the bar and disappeared for a minute or two. He wasn't too comfortable with his brother's request, because ever since his childhood, he had suffered a phobia of dark places where rats might be found. His inspection was cursory. He returned with the statement, "Cellar clear!"

Then he threw a thick rope over the beam that crossed the ceiling in the middle of the pub. One end was secured to the foot rail by the bar, while the other was wound around Chuck's ankles. He struggled, and was kicked and punched to the ground, and his torso was thudded mercilessly with Ali and Yusuf's rifle butts. His battered body was then hoisted upwards, so that he was hanging upside down from the beam.

"American man is bad man. This is what we do to American."

With wicked menacing smiles on their faces, Ibrahim, Yusuf and Ali then rushed towards the hanging victim and kicked, punched and rifle butted his body and face in an orgy of extreme violence. Gore and broken teeth splattered the floor. Chuck's baseball cap was rammed into his bloody frothing mouth.

Mohammed waved his hand to indicate a halt in the action. He whispered something in a gang member's ear, and then laughed.

The men threw another rope over the beam and bundled Clint to the floor ready to carry out the same hideous process. The crack of breaking bones could clearly be heard, as both of Clint's arms were smashed by rifle butts before he stopped struggling. Then he suffered exactly the same ritual humiliation as his fellow American.

Mohammed continued to laugh heartily, and then one of his cohorts whispered in his ear. He nearly fell off the bar stool he had been sitting on when uncontrollable delight overtook him.

"Now we play new game." he grinned through his perfect white teeth.

Ibrahim took hold of Chuck's shoulders, and Ali pulled Clint's body in the opposite direction. Mohammed held one hand in the air, and when he dropped it down, the 2 battered faces and bodies were swung towards each other. The ritual was repeated again and again and again.

Every time the bodies or heads made contact, there was a sickening crunch of breaking bones and screams from all the women.

Sir Eric whispered, "Barbarians!" under his breath.

Taylor concurred with "Animals!"

When the orgy of destruction had begun to bore the terrorists, Mohammed held up his hand signifying a halt. Then the Big Butcher tied a plastic bag tightly around each victims head, and stood amused and delighted, watching them slowly suffocate. To a man the pub punters cowered in horror and disgust.

Chuck Monteverde was first of the victims about to expire on taking his last breath. Then the bag was removed. When he was gasping for air again, Ibrahim took the Smith and Wesson model 41, held it at the side of Chuck's head, shouted, "Filthy, murdering American scum!", and shot him through his left ear. Blood spurted across the room in a strawberry coloured stream, as the body went limp and lifeless. The butcher seemed to be ecstatic at the thought of killing an American with his own gun. So without further ado, he repeated the whole ugly scenario, this time shooting Clint in the mouth with the Smith and Wesson SW1911.

There was fear and horror. There was whimpering and tears. No one dared move or breathe.

The leader scanned the room, pointed to indicate where he wanted his brothers positioned at each door, and spoke again.

"Now! We have understanding. I am boss. You do as you are told."

As he said that Ali and Yusuf went to stand by the front doors to the street, and little Ishaq guarded the door back to the garden. Ibrahim disappeared through the door upstairs to the living area. For a few minutes the terrorists busied themselves setting up trip wires by every exit, each with a grenade attached.

"There is no escape. All doors booby trapped. We stay until we get what we want, and every hour we kill 2 more."

Sir Eric raised his hand. "May I ask you a question?" he said.

Mohammed nodded.

"Would it be possible to remove the bodies of the poor souls you have murdered, so that the ladies don't have to look at this distressing situation?"

The slowly emphasised reply came with a quietly disrespectful and menacing smile. "No! They stay. Is example to heathen infidel."

Big Butcher returned with a bundle of clothing."

"Now! All women sit down. Whores must cover heads and legs. Do not show flesh, or we make trouble. Moslem girls are good girls, cover themselves. Only whores show flesh. You are promiscuous unsavoury bitches. We teach humble."

The clothing was handed out and every lady except Sophie obeyed. She stood up and said, "You have killed my husband. You have insulted my clients. You abuse the privilege of living in my wonderful and tolerant country.

I wonder whether savage bastards like you would at least allow us to go the toilet if requested?"

"Of course!" came a reply, "But, You! Come here! Now!!"

Sophie was forced to don a heavy overcoat. She was then tied to the bar, and before she could speak again, she had her mouth taped over with gaffer tape.

"Ishaq will watch if any of you go toilet. If you no return we kill this fat loud bitch. In my country woman only speak when man say is OK."

Chapter 4

The Captain's Table massacre

All the doors and windows were closed, and the tension filled atmosphere inside the pub soon became like a sauna. Crowded into the corners of the bar, people began to feel breathless and close to fainting. Little Ishaq was sweating profusely, and mopping his head with a bar towel. But throughout it all, Mohammed remained as cool as a block of Arctic ice; Arctic ice radiating all the quiet menace of a polar bear with a 3 day hangover.

Suddenly, the silence in the premises under siege was overwhelmed by the unmistakeable sound of sirens wailing, as police and armed troops converged on the area. The area around the Captain's Table was cleared and secured.

An exclusion zone was quickly set up. The throbbing blades of a helicopter were heard hovering directly overhead. The noise rattled the large windows of the old pub and came close to shaking the building. Heads were lowered in fear that one or more of the trip wires would be set off, and a grenade would explode in the confines of the room causing more carnage. There was a collective brief sigh of relief as the helicopter eventually moved away; the noise diminishing to a distant reverberation.

After that peak of panic had passed, echoes of courage returned to some of the hostages. Sir Eric looked at his Rolex watch. It was 8.15 pm; getting closer to the time that his captors threatened to kill 2 more hostages. Perhaps a distraction would at the very least delay further brutality.

He moved forward and addressed Mohammed face to face, "It's very uncomfortable in here; could I ask if drinks may be distributed in this stifling heat?"

Wheels turned in the Jihadi's brain as he remained silent, with a wicked smile on his face for a while. After a short pause, he replied sarcastically, "Don't want you to die of thirst, we would have no one to kill."

After another long pause he declared, "Yes, only coffee, tea, orange juice and lemonade; no Coca Cola or alcohol."

Charlotte and Emma had been cowering behind the bar, consoling each other in tears of horror for the murderous execution of their father. They were now instructed to cover their heads, and set up drinks for everybody along the bar. Then the pub telephone rang, and Mohammed nodded for Emma to pick it up. She immediately passed the receiver to the gang leader.

"We are Jihadi. You will do as instructed or we kill 2 people every hour."

He then reeled off a list of prisoners in Guantanamo Bay who he required to be released, before requesting 10 million dollars in used banknotes, and a safe passage to Afghanistan. He spoke quietly in imperfect English but with perfect menace.

Sir Eric did a calculation, and came to the conclusion that the terrorists would become increasingly desperate within about 12 hours. He quickly concluded that it didn't need a genius to work out that it was almost impossible to satisfy the Jihadi's demands in the time that it would take to execute everyone. By that time, their threats indicated a death toll of 25 including Wally, Chuck and Clint who were already dead. The thought of over 20 bodies, piled up across the floor cooking in the expected Sahara conditions of the next day, filled him with absolute disgust and dread. The room was already a stinky chasm of dried blood, spilt alcohol, shards of glass, and sweating trembling frightened bodies.

Now that the exits were secured, Ali and Yusuf were free to wander around antagonising their prisoners. Although they appeared to be giving grudging respect to the women that they had labelled as unsavoury bitch whores by only hurling further insults, they were not so sparing with the men. Grinning in their evil satisfaction, they began to frisk every man; stealing watches, wallets, jewellery; anything of value. Protests were met with a blow to the face or head with a rifle butt. After each man was fleeced of his belongings, their mugger barked, "Kneel, you dog!"

Resistance was met with further violence. Realising the predicament, many victims just began to throw their valuables into a heap on the floor, and to kneel without instruction. Eric and Taylor, relieved of their wallets and watches, knelt shoulder to shoulder in utter disbelief. But they were relieved that at least this process delayed the selection of 2 further sacrificial lambs. There seemed to a much desired lull in the brutality, while the delighted highwaymen inspected their spoils. Only Mohammed remained detached, cool and aloof from the work of his compatriots until he was handed Sir Eric's Rolex watch, and seeing the time, decided on further action. He began to inspect the contents of the 2 dead American's briefcase and rucksack, and found paperwork giving the names of Sir Eric McClintock and Taylor Brandon.

"Sir Eric McClintock, come here!" he instructed.

Sir Eric stepped forward.

"Taylor Brandon here!"

Taylor followed his boss.

"You have deal with Americans. I hate Americans!"

Ibrahim swung his rifle at Sir Eric breaking 2 ribs and then smashed Taylor in the face knocking out 3 teeth.

"Anyone with American friends is my enemy."

He asked Eric, "Do you have a gun?"

The breathless victim shook his head. The Butcher went through the high financier's pockets, finding the cigars he'd got from Sophie earlier. He threw them to little Ishaq who grinned and lit up.

"Time for more fun." declared the leader.

Ropes were untied from Chuck and Clint's battered bodies, and their corpses dropped to the floor in a lifeless, gore splattered heap. The sadistic butcher took great pleasure in kicking them aside. Sir Eric and Taylor struggled courageously, but to no avail. Courtesy of Ibrahim's inherent anger, they were dragged across the red rivulets of the stinking blood soaked carpet covered in splinters of glass. A few minutes later, they had been hoisted in the air, and were undergoing the same savage treatment as the 2 previous victims. The game was played out exactly as before until the 2 expensively dressed businessmen were pounded into a wheezing and whimpering bloody pulp of smashed heads and bodies. Then they had gaffer tape plastered across their mouths and noses and suffered near death through suffocation like their American friends, before they were executed with bullets through their brains. When the ritual of killing was over Mohammed declared, "This is what happen to bad men who bomb my country, kill my family!"

Suddenly Sophie began to struggle violently, and was obviously trying to say something through her taped up mouth. Helen bravely moved forward to help her mother shouting "You bastards! Can't you see she's in trouble?"

Ali blocked her way and waved a rifle in her direction, but she ignored the risk, glared at him and shouted, "OK! Shoot me if you want but I'm going to help my mother."

Mohammed nodded at his brother, and waved his hand to indicate letting her proceed. She pushed her tormentor aside, and peeled the tape quickly from her mum's red and swollen face, and quickly removed the heavy overcoat. But it was too late. In an uncontrollable spasm of relaxation, the landlady passed a hot stream of piss down both legs and then shat herself. A furore of repulsion and disgust with the treatment of mine hostess oscillated around the room.

The terrorist leader laughed, and then whispered something to his brother. He released Sophie's bonds, and then grabbed Helen by the wrists. She struggled vigorously; so vigorously that she fell in her mother's fresh excrement.

The head Jihadi laughed again.

Emma followed her sister's lead in not waiting for approval from her captors before helping.

"I've had enough of this!" she said, and told her mother and sister to go upstairs and clean themselves up. Surprisingly, there was no reaction from the terrorists. She continued, "Have you no sense of decency? You cruel hearted shit faced nobody!"

Mohammed just continued to smile.

Emma then brought a mop and water filled bucket out to clean up the mess.

When she had finished, Ali and Yusuf grabbed her and manhandled her roughly into position. She was tied to the bar in position, replacing her mother.

"You clean up!" he indicated to the soiled ladies, "If you no return, she dies!"

In the sanity of the world outside, the brilliant white sunshine of the day began to acquiesce for a golden glow, before converting to a warm red shepherd's delight, reflected in dazzling splendour from the tall glass-plated surrounding buildings. Inside the Captain's Table, for a short while, there was comparative calm. The body count was now 5, and the siege had been progressing for over 2 hours with no apparent positive reaction from the police and army, other than to set up a direct line on the pub telephone. Mohammed decided to remind the authorities of his demands. He barked them down the phone and slammed it down.

At 9.30 pm, the last light of a brilliant sunshine day dissipated into evening gloom. For the captives, the walls of the Captain's Table seemed to shrink inwards in a claustrophobic, sweat drenched, and all pervading crush. A crush accompanied by the dread of time moving towards another bout of brutality and execution. Nobody understood quite why there had been little reaction from the authorities outside controlling the situation. There was only a collective desperation at the hopelessness of their predicament.

When Helen and her mother returned to the bar area, having showered and changed, Sophie walked boldly behind the bar and poured herself a large brandy from the optics, swigging it back in one swallow. Collecting a disdainful look from her antagonist, she hurled, "So! Are you going to kill me for having a drink?"

Ibrahim rushed behind the bar, and in an angry outburst proceeded to smash every optic and every bottle with his rifle butt. Glass and spirits showered the area in his orgy of destruction, and crunched underfoot as he made his way back, herding Sophie and Helen before him to rejoin the other women.

With the death of Sir Eric, the captives had lost the only man present who was brave enough to confront the Islamists directly. Having witnessed the complete brutality of 4 executions, there was no longer any man who wanted to make himself conspicuous by addressing his captors. Ironically, it fell to Sophie to make any necessary verbal contact with her aggressors. In the previous few hours, she had seen her world of security shattered. Her 300 year old city wall had been breached as surely as if a cannonball salvo had smashed it to smithereens. She had been ritually humiliated to the point where she had soiled herself in front of her clientele. Her husband's body lay in a crumpled heap, where a bizarre pattern of bloody pools stained the carpet, and her daughter Emma was tied to the bar and gagged in a further ritual of brutality. But she was ever more and more determined to take what control she could of the situation and show the terrorists that in her pub, she was boss and no mistake. She owed that to her Wally.

"If you intend to hold us hostage all night, then we will need to make some arrangements to help my customers sleep." she said.

Mohammed, slow and methodical as ever, took time to consider her request. Then he barked back, "No sleep!"

"Don't be ridiculous," she replied, "In this heat and tension; these people can't stay up all night. They'll collapse on the floor. Some of them will die. You'll lose some of your hostages. At least, please let us all sit down comfortably."

Top man thought for a while, and then conceded, "OK! All sit!"

The command was obeyed, with much relief from the men and no questions.

The landlady had recorded a small victory, and she had accumulated years of experience in reading peoples thoughts and motives. Now, buoyed with a new confidence, she began to organise essential services like drinks and toilets, and cleaning up after the damage and devastation, without asking further permission. Although she was closely watched by all the terrorists, she soon manoeuvred herself into a situation where she had free movement.

As night began to set in, with still no move towards a resolution from the authorities, the selection of candidates for ritual execution continued. The terrorists were assisted in carrying out this process by inspection of the surrendered wallets. This enabled identification of anybody with connections with Sir Eric and the financial institutions he traded with. Before each new horror, Mohammed menacingly reiterated his demands down the phone, and issued a body count with every bulletin. Throughout, he remained cool and steady in his demeanour.

Little Ishaq smoked his way through all of Sir Eric's cigars, and slumped in a slobbish heap by the toilet doors.

Ali and Yusuf tired of their games of antagonism, and drank gallons of black sweet coffee.

Only the blood thirsty barbarian, Ibrahim, living up to his delight in butchery, found it necessary to maraud about the room, hitting out at anybody who made eye contact. He had become less amused by suffocating his hanging victims, and found new happiness in merely finishing his work by slitting their throats. The pools of blood continued to spread across the carpet, drying quickly in the heat of the summer night, and the mutilated broken bodies piled up in a vile stinking heap. The room itself seemed to be sweating in the gore drenched, damp and dusty, claustrophobic atmosphere.

The only apparent activity outside in the depths of the long night, consisted of a low rumbling and bright flashes in the skies, as a thunderstorm approached.

When the eye of the storm broke overhead at 3 in the morning, with a massively loud crash of thunder, all 5 terrorists jumped to their feet, fearing that the pub was about to be attacked by the SAS. All of the captives stayed put, cowering low in anticipation of gunfire. All at once, they were both in fear of their lives, but also relieved that something appeared to be happening at last.

Alas! No release from their captivity came, only the welcome cooling down of the building by the torrential rain that eventually accompanied the storm. All hope was extinguished, and a sanguinary hopelessness descended upon the hostages, and hung there like a choking fog over a frozen morning meadow. By 5 am the storm had abated, and the temperature in the pub started to rise again, as the sun quickly began to break through the remains of the storm's cloud cover, heralding the opening of another blistering hot day.

Chapter 5

Angels amongst us

The City of London began to stir. A confident awakening of the day cracked the skies like a thermal lance, making short work of sucking up the residual moisture of the overnight storm, and unveiling another ceiling of perfect blue heavens.

A rampant sun began to beat down intensely over the return of oppressively hot city streets. Saturday's streets might be free of the industrious activity of millions of commuters, but were still busy with the less frenetic curiosity of excited sightseers. A few miles westward of the City, in the Chelsea posh spots, 3 modern girls had risen from their slumbers.

Heidi-Maria came running into the room, and switched on the TV. She stood stock still and focussed her steely blue eyes on the screen.

"I heard about it on the radio. I couldn't believe it! O.M.G! I really can't believe it! It's terrible."

"What are you on about?" asked Courtney.

"There's been a terrorist siege at the Captain's Table overnight. They're saying that lots of people have been killed."

"What! It was only last weekend that we were all there together with Mike for Sophie and Wally's birthday bash." added Melissa from the kitchen doorway. "I do hope they're alright. They're a lovely couple. They might be oldies but they're such good fun."

Courtney choked on her cornflakes, picked up her mobile, and for a few minutes tapped away to no avail.

"I can't get through. I must have tried 10 times." she whined tearfully. She shrunk back into the huge pink sofa in distress, bringing her knees up to set herself into a foetal position. She hung her head and cried, as rivulets of mascara ran from her sorrow filled brown eyes. Her petite frame almost disappeared into the deep cushioning.

"But I thought you said that Mike would be OK." reassured Melissa, in her soft Irish tones, as she crossed the room, brushing her long auburn hair, and eating a slice of toast at the same time.

"I can't be sure. I don't know. I need to talk to Michael."

"You say that Mike could have been in the Captain's Table, but you can't be sure. And I thought you said that he sent you a text yesterday evening." the freckle-faced Irish girl replied, throwing herself down on the sofa, and brushing crumbs off her tiger-skin onesy.

"Yes, he did. But?"

"So what's the problem, Babychops?"

For a few moments, there was no response; just more sobs.

Then a reply came.

"Yes! I did get a text from Michael yesterday evening."

Melissa gave her pal a hug, "Alright then, show me the text." she said.

Green Irish eyes flicked quickly across the screen. She smiled.

"There it is in black and white, my dearie."

Courtney checked her mobile again and read out the text.

"Yes, here it is! He said, 'Sorry, I've got a monster of a headache. Can I put you on hold 'til tomorrow lunchtime? See you here at 11.' That was it."

"Check the time that it was sent."

She fumbled through the icons on the mobile. "It's timed at 19.23."

"So they said on the BBC news that the siege started at 7 and his text was sent at 7.23. I'd say that suggests he wasn't in the pub when the trouble started."

Courtney sighed. She only half believed what had just been determined.

"I suppose you're right, Melissa. Thank you.", she said.

"Nothing to worry about, Court." added Heidi with a confident swish of her long blonde hair. Melissa and Heidi-Maria instinctively hugged their friend.

It was only 5 miles to Michael's place from the flat in Chelsea that Courtney Channing shared with her 2 girlfriends and fellow business associates, but at that moment it felt like 10,000 miles. She wanted to wave a magic wand, and be transported across town to wake up in Michael's bed. She just wanted to be sure that he was safe.

For the time being she had to set her worries aside. There was work to do, and she had been at least partially reassured by her friend's words. The gaggle of young girls worked for Andersen, Biehn and Channing, a high class wedding planning agency, which they had established together with their senior partner, Dorseta Harrison, the owner of their flat and shop-cum-office premises.

A few minutes later, Dorseta arrived as expected to discuss their last project. She was the 40 something mother hen, always steady and trustworthy; the foundation of the business. She handled all the admin and paperwork. She was the accountant, she had the contacts, and she did the marketing and scheduling for all their projects. Her posh totty perfect English accent was Chelsea Blue through and through.

She breezed into the room in her Aztec motif hippie style dress and beads with a clipboard and several folders under her arm, and strode across the thick Persian carpet in her light brown suede boots, as she tied her long, thick, light brown hair, flecked with greying streaks, into a pony tail.

"Good Morning, ladies. How are we all? We've missed you." she greeted them. She always used the royal prerogative. Dorseta plonked herself on the massive sofa like a joss stick and patchouli weed amongst a bed of deliciously perfumed and coiffured flowers. Her tattooed eyebrows raised above her botox eyelids.

"Something wrong?" she asked seeing Courtney's distress.

"Court's worried about her man, Mike. Thinks he may have been involved in that terrible business at the Captain's Table last night." offered Heidi.

Sometimes, Dorseta was just too cold and unemotional. This was one of those times.

"He'll be fine," she asserted, "Bad things only happen to bad people. That's kharma!"

Her matter of fact air seemed to placate Courtney.

"Let's get to work." she said, "I had a call this morning from Mr Harcourt-Wilson. He's absolutely delighted with the work we did on his daughter Rachel's wedding. Were there any problems with the wedding project down in sunny Bourton on the Water?"

The Bohemian hippie chick knew that Courtney was the problem solver, the practical one, and an incurable perfectionist. Courtney realigned her focus on her work and replied, "I've made a little list of unexpecteds that we needed to overcome. We can write the solutions into future plans. But nothing spoiled the big day. I'll email the list to you with suggestions tomorrow."

Now that her mind had been focussed on work, Courtney thought of how wonderful it would be to marry Michael. They had been a couple for over 2 years, and the wedding she most dreamed of planning would be her own. But she wasn't sure that her beau was the marrying kind. Her small facial features, framed by her short cut plum brunette hairstyle softened, as she felt a wave of releasing tension flow through her, and tears welled up in her eyes again. But these were tears of relief. She thought about the text she'd received, and knew Michael well enough to understand that he wouldn't tell her lies to put her off.

"He couldn't have been in the Captain's Table." she thought.

In the natural pecking order of things that Dorseta understood, it was probably Heidi's turn to speak next, but Melissa butted in enthusiastically.

"It's a beautiful village, Bourton-on-the-Water, in the beautiful county of Gloucestershire. It's sometimes called the "Venice of the Cotswolds". The High Street is very picturesque, and quite unusual; honey stone coloured buildings, long wide greens and the lovely little River Windrush runs right through the middle. We organised the ceremonial throwing of the bride's bouquet on one of the lovely little low, arched stone bridges. We stayed in a beautiful B and B called Rooftrees, run by wonderful hosts Sylvia and Sean."

Dorseta knew that the County Mayo girl was a born romantic; a creative and often outrageous genius. Her fun filled and flirty nature had occasionally caused a few problems.

"OK, I get the travelogue." she smiled, "No problems then? And you managed to keep your man-eater emerald eyes off of the best man."

Melissa had something of a reputation for making sure she enjoyed the weddings as much as the invited guests. Her co-workers reached a mutual understanding that they would turn a blind eye if she had her heart set on the best man or any other handsome willing candidate in the congregation.

The cheeky Irish colleen laughed, "No; I conducted myself with an attractive and unobtainable aloofness. It was a perfect location and we had fantastic weather. Everything went like clockwork."

"Now, Heidi, what about your input?" Dorseta asked.

Heidi was the on the spot organiser. Her friends didn't nickname her Killer Queen for no good reason. She was caviar and cigarettes, well versed in etiquette, extraordinarily nice, not to mention fastidious and precise. Her contribution to the wedding projects always attended to everything in the finest detail. She cracked a perfect white teeth smile as she began her summation.

"The church of St Lawrence's was perfect. The vicar was a lovely lady, the

Reverend Rachel Rosborough. She had a wicked sense of humour. The bridegroom, Christopher and his best man, Ryan, drove up to the church in a silver Mercedes SLK. They arrived right on time. They, and all the other men folk, were attired in grey morning suits with top hats and lilac and gold cravats. The 6 bridesmaids wore lilac dresses trimmed with gold. They looked gorgeous."

She took a breath and laughed," The little one was only five, and she fell over in the church porch, and grazed her knee. But Court patched her up."

Dorseta waited until Heidi returned to her overview.

"The bride, Rachel, was completely stunning in her pure white and gold dress, and arrived fashionably late. After the ceremony, the happy couple left the church by horse and cart. It was a drayman's cart, beautifully adorned with white, lilac and gold ribbons, and pulled by 2 lovely dark brown shire horses. The marquee was set up in a buttercup meadow, and laid out expertly. The catering was done by Freshmans, a local company supervised by Anton Fellini, who was the best local chef we could find. The food and wine was expertly served by a locally recruited army of pretty waitresses. The 6 course menu and wine list, selected by the Harcourt-Wilsons, was well balanced, delicious and exquisitely presented. In short, everything was absolute top notch, even down to the lack of fighting at the evening reception, when some of the local plebs turned up. Court did a great job keeping them amused and plied with drink, without upsetting the invited guests. Mr Harcourt-Wilson and his wife Millicent were gracious and grateful throughout the day. Need I say more?"

The blonde, slim figured, model-like, Heidi-Maria knew she and her associates had done a fabulous job. Dorseta was delighted.

"Thank you girls; another one we can be proud of. Mr Harcourt-Wilson is sending over a banker's draft with a 10% bonus, and a glowing reference."

"Champagne all round then." grinned Heidi.

"Right girls, on to the next job then. We are all set for this big one in Scotland that we've had on the drawing board for a few months. I spoke to the McPhersons while you were away. The job's worth megabucks. Here are the folders with all the details, most of which you know already. The only major addition is that the bride and the groom have decided that they will be flying from the wedding ceremony at Gretna Green up to the reception at Auchencastle in a helicopter."

At 10.00 o'clock, Courtney drove across to the City in her white Fiat 500C convertible with a maroon roof and seating. It was hot. The air-conditioning was ineffective, so the roof was down. Before she arrived at Michael's, she took a quick diversion to see Karen Robbins, an old colleague who had been one of the Captain's Table hostages. Her friend talked about the tragedy, and was able to describe the ordeal first hand. She provided a welcome confirmation that Michael had not been involved in the atrocity, but she was scathingly critical of the situation that the hostages had been forced to endure by the authorities.

"I couldn't help but be totally disgusted with a whole night of inaction from the police and troops. It appeared that because there was no gunfire they made the assumption that the threat to kill hostages was a bluff. But they executed 2 men every hour of the time we were there. It was brutal, horrific, disgusting and sickening. The bodies just piled up in front of us. I have never been so scared. It just went on and on through the night, until someone managed to contact the police, explaining exactly what was happening in the bar. Up till then, they failed to make any movement. The authorities wouldn't reveal the true identity of the informant, but we were told by Sophie he was called Seth, and was taken on as a casual barman that evening. Eventually the SAS had to go in around 5 this morning to prevent any further bloodshed. When they came in, they were very quick and decisive, and killed all 5 of the Jihadis."

Chapter 6

Bubblegum and Candy Floss

On Saturdays, Michael's "daily", the super efficient Audrey Bairstow, usually made a quick morning visit to his apartment at 10 am to pick up and deliver the dry cleaning, and to get her pay in cash from her boss. But as Courtney arrived at just before 11, she was only just leaving.

"Oh, I'm so glad you're here. I didn't really want to leave Mike on his own. You've heard what happened last night at the Captain's Table?"

"Yes! It's terrible. We were there only a few days ago."

"Mike's taken it very badly."

Courtney didn't know exactly what she would find when she arrived, and although she was distressed after what Karen had related to her, she was relieved to find the love of her life in one piece; albeit at that moment in time, a very fragile and haunted one piece. She greeted him with a flurry of kisses and an emotionally intense hug.

"My Darling, Michael, I am so glad you're OK. I tried to call you, but the lines appear to be down."

"Yeah, I'm OK, Courtney, and all the better for seeing you. I tried to call you and got the same response, and when I tried phoning some of my work colleagues to check that they were alright, it was just the same. I think the authorities have shut down the local telecomms system for security reasons."

Audrey's work was done, and she knew that her presence was no longer necessary. "I'll leave you two young people alone now; don't want to play gooseberry," she said, "I'll be here as usual on Monday."

She waved and left quickly. The couple sat down holding hands on the couch.

"The news bulletins on the TV just continue to repeat the same things," Michael said, "They're not giving out much in the way of detail. I suppose they need to find out exactly what happened and who has been killed, before they tell the whole story."

"It's terrible! They estimate that at least 20 people have been executed, but so far they've only mentioned Sir Eric McClintock and several of his senior staff, and 2 American businessmen." Courtney replied.

"Yes, I know, and it shakes me to my foundations, because I was planning to be there with them."

"What! How come? Oh darling, are you kidding me?"

"Would I kid you about something this serious? No! Taylor Brandon phoned me yesterday about 6.30 and invited me to join them. We were going to discuss a slightly dodgy oil deal with the 2 Yanks."

"A dodgy deal? Oh Michael, you don't usually get involved in stuff like that."

"No, but Taylor explained it, and something told me to join them. Only thing is, I had to be there by 7 or I'd miss out."

Courtney then noticed the bump on the side of Michael's head. "How did that happen?" she asked, stroking the area gently with a soft hand.

"I'll tell you all about it."

"Let me make some coffee first. I'm very thirsty and it's so hot outside."

She went to the kitchen while he refocused on the TV. A few minutes later she returned.

"I dropped in at Karen Robbins place on the way here." she said, "She was in the Captain's and told me what went on in there. It was bloody sickening; stinking dead bodies piling up in the heat. All the men were beaten up and humiliated, and those selected for execution were hung upside down, and eventually suffocated with plastic bags, or had their throats slit. There were rivers of blood. Wally was killed first. He was shot in the head."

Michael sat there dumbstruck and stared into space as another wave of horror washed over him. Ever since he had first seen the TV news broadcast that morning, all the events of the previous evening had never left his thoughts. But whenever he tried to think the whole business through, it was like his brain was a churned up mixture of bubble gum and candyfloss. Sometimes in his drinking life, when he had seriously overdone it, he had woken the next morning with the same feeling. Not being able to remember everything clearly, and having it come back to him in little flashbacks over the next day or two; that was the way it felt to him. But at the same time he felt he had a desperate and all consuming need to remember.

"Are you alright, darling? You look very pale and your breathing is a bit shallow. Here! Drink some coffee."

She handed him a cup. His hands were shaking as he took gulps from it.

The Chelsea girl had a tough job on her hands. Here was the man she loved most in all the world in a bit of a state, and she felt that if anyone could help him at all, it would be her. After all she was Miss Fixit in her daily job, the problem solver, the pragmatic solution finder, and as a trained counsellor she knew all about people and their problems.

"OK, darling," she said softly," Just tell me what happened."

Michael took a deep breath trying to steady himself, placed the coffee cup on the table, and began.

"Well, like I said, Taylor told me to be at the Captain's at 7. It was very tight time wise. I set off and hailed a taxi, but it ground to a halt in the road works. So I was about half way there, and decided to run the rest of the way through Blenheim Circus Park. When I got to the other end of the park, the fucking gate was locked. I'd nearly run out of time, but I did a Usain Bolt back to the entrance, and then I tripped over my laces and fell arse over tit. That's when I got this bump on my head. Then, when I started running again, I found out I'd dropped my wallet. It was the Alexander McQueen wallet that you bought me. By that time there was no way that I'd be able to get to the pub on time to meet Eric and Taylor, so I retraced my footsteps and went searching for the wallet. A tramp called George was sitting on a park bench, and he had found the wallet. We had a little chat and then I went home. That's when I sent a text to you to say not to come till today. I had a splitting headache, had a shower and went straight to bed. When I got up this morning I found out what had happened at the Captain's last night."

Courtney had used all her listening skills to hear what her man was saying, and to read the expressions on his face as he said it.

"It seems to me that you've had a very lucky escape; providence, fate, kismet whatever you like to call it has intervened in lots of small ways to stop you being at the scene of the massacre."

"I understand that, Babychops. What I don't understand is why. Why me?"

"There are not always clear reasons for why things happen, but sometimes your inner voice tells you that you should or shouldn't go somewhere, and you ignore it. If you do the wrong thing there may be consequences. That's often when a guiding hand takes control and intervenes to stop you coming to harm."

"So you think that all the little things that stopped me getting to the pub we're meant to happen to keep me safe?"

"Yes, why not? That's a perfectly plausible explanation."

"But it still doesn't explain why!"

"Well, at the moment you perhaps haven't thought the whole series of events through clearly. Maybe as time passes more aspects will come back to you. And the bump on your head probably doesn't help either. For the moment I'm so glad that you have been saved. My world would be an empty place without you."

Michael felt reassured, but it occurred to him that some of the things Courtney was saying were wise words that he had heard somewhere before.

Later, Michael and Courtney were eating their lunch when she said, "Listen, darling, I think it might be useful cathartic process if we were to take a walk through Blenheim Circus Park this afternoon."

He had regained some confidence after the earlier discussion. "Yes, I think that's a good idea. Let's do it."

In the lift well they bumped into Charlie Evans.

"Mr Hartson, Good afternoon." he said, "Have you got a minute."

"Yes, Mr Evans, what is it?" came the reply with just enough disguised disinterest to be polite.

"Well, you remember I was going to discuss something with you yesterday, but you seemed to be in a bit of a hurry."

"Sorry! Yes! What was it you wanted to talk to me about?"

"Oh, it's not that important right now. But I just thought you might like to sign my petition."

"A petition, what for?"

"Well, as you probably know I used to work for the Parks Department. I'm a concerned that the local bigwigs at the Council want to start closing some of the parks earlier. They're having trouble cleaning up after the evening concerts. It's to do with a dispute between Parks and Cleansing really. The Parks people are experimenting with closing some of the gates at 7 pm. My petition is politely asking them to reconsider. I think it's unfair on the park visitors."

Michael felt a wave of horror roll over him. He thought back to Friday evening.

The terrible haunting idea shook him to the core that if Charlie hadn't delayed him by a few minutes, he might have been a hostage victim.

"But, but, but; are you telling me that you knew that the gate on Churchill Avenue at the end of Blenheim Circus Park was closed early on Friday?"

"Yes, Mr Hartson! That was one the gates selected for early closing."

Suddenly Michael had a flashback. He was back there running through the park and then hearing himself shouting, "The fucking gate's been locked." as he shook it in sheer frustration.

"Shit! Shit! Shit!" he thought. "If this very correct and always polite chairperson of the apartment block's management company had told me that on Friday; if I had just waited to talk to him and sign his petition, then what would have happened? Would I have avoided that gate? I'd have made it to the Captain's Table and been in the siege, and probably been executed along with a group of my close colleagues?

There were so many questions and only one conclusion he could draw.

"There was a whole inexplicable bunch of little events coming together to stop me being there." he thought, "Charlie's little delay, not knowing the gate would be locked, the road works, the taxi not being able to get through, finding the gate locked and turning back, tripping over my laces twice, banging my head, losing my wallet, sitting down on the bench next to George O'Donnell. Why? Why? Why?"

The financial whiz kid felt sick. The room swirled around him. He needed to sit down. It was obvious from his pale contorted face that he was in enormous mental turmoil. There was that feeling again; that desperate need to remember, but the bubble gum and candyfloss wouldn't disperse.

"Are you alright, Mr Hartson?" asked Charlie.

There was no reply. Courtney saw what was happening and took charge. "We'll catch up with you later, Mr Evans. Michael is not too steady at the moment."

And with that, the couple staggered back into the apartment.

Chapter 7

Revelation

Back inside the apartment, little Miss Fixit made some quick decisions. She had recognised her boyfriend's symptoms as a form of PTSD, and she was well aware that fervent curiosity guarded by confusion and a possible need for denial would require careful handling. She decided that for the rest of the day there would be no further discussion of his recent experiences and the Captain's Table tragedy. The TV was unplugged. She would control everything and look after him so as to let his thought processes catch up at a more gentle pace. They would just chill out together, with no pressure.

First, she ground the Blue Mountain Arabica coffee beans and made lots of coffee. They sipped, sitting closely wrapped in each other's arms while they listened to Bob Dylan and Roy Harper tracks on the superb Bose sound system. Then she made her beau's favourite evening meal; smoked salmon and prawn linguine, followed by white chocolate and cardamom tart with raspberry dust, which they both enjoyed with a nicely chilled bottle of Ramey 2008 Chardonnay. He was quiet and contemplative throughout the evening. Then they went to bed early and finished off the day in the best possible way with a long and gentle session of sensual lovemaking with Courtney taking full control. They slept well, entwined in each other and woke feeling refreshed and renewed.

The after breakfast washing up was finished, when Courtney smiled at Michael, with a question on her lips.

"Want to give it another go?"

"Give what another go?" he replied.

"Walking through the park, darling."

"Maybe."

"You're ready now, sweetheart. We've had a good night's sleep, and hopefully you are now ready to reconcile the events of the past few days."

He didn't need to think about it for very long.

"Yeah, come on. Let's go!"

Soon they were back out in the sunshine, dressed cool and casual. After the Friday night storm, the weather had reverted to a blazing hot Sahara style pattern, with perfect blue skies, sweltering heat, and a dearth of welcome shade.

Fifteen minutes later, they entered Blenheim Circus Park. Each step of the way Michael experienced a mixture of feelings. He felt an exaggerated sense of déjà vu, and an unsettling edge-of-a-razor-blade impatience.

"The taxi got held up a little way along the street there, and because it's a one way street we couldn't turn around. So I jumped out and started running through the park. When I came in through this gate, I didn't see or hear anything around me. I had one thought on my mind, and that was to get to the Captain's Table on time by 7 pm."

"How long did you have to get there?"

"About 10 minutes. But the laces on my new trainers came undone, and I had to stop by that bench and retie them. There was a dirty old tramp sitting there, and he tried to bum some cash from me; so I told him to fuck off and kept running."

"That wasn't a very nice thing to do. Was it?"

"No, but I was in such a hurry. I didn't have any time or the patience to patronise him."

Courtney gave Mike a scolding look as they continued their walk. He felt embarrassed for a split second, and then they carried on in silence until they neared the gate at the end of the park.

"Anyway, when I reached this gate it was locked. So I cursed and then had to turn back."

As if to illustrate the point, the end gate was locked again, and Michael needed to rattle the wrought iron bars, attempting to relive his previous frustration. Courtney watched, and when the time was right, she pointed out a small sign on the gate which explained that the gate was locked by the police for security reasons. After a minute or two, they retraced their steps.

"When I got back to where the tramp was sitting, the bloody lace had come undone again, and I tripped over, ripped my chinos, grazed my knee, and banged my head on that bin."

"You must have run out of time by then. Surely there was no chance that you would arrive on time for the meeting."

"Yeah, but I was so focussed on getting there, and by then I thought it might be OK to arrive a little late."

"So what happened then?"

"Well, the old tramp was still there, and he seemed to be laughing at me."

"And don't tell me; you swore at him again." she grinned.

"Bloody right, I did! Then I ran out of the park and shortly after that was when I realised my wallet was missing. I decided to go back to the park looking for it. That's when I gave up on any hope of getting to the Captain's. To cut a long story short, the tramp had picked up the wallet when I fell over, and he just gave it back to me."

He laughed as he explained, "But not before I'd abused him again. I called him an utterly useless pile of dog's vomit, and told him to shut his fucking dirty, ugly, mouth."

"Oh, Michael, how uncouth." Courtney shuddered.

When they passed the bench where Michael had encountered George O'Donnell two days before, a sense of instant reminiscence washed over him, like a warm wave in a tropical ocean, and for the first time since he had entered the park, he began to feel relaxed and contented.

He began to remember the incident in the park much more clearly, and what the tramp had said that provided a gentle persuasive compulsion to stay put.

He remembered how the tramp had spoken slowly, and with deliberation in short sentences in a soft, velvet smooth, enchanting voice.

He remembered every phrase, every nuance as if it was an imprint in his brain cells.

The couple sat down on George O'Donnell's bench, and Mike acted out every line of the words he had heard from the tramp. So far, while revisiting the park his recollection had been sparse, but now he had an inescapable need to explain every detail of the remainder of his experience to his companion.

He took a deep breath and looked around him.

He allowed himself to see what a beautiful world surrounded him.

He felt the warmth of the sunshine on his face.

He looked up and drank in the perfect blue sky.

He smelled the flowers and delighted in their colours and their aromas.

He sensed the easygoing happiness of passers by, walking together.

He heard the birds singing cheerfully in the trees, and some way off, he heard the ducks quacking on the pond.

He heard the music as a local group played on the bandstand, and listened carefully to the blend of music and words.

He sat there in silence, contented in just holding his girlfriend's hands and being alive.

Then he remembered wise words and repeated them to her out loud.

"Take your time.
Live your life at a stroll not a sprint.
You have been in a hurry; not just this evening, but all of your life.
Learn a lesson today.
You thought you needed to be somewhere at 7 o'clock, and you failed to get there in time. You will be glad that you failed, my friend.
Sometimes life tells you that you shouldn't go somewhere.
Instinct, a 6th sense, whatever it is, intervenes, and it is seldom wrong.
Sometimes life tells you to go somewhere, and you don't listen to that little voice. That's when you might get it wrong.
Life is a vast learning curve."

Courtney sensed from her training as a counsellor that her boyfriend had experienced a life changing event. However, she was wary of pushing the issue. Fascinated though she was, with a million questions passing through her brain, she used all her training to stand back into the role of good listener.

After a long silent spell, they exited the gate and walked along the road around the park perimeter. After they'd skirted the area of the Captain's Table, which was cordoned off with a massive presence of police and troops, they then decided to go to the nearby St Matthew's church, to light candles for the victims. Neither of them was of a particularly religious persuasion, but they had agreed it felt like the right thing to do in the circumstances. As they entered the church, they were greeted by the female vicar. She had super-size model good looks, false nails painted black, perfect understated makeup, long, out-of-a-bottle, dark blonde hair and was wearing jet black, highly polished Doc Marten's boots.

"Welcome to Saint Matthew's. I have not seen you in here before. My name is Phillipa Jackson, the Reverend Phillipa Jackson. That sounds very self-important but you can just call me Pippa. And you are?"

"Michael Hartson."

"And Courtney Channing."

Pippa seemed to be very proud of her church, and without prompting, began to illustrate its history.

"St Matthew's is an early 18th century building designed by James Gould, under the supervision of George Dance. The original chapel was of Roman origin, and was replaced by a Saxon church."

"Roman, Saxon and 18th century? I don't understand!" quizzed Courtney.

"No I'm sorry. Let me try to explain more clearly. The current church is located on the site of the 2 previous churches. The Saxon building survived the Great Fire of London in 1666, but fell into disrepair and was eventually demolished to make way for the current place of worship."

"Now I understand."

"Good! As you can see, the interior is aisled and galleried in the classic style, with a font, pulpit and organ which all date from the eighteenth century."

Neither of them knew what that meant, and Michael was becoming a little impatient with the vicar's enthusiasm.

"Thank you for your explanation." he said politely.

"Oh, don't mind me. I like to go on a bit about this lovely place. Tell me, what brings you both here?"

Courtney and Michael took a quick nervous glance at each other.

To Pippa it was a giveaway.

"I suspect you are here because you have friends who were involved in, or affected by, the awful events in the Captain's Table on Friday evening?"

"Yes, I work at Connor, Hartson and Bromberger Futures in the City. I have many friends who were in the Captain's when it happened."

"Essentially, the City of London financial hub has grown up around the church of St Matthew's, and it was much beloved by those patrons of the wealthy churchgoing community. Times change, and we serve many different purposes nowadays."

"We are obviously not regular church goers, but…"

Courtney was interrupted.

"That doesn't matter at all. My heart is with you and your friends. If you wish to say a prayer regarding anyone involved in or affected by the obscenity, then it would be most appropriate to offer your prayers directly to Saint Matthew. Prayers are considered more likely to be answered by asking a patron for intercession on your behalf."

"Yes, we would like to light a candle and say a prayer."

"We have a perfect place for just that. The stained glass window over the altar end of the church represents Saint Matthew." Pippa said, as she pointed to the window.

The couple both looked at the light streaming in through the stained glass, creating a wonderful picture to pray to.

"It's a beautiful window." said Mike.

"It certainly is beautiful, and extremely rare. Do you see how St Matt is depicted seated at a desk, with money spread out before him? That's not always the case. Usually in Christian Art, which might include paintings, stained glass windows, illuminated manuscripts, architecture and other forms the representation would be of him holding a purse or money-bag."

"How come Saint Matthew became the patron saint of finance?"

"The reason why he was adopted as the patron saint of finances and accountants is that he was originally a tax-gatherer, who collected money in the service of the Romans. Like many saints he was a martyr, and he was axed to death."

"Really! Thank you! I didn't know that."

Pippa's enthusiasm was beginning to grate a little, but she didn't seem to notice that.

"There are many patron Saints. They are all holy and virtuous men and women who are considered to be a defender of a specific group of people, profession, a cause or a country. There are saints days or feast days for all of them, and Saint Matt's is the 23rd of September."

"That's my birthday." exclaimed Michael.

"What a strange coincidence." replied the minister, "It was a Christian custom to recognise the annual commemoration of martyrs on the dates of their deaths at the same time celebrating their birth into heaven."

"Thank you. I think we'd like to pray together now."

"I'm sorry! There I go prattling on again. I'll leave you to yourselves now. Thank you for coming here today."

The two novices knelt before the stained glass window, staring at the patterns of light and colour and held hands. Prayers if any were silent and private. Then they both placed a couple of pound coins in an ancient metal box, before lighting two candles. There were quiet tears. Whatever they did seemed somehow inadequate in the circumstances. Perhaps there was a hint of embarrassment.

As they made to leave the church the Reverend Pippa approached them again.

"Can I advise you that that there will be a memorial service for the victims and their families on Wednesday afternoon?"

Courtney and Michael looked at each other.

"I'll be there." Mike confirmed.

"Sorry, I can't make that." frowned Courtney, "Work commitments, I'm afraid."

They were almost at the door when Mike had a sudden urgent need to turn around and go back to talk to the reverend. She was standing in the middle of the aisle looking up at the altar. He touched her gently on the arm and explained.

"I was supposed to be in the Captain's Table on Friday evening, but a succession of small events prevented me from getting there."

"You have been truly blessed to have escaped such brutality."

Michael opened his Alexander McQueen wallet, withdrew the little purple velvet star and showed it to Pippa

"Where did you get that?", she said with a smile...

"It's a long story," he said, "On Friday evening when I should have been in the Captain's Table, I met someone called George O'Donnell; an old tramp in the park. We had a very interesting chat, and when I returned home, I found this in my wallet."

She stared at the star and asked, "May I?"

Then she took the star from Michael's hand, and held it in a way that suggested it was the most precious thing she had ever set her eyes upon. Suddenly her face took on a whole new countenance. It was as if the brightest and most wonderful golden light shone through her. She handed the star back and clasped her hands around his, and looking deep into his eyes, she said, "Oh, that's wonderful, Michael. You really must treasure that."

Her hands felt like rays of warm sunshine, and for a few moments he was transfixed. Then he noticed a scruffily dressed man was weeping and praying alone in the back pews of the church. He looked somehow familiar. There was a strange, imperceptible aura about him; a kind of dim, but at the same time exceeding bright light surrounding his dishevelled and dirty appearance. A black light! Michael let go of Pippa's hands and approached the man, but he suddenly disappeared.

Chapter 8

Separate Heavens

On Sunday afternoon, after visiting the church, the couple made their way back to the area around the Captain's Table. Here, they found that the gate into Blenheim Circus Park had been reopened by the police. On the way through the park, a local folk rock band were performing on the bandstand.

"Hey, that's the band Melissa told me about; they're called "Redberryash", said Courtney, "Let's take a break from all this gadding about, and listen for a while."

"OK, sounds good to me." Michael replied.

"Are they famous then, this band?"

"No, but Melissa told me about how good she thought they were, and apparently they recently featured on the music programme "Later… with Jools Holland" on the BBC, after getting their first big break with a recording contract."

For the second time in an hour or two, the couple sat down on George O'Donnell's park bench. Immediately, that sense of crystal clear reminiscence washed over Michael again, but now it was more like a massive tidal wave in a tropical ocean. It was not a violent overwhelming, and not in the least aggressive. It was a wonderful, tranquil and soothing experience. While he sat there, the simple words of the creed permeated his whole being, as if they were part of him and he was part of them.

"Take a deep breath.
Look around you.
It's a beautiful world if you let it be.
Enjoy the warm sunshine.
Drink in the blue sky.

Smell the flowers.
Delight in their colours.
See the happiness of people together.
Listen to the birds singing and the ducks quacking.
Hear the music.
Feel the satisfaction in the blend of music and words.
Take your time.
Live your life at a stroll not a sprint.
Life is a vast learning curve."

Michael's brain was buzzing. He felt like he needed to learn something new, to open his mind to a greater understanding. He didn't have to wait for very long. When the band finished playing one of their own compositions called "Promises and Regrets", they introduced their new single. This was another group composition called "Separate Heavens".

The words of the song enveloped a willing consciousness. He yielded to their meaning.

"Someone opens up the book, and our pages slowly turn,
and as we take a closer look, there's so much more to learn.
Sometimes we follow dead-end trails in the shadows of our fears;
knowing that co-incidence can't be what it appears.

Yesterday's a place that we now think we understand,
and it's no good regretting or forgetting where we stand,
for when it's gone it's history, and can't be re-arranged,
what's done is done, the sun's set on it, and the past cannot be changed.

If life is just a lazy stroll around a crazy maze,
If time is just an instrument for counting out our days;
perhaps you're lost among the mist of possibilities,
or peeping round the corner into vast infinities.

So let's just walk a way together while we can,
and not head off to our separate heavens never holding hands.
Only a fool would bend the rules to return from whence they came;
today's the only way to play at winning in the game.

So let's just talk a while together and be glad;
thank our lucky stars for all the good times that we have.
Let no man steal the song you sing,
let no hand re-write your lines;
you'll never get to your own heaven,
if you ever change your mind."

Michael listened carefully. The words came to him all so clearly; almost as if George O'Donnell himself was saying those very same words in his quiet and persuasive way.

The couple weren't back at Michael's apartment for very long when the entry system phone rang, and when Courtney picked it up she found that Melissa and Heidi were waiting at the door.

"We've come over to make sure that everything's alright with you Mike." explained Heidi. Melissa nodded and gave Michael a cheeky wink. The other girls noticed, but were completely used to their friend and colleague's flirty ways. He looked back at her and smiled, remembering a recent Wednesday evening when, unbeknown to his girlfriend, they had shared a bed. He was enchanted by her emerald eyes and soft Irish lilt, but they both had to hide their physical attraction to each other for the sake of their relationships. It wasn't as if either of them hadn't played that game before with other partners and friends. Courtney made coffee, and as the four friends talked, Michael explained all that had happened in the past few days.

"It must be some kind of divine providence that you weren't able to get to the Captain's despite your best efforts." smiled Melissa, "The words you have illustrated that the tramp said to you are indeed a creed. They have certain similarities to something called Desiderata; although the tramp's words are much simpler and more direct. Are you familiar with Desiderata?"

"No, I don't think of heard of that."

"Well, it's a sort of poem, a creed, written by somebody called Max Ehrmann in 1927. It's used as a devotional, and I think somebody made a hit single of it in the 70's. Desiderata means desired things."

"What does it say?"

"Let's Google it on your computer, and then you'll see."

Even though they could have conducted their googling on a mobile phone in the room with the others, Mike and Melissa made for the study, and sat down at the computer, enjoying being close to each other, and exchanging knowing looks. As the other two girls began discussing plans for an imminent future wedding project, Melissa teased her prey by touching his hands and fluttering her long false eyelashes at him. He was careful not to make any inappropriate response. It was difficult to concentrate while being tempted by the beautiful colleen's advances, but he read the words of Desiderata over and over again.

"Go placidly amid the noise and the haste, and remember what peace there may be in silence.

As far as possible, without surrender, be on good terms with all persons.

Speak your truth quietly and clearly; and listen to others, even to the dull and the ignorant; they too have their story.

Avoid loud and aggressive persons; they are vexatious to the spirit.

If you compare yourself with others, you may become vain or bitter, for always there will be greater and lesser persons than yourself.

Enjoy your achievements as well as your plans.

Keep interested in your own career, however humble; it is a real possession in the changing fortunes of time.

Exercise caution in your business affairs, for the world is full of trickery.

But let this not blind you to what virtue there is; many persons strive for high ideals, and everywhere life is full of heroism.

Be yourself.

Especially, do not feign affection.

Neither be cynical about love; for in the face of all aridity and disenchantment, it is as perennial as the grass.

Take kindly the counsel of the years, gracefully surrendering the things of youth.

Nurture strength of spirit to shield you in sudden misfortune.

But do not distress yourself with dark imaginings.

Many fears are born of fatigue and loneliness.

Beyond a wholesome discipline, be gentle with yourself.

You are a child of the universe no less than the trees and the stars; you have a right to be here.

And whether or not it is clear to you, no doubt the universe is unfolding as it should.

Therefore be at peace with God, whatever you conceive Him to be.

And whatever your labours and aspirations, in the noisy confusion of life, keep peace in your soul.
With all its sham, drudgery and broken dreams, it is still a beautiful world.
Be cheerful.
Strive to be happy."

When Michael removed the small purple velvet star from his Alexander McQueen wallet and showed it to Melissa, her reaction seemed to be almost a carbon copy of the reverend Pippa's earlier on that day. She also held it in a way that suggested it was the most precious thing she had ever set her beautiful green Irish eyes upon. There it was once again for Michael to clearly see; the brightest and most wonderful golden light shone through her. She looked deep into his eyes, with a look that overwhelmed him and enveloped him in a feeling of sheer love and said, "Oh, how completely wonderful, Michael. Promise me that you will take that with you everywhere, and guard it with your life. Never let it go, and never be without it wherever you find yourself."

He touched her hands to retrieve the star. They were glowing like rays of warm sunshine, and for the second time that day, for a few moments, he was transfixed.

When they returned to planet Earth, he asked, "How do you know about Redberryash then?"

"Why do you ask?" she teased.

"We were listening to them in the park, and Courtney said that you were keen on them."

"They're a brilliant band. I saw them on that Jools Holland show, and loved their music and lyrics right away."

"The words are certainly very engaging. They make you think about things."

"I downloaded the album called "Separate Heavens" and I can't stop listening to it."

"Let's google it and see what comes up."

A few clicks and they were in the band's brand new website.

"I don't believe it," said Mike, "I went to school with the band leader, Neville Waterford. He was obsessed with music at school."

"Do you know him then?" Melissa enquired.

"No! We drifted apart after school; it's been 15 years since we last met. He hasn't changed much judging by that gallery picture."

After a while, the four friends came back together, and by this time, Michael had achieved an enormous sense of well being. He plonked himself down contented among the bevy of beauties seated on his Amode Italian designer leather sofa.

"It's lovely to see you all," he grinned, "And I'm beginning to understand what's happened, and just how lucky I've been."

"Mike's going to the memorial service at St Matthew's on Wednesday?" said Courtney.

"Yes, I forgot to ask you why you can't be there with me, sweetie."

The three girls all looked at each other.

"I'm so sorry, darling but we will be going away on Wednesday to organise a wedding at Gretna Green, followed by a reception at a Scottish castle."

That was a cue for Melissa's romantic overview, which soon overshadowed Mike's disappointment at having to attend the service without his girlfriend.

"You know all about Gretna and weddings over the anvil in the blacksmith's, but the bride and groom are having a second blessing at Auchen Castle. It's a wonderfully romantic place, set in the heart of Robert Burns country, not far from Gretna Green, and it's called the jewel of the Scottish Borders. There are Italian gardens and a private lake. The Beatles, the King of Norway, Margaret Thatcher, Barbara Cartland and Chris de Burgh have all stayed there. The descriptions and pictures are wonderful, showing spires, turrets, gilded staircases and panoramic views just as if it was set in somewhere akin to Disneyworld."

"The castle has a helicopter landing pad and parking for 60 posh cars." added the ever practical Heidi.

"Oh, and listen to this," enthused Melissa, "There's a falconry centre where the birds of prey have been trained to delivery wedding rings in a velvet bag at ceremonies in the garden."

"Wow!" said Michael, "And where is it exactly?"

"It's just over the Scottish border near to the town of Moffat." Heidi explained.

The group talked long into the evening, sharing wine and nibbles. Seeing the three girls together was a brilliant tonic. It was fun, and Mike's bubble gum and candyfloss brain fuzz from the previous day was now fully dissipated. When Melissa and Heidi left, Michael had sorted and filed everything that had happened neatly away.

Monday was always destined to be a difficult day. And so a difficult day dawned with a magnificent red and blistered orange sunrise, and a temperature in the seventies long before the city rush hour began. Michael woke up with a start and a sickening headache, after a fitful sleep interrupted with a series of short and terrifying nightmares. He felt as if he had slept on a conveyor belt of corrugated iron, and at regular intervals had been tipped off the end into a sauna inhabited by swarthy faced monsters carrying huge automatic weapons. After all the comforting experiences of the previous day, setting his mind at rest, fate seemed to have twisted his controls into a recurring and very vivid picture of him being trapped and tortured in the Captain's Table.

"I really don't want to go in to work today, but I know that I have no choice." he told his girlfriend.

She attempted to comfort him by replying, "Yes, I know it will be very distressing, but sooner or later you will have to face up to the consequences of Friday's disaster. You may even feel guilty for not being in the Captain's when it all kicked off, but fate played you a trump card in disguise. You did not have control of the situation, and you were a victim of it in a different context with, for you, an alternative outcome."

"You're right, sweetheart, but this morning it's very likely I'll find out which of my friends and colleagues I've lost, and that's going to hurt so bad."

"Sometimes in our lives we just have to face the music."

"The financial community is very close knit. We respect, even admire, some of our rivals as well as our own team members. It sickens me to know that I'll never see some of them again."

"You are stronger than you think, Michael. You will come through it, and Wednesday's memorial service at St Matthew's will provide some closure."

"I am fearful that I've already lost my best mate, Taylor, as well as my colleague Sir Eric McClintock, the man who everybody in the business aspired to equal."

"Wasn't he a bit of a rogue though?"

"Yes, of course, and he was definitely involved in some very shady deals, but nevertheless we couldn't have done anything else other than to look up to him. I don't know how his crew will get on without their Maverick Mack."

"It will take time for the wounds to heal, but you'll be OK, Mike. Come on, let's get up and have some breakfast."

"It may sound peculiar, but it's all made worse by the lack of information about the victims coming from the authorities on the news reports. They haven't told us exactly what happened, or issued a roll call of victims."

"It's an awfully large and complicated mess that needs to be sorted out. There may be some very good reasons why they're holding on to information. In these terrorist situations it's always possible that the Official Secrets Act needs to be applied temporarily, or even permanently. Dealing with vast amounts of money on a daily basis must by definition have a large element of secrecy or security about it."

"Yes, I know that they wouldn't want the news of losses of prominent dealers to affect the markets adversely. Look at what happened with the 9/11 tragedy. That had an immediate effect on the markets, but it was obviously an event on a much larger scale."

Eventually Michael went to work with a heavy heart. Some of his closest colleagues were missing, and he realised he would never see them again.

The bad weather threatened by the red sky sunrise, hung over the city like a dark blanket, as the brooding summer weather pattern oscillated thunderstorms through the streets, and cascaded rain in waterfalls down the sides of the financial district's tall buildings. All this adding the sense of doom and distress hanging over the premises of Connor, Hartson and Bromberger Futures in the City's financial heartland.

Michael met first with his senior partners, and was relieved to find none of them had been murdered, but there were empty seats behind desks where work colleagues had sat only a few days before.

Andrew McPherson, the right hand man to Bradley Connor had been one of the terrorist victims, and David Northcote-Green, a posh kid from Cambridge, and a recruit of Max Bromberger was also missing. Tears came to Michael's eyes when he learned that Wayne Chandler, an Essex boy, and his bright young thing, had also perished.

That day, separating his life into boxes did not come easy. Trying to focus totally on his business with no distractions, was impossible. The last things that he was likely to be were efficient, successful and bordering on utterly ruthless. At times, he felt that as far as his business associates were concerned, their expectation was that he would continue as usual. But he periodically had to ask himself whether his heart was in it. There were more empty seats in the workplace because C. H. and B Futures had made a concession that all survivors, if they wanted to, would be given a week off to allow them to get over the trauma.

As the day progressed slowly, contact with other traders revealed that the Untouchables had not only lost Maverick Mack and Taylor Brandon, but 2 more rival colleagues in Spencer Tavistock-Smith and Liam O' Leary.

Throughout the working day, and whenever the burden of losses pulled at his heart, he felt something compelling him to retrieve the small purple velvet star from his wallet, and just hold it in his hand for a while, until the stabbing pains of grief would ease. Michael was glad when the end of the day came and the storms overhead abated to reveal a humidity drenched silver grey cloudy sky.

The journey homeward and the rituals of early evening passed slowly, with no escape from the overwhelming sensation that the world had become a different place. A place with less happiness, less excitement and where anticipation of good things to come was sidestepped by the present sadness.

The phone rang. It was Courtney.

"How are you, Michael? Tell me about your day."

He proceeded to describe his day in great detail, even to mentioning the names of victims that his girlfriend would not know, and describing why he missed each and every one of them. She listened carefully, using all her counselling skills to take in and process all information and tone of voice without interruption.

"Do you want me to come over? I won't be able to stay long, but if you need me, I'll be there."

"No, that's OK, sweetheart. I have to go out anyway."

"Where are you going?"

"Something tells me that I must go to see Susannah, you know, Taylor's wife."

"Do you want me to come with you?"

"No, it's something I think I must do on my own. He was my best friend."

The huge, rambling house, in a posh North London suburb, had a Bates Motel aura about it, as Michael drove along the pretty, leafy, avenue at dusk. All the other houses had porch lights on, and signs of activity and life in their rooms and gardens. Taylor's pad was in complete darkness, a black hole in a universe of intermittent light. Michael clutched the small purple velvet star in his hand again for the umpteenth time that day, and rang the doorbell. He had only met Suzy a couple of times before.

Having rung three times with no sign of life, he was about to jump back in the car and leave when she appeared at the door. She was in a light blue Harvey Nicholls dressing gown and fluffy slippers. Her dark brown hair was uncombed, and her make up was in total disarray. Dark mascara caked her eyes, but did nothing to hide the tears that filled them. Her Italian good looks were smudged into an unattractive distressed and inconsolable expression. She was dazed and hardly coherent.

"Oh! Mike! It's you! Come in."

"Suzy, I'm so sorry…"

She stumbled slowly back into the living room ahead of him, unfocussed, not listening, entrapped in her prison of grief. Mike followed her. They sat down opposite each other. The thick curtains were drawn. A dim light from a table lamp just managed to pierce the gloom.

"Suzy, I'm so sorry about what's happened. Taylor and me were old friends. He was not only a work colleague, but my best mate."

She just stared into space, not able to muster a reply.

"I should have been there at the Captain's Table when it happened. Taylor phoned me only 30 minutes before to arrange a meeting there."

She stared across at Michael. Her eyes said nothing. The look was empty and desolate. He crossed the room and sat next to her, grasped her hands and made eye contact. She collapsed into his arms sobbing like a small, helpless child. She was trembling, cold and heavy against his body. He whispered soothing nothing sounds to attempt to console her.

For many minutes they clung to each other. Although they weren't that well acquainted, Suzy seemed to find some strength in being close to someone who had known her husband well. Then suddenly, she drew away still sobbing and cried, "Why didn't they go in earlier and stop the massacre? Why won't they release any information about what actually happened? All they've done is send someone round to tell me that Taylor is dead. They offered counselling, but said it would take time to arrange."

Michael sympathised, "I'm so sorry, Suzy, but I don't have any answers. I went in to work today, and everybody's in the same boat. No information; just continual news bulletins that repeat the same things, and then assert that the government will leave no stone unturned, and will strenuously seek justice for the victims. It's just not good enough!"

There was a short and very pregnant pause before the widowed spoke again, "And what about my boys? They're all at boarding school in Sussex. They'll have seen the news reports. What do I tell them? HOW can I tell them their dad has been murdered for what; being in the wrong place at the wrong time?"

Some of the hostages had been at work earlier in the day, and Michael had been piecing together bits of information from their experiences. Courtney had also told him what Karen Robbins had described about the brutal handling of victims. He had a pretty clear picture of what had happened during the siege, but he didn't want to provide any details to Suzy.

He asked, "Suzy, do you know Karen Robbins? I think she worked for Taylor."

"No!" she answered, "Why do you ask?"

"Well, Karen was one of the hostages who lived to tell the tale, and she told my girlfriend, Courtney, what actually happened."

He paused and wondered if he was doing the right thing. Then he continued, "Suzy, there may be very good reasons why the authorities are not providing any information to the public, but when you are ready, why don't you have a chat with Karen. When I get back home, I'll let you know her mobile number."

"I don't know if I want to."

"Tell you what. Wait until you have family and close friends with you and discuss it with them before you decide. You know it's not going to be pleasant."

She just stared at him lost in her thoughts and then she just replied, "OK!"

For a minute or two they just sat and looked at each other.

"Suzy, have you eaten today? Can I get you anything?"

"No, thanks, I don't feel like eating, but let me make you a cup of tea."

Michael didn't like tea that much, but he didn't refuse as he followed her to the kitchen. By the time they returned to the lounge she had gained a small measure of composure.

"I didn't ask you, Suzy, but is there anybody close by who can look after you?" Mike asked.

"My sister, Isabella is flying to London from Milan tomorrow, and my parents will be coming from Rome the day after."

Mike and Suzy made small talk about Taylor and the children for a while, and then it was time to leave. He was glad that he'd done the right and necessary thing, and promised to keep in touch.

Back home in his apartment, he switched on the TV and stood frustrated in front of it. In the endless TV bulletins the government continued to issue a bland statement about the tragedy, vowing justice for the victim's families. The authorities stressed the need for an adherence to the rule of law and the policy of no negotiation with terrorists. There was still an absence of personal detail other than the usual mention of Sir Eric McClintock. No attempts were made to describe the nature of the killings, other than to suggest brutality and random selection of victims.

Chapter 9

Dangerous Curves

All trading ceased at C. H. and B Futures as it did in the offices of all their rivals. On Wednesday afternoon at just before 3 o'clock, a stream of people from the City financial sector made their way to St Matthew's church. Most were wearing dark suits and ties, and carried themselves quietly, and with dignity to the memorial service. Michael was among them. The streets around the church were filled with troops toting automatic weapons. There was no hiding that this was a maximum security event.

The Reverend Pippa greeted Michael at the door, and insisted that he sit in the front row of the pews. Many of the mourners were recognised with nods, a few with saddened expressions and handshakes, but at least 20% of the assembly appeared to be from a collection of government security services. It was their dark grey suits, fixed and alert expressions, and bulging breast pockets crudely hiding small arms that gave them away. Very few wives or girlfriends were present.

"Thank you all for coming to this extremely sad and distressing occasion," the Reverend began, "I hoped that in my lifetime I would never have the need to conduct a service for this reason. But, we live in a world full of danger, where sometimes organisations plan and commit terrible and inexplicable acts of violence to pursue unreasonable goals. It may be of very small solace, but our Lord has stated unequivocally that vengeance is his alone. In our collective grief, we must restrain ourselves from any over-reaction, and trust in God to do as he sees fit to exact whatever retribution he feels is appropriate."

She paused and looked at heads hung low with pain and frustration at being helpless to make a response to the carnage. Then she asked for all to join in with a hymn.

"O God, our help in ages past,
our hope for years to come,
our shelter from the stormy blast,
and our eternal home:

Under the shadow of thy throne,
thy saints have dwelt secure;
sufficient is thine arm alone,
and our defense is sure.

Before the hills in order stood,
or earth received her frame,
from everlasting thou art God,
to endless years the same.

A thousand ages in thy sight
are like an evening gone;
short as the watch that ends the night
before the rising sun.

Time, like an ever-rolling stream,
bears all its sons away;
they fly, forgotten, as a dream
dies at the opening day.

O God, our help in ages past,
our hope for years to come,
be thou our guide while troubles last,
and our eternal home!"

Then she issued a roll call of the victims, reading slowly through the list of 22 names. For the first time since the tragedy occurred. those present had a full list of their friends and colleagues who had been murdered. Up until then, there had only been empty desks and piecemeal collections of names. Now at last, presumably under government direction, the full list was made public knowledge.

Prayers for the victims and their families were quietly observed, before Pippa turned to Mike and suddenly asked if he would like to say a few words. At first, he was reluctant to respond to such a casual and unexpected request, but something seemed to take possession of him and prompt him to retrieve the purple star from his wallet. When he opened the wallet to find the star, he was surprised to find a sheet of paper on which were the lyrics to "Only Turning Over Stones" another of the Redberryash group's new songs. Without having to think about it, he knew that he had to read it.

"We're lonely when we turn our heads,
Not hearing where our memories echo from,
And then we wonder at times of solitude,
Where all our good time friends have gone.
One day your heart stops singin';
It seems that time stands still,
Now you can stop and look back upon your life
as if watching from a distant hill.
Then it's time to meet the spirit in the sky,
To be gone,
No chance to turn around and say goodbye to anyone.
Why do we try to find the reason why?
There's not one.

When lowly souls just dream away,
Awake too late just howling at the moon,
And sadness waits for cruel fate;
All because our winter comes too soon.
When loves last brown leaf falls from the tree,
And away inside the wind she sweeps,
New snow will fill this window sill,
And deep upon the hill still sleeps.
Then it's time to meet the spirit in the sky,
To be gone,
No chance to turn around and say goodbye to anyone.
Why do we try to find the reason why?
There's not one

Careworn and windblown; it's only memories we own,
Turning over stones,
We all travel alone; destination unknown,
Turning over stones,
Foolish devil-may-care; rising up to the dare,
Turning over stones,
On a wing and a prayer; searching here, searching there,
Turning over, turning over, only turning over stones."

Soon the service drew to a close and the Reverend Pippa asked for the congregation to assemble outside on the small church forecourt. The assembly began to stream out of the church while the choir sang "Be Thou my Vision"

"Be Thou My Vision"

Be Thou my vision, O Lord of my heart
Naught be all else to me, save that Thou art
Thou my best thought by day or by night
Waking or sleeping Thy presence my light

Be thou my wisdom and Thou my true word
I ever with Thee and Thou with me, Lord
Thou my great Father, I, Thy true son
Thou in me dwelling and I with Thee one

Riches I heed not nor man's empty praise
Thou mine inheritance now and always
Thou and thou only first in my heart
High King of heaven my treasure Thou are

High King of heaven my victory won
May I reach heaven's joys, O bright heaven's Sun
Heart of my own heart whatever befall
Still be my vision O Ruler of all"

Outside the service concluded, as Pippa stood on a chair and proclaimed, "The dove is the universal symbol of peace, hope and freedom. Releasing doves can represent the release of the spirits of the deceased. Today we release 22 doves for the victims of the Captain's Table tragedy."

Above the porch of the church, 22 doves were set free, and flew off together into the clear blue London skies.

Pippa added softly, "Rest in peace."

As Michael was about to make his way back to work, an elderly man, very smartly dressed in a dark blue pinstriped suit, blue shirt and black tie, and super shiny black shoes approached him. The face was familiar but somehow very out of context.

"You don't recognise me, do you?" he said.

Well," Michael replied, "It may sound odd, but I do, and I don't at the same time."

The face just smiled. His teeth were dazzling, pure white; his features distinct and clean.

"Have a look in your wallet." he instructed.

The wallet was opened with shaking hands. The velvet star had disappeared. A flush of panic gripped Michael's senses as he wiped sweat from his forehead. He was puzzled, troubled, confused.

"Is this what you are looking for?" said the man, handing over the precious little star. Michael took it back with the most immense feeling of relief he had ever felt in his life.

"Know who I am now, do you?" came the question.

"Yes! You're George O'Donnell. We talked on a park bench a few days ago. But you don't look the same. What's happened?"

"Never mind that! You understand now how precious the little star in your hand is, don't you?"

Michael nodded. George turned and walked away.

One hundred and ten miles north of London, on the M6 near Birmingham, the weather suddenly changed. The city swelter, which had persisted for nearly a month, was broken once again by another storm. But this storm would be like no other Michael had ever experienced in his life before. It had only been a week since the Captain's Table incident, but in the emotional turmoil and grief of personal losses Michael's life was inexorably set on a different path. Sometimes it seemed as if his previous 30 years had been lived with eyes and ears closed, with a determination to follow a destructive dead end trail to nowhere; to pursue money, wealth, status, recognition at whatever cost. Many of those aspects of his being no longer appeared to be quite so important.

He had missed Courtney so much in the last few days; so much, that on this Friday evening he had acted completely on impulse. He decided to surprise her by driving up to Scotland for the wedding she was involved in organising.

He recognised that she would be at work, but he just needed to be near her.

His red Boxster Spyder had made excellent time, streaming out of London in the bright sunshine and continuously snarling evening traffic. Now the world darkened as the storm gathered in the northern skies. There was a brooding stillness; a feeling of impending doom about the way the tension of the coming maelstrom was building. He could see no lightning, hear no thunder, and smell no rain in the distance as he guided his car along the motorway. The darkness surrounded him, enveloped him like a huge blanket. It was only 7 pm. Sunset wasn't due until around nine.

An hour later, passing Manchester, there was still no break in the stretching of suspense. Michael switched on the radio and sang along to "Dangerous Curves", another track from the Redberryash album.

"I'm driving in my Porsche in the dead of night,
Roaring through the countryside, blazing headlights,
Pedal to the metal, squealing tyres and burning rubber,
Shifting through my gears beyond a hundred miles an hour,
I'm your tail gater and I'm bringing up your rear,
I don't want no motorways, no straight roads, or low gears,
Want to feel the G-force, the horsepower, and the swerve,
Man I'm just a petrolhead on dangerous curves,
Dangerous curves, dangerous curves,
Man I'm just a petrolhead on dangerous curves,
Running my wheels over dangerous curves,
Showing my skills on dangerous curves,
Moving in for the kill on dangerous curves,
Man I'm just a petrolhead on dangerous curves.

Dressed up in my finery for nightlife on the pull,
Wallet stuffed with ready cash, attitude full of bull (shit),
Not looking for that special someone, no just a one night stand,
No long term commitment babes, no-one ties my hands,

I'm God's gift to women, you know I'm the man,
Got the looks, got the dosh, aint no also-ran,
No computer dating, can't get what I deserve,
Looking for a lady with dangerous curves,
Dangerous curves, dangerous curves,
Looking for a lady with dangerous curves,
Kissing and caressing those dangerous curves,
Counting my blessings for dangerous curves,
Aint doing no confessing on dangerous curves.
Looking for a lady with dangerous curves.

I went to see the doctor, I was feeling below par,
Drove there at breakneck speed in my turbo charged car,
He fixed monitor wires to my body and my head,
He umm'd and ah'd, and took some notes, and this is what he said,
I've been looking at your test results, so let's not pretend,
Someone here's been burning the candle at both ends,
You'd better slow down my friend, you been living on your nerves,
There's overwhelming evidence for dangerous curves,
Dangerous curves, dangerous curves,
There's overwhelming evidence for dangerous curves,
Live fast, die young, on dangerous curves,
Won't last too long on dangerous curves,
One day you'll die on dangerous curves.
There's overwhelming evidence for dangerous curves. "

Somewhere near Preston, getting on for 2 hours since the storm had threatened, it finally broke with a massive overwhelming vengeance.

There was no need to count between lightning and thunder to determine distance away, There was no distance. The violent epicentre of the storm was directly overhead. Skies were filled with a wall of blinding light, as the air crackled with electricity, and thunder roared like the sound of a wave that could drown the whole world. Here was a monsoon of epic proportions. The motorway was a river. The windscreen wipers were ineffective. But doing the sensible thing and stopping at the next service area wasn't on the agenda for the Boxter driver. He was on a mission. He was unstoppable. He gripped the steering wheel, put his foot hard on the accelerator and went for oblivion.

Suddenly, all of Michael's senses tuned to full alert.

"So, my friend, we meet again." said the familiar voice of a man, who by some unbelievable magic was sitting in the passenger seat.

"Find the star in your wallet, Michael." said the voice beside him.

What was happening? Whose voice was that? He knew who it sounded like but he dare not look.

The voice continued, "Do you remember something I told you in the park? I said that sometimes life tells you that you shouldn't go somewhere or do something. Instinct, a 6th sense, whatever it is, intervenes, and it is seldom wrong. Sometimes life tells you to go somewhere, or do something, and you don't listen to that little voice. That's when you might get it wrong."

Michael listened, but he couldn't answer or take his eyes off the road.

"Now, trust me please and quickly find the star in your wallet, Michael." said the voice again.

With one hand gripped tightly on the steering wheel, the driver fumbled in his inside pocket for the wallet, and retrieved the star.

"Now, put it on the dashboard." came the instruction.

As soon as the little emblem was put in place, a myriad of a million blue and gold stars swirled around the car in spiralling circles. The terror and violence of the massive storm was instantly replaced with a warm, welcome feeling of security. It seemed as if the car was rising slowly from the road surface on an invisible continuous slope. Then the swirl of brilliant twinkling star lights broke from their circular formation and began to stretch out ahead of the car in two parallel lines, as if forming into train tracks moving into the distance.

It seemed like the car was flying on a soft conveyor belt above the motorway. There was no sense of danger. Michael felt completely safe.

The next thing that he knew was that the storm had abated and tiredness had overtaken him as he passed along the M6 close to Kendal. He was only 60 miles from the Scottish Borders, but it was nearly 11 pm. There was only just over an hour's driving time left to reach his destination, but by this time, even in the Boxter, he was unlikely to arrive at Gretna before midnight. Something told him to turn off at Tebay services and check into The Westmorland Hotel set back just 2 minutes from the motorway. He was upset that he hadn't the energy to complete the drive.

He slept like a baby.

The next morning when he woke up and switched on the TV, he had an enormous déjà vu moment from the previous Saturday. The news reported that during the night, there had been an unprecedented violent storm in the North West and a major pile up on the M6 after junction 40. More than thirty vehicles had been involved and at least 20 people were killed or injured. He asked himself, "What is happening?"

It seemed that he was being quietly guided into directions where he could avoid potentially lethal situations. He didn't take a lot of convincing that he was being somehow protected by the fantastic magical powers of the velvet star in his pocket.

Chapter 10

Don't You Wonder?

After the longest, hottest summer in living memory, November arrived with an apocalyptic shock. There was no sliding slowly down from the green and bright days of summer, through the cooler leaf-falling autumn days, and then slipping gradually into an increasing icy coldness of winter. It was almost as if somebody had switched off the warmth of the sunshine in Mike's world. The Indian summer of September and early October dropped within a few days over a precipice into heavy frosts, ripping hail, flurries of snow and the ice covered roads of winter.

That morning in November, Michael had woken up from a very vivid and detailed recurring nightmare. It was the same nightmare that he had experienced many times throughout the previous 6 months. He was in the Captain's Table, hanging upside down from a rope tied to his ankles, in agony from a succession of kicks, punches and rifle butt blows across his face and body, with a plastic bag over his head.

Suffocating, struggling to get air in vain; panic, sweating, blackness, dying.

This time it had ended differently. In the final death pangs of the nightmare, he had suddenly and reassuringly been at peace, while a quiet, soothing repeated message from a voice he had heard before filtered through to his senses. He had a vision of a derelict bungalow at an address in Barking. When he woke the image and location were indelibly imprinted in his memory. He had never been to Barking in his life before, but now he had the feeling that he was being drawn by some irresistible impulse to visit the place in his vision.

Soon, he was making his way out to Barking on the District Line tube. The train clattered its way along the tracks, making slow but persistent progress to the station. Upon arrival, the bleak, unwelcoming terrain of suburban East London bade him no greeting.

He staggered with difficulty through the chill, frosty, morning air, pulling up the collar of his woollen black coat against the cold. He was making for a small derelict bungalow in Oaktree Avenue, on the other side of the deserted park. A camaraderie of sullen looking ducks was silent on the lake, scratching at the sheet of ice which had invaded their habitat over night. The path side trees loomed like dark foreboding skeletons in the frozen atmosphere. His head was throbbing from where he had fallen on the ice while entering through the park gates. He had to get to the bungalow and safely indoors quickly, and each breath was becoming harder to wrestle into his lungs. His legs were heavy and shaky. He felt an immense sense of relief that his walk was over, when at last he matched the image in his nightmare to the building that confronted him.

A garden gate hung on one screw of a bottom hinge. He entered a front garden that was overgrown with brambles and sparse bushes, edging a concrete path, green with age and algae. Two windows stared at him like big sad eyes with grey, cobwebbed net curtains at their edges. A huge, ancient front door had patches of bare wood showing through the peeling dark brown paint. The door was ajar. He entered.

A long hallway of bare boards and peeling magnolia emulsion led him to a large room overlooking the back garden, features obscured by 3 foot high grass matted in November frosts. The large room was decorated with mould stained floral wallpaper. It was cold and empty apart from 2 wicker chairs.

Something told him to sit down and wait. Wait in this dirty, unkempt, smelly, uncomfortable and gloomy place; so different from his plush, sterile, squeaky clean, luxury apartment. He wrapped his coat tightly around him, folded his arms, and shivered. He fought for every breath of Arctic air, and watched as it streamed out of his body like a damp smoke. Was it colder in there than outside? He heard the swirling wind rattling the windows and doors.

He wondered; "Why this place. Why had I been drawn here?"

He rubbed the swollen lump on the side of his head. It hurt so much. He replayed the fall in his mind; over and over. His eyes closed, and his mind wandered. He remembered the words he had spoken at the memorial service for the Captain's Table victims in St Matthew's church six months before. It was as if George O'Donnell was reading them in his brain in that soft, persuasive voice.

"We're lonely when we turn our heads,
Not hearing where our memories echo from,
And then we wonder at times of solitude,
Where all our good time friends have gone.
One day your heart stops singin';
It seems that time stands still,
Now you can stop and look back upon your life
as if watching from a distant hill.
Then it's time to meet the spirit in the sky,
To be gone,
No chance to turn around and say goodbye to anyone.
Why do we try to find the reason why?
There's not one."

"You see Michael, that the most important thing in anybody's life is people; family and friends, workmates and colleagues. Life is so very short and we all seem to grow up and grow old very quickly. There must always be an end to this life and it may be sudden and premature. There may be no chance to say goodbye. It is beyond our imagination to fathom a reason why things can be this way."

"When lowly souls just dream away,
Awake too late just howling at the moon,
And sadness waits for cruel fate;
All because our winter comes too soon.
When loves last brown leaf falls from the tree,
And away inside the wind she sweeps,
New snow will fill this window sill,
And deep upon the hill still sleeps.
Then it's time to meet the spirit in the sky,
To be gone,
No chance to turn around and say goodbye to anyone.
Why do we try to find the reason why?
There's not one"

"When we are left behind in this world, after people we have known or loved have said goodbye, we have a difficult burden to bear. But in the fullness of time, we will all meet again with those we have lost. In a beautiful paradox, when the time comes for us to leave the world behind, we pass the burden, the grief of loss to others we have known who live on."

"Careworn and windblown; it's only memories we own,
Turning over stones,
We all travel alone; destination unknown,
Turning over stones,
Foolish devil-may-care; rising up to the dare,
Turning over stones,
On a wing and a prayer; searching here, searching there,
Turning over, turning over, only turning over stones."

"We all arrive in this world, naked, and with nothing to bring except ourselves, and we leave with only memories. But memories are shared, and they don't die with us. When we leave the Earthly Realm, however hard we may search for it, our destination is unknown. But, my friend, be assured. There is a common destination."

Then there was silence; peace and quiet. Michael opened his eyes. George O'Donnell was sitting in the other wicker chair. Once again, he bore the exact dishevelled appearance of the tramp in Blenheim Circus Park; scruffy clothes, a weather-beaten and grimy face, yellow teeth in a broad smile. The strange, imperceptible aura surrounded him; a dim, but at the same time exceeding bright light. A black light!

They smiled at each other.

"Hello, my friend. Do you remember me?"

"Yes! You are George O'Donnell."

"I'm so glad you remembered the poem you read at St Matthew's 6 months ago?"

"You put it in my wallet; didn't you?"

"I may have done."

"And you knew that the Reverend Pippa would ask me to say a few words; didn't you?"

"I may have done."

"You were there in the church."

"Yes, I was indeed."

"And you sat beside me in that storm when I was driving up to Scotland later that week."

"Yes, I did."

"What's all this about then?"

"I'm sorry!"

Michael opened his wallet and removed the small purple velvety piece of fabric in the shape of a 6-pointed star upon which was written in gold script "Look! Listen! Learn!" with the initials "G O'D" underneath. He offered it in the tramp's direction.

"This! The little star that you gave me seems to be a talisman. It has some magical properties. It protects me in harmful situations. It's a shame that it didn't stop me falling over this morning and banging my head."

"Yes, I'm sure you are right. But we have more important things to talk about right now."

"What do you mean?"

"Well, my friend, the last 6 months since we met in the Park in the summer were all part of a learning curve for you."

The tramp beamed a massive smile at Michael, and the black light seemed to suddenly swirl around and envelope him. In his mind he was transported back to the incident in the park 6 months before, when George had spoken in a way that provided a gentle persuasive compulsion to stay put on the park bench and listen. His words were spoken slowly, and with deliberation in short sentences in a soft and velvet smooth, enchanting voice. He heard those same words again.

"Take a deep breath.
Look around you.
It's a beautiful world if you let it be.
Enjoy the warm sunshine.
Drink in the blue sky.
Smell the flowers.
Delight in their colours.
See the happiness of people together.
Listen to the birds singing and the ducks quacking.
Hear the music.
Feel the satisfaction in the blend of music and words.
Take your time.

Live your life at a stroll not a sprint."

The orator continued.

"You have been in a hurry, not just this evening, but all of your life.

Learn a lesson today.

You thought you needed to be somewhere at 7 o'clock, and you failed to get there in time. Am I right?"

"You will be glad that you failed, my friend.

Sometimes life tells you that you shouldn't go somewhere.

Instinct, a 6th sense, whatever it is, intervenes, and it is seldom wrong.

Sometimes life tells you to go somewhere, and you don't listen to that little voice.

That's when you might get it wrong.

Life is a vast learning curve."

Michael reflected again on those words, just as he had many times in recent months.

"George O'Donnell is just a sort of reverse acronym for God isn't it?"

"Is it? Do you think so? That's very flattering. Thank you!"

"You are God! Aren't you?"

George smiled and then laughed.

"No, Michael. But he is a very good friend of mine."

"OK, so why did you bring me here, to this awful place?"

"You came here of your own accord. Something told you to come here, but you made the choice, my friend."

"Again, why am I here?"

"We are all running towards something, Michael, but at the same time running away from something else. Do you understand?"

"I'm not sure that I do."

"I have been your guardian angel, but now I am sorry to tell you that the time has come when you must soon move on to a better place. And I, I also must move on. It may seem cruel that your Earthly life must end, but be assured you will be going to a better place, and you will have a real purpose to fulfil on arrival."

"Are you telling me that I'm going to die?"

"Do not be afraid. This must come to all."

"But.. but.... but....but!"

So many questions, but no answer to the big one, "Why!"

The black light swirled around Michael again, as if he was being released from a comfortable and reassuring grip. He flopped back in the wicker chair; exhausted, confused, annoyed. George had disappeared. He sat alone with his thoughts, his fears; his questions. He sat there for a long, long while, frightened to move.

Eventually, he staggered out of the bungalow, tears freezing on his face as quickly as he cried them. He hobbled through the park between the foreboding lines of bare, black, trees, past the frozen lake where the ducks still scratched and slipped, and up the hill to the station. Intense cold bit at his bones, and his expensive woollen coat was no barrier against the cruel all permeating wind. Skies above were pearly white and full of imminent snow. Within yards of the station, a hailstorm erupted over his head, and he was being pelted with hailstones the size of golf balls. They soaked his coat, and ripped at his face and hands. He decided to pop into the Spotted Dog pub, and warm up with a coffee and a brandy while the storm subsided.

"What'll it be?" said the barman.

"Can you do me a cappuccino please, and a double Hennessy's Cognac."

"Good choice, sir. Bloody cold out there, isn't it."

Michael sat down next to the open fire, and sipped at the brandy. He felt the chills receding as the fire warmed him on the outside and the brandy warmed him inside. The jukebox was playing a familiar tune; another track from the Redberryash album. He listened while the words of "Don't you wonder?" spilled over him. Somehow, they seemed so completely apt.

"So your mind wanders empty, there's ice in your veins,
Staring eyes cold and angry, see your spirit in chains;
But your heart is on fire crying out to be heard,
Just the way that you play and fine words that you say in your songs;
And you've stood on the edge for so long, just tryin' to be strong -
Don't you wonder?
Don't you wonder?
Don't you wonder?
What went wrong?

A small voice in your head just won't go away,
You've a choice to take chances; ev'ry dog has its day,
But you choose not to gamble, win or lose, it's OK;

At the point of no return, the return of no point is so strong;
And you've stood on the edge for too long, to be rushing headlong -
Don't you wonder?
Don't you wonder?
Don't you wonder?
What went wrong?

And so every day I tear out my soul and display it for you to review.
I keep hearin' you say you think it's OK, but not what you're looking for;
So what's new?
So what's new?

We all pray for the circle remaining unbroken;
And so may the broken stay unchained and encircled;
If the game's worth the candle, we'd just better play on,
Or put out the fire, shake the bird off the wire and be gone;
'Cause we've lived on the edge for too long and we've gotta stay strong -
Don't you wonder?
Don't you wonder?
Don't you wonder?
What went wrong?

You know there's only one way that you're gonna pay the fare that you owe,
For the ride.
When you've been there before, your heart dropped to the floor and your
spirit's all broken;
Inside,
Outside on your own,
Where have you been?
Outsider alone;
Still lookin' in;
Cut down to the bone; head in a spin,
Face turned to stone, you never can win,
Just a voice on the phone, not listenin',
For reasons unknown, still wonderin',
Outside on your own, still wonderin'."

"Your coffee, Sir." said the barman as he placed the cup on the table by the jukebox. "Enjoy!"

Michael soon learned that the Spotted Dog had made him a cappuccino to die for.

Chapter 11

Catch a falling star

Outside, snow had fallen over night and settled on the open spaces of the city. The panorama was almost like a classic scene on a Christmas card. Skies overhead were cloudy white, with more snow ready to fall. A weak, yellow sun reflected off the bright, white surfaces. Inside, St Matthew's was filled to bursting. Every pew, and every nook and cranny was occupied with mourners. It was gloomy. For some reason, the beautiful stained glass window at one end of the church, depicting St Matthew, was hidden behind a heavy black velvet curtain. Consequently, the place of worship seemed much more dark and dismal than usual. Only a few church candles flickered their faint light across the faces of the congregation. On that day, many of the same faces were present that had attended the memorial service for the victims of the Captain's Table massacre six months before. Only one significant face was missing from the throng. His face, his body, his heart, his soul, his very being, had arrived in a fancy box, fashioned in solid redwood with ornate brass handles. Michael Hartson was that face. Michael Hartson had died, the unfortunate victim of a brain haemorrhage, and mourners were weeping for a good man, a fine friend, a loyal work colleague, or a respected competitor, who had gone to meet his maker.

Just before the service began, an elderly man, very smartly dressed in a dark blue pinstriped suit, blue shirt and black tie, and super shiny black shoes entered at the back of the church and clanged the large wooden door shut to keep out the cold. He wasn't recognised by anyone. He had met Michael for the first time on a park bench about 6 months before. His name was George O'Donnell.

The minister emerged from a side door out of the darkness, splendidly attired in her best ceremonial robes, and made her way carefully to a position behind the lectern. She lit 2 large candles to illuminate her presence, and her long dark blonde hair framed an almost ghostly pale face.

"Good afternoon, ladies and gentlemen. Thank you all for coming. It's heartening to see a full church even in these sad circumstances. My name is Phillipa Jackson, the Reverend Phillipa Jackson. That sounds very self-important but you can just call me Pippa. Today I have the sad duty of conducting a funeral service for someone special. I only met Mike 6 months ago when he came together with his partner, Courtney, to light candles and offer prayers for the victims of," she paused and pulled a face, "Well, you all know what!"

People shuffled in their pews, reminded again of a fateful day 6 months before that had changed many lives forever.

The Reverend continued, "My first very impressions were that they were a lovely couple who seemed to be absolutely right for each other. Michael's passing on is a tragic loss. The loss of someone still young with so much living still to do. Memorial services traditionally follow a set route. I am supposed to pretend that I knew Mike very well, and to describe some details of his life as if he was my best friend and a regular churchgoer. Well! He wasn't, and I am not a traditional vicar. So we are going to things differently. We are here, first of all, to celebrate a life. So let's do that."

There was a long pause. All that could be heard was breathing, a few people coughing, some weeping quietly. A growing air of expectation filled the church. Then the words of a Westlife song filled the void.

"Everybody's looking for that something,
one thing that makes it all complete…"

Faces turned to smile at each other in the darkness. The beauty of the song, and the significance of the lyrics, warmed the atmosphere and broke the tension.

"…I'm flying without wings,
and that's the joy you bring;
I'm flying without wings."

The song finished. There was another pause before the Reverend Pippa resumed her address. She shuffled some papers, cleared her throat and looked up.

"Mike's mum, Dierdre gave me this to read to you. These are her words, not mine." she said, waving a single sheet of paper in the candlelight.

"Michael was born in Brentwood, Essex on 23rd September 1983. He was an only child. He went to school at St Martin's, and left with 10 GCSE's to work in the City's financial sector. His talents were very quickly recognised, especially by a colleague, Sir Eric McClintock.

When Michael's dad, Henry, died just over 10 years ago, he was a tower of strength. Henry was a massive influence in Michael's life. I think that's where he first found an interest in mathematics, computers, and finances. We were both very, very proud of our only son and the way he had made a success of his working life. When he was younger, he was a determined, sometimes ruthless man. But he was never, ever nasty or vindictive. After the Captain's Table, something changed him. He seemed to mellow, to become more relaxed and at peace with the world. For some reason which is a complete mystery to me, a few weeks ago Michael made a visit to Barking, and collapsed in the street outside a pub called the Spotted Dog, near Barking Station. He was taken to hospital, and died the next day. I was at his hospital bedside when he passed away. He wanted to show me something in his pyjama pocket just before he died. But he ran out of breath before he managed it. The nurses found this small piece of velvet in the shape of a star in his pocket. On it, are inscribed the words "Look! Listen! Learn!" and there are the initials "G. O'D. Courtney tells me that this emblem was very important to him."

Pippa held up the talisman, and then called Courtney to the lectern. Her makeup was smudged by tears, but otherwise she was immaculately attired all in black. She composed herself, and with great dignity addressed those present, saying, "These are the words of a song from Michael's favourite band Redberryash."

"The horizon is not at the end of your nose,
Or the tips of your fingers, or tips of your toes,
The horizon is set at the end of a rainbow.

In placid blue waters moving quiet and lazy,
In rugged red deserts shimmering rude and remote,
In lush, warm, green forests spreading far past your gaze,

In sleek silver clouds floating high and aloof,
In distant white mountains guarding treasures undreamed of,
In precious gold sunsets blazing day's glorious end.

The horizon's as far as your mind's eye perceives,
It's as wide as the truths, in which you believe,
It's as high as the ideals you seek to achieve,
It's as deep as the sorrow you feel when you grieve,
It's as big as the love that you give and receive.

The horizon is always just out of reach,
It's as bitter as vinegar, sweet as a peach,
An elusive illusion beyond pure extremes,
To bring into focus our hopes and our dreams."

She left the lectern as tears welled up again, and rejoined the front line of the congregation. There was a pause in the proceedings as if the world was taking another breather.

Then the Reverend reappeared at the front with a huge beaming smile on her face. She said, "Thank you, Courtney. I have a very nice surprise for you."

The chief mourner looked confused.

"As you said earlier, Michael's favourite band was Redberryash."

There was another pause, and a continued smile from the minister.

"Well, here they are to sing a couple of songs from their recent album."

The curtain covering the stained glass window opened at the back of the church. Light streamed through the window and the image of St Matthew, sending streams of white, gold, green, red, blue, all the colours of the Universe, onto the congregation. Eyes squinted in the sudden flood of magical colours, glistening and flickering through the church, and out of the blaze of light four figures appeared sitting on stools, smiling, prepared. The air of anticipation was touchable.

Then they began to sing the song "All you can become"

"And in the end my friend all you can become
is the sum of all the words you've said,
and all the deeds you've done,
of everyone you've ever met,

and everything you've seen,
the depths of your experience,
and the places you have been.

Your value is in who you are and how you became that way,
and one day you may understand why it has to be that way.

And in the end my friend all you can become
is the sum of all the words you've said,
and all the deeds you've done,
of every blade that cut you,
and every word that soothed,
of all the times your heart stood still,
and the times your spirit moved.

Your value is in who you are and how you became that way,
and one day you may understand why it has to be that way.

And in the end my friend all you can become
is the sum of all the words you've said,
and all the deeds you've done,
of all the love that you poured out,
and gathered in together,
of every breath you ever breathed,
and every trial endeavoured.

Your value is in who you are and how you became that way,
and one day you may understand why it has to be that way.

And in the end you know my friend what you'll become is not
the sum of all your treasures and the riches you have got.

Your value is in who you are and how you became that way,
and when you understand my friend I've nothing more to say."

At the end of the song, the leader of the band, Neville Waterford, moved to the lectern and began to speak.

"Michael and I were at school together. We were true Essex boys. Mike was always a very determined and focussed schoolmate. He was captain of the rugby team, even though he hated rugby, and really preferred football. Pissed off that he never got to be head boy. Always immaculately turned out. He looked smart and he was smart. He was a babe magnet and all of us ugly boys envied him."

A giggle rippled through the females in the congregation. The speaker wasn't in the least bit ugly. He had tight-curled long blonde hair, broad shoulders atop a slim, tall frame and a face that would have adorned a classical Greek statue.

"We drifted apart after school. I went into music; he went into finance. He was very successful and made a small fortune, and I scraped along in various bands, finally ending up forming Redberryash. We were relatively unknown until very recently when we were lucky enough to get a spot on "Later with Jools Holland Show on the BBC". I'd like to think that Mike played a part in the bands' current success, because when we were at school together, he always encouraged me with my interests in music and playing the guitar and singing. In the last six months, we met twice when he came backstage at our concerts at the Queen's Theatre in Hornchurch and the Civic in Chelmsford.

It was like we'd never been apart. We hit it off again right away. It's truly a great privilege to play for you all today to remember a good friend. If only he was still here to enjoy it. But, I'm sure that now he'll be somewhere safe and beautiful listening. Thank you, Michael. This is especially for you."

Then Neville returned to the space underneath the window and the band played a song called "Everlasting Light".

"Found a fairy circle in the meadow,
Fresh and wet, with new morning dew,
So I stepped inside this magic little spotlight,
Made a wish, and then I thought of you,
Then turned around, one, and two, and three,
Warmed in watery, summer's-gone sunshine,
Sealed the wish into my achin' heart,
And now it's just a matter of time.

Beside a secret garden's wishing well,
Almost hidden by a tangled leafy hue,
We kissed, and then I risked a lucky penny,
Made a wish, and then I thought of you,
We held our breath while waiting for the splash,
Of my penny falling far below,
Until the rippling echoes of the water,
Told me now it's time for you to go.

You left a howling hollow in my heart,
An empty vacant space, so icy blue,
I wandered lonely underneath the tall skies,
Whispered a prayer, and then I thought of you,
Then shivered in the green tree shade,
My broken heart was pounding fit to burst,
I saw a chequered road stretching out afar,
And disappearing into distant dust.

Now a holy beacon shines my way,
A bright guiding light there to see me through,
And as sure as sunset follows sunrise everyday,
I say a prayer, and then I think of you,
Amongst the busy turmoil of my days,
Against the darkest forces in my nights,
Leaving pale and faded shadows to the past,
Towards the everlasting light."

The service continued when the Reverend compassionately declared the 23rd Psalm.

"The Lord is my shepherd; I shall not want.
He maketh me to lie down in green pastures:
he leadeth me beside the still waters.
He restoreth my soul: he leadeth me
in the paths of righteousness for his name's sake.
Yea, though I walk through the valley of the shadow of death,
I will fear no evil:

for thou art with me;
thy rod and thy staff they comfort me.
Thou preparest a table before me
in the presence of mine enemies:
thou anointest my head with oil;
my cup runneth over.
Surely goodness and mercy
shall follow me all the days of my life:
and I will dwell in the house of the Lord for ever."

Then the service was concluded with the wonderful words of Ruth Burgess:

"Into the freedom of wind and sunshine
We let you go
Into the dance of the stars and the planets
We let you go
Into the wind's breath and the hands of the star maker
We let you go
We love you, we miss you, we want you to be happy
Go safely, go dancing, go running home."

A small select few gathered afterwards together with Pippa in the reverend's small apartment; Courtney, Heidi, Melissa, Taylor Brandon's widow, Susannah, and Dierdre Hartson all dressed in black. Only Melissa provided an exception by wearing a wide, shocking pink headband in her auburn tresses. The ladies drank tea, and nibbled at smoked salmon sandwiches, while talking quietly.

"So, Michael was supposed to be in the Captain's Table when the terrorists took over, but he didn't get there for some reason, and that's when he met this George O'Donnell character, who somehow managed to put the little star in his wallet?" said Dierdre.

"Yes, that's exactly what happened. He was mysteriously prevented from getting there, by a series of little insignificant events." said Courtney.

"He was going to meet my Taylor there to discuss an oil deal with 2 American businessmen." said Susannah.

"That's right! Michael and Taylor were great friends, even though in many ways they were competitors for business." Courtney replied.

Suzy's faced screwed up before she continued, "Taylor was one of the victims of the terrorist's brutality. I found out from Karen Robbins what actually happened. It's so horrific that the authorities have never revealed any details about the true extent of the tragedy. I'm glad that when the SAS finally went in, they killed them all. I have no mercy in my heart for them. They took my husband, a good man, away from me and my 3 sons."

The minister felt that she needed to provide the basis of some solace for the bereaved and offered, "It's understandable how you may feel about that now. Time will be the healer, and we must all take faith from the Bible teaching that our Lord God said, "Vengeance is mine!" Hate can only be a negative force. We must forgive however heinous the offence."

It didn't work! Anger quickly came to the boil.

"I will never forgive the terrorists, and I think the authorities are just as much to blame." Suzy spat, she jumped to her feet, her eyes wild with fury.

"Can you tell us why that is?" asked Courtney, as Pippa nodded.

"I don't understand why the SAS didn't go in sooner?"

"Would that have helped?" asked the Reverend.

Taylor's widow became even more agitated; her temperature was rapidly rising. She almost shouted, "The terrorists separated the men and women, and made the women watch as they beat up the men and ritually humiliated them. The men were executed when a rope was flung over a beam in the tavern, and each victim was then hung upside down by one leg while they punched and kicked his head. Finally, each victim had a plastic bag placed over his head, and was slowly brought to a point of near suffocation, before they then had their throats slit. That is how my husband died. How am I supposed to feel about that?"

All the ladies in the room were stunned into silence. The irate mourner continued, "The Jihadists threatened to kill 2 people every hour until their demands were met, but because there was no gunfire, the authorities assumed it was a bluff, until someone as yet unidentified managed to get a message out to the police describing what was happening. Then the SAS had to go in to save any further bloodshed. They should have gone in much, much, sooner, and then my boys might still have had a father today."

Silence reigned for a few seconds. It wasn't golden.

"I can fully understand how you could be so very angry at the loss of your man in those circumstances." appeased the hostess.

That was it. The floodgates opened. Susannah began to sob uncontrollably and Pippa moved in the comfort her. Instinctively the other ladies followed until they formed a protective circle around their friend in a large group hug. Prayers were whispered. They stayed holding each other until the sobbing subsided.

Then Susannah composed herself, sat back down, and quietly said, "I'm sorry!"

More tea was poured, and another round of sandwiches offered, as all the ladies sat down again.

Courtney began to explain, "On the Friday evening when Michael should have been in the Captain's Table, he met someone called George O'Donnell; an old tramp in the park. He said that they had a very interesting chat, and when he returned home he found a little velvet star in his wallet."

"That little piece of fabric seemed to be very important to Michael, and I don't really understand why." Dierdre said.

"Well, it's what you might call a talisman," said Pippa, "I know as a minister for Christ I'm not supposed to believe in superstition or magic, but after all, what is a crucifix but just another form of talisman. It's an item with magical, sometimes protective properties."

"But, what does it mean? Why was it so significant in his life?"

The Reverend stood up facing her friends, and retrieved something from her robes and held it very carefully in her right hand. Suddenly her face took on that new countenance. The brightest and most wonderful golden light shone through her. She held her hands out in front of her, and instinctively all the other ladies stood up and brought their hands out to touch a star that was the exact copy of the one that Michael had treasured. The girls, without thinking about it, had formed into a circle again to sense the preciousness of the star, as if performing some ancient religious rite. They stood in the circle for a few minutes, looking at each other smiling, feeling absolute joy. It was as if all the beauty and wonder of the Universe were coursing through their veins, permeating every cell of their bodies, enveloping their hearts in a feeling of complete love. The light shone through every one of them, and their hands were glowing like rays of warm sunshine. There was a completeness. Tears of joy flowed from every eye as the circle began to break.

Melissa grinned and said, "I told Mike how completely wonderful it was to be blessed with having his little star. I made him promise me that he'd take it with him everywhere and guard it with his life, never let it go, and never be without it wherever he found himself."

Book Two

Between Two Realms

Changes and Challenges

Chapter 1

All the Stars in Heaven

(Time without beginning or end)

Night fell so heavily. It fell for me like it had never fallen before. One second I was reaching for something in my pocket, and the next all there was around me was darkness. There was a complete nothingness; for a moment my mind was totally blank. Then it began. So black and impenetrable was the darkness that all I could feel was its claustrophobic intensity all around me, gripping me tight like I was floating in treacle. Black, black, and more black tumbled over me in undulating waves, squeezing and scrambling all my senses into one; just a pure sense of being. But I was not afraid.

In the blackness I felt as if I was being pulled and persuaded very gently towards something exciting and new and wonderful, without actually knowing what that thing was. There was no fear or hesitancy or reluctance to go along. I had no choice in the matter, but my being told me that I must submit myself willingly to the dark, surrender to the unknown.

The darkness swirled, and I began to fall, spinning faster and faster. I was falling, plummeting, and spinning, tumbling forever.

And then I heard a sound, I felt a sound, I smelled a sound, I tasted a sound, I touched a sound; a beautiful sound. The most beautiful sound I have ever heard.

It was like a whisper, "Michael! Come home!"

But I felt the sound - like warm waves in the ocean washing over me; like a cool, refreshing breeze on a warm day blowing through me.

"Michael, Michael! Come home, come home!"

The sound filled my nostrils with the homely smell of new baked bread; with the essence of vanilla; with the heady perfume of jasmine and patchouli; with the bouquet of Ramey 2008 Chardonnay.

"Michael, Michael, Michael! Come home, come home, come home!"

The sound made my taste buds explode with the luscious tang of the sweetest flower dew honey; with the flavour of fresh fish and chips with lashings of malt vinegar, eaten by hand from a newspaper; with the taste of freshly ground Blue Mountain Arabica coffee beans.

"Michael, Michael, Michael! Come home, come home, come home!"

The sound was smoothing, wrapping my being in the softest velvet cushioned blanket; caressing me in a universe of cotton wool; anointing me in an ocean of the most precious aromatic oil.

Then I saw it. There was the merest pinprick of light, and I was being drawn towards it. Ever so slowly it came, like a billion of the brightest stars in the Universe, cascading into my being one at a time through the tiniest of tiny holes in the blackness. I didn't see it with my eyes. I saw it with all of me. My sense of being overwhelmed me. All of my experience pulled me towards this growing, glowing and bright fantastic light that permeated my being as if I was melting ever so slowly into it. And all the time, I was not afraid.

Billions of stars, billions of planets, billions of moons, circled my being in a gigantic swirling lightshow. All the galaxies of the Universe surrounded me in a warm protective glow. I was suspended for a moment at the centre of all creation.

When the light had totally enveloped me, I began to sense colours, every colour imaginable. With a whoosh the colours separated, and a huge vibrant exceeding beautiful rainbow spanned the skies. Then I found myself standing at one end of the rainbow. I could touch the colours, and they responded with the sounds of all positive emotions; love, hope, faith, peace, longing, belonging, being; with wonderful smells, and tastes, with soft and gentle caresses. My being rose steadily through the space below the rainbow, until I was standing on the highest point of its arch.

I glided through the air like an albatross, and saw a vast ocean below me, where placid blue waters were moving quiet and lazy. The ocean rose up into a mountainous swell, and I plunged into the depths like a cormorant and swam underwater. I gyrated and tumbled with massive shoals of small fishes. I danced and sang with pods of playful dolphins. I waltzed in the depths of the ocean with families of blue whales.

Then I fluttered like a butterfly, high over rugged red deserts, where the heat of the midday sun painted mirages, shimmering rude and remote, on distant horizons. Then I flew above lush, warm, green forests which spread far past my gaze, into infinity. I soared through perfect blue skies, among a flock of birds migrating south for the winter, under sleek silver clouds that were floating high and aloof. In the distance, I touched the summits of gigantic white mountains, as they stood like formidable giants guarding treasures undreamed of. And all the time, I knew I was making my way homewards, towards sunsets that were setting the skies fire red, and then turning to precious gold, blazing day's glorious end.

I landed at the opposite end of the rainbow, and looked back to see the magnificent arch of colours stretching forever, high and brilliant across the skies. All at once I knew that I was making a journey to somewhere new and exciting. I heard a voice.

"Welcome, Michael! You have been on a long journey, a journey of transition from Mother Earth to Father Heaven. You have been going away to home. We have been expecting you, my friend."

"Who are you?" I asked.

"My name is not important. Let's just say that I am an angel on reception duty today, and you have arrived at these magnificent golden gates which guard the way to Heaven."

The angel who stood before me was radiant and beautiful, but somehow looked familiar. It seemed as if a black light shone through him rather than on him. He spoke again.

"I must find out more about you, my friend, before you can be permitted to enter through these gates."

Then, thoughts and questions flooded my sense of being. I heard a soft voice that I had heard before, asking me the questions in a gentle, thought provoking way. The questions invaded me, but I felt safe in submitting to them. I knew I must tell the truth. I answered every one instantly, without having to think much about what I was saying.

"What have you said and done in your life?"

All the words I had ever spoken, and all the things I had done, flashed before me in an instant.

"Who have you met on your way?"

The faces of all the people I had ever met passed quickly in front of me.

"Where have you been?"

All the places I had ever visited in the world were laid before me.

"Do you understand who you are?"

At that moment, my being knew exactly who I was.

"Do you know what your values are?"

I had a feeling that I was very, very small, but oh so special.

"What blades have cut you?"

I remembered every time I had been wronged, but I forgave all those who had wronged me.

"What words have soothed?"

I remembered all the times that someone had spoken to me quietly.

"How many times did your heart stand still?"

I recalled all the times when the world seemed to stop spinning.

"How many times did your spirit move?"

I recalled all the times when wonderful things had happened to me.

"How much love did you pour out?"

My heart was bursting with love.

"How much love did you gather in together?"

And I gave all the love back to others.

"Was every breath you took worthwhile?"

There had been times when I felt worthless.

"What trials did you endeavour?"

There had been times when life had kicked me in the teeth,

"Do you really understand who you are?"

Again, at that moment, my being knew exactly who I was.

"Do you really know what your values are?"

I had a feeling again, that I was infinitely small, but oh so special.

"Do you understand that all your treasures and riches now count for nought?"

I gave no thought to all the treasures and riches I had accumulated in my time in the Earthly Realm.

Suddenly there was a fanfare of trumpets, echoing through my being like a fire in the wind, and the golden gates opened slowly before me.

"Please, Michael; feel free to enter." said the angel, holding out his wing to beckon me in. Then the gates closed behind me, and at last I felt as if I had come home and my journey was over.

I heard another voice; the voice of an angel; soft, gentle, comforting.

"You have arrived here in Heaven because once upon a time you could have become a greedy, hedonistic and power crazed man. But that was not you, and because of that there was a potential spotted from above. That is why our good friend George O'Donnell put a star in your pocket."

I looked in my right hand, and there it was; the little velvet star, inscribed with the words "Look! Listen! Learn!" with the initials, "G O'D" on it.

I remembered words that the Reverend Pippa had said to me.

"Oh, that's wonderful, Michael. You really must treasure that."

I remembered the words that Melissa had said to me.

"Oh, how completely wonderful, Michael. Promise me that you will take that with you everywhere, and guard it with your life. Never let it go, and never be without it wherever you find yourself."

The angel before me spoke again.

"My name is Sebastian, and I have been assigned as your guardian. I have been watching over you for a long time, and I know everything about you."

Immediately I felt I could place my trust in this Sebastian.

He began to explain how the band of angels were always working to bring new recruits to Heaven, and how they had recognised me as a perfect candidate.

"The star you hold in your hand; you have looked after it well. It is why you are here. Let me give you a safe place to put it."

He handed me a little pouch, saying, "Place your purple star carefully in this special bag, and then put the cord around your neck. Keep it with you always."

I followed his instruction.

"Now let us clear up something for you. You will remember, that the evening when the Captain's Table tragedy occurred, was when you received the star. You failed to reach your destination in time for your appointment. That was when you met a tramp, in the Blenheim Circus Park, and your life began to change. George was your guardian angel on Earth. He put the star in your pocket, looked after you, and guided you for the short few months that were the remainder of your life."

"Yes!" added the angel who had questioned me before I entered, "Our friend, Sebastian was there in the Captain's Table. He was the unidentified someone, who managed to convey details out to the police describing what was happening. As the thunderstorm raged overhead, he managed to unlock the cellar trapdoor."

Sebastian continued, "I had been sent there early in my angel training. That day, I had been taken on by Sophie as a temporary barman. I had been in the cellar when the terrorists took over the pub. I was almost helpless to do anything, but I heard very clearly what was going on. When a man called Ibrahim was sent down to check the cellar, I hid in a small cupboard. Eventually, I managed to open the trapdoor which was used as the entrance for barrels of beer, and I let the SAS into the pub through that opening. This had to be expertly timed. The thinking behind it was that the Jihadis would have been startled by the noise of the thunderstorm, thinking that they were being attacked, but then lulled into a false sense of security when the storm abated. Also, it is common knowledge that the best time for an attack is just as the sun is about to rise; in this case just after 5 am. The SAS snipers crept up the stairs of the pub cellar, and targeted each terrorist individually, sending them all back to their own God with a single shot, with the exception of the man called Ibrahim, who took 5 shots to die. The aim was to minimise the chances of injuring or killing any of the hostages."

I was surprised at the casual way in which my new friend described what had happened in such detail, and asked him, "Couldn't you have stopped the massacre in some way. Don't you have special powers as an angel to intervene?"

"No, my dear friend, it does not work like that. We cannot intervene to prevent something happening. We can only help in small ways to minimise the effects, and hope for a more acceptable outcome. As an angel, you will learn that is the way of heavenly beings. It can be frustrating, even distressing, but that is all we can do to help."

I thought carefully about what he had just said.

"Now, there is work to be done." added Sebastian

He smiled, and explained with every gentleness, "As you are a new recruit, we must initially bring you to a place of beautiful graceful naivety. First of all, you must have your innocence and naivety replenished."

"How will you do that?"

"It's not what on Earth you would have called brainwashing! You will still have self-determination as to whether you decide to do good things or not."

"How will I know what to do?"

"You will spend a long, long time training to be an angel, so that when the time comes for you to go back and help in the Earthly Realm, you will know what to do."

"Tell me more about this beautiful graceful naivety."

"Well, the easiest way to look at it is by regarding yourself as a beginner. A beginner is just starting to learn how to do something. If we use the letters of the word 'begin' to remind us, we get:

B for beautiful,

E for enlightened,

G for graceful,

I for intelligent, and

N for naivety.

Keep that in mind, and you will begin to understand."

I grinned. This seemed so simple and obvious.

My teacher continued. "This training must happen before you can move on; so that you will be better equipped to deal with the tasks you will be set. The newly opened eyes of a child will be more receptive to the situations you find yourself in."

Something came quickly to my mind, I found myself saying, "On Earth, a man called Alexander Pope said, that a little learning is a dangerous thing, or is it a little knowledge is a dangerous thing?"

"He was very wise. Think about what that really means, Michael."

"OK! When will I be set these tasks?"

"Only when the time is right. There is no such thing as time in Heaven; at least not how you have known it in the Earthly Realm. Things may happen to you out of Earth time order."

"That sounds very confusing."

"Yes, it does, but now I have to ask you an important question."

"OK! What do you want to know?"

"Michael, bearing in mind all the things we have just described to you about your training and bringing you to a place of beautiful graceful naivety; do you want to become an apprentice angel?"

"I think so. Yes!"

"But you look troubled, my friend. Is there something that is bothering you? Do you have a question perhaps?"

"Yes, I do have a question. I am not sure why I have been chosen?"

"I believe we have already explained that, but haven't you guessed by now? Everybody who leaves the Earthly Realm with a star in their pocket can become an angel. First, they must complete their tasks to earn the Angel's Rainbow."

"So it is the star in my pocket that makes me eligible, is it?"

"Yes, my friend. Let me ask you again. Do you want to become an apprentice angel?"

I didn't need to deliberate over this question any more. To me, it seemed that the answer would be obvious.

"Of course! Yes, I want to."

"Good! Now you are one of us, and you have the opportunity to train to be an angel. After your initial training, you will undergo a series of tests to achieve your wings."

"Thank you, when and where do I begin, and how long will it take to qualify as an angel?"

"Well, guardian angel training will begin very soon with small tests. The length of time it takes will depend entirely on how you respond."

"But, I thought you said that there was no time here in Heaven."

"It may be difficult for you to understand at the moment. Let's just say that time doesn't work in quite the same way as you knew it before arriving here. When you have served your apprenticeship, then we'll move on to the tests for each colour of the rainbow in a set order. For each colour, you will be transported back to the Earthly Realm, to see what you can do to help people in critical situations."

"Wow! That sounds exciting."

"Once you've passed all those tests, you will be a fully fledged angel, and you will achieve your wings."

"I can't wait to start."

"But right now, my friend, you look a little tired, and you have been on a very long and difficult journey. Come with me, please."

I was taken to a lovely place on top of a very tall fluffy white cloud, where I fell asleep almost immediately. That night, I had a very vivid dream. It was the end of summer, and the sunshine was barely warm. I stood inside a fairy circle of mushrooms in a wild flower meadow, then turned around three times, and made a wish that my precious Courtney would be safe. Somehow, I knew my wish was heard. Then quickly, I found myself beside a wishing well, in a secret garden with my loved one. We smiled at each other, and holding hands, we dropped a coin into the water, and watched the ripples after the splash, knowing that something was coming to an end, and something new was beginning at the same time. My heart felt empty and heavy, and I found myself wandering alone, in a vast open landscape. A difficult unknown path stretched out before me, and disappeared over a faraway horizon. As I travelled along the path alone, something persuaded me to continue no matter what. I felt safe and valued, and even though I was leaving many things behind, I knew I was heading for a better place, where there was everlasting light.

When I awoke, Sebastian was sitting beside me, smiling. As I gathered my senses, I had one more question.

I asked "When I was in the Earthly Realm I was flesh and bones, but what am I now?"

Sebastian replied, "Why isn't it obvious, Michael? You are stardust, the essence of the Universe that fills the void and gives meaning to all life."

Chapter 2

Red Star - 15th April, 1989

It had been a very long, time that I'd been training to be an angel, and I have to say that I have enjoyed every minute of it. I remember that I started with simple things, like sewing crystals made from raindrops on the edges of clouds, so that they would all have a silver lining. I spent some time knitting sunbeams together in the right order, to make rainbows, and making sure that they were positioned not to touch the ground, so that another angel didn't need to hide a pot of gold at each end. I loved all the nights I spent catching falling stars, and putting them in my pocket, and saving them for a rainy day. I became so good at it, that Gabriel gave me a special pouch with rainbows all around it, to put my falling stars in, so that they would never fade away. He said they were very special, because when I needed them, I could use them to perform magical deeds. When I wasn't doing these things, I would often be found sitting on a favourite cloud, playing on my very own harp, and winding harp strings from angel hair.

There was no warning that I would suddenly be transported back to the Earthly Realm, and into the real circumstances of an event where I had to do something to earn a star. I knew that the first task would be to earn the red star; the first colour of the Angel's Rainbow. My angel training had prepared me for a beautiful graceful naivety in this situation, so that the knowledge I had was minimized to a kind of pure and unadorned necessity.

That's how I got to be on a coach, heading for a football match.

I was a little uneasy in this company, and for some reason I was wearing a red baseball cap. There was only one vacant seat left on the coach number 7, about half way up the aisle, and I sat down next to a 30 something gentleman, dressed from head to foot in red. I had found myself on a coach, bedecked in red scarves, with 49 other football fans, all chattering excitedly about the forthcoming epic battle. In another life, I had occasionally brushed alongside the euphoria of England's exploits in the Euros or the World Cup. It had been difficult not to be swept along by the air of joy and expectation, to bathe in the national pride, and sink a few beers in the process. But my game had always been squash; intense, individual, fast, and single-minded. Sport wise, I had been a loner. It was only when I had been at work in the financial sector that I had regarded myself as a team player.

On this warm and sunny day, I had boarded the coach at Lime Street Station in Liverpool, to make the 100 mile trip around the southern edge of Manchester, and out into the wide open spaces of the Peak District, towards the destination in Sheffield. Scheduled journey time was about 2 hours and 30 minutes, but this was an important F.A. Cup match, and there would be a big crowd of about 50,000, including up to 25,000 Liverpool supporters. Delays and congestion were expected and inevitable. Therefore, the coach had left at 11 am; leaving plenty of time to get to the stadium by kick-off at 3 pm. Some minor delays on the motorways, around the sprawling urbanity of Greater Manchester, eventually gave way to steady progress eastwards into a rustic green panorama.

"You're not a scouser, are you?" enquired the friendly face in the seat next to me.

"No! You're right, but does it matter?" I replied softly.

"Well no. It means you're not likely to be a toffee tosser, and don't worry, pal; as long as you're one of us today, we'll look after you wherever you're from."

"I'm from London actually, but I'm not a big football fan."

"That's OK, as long as you don't follow then scumbags from Arsenal; stuck up wankers, they are."

"Yes, I'm sure you're right."

I didn't want to antagonise any of the ardent supporters in my close vicinity, and so agreeing with whatever they said seemed to be the best course of action. My new friend seemed to like that, and offered a handshake.

"My name's Will, Will McCluskey." he said.

We shook hands.

"I'm Michael Hartson."

"Know much about our glorious team, do you?"

"No, I'm afraid I'm a complete greenhorn, Will, but I'm sure you can educate me."

Will raised his voice to the people surrounding him.

"D'yer hear that lads? Michael here's a scouse virgin, and wants me to educate him."

"Make sure you use a condom." offered a nearby joker to the rear.

"Go easy on the lad." came from a more mature fellow traveller near the front.

The boys on the coach were a strange eclectic mixture. In the front seats were a gaggle of older fans, equipped with coats and jackets, thermos flasks and sandwich boxes, mostly only sporting team scarves. At the back, was where the younger contingent sat; a massive splurge of red replica shirts, jeans and trainers. They didn't come prepared food and drinkwise. They were the pie and burger and hot dog brigade, feeding and watering themselves on the way into the stadium. There was just a small band of more, mostly anonymous, fans making up the centre circle, where I was seated. In amongst them, Will McCluskey was a recognisable exception. He wore red from scouser head to scouser toe, sipped constantly from a large bottle labelled Irn Bru, seemed to know everybody on the trip, and as the destination drew nearer, I would learn that he would be delighted in leading the chanting and singing.

"Right, pal," said Will, "First there's the gaffer, Kenny Dalglish, fantastic player for the 'Pool, and now he's the dog's bollocks as our player/manager. Shankly was a magician, Paisley was a marvellous tactician, but Kenny, he's Lord of the Universe. If he was an MP, everybody would vote for him by a landslide majority. If he was a singer/songwriter, nobody else would get to the top of the charts, and he would sell a million every week. If he was my best mate, well. I wouldn't want for anything. He's the top man."

I couldn't help but be excited and amused by the enthusiasm and eloquence with which Will was beginning to state his case.

"OK, what about the players?" I asked.

"All you need to know about goal-scorers is two names; John Aldridge and Ian Rush. They score goals as easy as drinking cups of tea through a straw. Then there's Alan Hansen, defender. He'll chop your legs off for a penny chew. And our goalie is the mighty Bruce Grobbelar. He's definitely not a nice South African, but he can stop shots blindfolded in a hurricane."

"Thanks for that information, Will." I said, "I suppose your disdain for the opposition, is as enthusiastic as your pride and pleasure in your team?"

"Too right, pal; the Forest no-hopers are managed by old big mouth, Brian

Clough, and they don't have any star players; they're also-rans, upstarts, complete wankers. You know what they say about Cloughie don't you?"

"No, but I'm sure you're going to tell me."

"Yes, I am! Our Brian wants to be the England coach, and I think it's a great idea. All you need to do is take his teeth out of his big gob, and put seats in."

It was obvious that this supremely ardent Liverpool fan didn't want to speak quietly, he was used to spouting his partisan views for all to hear, and although he'd told that joke scores of times before the surrounding fans all laughed or smiled in appreciation.

"Anyway," he continued, "We didn't want effin Nottingham Forest in this semi-final. We'd all been hoping that they'd be beaten in the quarters, by those smelly, useless, morons at Man U. Old big Gob must have spiked the Mancunian moron's half time tea for his mob to win it. We were all longing for a chance to beat the old enemy in the semis. Isn't that right lads?"

I sensed and heard all round agreement.

"It's been a tough road to get here, we've had to play away at that shit heap in Carlisle, that derelict refugee camp at Millwall, and then against them Yorkshire wife beaters at Hull, before we got a nice easy one, beating those southern softies from Brentford 4-0 at Anfield. I suppose, if I was to look at it with a friendly face, I'd say that the Forest scumbags had a tough road too, and I'll admit they did us a favour, by knocking out some much better teams. They've beaten Ipswich, Leeds, Watford and Man U to get there, and that's the beauty of the F.A.Cup. On the day, any old second rate upstarts can get an unexpected win."

Will was getting to the stage where his soapbox was increasing in height by the second. His hubris for the lads was unshakeable. He continued.

"And talking of any old second rate upstarts, the best thing about the semis now is that we have a great chance of meeting our other nearby rivals in the final, when we've seen off Brian Clough and his merry men; 'cause the other semi is Everton versus Norwich. Those toffee tossers should be able to beat the carrot crunchers, and then we'll be crowned as the pride of our great city, when we win the final at Wembley. Am I right again lads?"

A united cheer went up from the assembly.

Soon the green rustic calm of the Peak District was giving way to the busy urban outskirts of Sheffield's steel city, and it was time for the glorious leader to start the chanting and singing.

Most of the chants were suitably obscene, questioning the parentage, pedigree, sexuality and intelligence of the opposition, but the ragged choir that sang "You'll Never Walk Alone" was a beautiful experience, and the bandmaster conducted them with well-practiced timing and precision.

A quick glance at the coach clock gave the time as a few minutes before 2, and the merry mob were at a standstill in a set of road works on the A6102 near Middlewood Park. It was a very slow crawl from there to the junction with Leppings Lane, and by the time the coach was stranded at that spot it was approaching 2.30. The coach driver, Bernie, made an announcement after standing still for nearly 10 minutes with no indication of any possible forward movement.

"OK, lads I'm going to drop you off on the corner here, otherwise you might not make the kick off. It looks like there are so many people here that I'm not going any further for a while."

The 49 strong scousers plus me, a bemused straggler, spilled diligently off the coach, and quickly joined the tidal wave of expectant fans, making the short walk to the turnstiles. Progress was slow and difficult, and the crowd surged in small erratic waves, only generally moving in the desired direction. I was sure that at times, I moved along in the collective momentum without my feet actually touching the ground, carried mostly forward, sometimes sideways, in the midst of the group that had stepped down from the coach. They all moved together; a bit like a huge upright rugby scrum, unified in purpose, straining against the resistance of thousands of moving bodies, heading like lemmings for their common destination.

"Stick close to me, and I'll see you there alright." Will urged confidently, "This lot at Wednesday always herd us like cattle. It's like trying to push a Mersey ferryboat through a canteen serving hatch, and it doesn't get much better in the ground, 'cause they've got 10 foot high fences all around the pitch to make sure we can't stop the game with a pitch invasion, or join in the celebrations when we win. I ask you. Whose game is it anyway? Football belongs to the terrace supporters, not the effing blazers and bowties in their plush upholstered heated seats, scoffing their prawn sandwiches, and sipping glasses of Cabernet Sauvignon. It's our game, not theirs. We are the backbone of the club."

I found the relentless surging movement of this sea of people utterly terrifying, and the use of massive police horses to exert some control even more alarming. As much as I tried to avoid getting anywhere near a horse, after

10 minutes of pushing and shoving I found himself at the rear end of a huge brown beast, just as it decided to empty it's bladder. Gallons of steamy, smelly horse pee splattered on the ground, and there was nowhere for anyone to take refuge. As if that wasn't bad enough, the poor horse was barely under control and began to panic and rear up with the next movement of the masses. Then it farted like a trumpet in a wind tunnel, and dropped a great steaming pile of fermented grass out of its rear end. In a supreme effort to draw away in the mass of humanity, the coach group swayed violently to the left. Both Will and I fell over in the slimy, pungent mixture of equine excrement, and disappeared for a few moments underneath the horse's rear hooves. Above the noises of the crowd and the disturbance of the horse's panic, I clearly heard it. There was a loud crack, which was followed by something that sounded like a banshee howl, as Will cried out.

My new friend was in serious trouble, and when we resurfaced the look on his pale and contorted face confirmed his distress. I dragged myself up to a standing position, and when I put weight on my feet, a bullet of searing pain shot through the bones where I had twisted my ankle under the crush of the horse's bulk. I tried to take off my baseball cap, and noticed that the ring finger of my right hand had had a disagreement with his finger friends, and was pointing alone at the sky, while the others gripped the headwear. Waving the red cap frantically in the air, I shouted "Help! Help! There's a man down here! Help!"

A small piece of cloth in the shape of a red star fell out of my cap and floated softly to the ground. Suddenly, a fluorescent swirl of bright shimmering light circled around me, and a whooshing stream of a million blindingly bright twinkling red stars curved in a magnificent continuous lightshow, and began to cascade like a silent waterfall from the skies above. Then, the early spring sunshine quickly dimmed, almost as if someone had switched off a light. At the same time, the temperature dropped to a winter shiver, as the blanket of mist and red stars seemed to fall over the throng in an instant. I felt cold and re-seated my cap, and turned up the collar of my jacket against the sudden chill, as a piercing gush of wind began to blow the stars around. At first, a small gap in the crowd appeared; created by the horse rearing upwards and forwards. Then, magically, the red sea of agitating bodies parted, and the stars settled on the ground to form a narrow path.

All the fellow travellers from the coach surrounded their cheerleader in his distress. Then, 4 men lifted him up and carried him back towards the coach, and as if in triumph, they began singing as they walked through the star strewn corridor backwards towards safety. Somehow, the contra flow of the rescue band went totally unnoticed by the majority of bodies flowing towards the stadium entrance. It was almost as if the coach party was a single minded ghostly invisible ribbon in an ocean of zombie-like constant and opposing movement.

"When you walk through a storm hold your head up high and don't be afraid of the dark..."

I followed instinctively, hobbling along on my twisted ankle.

Back out where the crowd became more sparse, they laid Will down on the ground, just as they reached the climax of the chorus.

"And you'll never walk alone. You'll never walk alone."

Will's red outfit was soaked and plastered with a mustardy coating, and he laid there clasping his right leg below the knee. The blanket of stars disappeared. The air stilled, and the sunshine returned.

"I'll get some help." I said, at that moment realizing that I too was contaminated by the panicking horse's effluent.

One of the Liverpool lads took a quick look at Will's leg, and declared, "Too bad, pal, your leg is broken in 2 places."

"We won't get into the ground unless we go now." Will answered.

"But, you're not going anywhere, my friend; not on a broken leg."

"It fuckin' hurts like hell, but I'm not going to miss this battle."

The injured fan attempted to stand, his face straining every sinew with the effort, and then promptly fell over screaming and clutching his damaged leg.

I asserted, "Like our friend said; you're not going anywhere. Sorry!"

He didn't move again, and said nothing, exhausted and in tears.

A St John's volunteer was quickly found, who confirmed the seriousness of his injury.

Somewhere close to where the coach party had been a few minutes before, a gate had been opened to ease the increasing pressure on the frustrated and angry masses. The violent unstoppable surge into the void created was clearly visible from our safe viewpoint. It was like the start of the London Marathon, the battle of the Little Big Horn, and the charge of the Light Brigade, all rolled into one single-minded and untamed release of tension.

An ambulance was called. In the melee of traffic and congestion, it took over half an hour to arrive, but we all stayed with our injured friend, and then I accompanied him to the Royal Hallamshire Hospital. After all the build up and excitement, both myself and Will had missed the match, and it was doubtful that any of our friends on the coach would manage to get into the stadium.

A few hours later, Will had had his injured leg reset, and was sitting up in his hospital bed. My ankle had been examined, and declared to be a minor sprain. The hospital staff gave me a walking stick to assist my mobility

"How are you now, Will?" I asked.

"I'm OK, I suppose, but pig sick that I missed the match."

"Yes, so am I." I sympathised, knowing that there was worse to come. I had heard the news reports flooding into the hospital, and seen the avalanche of casualties arriving.

Will raised a thin, ironic smile.

"Not a good day, the 15th of April, is it? That's the day that the Titanic went down in 1912, but never mind that now. What time is it? Has the match finished? Did we stuff Clough's wankers?"

My eyes filled with tears, and I didn't quite know how to break the news, but there was no way I was holding it back from him.

"Will, something terrible has happened. Nobody knows quite how bad it is yet, but people have died, and lots of them have been injured."

"I'm sorry, but what's that got to do with the match? Did we win?"

Then I told him the facts as I knew them at that time, from the news that had been filtering through on the radio, and from the hospital staff as they admitted and attended to living casualties.

"The match was abandoned after about 10 minutes. There was a crush in the pens that they allocated for Liverpool supporters. Too many people! The police lost control. It appears they just stood back and let it happen. They wouldn't open the barriers at the front of the pens, and people were crushed to death. The fans tried to climb out of the pens and over the fences and even up into the stands above, but there were just too many people."

Will's eyes filled with tears. He sat stunned into silence. I didn't know what else I could say. Information was so sparse and sporadic, and at that time that was all I knew. It was several minutes before he spoke again.

"Shit! Shit! Shit! All my mates on the coach were in there. Oh No! It can't be!" he said.

I thought carefully about how to reply.

"We won't know about that. The situation as to who exactly the victims were is totally confused, and will be for sometime. Let's just hope and pray that they're all safe."

Will looked at me strangely, "I'm not a religious man, but praying seems to be the only thing we can do now." he said.

We both closed our eyes, put our hands together and fell into a silent, very personal, tear filled prayer. I'd like to think that somehow he heard my prayers, because I most certainly heard his.

After a while, Will said, "You'd better be getting back to the coach. Sure as hell I'm not going anywhere for a few days."

Just then a nurse came into the room, and, after checking on Will, looked at me and smiled.

"We'd better have a look at that finger before you go." she said.

I was led away to a small room, where they determined that I had dislocated my ring finger.

"I've given you a small injection on either side of the finger root to deaden the area, and once the drug has taken effect, we'll pull and click your finger back into place. It shouldn't hurt too much, but it gets harder to relocate the longer it's been out of position, and it's been a few hours now." she declared, and then added with a cheeky smile, "By the way, did I tell you?"

"Tell me what?" I asked.

"You don't half stink!" she laughed, "What it all that gooey, yellow stuff on your coat?"

"Oh! Both me and Will fell under a horse, just after it had decided to empty its bladder and then its bowels."

"Yuk!" she replied, and then she made a quick attempt to yank my finger back into position.

The distraction didn't work, and I nearly jumped off the bed and through the ceiling with the pain.

"Brace yourself, and I'll try again." she instructed.

She pulled my finger again and the room swirled around and bucked up and down like a roller coaster out of control, and I passed out. There was a loud and persistent ringing in my ears like a fog in sound form. Gradually the fog cleared, and the sounds became far more distinct, building to a triumphant positive crescendo.

"When you walk through a storm, hold your head up high
And don't be afraid of the dark
At the end of the storm, there's a golden sky
And the sweet, silver song of a lark
Walk on through the wind
Walk on through the rain
Though your dreams be tossed and blown
Walk on, walk on
With hope in your heart
And you'll never walk alone
You'll never walk alone
Walk on, walk on
With hope in your heart
And you'll never walk alone
You'll never walk alone"

When I opened my eyes, I was back on my favourite cloud, and my good friend Sebastian was sitting next to me. I looked at my hands and felt my ankle. Everything was perfectly as it should be.

"Think about what you have learned, my friend." he smiled, "How do you feel about horses?"

And with that, we carried on catching falling stars and putting them in our pockets, and saving them for a rainy day.

A few days later, we were back on the cloud, talking about my adventure, when Gabriel turned up.

"I am very pleased with you, Michael," he said, "It may be difficult for you to understand what important part you played in the tragedy you have experienced. But there are very, very good reasons why we put you in that situation."

"You are so right! I don't know what the point was really?" I asked; a little confused.

"Ah, well," Gabriel explained," You see, you rescued your friend, Will, from under the horses hooves, and he will live a long and healthy life."

"Is that all?" I asked.

"No, there is much more. Every single one of the people on the coach failed to get into the ground, and so they all returned safely home. You see, they moved through the crowds as a group, all for one and one for all. They travelled that day for joy and expectation through competition and belonging, and their plans were interrupted by tragedy."

"I think I understand what you are telling me," I said, "But what about all the people that died or were injured?"

Gabriel looked me straight in the eyes and explained gently.

"Everyone who died has a star in his pocket. They weren't selected to receive this, but came to earn it through a life cut mercilessly short, as they became victims to incompetence and intolerance and misunderstanding. Every man has God's love, but his own self-determination. In this situation, you appear to have been totally helpless, but you have witnessed a great tragedy, and felt the pain and suffering to earn your red star. The little that you felt you were able to do has true significance."

This brought a big smile to my face, but it wasn't as big as the next smile when Gabriel said to me, "Michael, we are very pleased with you. You have passed your first test on the Angel's Rainbow, and we can now award you your red star."

I was beside myself with excitement. "When will that happen?" I asked.

"Oh, in a few days time. We are arranging for someone very special to present you with your red star; someone who will be so pleased with what you were able to do for people for whom he has a great love."

"You must tell me please; who will that be?"

"A very great man, called Bill Shankly."

Chapter 3

Orange Star - 22nd April, 1986

My angel friends and myself had been having a wonderful time spinning clouds, and sewing them together in different formations. At the start, we were taught to make cirrus clouds; thin and wispy strands, like a ringlet or curling lock of hair, which we called mare's tails. They needed to be assembled in tufts, in a pattern from west to east across the skies, and point towards fine weather. Cumulus clouds were fun, but took much more time to make, because we had to pile them up into large heaps, so that they were puffy and fluffy like pieces of floating cotton wool. It was important to make sure that these clouds had flattish bases and tops like rounded towers. Sometimes when we overdid it with the cumulus clouds, they got too big and turned into cumulonimbus. These were storm clouds, which we called thunderheads, and had to be handled with great care, because they could generate lighting and tornados. Then there were grey or bluish-green clouds called altostratus. I liked making the thin ones, because you could see the sun through them. There were lots of other types, some more difficult to make than others, and making them was always very relaxing and therapeutic.

The cloud duty gave me a chance to reflect on the task I had undertaken at Hillsborough to earn my red star, and to remember how it was to be presented to me by a great man called Bill Shankly.

So there I was, flying around the cloud stores, happily inspecting all the work I had been doing, when the man himself suddenly appeared out of a cumulonimbus. He shook my hand as he introduced himself quietly and politely. We had a very interesting conversation.

"Aye, lad, I remember it well. I went to Liverpool as their manager on 14 December 1959. I'll tell you, it wasn't Christmas at Liverpool that year. We had been defeated by non-league Worcester City in the F.A. Cup the previous year, were a non-entity 2nd division club, and everything about the place was pure 2nd class."

"What did you do while you were there?"

"I changed everything, made them believe in themselves, and got them promoted. Then we went on a cannonball run for football glory."

"What happened?"

"A lot of football success is in the mind, my boy. You must believe you are the best, and then make sure that you are. So we just developed a winner's mentality, and then we kept on winning and winning. While the Mersey Sound led by the Beatles was conquering the world, and the great city of Liverpool arrived on the world map, we won the league three times, the F.A. Cup twice, the Charity Shield three times, and then finally the UEFA Cup in 1973."

"How did you make that possible?"

"I'm a people's man - only the people matter."

I smiled at him, and he grinned a knowing grin back.

"Let me give you some advice, lad," he added, "Believe, and your half way there!"

"I can see that."

"Aim for the sky and you'll reach the ceiling. Aim for the ceiling and you'll stay on the floor."

"Yes, I think I understand."

"Anyway, laddie, I've got something for you here. You've done a wonderful thing for people that I'll always love, so I'm pleased and honoured to be chosen to give you your red star."

He took a little shiny red star out of the pocket of his grey suit, and placed it carefully in my right hand.

I stared at it, mouth agape. It was so beautiful. It radiated a warm and soft glow.

"Look after this lad." he said.

"Oh! I will!" I replied.

"Before I go then, let me say that I've made some great friends along the way and there's someone special I know called Muhammad Ali, and he told me something that I really like, that I'd like to pass on to you."

"What was that?"

"He told me 'The man who has no imagination has no wings.', and he was so right, laddie."

Then he was gone, and I was left with the little lessons he had just laid on me. I sat down on top of a cumulus and thought about our meeting, while tucking my red star carefully into a purple pouch that Sebastian had given me.

I hadn't been there for very long, when the clouds all began to swirl around me like horses on a merry go round. I heard wind rushing in my ears, the roar of a waterfall, peals of thunder crashed around me and lightning blinded my eyes. I was whisked in the vortex of a tornado being pushed downwards. Down, down, down I fell, circling, round and around, again and again. Then it stopped abruptly, and I floated gently down to a place on Earth in the sunshine of a late April day.

I found myself standing on the corner of a wide and busy street called the Khreshchatyk, in the Ukrainian city of Kiev, looking towards the Bessarabska Square. It was a few minutes after midday, and the sun shone down lazily on the noisy bustling streets. I had been sent there to meet some people travelling in a two-tone grey UAZ minibus. I looked around me, and saw it parked just around the corner. As I walked forward, closer inspection revealed that it was really a three-tone minibus, where patches of orange rust infiltrated upwards from the bottom edges of the metalwork of the battered old vehicle. Leaning casually across the front of the van, like a giant slug, was Leonid Kedzierski; his lack of sartorial elegance making a bold and arresting statement.

Down at heel brown sandals with no socks, framed dirty feet with long yellowing toenails. His crumpled grey trousers were secured with a piece of thick brown rope for a belt across his expansive stomach. It was clear for all to see, that Leonid had a passion for food, and consequently he ate for Russia. His once white shirt had leather armpits, where months of sweat had hardened. His face seemed to be wider than it was long. It was a face that had launched a thousand vomits. He was blessed with a flat nose, huge jug ears, piggy eyes, and all his upper front teeth were missing. A series of wavy parallel lines on his forehead combined so well with his warts and other big red blobs, that it looked like a stave with two bars of a Rachmaninov symphony written across it. The top of his head sported not a single hair, but delighted in oozing a continuous stream of sweat, which he frequently wiped with a large grey green handkerchief.

"Dobroho ranku." I greeted him, extending a hesitant right hand.

He ignored my gesture, gave a mock salute and returned my introduction with, "Ahov, Jak tebe zvaty?"

I introduced myself as Mikael Kuzma from Minsk, and explained that I had been assigned as a guide by the state tourist agency. He replied that he was responsible for transporting a small group of students from a town called Pripyat, about 150 kilometres north of Kiev, on the minibus, for a short cultural visit. They had arrived in Kiev after a 3 hour drive, and would be visiting a number of places in the city over the next four days. I advised him that I had the full itinerary from the tourist agency, and at the end of the visit would be travelling back with them all, before returning to Minsk. He shrugged. It appeared he resented the fact that I existed, and that I knew exactly what tasks I had been assigned to.

He banged his fist on the side of the corroding door, and as he lit a cigarette and began to wheeze his way through the tobacco haze, the four teenage students piled off the minibus. There were two boys; Kazimir, tall, broad shouldered, curly headed and dark featured, sporting a juvenile growth of facial hair, and Yaromir, smaller, blonde, pale and skinny. They both greeted me politely with smiles, and shy and limp handshakes. Then there were two girls; Irinushka, a petite, dark haired girl, with a little nose and deep brown eyes, and Gavriila, an athletic, tall, and well built girl with an alluring smile and perfect white teeth. The young ladies giggled and smiled with polite nods.

There was a good reason why we had met in this particular place. It was because our first cultural visit was to the Besarabsky Market, also known as the Besarabka. Everyone in the Ukraine knew about the Besarabsky Market; a huge indoor market which had been in existence for years. The wonderfully solid and impressive building, with tall windows and a high arched roof had been constructed in 1910-1912, to a design of Polish architect Henryk Julian Gay. The market was well known for selling the best produce in the country.

Leonid decided that he'd spent enough time looking after the four students, and declined to join us in the market, declaring "All rynoks are the same. I've seen them all."

He then said that he would get into the minibus and have a sleep. I took the four students on a tour through the market. We stopped to talk with many of the babushka; the old peasant women, wearing triangular headscarves tied under their chins, who sat outside the market place, trying to sell their flowers. Gavriila in particular, spent a long time chatting and laughing with the babushkas. After a while, wandering round the market stalls as a fivesome, Kazimir decided to break off from the group and go it alone. I'd already identified that he was a bit of a loner, difficult to impress, and likely to be less sociable than the others. I instructed him to meet us back at the minibus by 2 pm. The rest of us moved slowly around from stall to stall, enjoying the sights and smells of a huge variety of fruit and vegetables from the four corners of the world, displayed in every shade of red, orange, yellow and green, and arranged in mountainous piles. We also enjoyed sampling a vast range of tiny pieces of smoked meats and cheeses. The market traders continually haggled with prospective buyers. There was a unique, cheerful and engaging buzz about the place. There was also fresh meat, fish, honey, and dairy products, such as milk and home-made smetana (sour cream). We also found stalls selling caviar, cut flowers, house wares, tools and hardware, and clothing.

Yaromir and Irinushka seemed to be very fond of each other, often touching, and on occasion holding hands, and looking very intently at each other, eye to eye, with broad smiles. Gavriila acted as mother hen, herding us all around, and deciding which way to go through the endless maze of colourful stalls. Time passed very quickly, and soon it was getting close to 2 pm. When we left the rynok, armed with apples and bananas, and jars of honey, and a few souvenir trinkets to take home, we found Leonid fast asleep, and Kazimir nowhere to be seen. I banged on the side of the van, and a bleary eyed Leonid slowly rose from his slumbers, and with an air of reluctance, opened a door. A fug of sweat and cigarettes flowed sluggishly into the city air as we climbed aboard. Fifteen minutes later, Kazimir appeared walking ungainly towards the van, with a small bottle of vodka projecting from the top of his jacket pocket. He nonchalantly climbed into a seat without a word, took a swig from the bottle, and closed his eyes. Gavriila rolled her eyes in disbelief. Yaromir and Irinushka were too wrapped up in each other to take any notice.

Leonid started the noisy and dirty engine of the UAZ, which juddered and smoked its way along the Baseina Street, and off to the next venue on the itinerary. The Slugman's driving was as erratic and disgraceful as his appearance. He negotiated the short journey as if he were Marshall Rokossovsky, driving a T34 tank against a relentless Nazi foe in the battle of Kursk. The assembly arrived unscathed, despite his best efforts. I worried about how I would survive another 3 days and a long drive north back to Minsk, with this tyrant at the wheel.

Thankfully, it wasn't long before we arrived outside the Kiev Academic Puppet Theatre in Shota Rustaveli Street, in the historic Podil district of the city. The oldest puppet theatre in the Ukraine was founded in 1927, and was housed in the Great Choral Synagogue of Kiev, built in the Romanesque revival style, resembling a classical basilica, between 1897 and 98.

"We are at Brodsky Choral Synagogue," my new fat friend quickly pointed out, and then added with a smirk to imply that he was more knowledgeable than me, "Did you know this is the largest synagogue in Kiev?"

It amused me that he was intent on doing my job as a state tourist guide, and I wondered if he really knew that the sugar magnate and philanthropist Lazar Brodsky had financed the synagogue's construction.

Kazimir had fallen quickly into a drunken sleep, and when we attempted to wake him, his grunts and groans indicated that he wouldn't be going into the theatre with us. Leonid insisted on going in his place.

We were booked to attend a performance of "Three Little Pigs". The puppets, some of which were many times restored, and up to 60 years old, were truly magnificent, as was their expert handling.

Kazimir's substitute sang all the songs, and booed, hissed, cheered and clapped his way throughout the show. When the exchanges between the wolf and pig were repeated, he chanted them louder than the performers and any of the attending children, much to everybody's embarrassment.

"Little pig, little Pig, let me come in."

"No, no, not by the hair on my chinny chin chin."

"Then I'll huff, and I'll puff, and I'll blow your house in."

He revelled in playing the wolf and huffed and puffed with asthmatic enthusiasm, laughing insanely all the way through the performance like a 7 year old with ADHD.

Despite the non-puppet understudy's behaviour, we all managed to enjoy the wonderful experience.

Then it was time for me and my little crew to risk life and limb again in the UAZ, making our way 20 kilometres southwards out the city, towards Camping Number 1 "KYIV", along the Akademika Zabolotnoho Street, in the Holosiivs'kyi district. This was to be our overnight billet for the next 3 days, from 23rd April 'til the morning of 26th of April 1986, when we would make our way back to Pripyat.

After reporting to reception, we were shown to our caravan. Each of the small bedrooms was basic and functional; 2 narrow single beds, one shared bedside table in the middle, thin plain white walls, one small mirror, and a shower room with toilet. There was a place for the girls, one for the boys, and much to my delight, I had the pleasure of sharing one of the miniscule cardboard boxes that passed for a bedroom, with Leonid. Outside the caravan was a small patio, with a plastic topped table and 6 garden chairs. Nearly all the youngsters were excited at the prospect of staying at the campsite, and were keen to explore the surrounding areas of forests and lakes. That thought pleased me, but the prospect of spending the night in close proximity to the Slug horrified me. He sat outside the caravan smoking his 40th cigarette of the day, while the rest of us stretched our legs and expanded our lungs with fresher air on an hour long stroll around the campsite. Kazimir went along with some reluctance.

Later, we filled our stomachs at a local cafe, enjoying kapusniak, a soup made with pork, salo, cabbage, and served with smetana. This was followed by an Olivier salad made out of cooked and chopped potatoes, dill pickles, boiled chopped eggs, cooked and chopped chicken, sliced onions, canned peas, and smothered in mayonnaise.

Leonid had to be different, and thoroughly enjoyed his pyrih: a massive pie filled with potato, onions and pork. He then ploughed his way through a huge portion of salo, a disgusting concoction of cured slabs of fatback, which he washed down with a large Obolon beer.

I could say that we shared a plate of the doughnut-like pampushky for dessert, but that's to deny that we had one each, while our driver finished off the other 5. I don't know what was more sickening to observe. Was it the myriads of many coloured food specks on his shirt, or the greasiness of the salo impregnated with sugar crystals from his pampushky, speckled across his slimy chin?

Soon the skies began to darken, and our tank commander went off to the minibus to smoke another packet of cigarettes before retiring.

"I go to service the minibus." he lied. The minibus hadn't had a service in decades.

The rest of us sat outside the caravan in the twilight, drinking the local Morshynska mineral water.

"How have you all enjoyed the day then?" I asked

"The Besarabka was wonderful, and I loved talking to the babushka." said Gavriila.

"Yes, we enjoyed that too!" agreed Irinuschka, obviously talking for her new beau as well as herself.

The young boy, nodded his head and added while munching at a large red apple, "We bought some lovely fruit there; the biggest apples I have ever seen."

Kazimir just sniffed the chilling air and emptied the final glug from his vodka bottle, while staring into the distance looking as if he wanted to be on another planet.

"You're such an oaf." said Gavriila, "Bottom of the class at college, only interested in getting drunk, and completely devoid of any saving graces."

"What's it to you?" he replied, rising up in his seat, ready for a confrontation.

"Kazi, we are here together, and you want to spoil everything with your bad habits. Just look at yourself. Examine! In a few years time, you'll be a sad specimen, just like an apprentice version of Leonid the slug."

"Gavri, my dear, go jump in the lake. You are nothing special. You walk around like you own the place, and nobody and nothing is anywhere near good enough for you."

Irinuschka and Yaromir leaned closer to each other, and bit their lips sensing a big argument brewing.

I tried to stop the bickering, saying, "Come on boys and girls, we need to be happy with each other for the next few days. Let's not start a major incident over nothing."

"I know why you didn't want to go to the puppet show." Gavriila continued.

"It's for kids, and morons. That's why you loved it!" Kazimir replied.

"No, Kazie, it's because you are hollow, just like the puppets. Who knows, they might have roped you into the show, and kept you there. Your brain is like the great Manchurian yeti. It doesn't exist!"

"Oh, give it a rest. You sound just like my mother. Come to think of it, you're so ugly; you even look like my mother."

"I'm going for a jog, before I say something I might regret." said Gavriila as her eyes filled with tears. She stood up, and jogged away into the forest behind us, where a red sun was flickering its last few rays through the gloom of a stand of tall pine trees.

"Will you be in a better mood, and a bit more sociable tomorrow?" I asked Kazimir.

He thought for a moment, looked at me down his nose, and replied, "Why, yes of course! Tomorrow we go to the National Museum of the History of Ukraine. It will be a day for men, not silly little boys and girls."

"Is that what you have been most looking forward to then?"

"Well, it is the main day of our tour."

"The highlight?"

"Oh no! That will be the next day when we go to the Dynamo Kiev stadium."

He looked at me, smirking, "When we go there, I will be a saint."

"What magic will bring about that change in your demeanour?"

"I am the first choice goalkeeper for the best team in Pripyat, and one day I will be famous, when I am playing for the Dynamo."

"Really? I think you'll find that footballers have to act as ambassadors for their team, and I don't imagine that they drink neat vodka on a regular basis."

"Maybe not!" he answered, "But when I am there, I will have the opportunity to introduce myself to people who will recognise my talent."

Then he stood up and climbed the 2 steps into the caravan. The 2 remaining youngsters looked at each other, and holding hands, followed suit.

"It's been a long day, and we are tired." offered Irinuschka for the pair of them looking at me over her shoulder, as they disappeared through the narrow door.

It was nearly dark, and I began to worry about what had happened to Gavriila.

I moved towards the forest, and caught a brief glimpse of a white and blue tee shirt flitting quickly through the trees. A sigh of relief escaped me as the athletic girl emerged from the foliage, slowing in her jog towards me. She was only feet from me when she let out a yell and almost fell into my arms; her jog dissipating into a limp in a few steps. She sat down clutching her left leg, with tears of excruciating pain welling up in her eyes.

"I've been stung by a bee or a wasp or something. My God, it hurts! It feels like my leg is on fire. Please, please. Help me!"

I pulled her leg up onto the picnic table, and in the dim light examined her calf finding a bee sting still pulsating and pumping its poison into her.

"Do you have any tweezers in your bag? I need to pull the bee sting out of your skin."

She was on the verge of fainting, and her face was contorted by the pain, but without saying anything, breathing and swallowing hard, she pointed to her shoulder bag. I upended the bag on the table, and rummaged through the spilled contents. There!

I positioned the tweezers and twisted the sting carefully out of the swelling reddening blob, and then attempted to suck the poison out of the wound, spitting it out on the ground.

Gavriila began to scratch at her face and eyes. Her breathing became even more shallow and laboured. Within a minute, she was clutching at her throat gasping for breath. Red swells appeared underneath the skin on her leg. Then she suddenly lurched forward in the garden chair, and vomited violently all over my shoes.

I had never seen anyone in this kind of distress before, and the thought never occurred to me that what Gavriila was experiencing was anaphylactic shock. But it was obvious that I needed to do something quickly.

There was an empty plastic cup on the table. I put my hand into my special rainbow bag, and clutched at a handful of falling stars. Carefully I emptied them into the plastic cup, and then filled the cup with mineral water, and brought it up to Gavriila's mouth. By this time, she was incapable of sipping at the concoction. So I very slowly tipped the cup up towards her lips, and let the contents drip into her mouth little by little. Seconds passed like days. She coughed and her eyes rolled upwards, before they flickered open and closed many times, like the shutter of a camera taking a succession of snaps. Her head lolled to one side, and she slumped in the chair.

To my west, the last few rays of a golden sunshine day melted through the fast fading twilight, into the impending gloom of night. A large flock of birds squawked in unison, and flew off in formation from branches in the treetops of the nearby forest. Black winged shapes circled overhead, as if the harbinger of a tragic outcome, and then vanished as quickly as they came. To my east, a pearly white crescent moon rose lazily from its slumber and reflected a shimmering cold light across the still waters of a mirror lake.

Then, silence!

A silence so deep and heavy, that the air around the two of us seemed to have solidified

The awful thought came to me, that I had acted too late to save this young and vibrant girl with all her life ahead of her. I hung my head and tears came.

In a flash Gavriila stood up, her eyes fixed and focussed, pupils dilated, and she was staring straight ahead. She began to turn, to rotate in a circle of ever increasing speed. A loud buzz, increasing steadily in volume filled my ears. It looked as if she was surrounded by a massive swarm of excited, but not angry, bees. I took a step back, not sure of exactly what was happening.

She disappeared in the swirl and just became a very loud whirling mass. Then the noise ceased and the vortex instantly transformed into a tall conical shape like a volcano. In a split second, the volcano erupted with an intermittent orange stream of stars whooshing heavenwards, and bursting in the skies above us, just as if I was watching a giant roman candle. The stars fell back to the ground, and one by one formed a glowing circle around the girl. Smoke encircled her, and rose up in spiralling orange plumes around her. She emerged from smoke and stepped towards me. She smiled at me, and I smiled back.

"That was a lovely run through the woods." she said, "Has everybody gone to bed?"

"Yes, all except for Leonid." I replied.

"I'm pretty tired myself now, I think I'll turn in as well." she said, and leaned forward, kissing me on the cheek. As she did so, she scooped up the contents of her duffle bag, and slung the bag back over her shoulder as if nothing had happened.

"Na dobranič!" she said

"Yes, good night, sleep well." I answered.

I was left alone in the fast chilling night air and it occurred to me that her name meant "God's bravest woman". In a strange way she had certainly lived up to that name.

Soon I had tidied up outside, arranged the garden furniture neatly, discarded any accumulated rubbish in the nearby bin, and climbed into the caravan. I took a quick shower, and went into my bedroom, where I found my new companion of the night, slumped resplendently on his camp bed fast asleep. A small bottle of vodka sat on the shared bedside table, alongside his bottom set of dentures. His brown and very dirty shoes needed fumigating so I put them outside. It was obvious that personal hygiene was an alien concept to this man. I soon found out that he not only ate and drank for Mother Russia, but he snored and farted for her as well. I did my best to get some sleep, almost longing for morning to break early and release me from the sweaty imprisonment in this son of Rasputin's boudoir. Luckily, my companion's collection of addictions only allowed him to sleep for a maximum of four hours. I heard him get up just before 4 in the morning, and he didn't return to the room, so I managed to catch a few hours well-earned shuteye.

When I got up at about 8 the next day, Leonid was dozing outside on a garden chair. He'd smoked his way through a half a packet of cigarettes, and there was the ever present bottle of vodka on the table. I don't know whether he'd warmed to me because of our close proximity through the early part of the night, but surprisingly he spoke to me as soon as he saw me.

"Dobroho ranku!" he said with a slimy grin, and added, "So you are a son of Minsk, are you?"

My graceful naivety only allowed me to know a little about my background for this task. I was wary of too many questions.

"Yes, I am," I answered, guarded, adding, "It's a beautiful city."

"Not so beautiful, I think," he answered with a derisory laugh, "Stalin rebuilt it after the war in his own image. Block headed, ugly and over industrialised."

"But it's where I grew up, and I love it."

"Each to his own. One man's Bolshevik utopia is another man's communist hell."

"Have you been there?"

"My family were at home there before the war. My father was a Bolshevik; a government official. Minsk was the cradle of the Russian revolution, and he was an active political campaigner. He was from peasant stock, and told me all about how the Tsars ate caviar and drank champagne in their golden palaces, while the peasants starved in their mud and straw hovels. I was born in Minsk in 1930."

"That makes you 11 when the German war against Russia began. How did your family survive?"

"It took the Nazis just 4 days to roll their disgusting fascist war machine to the gates of our city. My father had friends in the Politburo. We escaped by the skin of our teeth, and were transferred east to Stalingrad."

"I heard that the Nazis were truly monstrous, that they murdered millions, and had a scorched earth policy in Russia. They didn't take prisoners. They just killed everyone who opposed their regime."

"Too true! When they surrounded Stalingrad, in January 1943, my father called in favours again, and we were moved a long way east to Gorky. We were safe there, at least from the Germans."

Leonid looked distressed. He lit another cigarette, and puffed hard on it staring into the distance. It felt like he wanted to say more.

"Why do you say that?"

"What?"

"At least from the Germans?"

"Well, it's a problem if you call in too many favours from Politburo members. Joe Stalin always got nervous if you stayed around too long, and knew too much, or too many of the favoured few. My father's friend in the Politburo fell victim to one of Stalin's purges, and then the bigwigs wanted to transfer him way out to Siberia to manage a gulag. He refused to go."

"What happened then?"

"The KGB came to collect him in the middle of the night, in February 1950, and we never saw him again. It was rumoured that he was taken to Llubyanka, where he was tortured, and then shot by a firing squad. Stalin is supposed to have personally signed his death warrant, but then he signed thousands of similar decrees every week. To him it was just another piece of paper to effect the removal of a minor nuisance."

"What became of your family?"

"My two older brothers, Andre and Yuri, were both killed during the war. My mother and I were thrown out of our dacha, and forced to work in a labour camp. She died of tuberculosis in the winter of1952."

"And you?"

"I am a survivor. I became a beggar, a scavenger, a permanent refugee in my own country. Then, in 1953, salvation! Stalin died, and gradually things improved, until under Khrushchev and Kosygin, I was able to re-enter society."

"How did that come about?"

"I became a construction worker at Chernobyl. First, on the nuclear power station, and then, on the building of a city to serve the station's needs, at Pripyat. Now I live there in Prypyat. My life is not brilliant, but at least it is predictable. I don't have to fear that the KGB will come looking for me."

Leonid had finished his tale and lit another cigarette. He had spilled his tragic life story out to me in a few minutes. Now, despite all his outward repugnance, I suddenly felt very sorry for this man, and the difficult life he and his family had endured. The plastic tumblers from the previous evening were still upturned on the table. He turned two of them upwards, and sloshed a large gulp of vodka into each. He handed me one, and held the other up towards me. We clinked plastics in a toast.

"Nasdrovie, my Minsk friend." he said.

It was utterly disgusting, but I had made a new friend.

Soon, the small patio by our caravan burst into life, as the youngsters emerged one by one from the cardboard box that served as our holiday home. Gavriila came out first, looking fresh and sparkling with rude health, showing no signs of the ordeal she had endured only hours ago. Then, the petite, dark haired Irinuschka, and the pale and skinny Yaromir appeared, still holding hands and looking very pleased with each other. Finally, with a lethargic slump down the steps, holding his head, and looking pale and stressed, Kazimir joined us at the table.

After breakfast, we journeyed the 20 kilometres across the city to the Pechersk district of Kiev, to visit the Park of Eternal Glory and the Museum of the Great Patriotic War. It was a blisteringly hot day of magnificent sunshine and a light warm breeze, made all the better by spending our time wandering slowly around the 2 museums on the picturesque verdant hills overlooking the right bank of the Dnieper River.

The tall azure skies were fringed with mare's tails, spread across our gaze from the sprawl of the city to the west, to the green open spaces beyond the Dnieper River to our east.

We visited the Park of Eternal Glory, where we enjoyed a spectacular view of the city, from a wonderful viewpoint on a steep slope on the river bank. The central place in the park was the site of the Glory Obelisk, at the pedestal of which was the Grave of an Unknown Soldier. Our two most ardent Russian patriots, Leonid and Kazimir stood in silence here. Then with all due reverence, they laid flowers they had bought at a nearby kiosk, at the foot of the monument. Despite his obvious hatred for Stalin's brutal regime, Leonid displayed a true love of his country and a comprehensive understanding of its recent history. My role as a guide appeared to be surplus to requirements, while my new fat friend endeavoured to explain everything.

"We should be immensely proud of Mother Russia and our magnificent achievements since the 1917 revolution." he advised his young comrades in arms, his face beaming with pride.

"My father told me, that millions had sacrificed themselves to history to make our country the great nation it is today."

Kazimir smiled, as he raised his right hand, palm downwards to salute his war heroes. All the others followed suit. Yaromir had spoken very little so far on the tour, often allowing Irinuschka to speak for him. As the youngest and shyest member of the crew, he had been quiet and restrained. But even he became an enthusiastic patriot when we turned towards the grandiose Motherland statue, in the nearby Museum of the Great Patriotic War.

"Oh Wow! Look at that! It's breathtaking!" he spouted, as he led our way towards the one of the best recognized landmarks of Kiev.

A short walk later, we stood before the monumental sculpture. Once again I had no need to explain, as Leonid acted as guide by saying, "The "Motherland" was built by Yevgeny Vuchetich."

"It's very tall." said Irinuschka, looking upwards, and shading her eyes in the bright sunshine.

"Yes, it stands 62 meters upon the museum building, and the overall structure is 102 meters high."

"It's massive." said Yaromir, gazing skyward in awe.

"It weighs 530 tons." said the heaviest member of our group.

"I am so proud to be here today," enthused Kazimir, "This makes me burst with pride for our people and our achievements."

Leonid continued, "The sword in the statue's right hand is 16 meters long, and it alone weighs 9 tons, and look, the left hand is holding up a gigantic shield, displaying the Coat of Arms of the Soviet Union."

We walked around the perimeter of the monument in a complete circle, admiring its awesome presence from every possible angle.

"Let's go into the museum building." said Gavriila.

Our little group were grateful to spend some time out of the sun, inside the Memorial hall of the Museum, looking through the marble plaques with carved names of more than 11,600 soldiers, and over 200 workers of the home-front, honoured during the war. Each of us was looking to see if any of our namesakes or family members had been recognised with the title of Hero of the Soviet Union or Hero of Socialist Labour. Leonid looked for his brothers, but he did not find them. He remained nevertheless, a complete martyr to the cause. By the time we emerged back into the sunlight, it was midday. We needed to find somewhere to have lunch.

In the afternoon, there was much more to see and to marvel at. We walked through the memorial's main square, and the "Valley of Hero-Cities.", before we were then confronted by the giant concrete bowl that contained "The Flame of Glory".

Leonid was overcome with emotion, choking his words, and holding back tears as he explained, "This museum complex was opened on 9th May, 1981, the glorious day of our victory against the evil Nazi regime, by our Soviet leader Leonid Brezhnev."

"Is he a good man?" asked Yaromir innocently.

"Of course!" answered Kazimir without thinking, "All our glorious leaders are good men."

"Sometimes good, sometimes bad, very bad." corrected Leonid.

"Why do you feel so especially sad here?" said Gavriila.

"The flame for ceremonial opening of this museum was brought directly from the Mamaev barrow, from the field of the Stalingrad battle, and I was only 13 when I lived for a while in Stalingrad."

Our tour continued for the rest of the afternoon, and everywhere we went in the museum, whether it was outdoors or indoors, there were larger-than-life depictions of Soviet strength, courage, and sacrifice. Among the exhibits, we were able to examine, were tanks, other military vehicles, helicopters, planes, massive guns, statues and sculptures. And all the time, military music echoed loudly from speakers between the sculptured open-air walls.

There was no let-up in the warmth of the April sunshine, as we set to leave the area at the end of the afternoon. We had walked miles, and it felt like we had covered every inch of the 10 hectares of the memorial complex, and seen nearly every one of the 300,000 exhibits. My little party had all been filled to overflowing with patriotic pride, and all the youngsters had taken great advantage of the sunshine. Gavriila looked even more attractive with a healthy tan. The pale skinned pair of Irinuschka and Yaromir looked like two lobsters. I was unaffected by the sun, and the other two men would only confess to slight discomfort. We made our way back to the campsite, after a full and very emotional day. As we travelled, an enthusiastic Kazimir led the singing the Russian national anthem.

In the fading sunlight at the end of a glorious day, we had a quiet and contemplative evening sitting on our caravan patio.

I opened a discussion with, "Everybody enjoyed our visits today, I think. But what was the best bit?"

Kazimir was eager to answer first, "The Flame of Glory, for me.", he said while Leonid grunted agreement.

"But I also felt immensely proud at the "Grave of an Unknown Soldier" when we placed our flowers."

Gavriila added, "Looking through all the plaques in the Memorial hall of the Motherland Museum was very sad. All those millions of people died in the war, and the plaques could only represent a small number of them. To go in there and search for a particular name is a very chilling experience."

"We liked the Motherland monument." said Irinuschka, speaking for herself and Yaromir again, as he nodded beside her. The sunburn seemed to have affected him quite severely, and he didn't look at all well.

"Are you OK?" I asked, "You look a bit hot and bothered."

"I've got a headache, and I feel a bit dizzy." he answered. Then he attempted a reassuring smile.

It required some effort for him to slowly drawl, "I am looking forward to going home to Pripyat, and talking to my dad about all the things we saw today."

"Yes! Our little holiday is very exciting, but it will be lovely to go home again." added Irinuschka.

"I remember when Pripyat was just a river in the wilderness, a watery marshland." piped up Leonid.

I sensed that he was about to go into tour guide mode again, and sat back to listen to his eloquence.

"You children will not remember, because you were still in nappies at the time, but I was a part of the huge construction team assembled to build the city in 1970."

He was right. Yaromir hadn't even been born, and all the other youngsters were under 2 years old.

The lecture continued. "Today the city has 50,000 residents; people who moved in from all over Mother Russia, to serve the Chernobyl Nuclear Power Plant. Pripyat is the ninth nuclear city in the Soviet Union."

"We should be rightly proud of our national achievements with nuclear power." asserted Kazimir.

"I'm not sure that it's completely safe." queried Gavriila.

"Don't be stupid, woman," Kazimir spat, "Of course it's safe. It's only ignoramuses like you who would spread lies about it."

"It's time for my evening jog again, I think." she replied, smiling as she walked away from her antagonist.

"Make it an evening stroll, and we'll come with you." said Irinushka.

"OK", came the over shoulder reply.

The three of them set off into the woods. Leonid and Kazimir continued to share a bottle of vodka. I went for a shower.

Half an hour later, I had just got dressed again when I heard some commotion outside. Irinushka came rushing up to the caravan, breathless and very agitated, shouting, "Help! Help! Please help!"

"What's wrong?" I asked.

"It's Yaromir! He has collapsed over there by the picnic table; come quickly."

Quick action was required. I worried about another stinging accident.

"Go and find Leonid and Kazimir. They're probably over by the minibus. We might need to take Yaromir to hospital." I told her.

Then I ran over to the edge of the trees. The victim was prostrate on the ground. I turned him face upwards. It was only then that I realised how badly sunburned he was. His face was very red, and his skin was dry and very hot to the touch, but he was shivering uncontrollably. I felt for a heartbeat. It was rapid and irregular. His breathing was quick and shallow. He was obviously suffering from dehydration and heatstroke. I needed to do something to save his life. For the second time in 24 hours I put my hand into my special rainbow bag and clutched at a handful of falling stars. I scattered them all over his body from head to toe.

"Gavriila, please give me a bottle of water." I said. She smiled a knowing smile.

I took the bottle, opened it swiftly, and sprinkled the water all over the length of his body.

The sky overhead was cloudy and overcast, growing darker by the minute, threatening a thunderstorm.

There was no moon to be seen, but the dim light from nearby caravans danced eerily on the nearby lake.

There was a rush of air, as a large flock of water birds took off together from the surface of the lake and flew towards us. They circled over Yaromir, creating a swirling cool movement of air over his body. I took another bottle of water from Gavriila's shoulder bag, and told her to dribble the contents slowly over Yaromir's face and mouth. The birds began to sing. They sang a sad, gloriously moving tune. It sounded like the national anthem that we had heard frequently throughout the day.

Once again an awful thought came to me, that I had acted too late to save this young man, so quiet and shy, and hardly more than a child. I hung my head and prayed silently.

When I looked up, the boy was standing up, and his shape was wrapped in a diffused orange blanket of light, where a stream of stars made spiral shapes around him. At first they were miniscule pinpricks of light. But they grew, and grew, and grew, until Yaromir became one fantastic bright shining star, rotating slowly on the spot. Then, very gradually the blur of light came to a halt, with stars falling off his body like raindrops dripping off an umbrella. A fork of lightning struck the tallest tree a few meters along the forest path, followed in a split second by a loud crash of thunder in the skies above. The tree began to fall towards us, and instinctively Yaromir ran towards the caravan. We followed him with all due haste. I banged the door shut and moments later it burst open again as Irinuschka, Kazimir and Leonid rushed in out of the rain.

"What's going on? Is Yaromir OK? I thought he needed to go to hospital." asked Kazimir shotgun style.

I answered him calmly, "No, I think he just fainted. He was a little bit dehydrated. It's been a long, energetic, and very warm day."

Irinushka snuggled up to the boy and held both his hands. "Are you really OK?" she asked looking deep into his eyes.

"There's no need for any fuss, I'm fine," he said, "Sometimes I get a bit nervous when there's a storm brewing. I just need a good night's sleep, and I'll be right as rain."

Another flash of lightning lit up the sky and thunder crashed so loudly the caravan shook. Gavriila said nothing, and gave me that knowing smile again. Soon after, we all retired. The storm moved away, after sounding like boulders were crashing on our roof for a while. I looked in on Yaromir 30 minutes later, and he was sleeping soundly as any "man of peace" should. All the effects of his sunburn and heatstroke had disappeared. I felt sure that he would not remember his recent dangerous experience.

Perhaps I was getting used to my Minsk friend's snoring and farting, perhaps it was all the walking about in the sunshine, but I also slept very well.

After the patriot's day our party had just experienced, we were set to have a complete contrast the next day. What was planned was a day filled with entertainment and leisure pursuits.

Another 20 minute drive would bring us back to the city on the banks of the mighty Dnieper River, to the home of Dynamo Kiev. The most excited member of our crew on the journey was Kazimir.

"Dynamo Kiev are the most successful football club in the Soviet League, and they've won the Championship, the USSR Cup, and the USSR Super Cup, more times than any other team."

I asked, "Who's your favourite player?"

"Isn't it obvious? It's their goalkeeper, Viktor Chanov."

"Yes, I suppose it is obvious; you being a goalkeeper for the Pripyat team."

"And one day I will play for the Dynamo." he asserted, with a joyful sneer.

It was time for Gavriila to turn the tables on her antagonist.

"But why would they want you in their team. With a surname like yours, you'd be a laughing stock every time you let a goal in."

"I won't let any goals in. So that won't happen."

Gavri laughed. "I'm sure that a great team like Dynamo Kiev wouldn't want a Pasternak between the sticks. You do know what it means don't you?"

Kazi shuffled uncomfortably in his seat.

"What does it mean?" asked Yaromir, innocently.

The aspiring goalie's bête noire whispered something in the boy's ear. She whispered it loudly enough for every one to hear it.

"Turnip!" she said, "Pasternak means turnip."

The whole crew, except me of course, chanted, "Kazi is a turnip. Kazi is a turnip."

He scowled, and remained silent for nearly all of the rest of the way there.

The Russian tourist office must have pulled a few strings to organise this visit. It wasn't usual for ordinary folk to have the privilege of not only being shown around the stadium, but to also meet and talk to some of the players.

Out of the blue, Kazi broke his silence with, "Anyway, ignorant people, I have to tell you that in the last few weeks, Dynamo have knocked out Dukla Prague, in the semi-finals of the European Cup Winners' Cup. They won 3 - 0 in the first leg on 2nd April, at home, with goals by Oleg Blokhin and Aleksandr Zavarov. Then they went to Prague, and drew 1 - 1 on 16th April, with a goal by Igor Belanov. So with a 4 - 1 aggregate win, they go to the Stade de Gerland, in Lyon, France, for the final against Atletico Madrid, on 2nd May, which I think they will win easily."

Nobody said anything. His facts were true, and there was no need for any further argument.

As we pulled up outside the stadium, Dynamo's most ardent fan pulled a bottle of vodka from his pocket, and took a large slug. He looked at the others, and said, "For Dutch Courage! Today I get signed up by the mighty Dynamo."

We were greeted by an official from the football club, who introduced himself as Konstantin Andropov, and showed us to a darkened room, where we sat through a 40 minute film, illustrating the history of the club. Bottles of water and orange juice were offered as refreshments. Then we had a stadium tour. Everywhere we went, the club's colours of white and dark blue were emblazoned across every possible surface. As we toured, Konstantin explained that the club was founded in 1927 and had been at the stadium since 1934. He advised us that the capacity was now about 17,000. There had been a rebuilding programme after the war, which reduced the capacity from 23,000.

He asserted that the stadium was too small for a club with the highest profile in Soviet football, and hinted that a move to a bigger venue was always in discussion. Then he gave us all copy programmes from the 2 recent semi-finals in the European Cup Winners' Cup.

There were some players out on the pitch, and Kazimir recognised them.

"That's Oleg Blokhin," he said, pointing at a player to his left, "And, look, that's Igor Belanov on the ball."

"You know your players then?" asked our guide.

"Yes, I follow every match the Dynamo play in, but I've never been to one of your games."

"Where do you live, son?"

"In Prypyat, and I play in goal for the best team in the city."

"So that's about 150 kilometres away. All the people that live there are radioactive. Aren't they?" he joked.

Ignoring the joke, Kazi asked. "Where's Viktor Chanov? I can't see him out there."

"He'll be out there soon. He's on the treatment table at the moment."

"And will Valeri Lobanovsky, the manager, put in an appearance today."

"I'm afraid not, son. He's very busy planning for our game against Atletico Madrid."

"Can I speak with Chanov when he comes out?"

"No, we don't allow visitors to disturb the player's concentration. But we have autographs for all the first team players in the boardroom, for you to take away."

"I must talk to Chanov. I'm going to play for Dynamo one day, and he is my idol."

"I'm sorry! You can't talk to him." the guide asserted.

"Why?" came an indignant reply.

"I've told you, son. We don't want to disturb the player's concentration."

"That's not fair!"

"Maybe not! But it's the way it is."

There were a few minutes sullen silence, then Viktor Chanov ran out, and positioned himself in the goal directly in front of our little group. Kazi spotted him and attempted to climb over the perimeter wall. A massive, muscle-bound steward appeared out of nowhere, and held him back easily with one hand. He looked like the sort of man who would enjoy working at Llubyanka, pulling out toenails with pliers and snipping off fingers with garden shears.

He just smiled derisorily, and sneered, "Go away, little boy, before I get angry."

Konstantin pulled Kazi away, and dragged him off to the boardroom. We all followed, knowing that the tour would be prematurely over. Soon after, we were shown back to the car park.

There was a parting shot from our guide, directed personally at an aspiring Dynamo goalkeeper, whose dreams had been stifled. "By the way, sonny, let me advise you of something important."

"What?" snapped the boy.

"If you want to be a footballer, then lay off the vodka. I can smell it on your breath."

There was a fixed unfriendly stare between man and boy.

"Footballers need to be supremely fit, especially goalkeepers, and they don't argue with the rules. Lobanovsky is a stickler for discipline. You don't argue with the manager, if you want to be selected to play. We are ambassadors for the club, and for Mother Russia."

Then Konstantin waved the party goodbye, with, "I hope you found the tour interesting, and that you enjoy the rest of your holiday."

We set off a little earlier than expected for our next venue. There was a lengthy period of silence in the minibus, until Yaromir piped up, joking with Kazimir, "I suppose you'll have to support Metalist Kharkiv now."

Everybody except one laughed. He added, "Anyway, the Weasels were founded in 1925; 2 years before the Dynamo."

There was no consoling the rejected goalkeeper, and to everybody's disgust he was not the least bit aware that he had brought about a curtailment of the stadium tour. He remained disgruntled all the way through the short drive to the Hydropark, a water theme park on the Venetian and Dolobetsk islands, in the Dnieper River. Detached from the rising excitement among the other youngsters, he swigged frequently at his small bottle of vodka, until he had fully drained its contents. The driver dropped us off at the amusement park, and went off to meet an old friend after arranging to pick us up later, to take us to the evening venue. Our first stop after parking was to buy 10 bottles of water from one of the kiosks. There was going to be no repeats of dehydration dramas today. Once again the April sunshine beamed its flamethrower energy down from a metallic blue and cloudless sky. It was destined to be another absolute scorcher of a day. The atmosphere at Hydropark was lively; quiet chatter, laughter, people enjoying themselves on the rides, or splashing in the water. Ice-cream and doughnuts were everywhere. There was a pleasant middle of the river cool breeze, lessening the glare of the sun.

We spent a couple of hours enjoying the rides in the amusement park , all of us wondering whether Kazimir would stay the pace, or suddenly find his stomach rejecting its contents on one of the wilder rides. To our surprise he remained composed, albeit silent and surly. Then we enjoyed a leisurely snack lunch on the large patio of one of the cheaper restaurants.

"What shall we do after lunch?" asked Gavri.

"I want to go for a swim." said Kazi. It was the first time he had spoken since we left the stadium.

"That's not very wise immediately after we have eaten." I advised, "Let's give it an hour before we go swimming."

He looked at me like I'd stolen his bicycle.

"It's time to stop sulking now," said Gavri, "I'll tell you what, let's have a table tennis tournament."

Again, the dissident protested; this time with a scoff.

"Are you afraid that I will beat you at ping-pong then?"

"No, of course not. You stand no chance."

"We'll see."

"You will eat humble pie, little girl. You cannot beat me."

Gavrii turned towards me.

"You'll play Mikael, or do you want to be the referee?"

I didn't want to be either. I had never played.

"OK, I'll be the referee." I answered reluctantly.

An order of play was decided, and it was agreed that the girls would play each other, followed by the boys, and then the winners would play each other. The girls played a cheerful and friendly match, which ended 21 -17 to Gavriila. They laughed all the way through, and the referee's services were redundant. The boys played a tight needle match, where Kazimir disputed every point given against him. Yaromir maintained his cool and played some fantastic shots, which took his opponent by surprise. Slowed down by the morning alcohol, the older boy got more heated as the game reached its climax, but he eventually won 21 -19. The two defeated players were delighted that they could sit and watch the final, holding hands and sitting in the shade close to each other. Play began with a confident smile at one end and a defiant frown at the other. Every point was a microcosmic World War 3 in tension and conflict, with each player determined to win. One played with hubris and bluster, and the other with athletic talent and brilliant hand to eye co-ordination. Predictably, the loser smashed his bat on the table and walked away in a huff, cursing under his breath as he lost 21 - 19. This was his cue for another major sulk.

"He thinks he's such a big man and he's just a silly little boy grown too big for boots." Gavrii laughed, "And there's his second lesson in being humiliated today."

Minus one of the crew, we made off to the changing rooms to prepare for a cooling swim from one of the island's beaches.

At that time, none of us was aware that about 150 kilometres, away at the Chernobyl nuclear power station, unit 4 of the reactor was shut down for the purpose of a routine maintenance. The engineers began to conduct an experiment, which required the shutting down of the reactor's emergency core cooling system (ECCS). They wanted to determine whether the cooling system would still be able to cool the core, in the case of a power reduction or emergency. At 14:00 p.m. they set the reactor to operate at about half power, and the ECCS was switched off.

Almost half an hour later, the four of us were all happily splashing about with a beach ball, enjoying the cool and soothing textures of the river water running over our skin, like a playful pod of dolphins. Kazimir came galloping through the shallows towards us with all the subtlety of an angry tyrannosaurus rex, and ripped a tidal wave through the middle of our happy and contented little party.

"Come on you lot, let's go for a proper swim. I'll race you all out to that pontoon in the middle of the river."

We all looked at each other, and then swam slowly after him. Nobody was racing. When we got to the pontoon and climbed up onto the wooden planked surface, Mr Bigwig jumped back in and swam back to the shore. He stood on the beach about 100 meters away, and seemed to be goading us to follow him over.

"He lives up to his name doesn't he?" said Gavrii.

"What do you mean?" I asked.

"Well, Kazimir means either keeper or destroyer of peace, and I'll leave it to you to guess which one you think he might be today."

With no response from us to the encouragement to follow him, the destroyer splashed madly into the water, and swam back towards the pontoon. But he didn't get there. He surely was a strong swimmer, but only five meters away from safety he suddenly stopped. His head bobbed in the gentle current; he coughed and his eyes rolled, he looked distressed and then disappeared under the water. Everybody thought he was playing another silly game, perhaps trying to swim under the pontoon, and to come up behind us. Seconds passed all too slowly. But he didn't resurface. We looked around, and there was no sign of him in or above the river waters, either in front or behind us. The lifeguards were some distance away, and they all appeared to be preoccupied talking to a gang of girls celebrating a birthday party. The sun went into hiding behind the massive pile of a cumulus cloud, skies darkened, the happy hubbub of people enjoying beach and river seemed a million miles away, and it felt like we were in a bubble, isolated from the rest of the world.

Before I could react in any way, both Gavriila and Yaromir dived in, and disappeared underwater.

Irinuschka screamed and then shrieked at me, "He's not a strong swimmer! Do something."

For once I was powerless. My rainbow bag, and the contents that had saved the day twice already during this little tour, was back across the river in the locker room, where we had all changed. I felt sick. I felt that perhaps I had failed. The distressed teenager hung on to me shaking with fright that her young love had put himself in real danger. I considered diving in myself, but angels don't swim that well, and besides that, the young girl would then have been left on her own. Another thirty seconds passed, and then there was the faintest almost undetectable ripple in the waters; then another ripple, larger, then another larger still. Moments later, the ripples merged together, so that the surface seemed to be boiling in a great frenzied whirlpool, the force of which was so intense that the pontoon swayed violently from side to side, and became so unstable that we had to sit down and hang on. Then, out of a noisy, frightening chaotic swirl of foaming water Kazimir's body suddenly bobbed up face downward, flat and lifeless upon the water, with Gavrilla and Yaromir holding his arms on either side of him. The circular motion of the maelstrom ceased, as if someone had flicked a switch, and then the water bubbled and fizzed underneath Kazi as he floated towards the edge of the pontoon. As the 3 swimmers drew nearer, a huge wave at their stern pushed them forward and upwards, right up onto the pontoon. Behind that procession, the water churned and chopped with hundreds, possibly thousands of fish from small tiddlers up to 3 foot long carp and pike. In an instant, seeming to understand that their purpose had been served, the vast shoal of fishes dispersed.

Now there was a serious matter to resolve, and without hesitation Gavriila took charge.

"Yaromir, stay calm! I want you to swim over to the lifeguard station, and tell those idiots to stop flirting and get here quickly."

The boy nodded, dived back in, and swam back to the beach. Irinuschka bit her thumb, and stood there shaking with worry.

"Mikael, I think he's stopped breathing, and I can't feel a pulse. We need to start CPR."

"OK, what do you want me to do?"

She showed me where and how to place my hands, and said, "Press firmly down and release. Do that 30 times in quick succession."

While I was doing that, she tilted the boy's head backwards, cleared his tongue out of the way, and checked for breathing. I'd done 30 compressions by then, so she pinched his nostrils and took a deep breath, and started to give him the kiss of life. Still no pulse.

"Again!" she said.

This went on for about 2 minutes, during which we diligently repeated the process. The lifeguard had not arrived yet, but I could see him approaching the pontoon. As Gavriila went to place her mouth over the victim's mouth again, he suddenly spluttered, and began to cough up water. We rolled him on his side. His face was strained in a painful grimace, his skin grey and bloodless. He coughed and wheezed and moaned, as he lay there gasping for air. Gavriila let out a yelp of joy, flung herself at me, and embraced me in a huge hug, tears on her cheeks, but smiling at the same time.

"I've never done that before." she whispered.

"Well done! You were so confident and truly brilliant." I replied.

Yaromir returned breathless and exhausted, and hugged a relieved Irinushka. The lifeguard took over.

"We will take him to the First Aid post, and then he may have to go to hospital." he said.

Another lifeguard arrived in a large inflatable, and they lifted Kazimir into it, and as they paddled away, the drowning victim looked up at Gavrii. None of us had ever seen that look before. His eyes were like saucers, radiating warmth, with humility and admiration, and heartfelt gratitude.

He mouthed, "Thank you! Thank you Gavrii. You saved my life!"

Kazi went to hospital. We returned to the shore, and after changing, we sat in one of the little cafes, eating ice-cream and drinking orange juice. Here we reflected on the events, not just of the day, but of the few days we had been together on holiday. Most of all, we discussed our companion Kazimir.

"He has had a terrible childhood. His father was a drunk, and beat his mother up. His big brother, Yuri, whom he doted on, has been away in the army for 2 years. His little sister, Yelena was born with a spinal defect, and is crippled." explained Yaromir, "Yuri was his mentor, kept him on the straight and narrow. He's only gone off the rails since his brother was conscripted."

"I do hope he's going to be alright. He's been so difficult to get along with, but he is one of us." added Irinuschka.

"There's good and bad in everyone, "said Gavrii, "And today our friend has had 2 quick and shocking lessons in humility. Let's hope he learns from the experience."

I sat there and nodded in the right places. This wasn't my gang or my time, but I was proud of how these young people searched for saving graces in their friend's behaviour, and rejoiced at his salvation.

The evening was supposed to be a grand finale, but it turned out to be a subdued affair. The plan was to go to the centre of Kiev, in the area of Independence Square and Khreschatyk Street, which always became a large outdoor party place at night during summer months. Thousands would congregate to have a good time in nearby restaurants, clubs and outdoor cafes. The central streets were closed for auto traffic on weekends and holidays. In addition, we had planned to stroll around Andriyivskyy Descent, one of the best known historic streets, and a major tourist attraction in Kiev. No one felt like having much fun, with one of their number missing in hospital. We wandered around together, soaking up the party atmosphere in the Square and the taking in the interesting delights of the old town. It had been a strange kind of day, at the end of a hectic few days of sightseeing, and we were all a little tired and emotional. We returned to the campsite earlier than planned and soon we were all sleeping soundly.

As we slept, critical events were occurring at Chernobyl. The engineer's experiment reached a point of critical mass at about 1.23 am, when emergency procedures were activated. The reactor core was destroyed and one minute later, a massive explosion sent fuel, core components, structural items and highly radioactive debris into the air, exposing the destroyed core to the atmosphere. A plume of smoke and radioactive debris rose up to about 1 kilometre into the air, and fire broke out in the remains of the Unit 4 building.

We awoke the next morning, completely unaware of what had been happening during the night. Leonid was up early as usual, coughing and wheezing his way through a packet of cigarettes, and a gallon of coffee. Irinuschka and Yaromir eventually appeared, looking very pleased with each other again. Perhaps there had been explosions of another kind overnight, in the room that Yaromir would normally have been sharing with his male friend?

There was no hurry to have breakfast or to pack. We didn't need to set off for home until the afternoon, and we would need to go to the hospital to collect Kazimir. We had all day to get back to Pripyat. The youngsters were all chattering excitedly at the prospect of going home, reuniting with families, and seeing their friends. I was concerned about our driver. He looked even worse for wear than any of the previous mornings.

"You don't look too well, Leonid. Are you OK to drive?"

"I have been driving the road from Kiev to Pripyat and back for 30 years. It is no problem. I have a little tummy ache. That's all!"

"As long as you are sure?"

"Let's get going to the hospital. Then it's only 150 kilometres to home, about 3 hours."

Our missing person was discharged from hospital, and greeted his companions with a warm smile. It was the most relaxed I had ever seen him. He thanked everybody for saving him, and was especially charming to Gavriila.

"So you gave me the kiss of life, did you?"

"Yes, and it was one of most horrible experiences of my life." she joked.

"It wasn't that great for me either."

"You reeked of vodka."

"It smells better than your perfume."

They smiled at each other, and spontaneously hugged.

"You argue like my mum and dad." said Irinushka, "I think you two should get married."

Yaromir looked at his girlfriend, and grinned.

"Will you marry me?" asked Kazi looking at Gavrii.

"Certainly not!" she replied, "We are too young. You drink too much vodka and besides, you have a glamorous career as a goalkeeper for Dynamo Kiev ahead of you. I don't plan to be a football widow. I'm going to University to study biology. Then I'm going to set about saving endangered species."

"I think me and vodka had better sue for divorce. I need to straighten myself out and not be such an obnoxious prat." said Kazi.

Nobody answered. It wasn't necessary. There was a pause in the conversation, as the minibus shuddered its way north.

"Would you mind if we stopped for a little while at Independence Square? I missed that part of the trip last night.", the destroyer of peace turned keeper, asked.

Our driver shrugged, and uttered a quiet, "OK, but not for too long."

"I want to see Khreschatyk Street, and take a little walk along Andriyivskyy Descent. My good friend Gavriila can show me around."

Leonid parked, and then told us he was going off for petrol and would return in an hour. The area around Independence Square still bustled with a lively atmosphere, a magnet for tourists and locals alike. I wasn't sure, but I thought I saw two couples holding hands as they enjoyed the sights and sounds. It brought a lump to my throat.

Meanwhile, a few miles from Chernobyl, the army had begun to evacuate everybody from the City of Pripyat, with a task force of 20 buses and 5 lorries.

At 2 pm, our driver returned and we began the return journey. We soon found ourselves heading north, in the continuous sunshine on the wide city perimeter road that hugged the banks of the river. We passed by the bridge that spanned the river at the Hydropark and followed the Naberezhno Highway, until it became national route P02. Once out of the city, the roads got worse. The P02 was a fairly wide single lane highway, fringed by trees in places and interspersed with open areas, in the flat and scrubby landscape.

At first, it would have been difficult to notice whether Leonid's driving was any worse than normal, and the expectation was that once we were clear of the busy city traffic, he would become more relaxed. But the further we drove, the more he groaned and appeared to be cursing at other road users. The kids all seemed so happy to be going home after their four day adventure, and we seemed to be making good time dodging potholes and drawing ever nearer to our destination. I was sitting in the front passenger seat, watching carefully for any signs that our driver might display, to illustrate that his tummy ache was getting worse. His swearing and cursing was unabated.

"What time do you think we'll arrive back in Prypyat?" Irinuschka asked me, "Only, it's my little sister's birthday, and I want to be back for the party."

I turned to answer her, "All well and good, we should be back soon after 5."

My attention was diverted only for a second, but then the minibus veered off course, screeching off to the left, into the oncoming traffic, and narrowly missed a truck coming in the opposite direction. I grabbed the wheel, and with all my might managed to guide us back to the correct side of the road. Leonid had collapsed at the wheel. He slumped forward. I took the minibus out of gear, and guided us to halt as quickly as possible. We made a combined effort to pull our driver back to upright in his seat; me pushing and the others pulling, and then attempted to revive him. Water was not his drink, but splashing him in the face with it seemed to work. As soon as he came round, he groaned and wretched violently out of the window, while holding his expansive stomach. He got out of the minibus, and on unsteady legs, walked a short way into the copse at the side of the road. Then he bent over double and wretched again. After a short while, he lit a cigarette and came back.

"I am not well, and I can drive no further, Mikael you will have to take over." he whined in a low voice.

"What is wrong? Have you eaten something bad, or is it an ulcer from the vodka?" asked Gavrii.

"No!" he shouted, beginning to wretch again.

"Show me where the pain is. Point to it?" she instructed

He pointed to the lower right side of his belly, and moaned again. Clearly he was in absolute agony. We all helped him carefully into the back of the minibus.

"I don't like the look of him. He may have appendicitis." said our unelected nurse, looking at me, "He's right, you had better take over, and get us to a hospital."

"But I don't know the way!" I protested.

"Follow the state road P02 to Ivankiv. There is a hospital there." said Irinushka.

"How far away is that?" I asked.

"Well, we've done about 60 kilometres since we left Kiev." said Yaromir, "Kiev to Ivankiv is 83 kilometres. We are more than two thirds of the way there. I think from here it's about 20 more to Ivankiv."

"OK, it doesn't look as if I have any choice in the matter." I said, getting into the driver's seat.

"When we get to Ivankiv, we will need to turn right. I'll show you where to go when we get there." said the youngest boy confidently. He had recently had the unfortunate experience of having his tonsils removed at the Ivankiv hospital.

Leonid passed out and there was no conversation as we made progress. It was slow, because unlike our critical passenger, I was not familiar with the road. He had shown an extremely detailed knowledge of where the potholes in the road surface were all the way out of Kiev. Half an hour later, we pulled up outside the hospital and the girls ran inside to summon emergency assistance. Leonid was trolleyed away and we waited for a diagnosis. After an hour, a nurse came out to our crew and confirmed acute appendicitis. She said that our driver would need intensive care to prevent the situation developing into septicaemia, before the appendix was removed. He would need at least a 2 week stay in hospital. It was now my responsibility to safely return these youngsters to their homes in Pripyat. There was another 70 kilometres to go via Chernobyl.

It was after 5 pm, and the evacuation of nearly 50,000 people from Pripyat had almost been completed. A massive fire, which had burned in the ruins of the nuclear reactor, had been extinguished overnight by a team of up to 250 firemen, but a radioactive cloud enveloped the immediate area and began to drift north-westwards.

Again, we made slow progress along the badly maintained road avoiding the potholes. We had travelled about 20 kilometres when a squally rainstorm blew up from nowhere, making the single windscreen wiper work overtime. I was just thinking to myself that I had better pull over and wait for the mini-storm to pass, when the worst happened. The minibus hit a massive pothole, and lurched violently to the right onto the roadside verge. I waited a few minutes, and the rainstorm stopped as quickly as it had started. I climbed out of the seat and walked around the vehicle. The pothole had shredded the front nearside tyre. When I inspected the spare, it was tread-less and flat. There was no point in changing the wheel.

"What are we going to do now?" asked Kazimir, "Shall I go and get help? It's not that far back to Ivankiv."

"Maybe that's the only solution." I replied.

"We might be better off sitting tight and waiting for help to come to us."

added Irinushka, "It looks as if there's a bigger storm brewing up ahead. Let's wait a while."

All agreed to wait. We had been there about half an hour. Some vehicles had passed us without stopping. We realised we would need to flag someone down to get help. Our woman of peace, Irinushka, was right about another rainstorm, but Kazimir jumped out with his coat above his head, as he saw a large lorry approaching our position from the opposite direction. The rest of us witnessed a short conversation between him and the lorry driver, before he returned to the minibus.

"Well?" asked Gavrii.

"He said that he's on his way into Ivankiv and he'd call at a motor garage when he got there and let them know we needed help." explained the young man.

"Good! Well done Kazi." she replied.

"But there's more."

"What?"

"I'm worried. He told me something else."

"What? Tell us what is wrong."

"He said there was something bad going on at Chernobyl. Local hospitals are on alert. People are being moved away from the nuclear power plant. Pripyat has being completely evacuated."

"Well, let's not worry about that yet. We need to get the minibus fixed before we can go any further."

That was good advice. We sat and waited. Hours passed. The evening skies began to darken. The volume of traffic heading from the direction of Chernobyl steadily increased.

"It's been a great little holiday," said Irinushka, "And you have been an excellent guide and a lovely and gentle person to know. I am so glad that we have met you, Mikael."

I smiled and just said, "Thank you, that's very nice of you to say so. I've enjoyed meeting with all of you."

"It's getting dark soon, but I know you will look after us whatever happens." she continued.

"What makes you say that?"

"I've only known you for a few days, but I'm sure there is something special about you."

"I'm not special; I'm just doing a job, and then I have to go back to Minsk."

She laughed. "What do you have in the purple pouch around your neck and in the rainbow bag that you carry everywhere, Mikael?"

She smiled a knowing smile. I smiled back.

The conversation was over without either of us saying another word.

One by one, my companions fell asleep as night fell and the wait to be rescued continued. It looked as if help would not arrive until the next morning. Finally I also fell into a deep sleep.

When I woke up, I was back on my cloud, and Gabriel was standing next to me. My immediate thought, was that I had abandoned the youngsters, but I was quickly reassured.

"They are all safe, and although they can't go home, every one of them has a star in his or her pocket."

"I'm not sure that I was always able to give the right help in all circumstances."

"You did everything you could, my friend; saved Gavrii from the effects of the bee-sting, and saved Yaromir when he had heat stroke. You got Leonid to hospital. What else was there?"

"When Kazimir nearly drowned I couldn't do anything."

"You didn't need to. Gavriila and Yaromir did it for you. They used their residual magic from their own rescues, to summon the fishes to help. Sometimes your direct intervention and the use of stars is unnecessary, my friend."

"Yes, I think I understand."

"Before this assignment you had been working with clouds. This was a cloud that you did not help create; a very dangerous cloud that will affect many, many people for many years. You were powerless to prevent that happening. There is a lesson here, but it's not really for you, it's for people in the Earthly Realm."

"What is the lesson, Gabriel?"

"Man is not infallible and will make mistakes which have wide ranging impact upon others. Doodling with things they do not fully understand can be disastrous."

"And what about my new friends?"

"Leonid will recover, and the four youngsters may have lost or become temporarily separated from their parents. Some may become orphans, but they have not lost their lives. A succession of small and unrelated events kept them away from the disaster area. Sometimes things just happen like that."

"As usual, you are right."

Gabriel went to fly away, and then looked back at me and added, "By the way, Michael, or should I say Mikael, you've earned your orange star, and it will be presented by a namesake of yours."

"Who will that be?"

"A great man called Mikhail, Mikhail Gorbachev."

Chapter 4

Yellow Star - 24th December 1943

Guardian angel duty was always very rewarding. All angels got special little assignments looking after someone who needed a bit of help. It was especially wonderful sitting over someone's shoulder and whispering to them to save them from harm or danger. Sometimes, it was just a matter of creating a timely distraction, like a sudden burst of sunlight through the clouds, or a breath of a cool calming breeze on a very hot day, maybe a snowflake landing on an eyelash, or a bird suddenly starting to sing in a tree. Anything that was a nice surprise, just to stop them for a moment until the danger had passed. I loved this kind of angel work.

I began to understand how time in Heaven was not linear, and it worked in a completely different way to time in the Earthly Realm. It was almost like there was no time at all and every possible time that could be imagined throughout creation. Both these parameters of time were working in parallel alongside each other. That made it possible to meet people who had not died yet or indeed had not yet been born. Often these people came with the wisdom they had accumulated in their Earthly lives. What made that really interesting was that, because I had the blessing of graceful naivety, all words of wisdom could be considered as totally new and refreshing.

At the end of one day, as I was just idly swinging on a star, Mikhail Gorbachev came walking across the twilight skies towards me. I could see he was carrying my orange star in his left hand.

"Hello!" he smiled, "You've just completed a mission to the Ukraine at a very difficult and dangerous time, haven't you?"

"Yes! I managed to help a few young people while I was there and subsequently, they were diverted away from danger by a series of small but significant incidents."

"I am so grateful for your interventions, my friend. But don't forget that you saved that old vodka swilling grouch, Leonid as well."

He laughed, and mimicked drinking vodka from a small bottle.

"How could I forget Leonid?"

"Unforgettable, he certainly is." He paused and just looked at me portraying his quiet and thoughtful demeanour.

"Now!" he continued, "I have great pride and pleasure in presenting you with your orange star."

"Thank you, Mikhail." I replied.

"As you probably realise by now, my friend, a star always comes along with wise words, and I have only a few for you."

I listened, and he paused again before he spoke.

"First of all," he said, "If what you have done yesterday still looks big to you, you haven't done much today."

"I know," I replied, "Yesterday was a very big day and today was much less challenging."

"Not all our days can be the same. Imagine what they must have been like for people on Earth when Jesus was around."

"Much harder, although simpler, and people were much less worldly wise. It was a time of innocence."

"Think about it," he added, "Jesus was the first socialist, the first to seek a better life for mankind."

"Thank you for your wise words."

We sat there thinking for a moment.

"One more thing before I go."

"What is that?"

"A very close friend of mine, called Nelson Mandela, told me something very special and it fits in well with what you are trying to achieve by earning your stars."

"What did he say?"

Mikhail beamed a warm smile at me, and said, "After climbing a great hill, one only finds that there are many more hills to climb."

Then, quick as a flash, he was gone. I put the orange star in my purple pouch, and thought about how glad I was to have met him.

It wasn't much later when I was asked to go and see Gabriel. He told me that he was so pleased with my progress that I had been assigned a holiday.

"What is a holiday?" I asked Gabriel, "And what will I be doing?"

He just said I'd have to wait and see, because holidays were always great mysteries, were randomly allocated, and he couldn't tell me where I would be going, just that it would be very soon. Then he handed me a tiny little jar with a golden top.

"You'll need this for the moonbeams." he said, and then he was gone.

I went back to my duties.

I was carrying some moonbeams home in a jar, wondering what my holiday would be, when I bumped into my old friend Sebastian, and he told me what an honour it was if you were assigned a holiday. He advised me that it gave you a chance to do something truly special, but that you had to very, very careful because there were always consequences.

I pressured him into telling me about his last holiday, and after a great deal of persuasion, he swore me to absolute secrecy. Then he said that on his last holiday, which seemed to have been three aeons and a day ago, he had been sent to Jerusalem, where he had been a Roman soldier on crucifixion duty. The job he was assigned to do was to hammer in one of the nails that put Jesus on the cross. But he wouldn't go into any more detail about what happened. He just said "You'll be fine my friend, if you do the right thing!"

When I tried to sleep that night, I was nervous and excited and I kept waking up with a strange word resounding in my head. It started as a whisper, and then each time I woke up it got louder and louder and louder.

"Oswiecim"

"Oswiecim"

"OSwiecim"

"OSWIECIM!"

The next morning, I wasn't on my beautiful cloud with a silver lining sewn by my own fair hand. I was in a very different place. It was a crude wooden hut, and I was wearing a smart black uniform. It was very cold; snow had fallen overnight, but strangely it was covered by a layer of grey ash. There was an awful burnt, charred, sickly smell. I was very afraid.

Suddenly, there was a lot of commotion and shouting outside, and the metallic clanking, squealing, rushing steam noises of a train arriving. I heard strange words like, "Raus! Raus!" and, "Schnell! Schnell!" ringing in my ears. The door of my hut burst open with a rush of icy chill which cut right through me and then someone came in to get me. He had a stern, grim face and he ushered me out into the cold and told me where to stand.

Lots of very sad bedraggled people piled off the train and were quickly led up to a very important looking man at a desk. He waved any man who looked big and strong to his right. All the puny, or disabled, or weak old men, together with all the women and children, even women with babies, were herded to his left. Any belongings or suitcases they had brought with them were quickly stacked up and then taken away. Anyone who made any fuss or protest was frogmarched behind a nearby wall and behind that wall I heard screams and shouts and gunshots. Most of the people on the train had crude badges sewn on their clothes, a six pointed star; the Star of David, coloured yellow with the word "Jude" inscribed in the centre. A few of the train passengers had a different badge, a brown or black or pink triangle.

Snow and ash were both still falling, and it was bitterly cold. The wind howled cruelly between the buildings in the darkness of a gruesome early morning. There were no smiles, no affection, and no compassion in this terrible place. The left hand queue were led away and ordered to strip off, and when they asked why, they were told with cynical sneering looks that they were going to be showered and deloused. The black uniformed officers were assisted in this processing by a small group of grey-faced, emaciated, shaven headed men in striped pyjamas and wooden clogs.

An old grey haired man, in a tattered black three piece suit, had injured himself jumping down from the cattle truck train carriage. He had lain on the ground shivering. He struggled to get up and then limped over to me. There was a frightened, pleading look in his yellowed eyes.

"Please, Sir, I am Jacob, Jacob Bettelheim from Bratislava. Can you please help me?"

I could only stand and pity him. With great dignity and politeness he continued. "My wife Magda; she needs her pills. It's her heart. She is not well. The pills, they are in my bag. I don't know where she has been taken. Please!"

Before I was able to react, one of the black uniformed men came over and without the slightest provocation removed a truncheon from his belt and battered the old man across the back of his head twice.

"Get in line, you Jewish pig dog. No talking!" he spat with a wicked smile.

Eventually, the naked assembly was led down some steps into a big very bare room, with water pipes sticking out of the ceiling. Once everybody had been herded inside, two sets of heavy double iron doors were closed and a straight iron bar placed across them.

"You! You're new aren't you?" said Mr Important, looking at me.

"Yes sir" I responded, scared out of my wits.

"You can do the dirty deed then." he instructed.

He snarled each instruction in short sentences and phrases.

"Climb up that ladder to the top of the roof. Up there, you'll find a pair of heavy gloves and a mask. Be careful to put them on. Then take one of the cans from the top of the roof. Twist the top, turn it upside down, and drop it through the hole. Leave the gloves and mask up there. Hold your breath. Climb down as quickly as you can."

I did as I was told, terrified, to shouts of "Schnell! Schnell!"

Just as I was going to drop the can, Mr Important shouted "Halt!" and everybody ducked.

There was a very loud rumbling noise coming from the East, as a stricken plane coughed and spluttered over, flying very low, with thick black smoke belching out of its engine. Everybody looked up and felt sorry for the poor pilot trapped inside and then it crashed in a ball of flame and an awful ground shaking explosion a few fields away.

Moments later, Mr Important nodded at me, and I carried on as instructed.

"Let's go for breakfast, and come back when it's over," suggested one of the black uniforms, "I don't want to listen to THAT again and again."

We all shivered our way into another large wooden hut. There was a small wood burning stove in the corner, some bare wooden tables and stools, and at least it was some respite from the all-pervading stench of burning and the unrelenting bitterness of the wind. There was a calendar on the otherwise bare wall and I sneaked a look at the date. It was December 24th 1943. The calendar didn't have a picture of a lovely landscape, or seascape, or flowers, or happy smiling faces, just a very stern looking man, with a peculiar moustache and pure evil in his eyes. We ate quietly; each man had a small piece of sausage, a lump of stale bread, and some ersatz coffee.

"A Messerschmitt ME109 wasn't it?" questioned one of the black uniforms, "Coming back from the Russian front."

Nobody answered. "Poor bastards!" he continued.

Breakfast was over soon enough.

"Now the gruesome work begins." muttered another black uniform, as we all moved back out into the cold. He moved the big iron bar, and opened the first set of double iron doors. There was a strange translucent yellow light just visible through the small cracks in the second set of iron doors. With a great heavy clang he threw them open and took a deep breath, before stepping down into what was to him an every day, several times a day, sight. But instead of the expected pile of contorted bodies with tortured screaming faces, and the stench of prussic acid and shit, he found the room was empty.

As he focussed his eyes in utter disbelief and hesitated on the second step down, the yellow light seemed to swirl like a ghostly whirlpool. Then a stream of a million blindingly bright twinkling stars, curved in a magnificent continuous lightshow, out of the opened doorway, making their way in a glorious triumphant free ribbon, up into the blackness of the heavens.

"What's going on?" roared Mr Important.

"I don't know," answered the black uniform in the doorway, "But the room is empty."

"That's impossible!" hurled a now very angry voice.

"Come and look for yourself." was the reply.

All the other black uniformed men stared into the room and for a short while stood there baffled. What none of them knew, was that when they were all distracted by the plane's swansong overhead, I had quietly and quickly put the can back on the roof and retightened the top. Then without anyone noticing, I took my rainbow bag out of my pocket and emptied my collection of falling stars into the hole in the roof instead.

The black uniforms all gathered around Mr Important and they started shouting and pointing at me. I stood there shivering in the cold and then they ran over to me, still shouting and dragged me away. They tied my hands behind my back and placed me up against a wall. Weapons were primed, as they assembled for a firing squad, but even then for some reason, all my fear had left me.

I prayed quietly to myself, closed my eyes and waited for the bullets to rip into me. But as I felt each one go into my heart, I found it didn't hurt. No! Not at all!

Each bullet felt like someone was kissing me very gently and when the last bullet hit me right between the eyes, then the whole Universe swirled round and round for what seemed like ages.

When I opened my eyes, I was back on my favourite cloud and Sebastian was sitting next to me. "How was your holiday?" he asked smiling.

"Er, OK" I replied, obviously looking a bit confused.

"What's the problem?" he said.

"I thought you said that on a holiday I'd have a chance to do something truly special?"

"Well, you did, my friend. You did something wonderful and marvellous. Well done!"

I grinned at Sebastian, "I see! You were winding me up."

"No, not at all. You must remember that I also said you had to be very, very careful because there were always consequences? You did the right thing, my friend."

He smiled again, "Or you wouldn't have earned your star."

And with that, we carried on catching falling stars, and putting them in our pockets, and saving them for a rainy day.

Later that day, Gabriel came to see me.

"Once again, my friend, we are very pleased with you. You have earned your yellow star, the third star of your Angel's Rainbow. Congratulations!"

"Thank you so much. I am so pleased to be making progress towards achieving my wings."

The black light that radiated around Gabriel seemed to be extra bright that day.

"There is a lesson to be learned from your recent visit back to the Earthly Realm, and it's a very important one." he said.

"Please, tell me what the lesson is. I am keen to learn."

I knew by now that Gabriel was very good at ensuring that a lesson was learned from every new experience

"Think about this, Michael. It's very important." He looked at me very seriously and said, "Man's inhumanity to his fellow man separates him from God."

Having said that, he just stood there and smiled at me. Then he turned to fly away. Just before his feet left the ground, he looked back at me and added, "Did I tell you, that the man who will present you with your yellow star, is someone called Winston Churchill?"

Chapter 5

Green Star - 21st October, 1966

I was falling feet first, arms outstretched, gently gyrating, softly oscillating, like a slow motion movement of a sycamore seed, falling to the ground on its maiden and only flight. I fell through a thick cloud base filled with raindrops; nothing but greyness all around me. Greyness and damp filled my eyes, until suddenly; I broke through into sunshine; sunshine; yellowish and watery. My sycamore gyrations afforded me a panoramic view. Tall majestic mountains stood proud to my north, and to my south a wide estuary opened its mouth to the ocean. Below me, I could see green mountain ridges, and winding rivers running south in wide valleys, interspersed with little villages of small terraced houses. Villages that were home to men at their daily toil, women baking bread and going about their housework and children skipping their happy way towards the last day at school before half term.

Closer to the ground, I noticed that the green mountain ridges were spoiled and scarred by huge piles of grey and black debris. Huge piles of slag, carelessly dumped in unnatural and ugly formations on the sides of hills; were hovering ominously in a delicate balancing act, casting long shadows over the villages below.

After a long slow fall and a smooth flight, my feet touched somewhere that would be significantly less than terra firma. I landed on a hillside towards the top of a slag heap, on the side of Mynydd Merthyr. I made my way towards a cluster of crude metal huts laying a few hundred yards uphill, on a flat area surrounded by machinery.

The watery sun cast its feeble rays upon the broken ground which crunched underfoot. I was grateful for the stout boots and thick warm workman's jacket I was wearing. The smell of coal dust filled my nostrils. I looked down to the valley below and saw a thin mist swirling above the neat rows of terraced houses. High above them, men in the tipping gang on tip number 7 were busy in their never ending labours of piling up and stabilising the spoil from the coal mines of the Merthyr Vale Colliery.

I entered a hut. It was gloomy inside. When my eyes had begun to adjust to the lack of light, I saw there was a metal table with a chair either side. Behind the desk was a large man in a thick dark blue suit and a bowler hat. He had puffed out cheeks, and was smoking a large cigar.

"Hello, my boy, I'm Winston Churchill." he said, as he waved his arm bidding me to sit down.

"Oh, yes, Gabriel told me that you would be paying me a visit. But I'm confused! All of my stars have so far been presented to me in Heaven, usually on a cloud somewhere. This feels to me like I'm on another mission, to do what I can to help."

"Well, Michael, you see, it's all part of this 'time doesn't work in the same way as in Heaven business that they keep discussing with you. And it comes in combination with the beautiful graceful naivety that you've experienced elsewhere."

"I suppose the uncertainty of the way things happen and the shift in timeframes is just to keep me on my toes then?"

"Precisely!"

He smiled and chomped diligently on his cigar, sending clouds of aromatic smoke billowing upwards. Then he said to me, "Don't be confused, you must always be ready to learn, although you might not always like being taught."

He took a yellow star out of the pocket of his suit, and held it towards me in the palm of his hand.

"I believe this is yours," he grinned, "You certainly deserve it. It was a truly wonderful thing that you did in that bloody awful place. We had suspicions that the Nazis were exterminating undesirables all through the 30's, but the scale of their dirty deeds at Auschwitz and all their other death camps, was a horrific shock to us all."

For a moment I was back on the platform in December, 1943, watching as a train load of poor, bedraggled and confused people arrived, completely unaware that they were to be quickly dispatched in a gas chamber.

"Thank you," I answered, taking the star and placing it carefully in my purple pouch.

My new friend continued, "In the early days of Mr Hitler's reign, many people, even in our sceptred isle, thought that he was a true statesman, a great man. But we soon learned that great and good are seldom the same man."

"When I went to Oswiecim, I only did what I thought was right at the time. The graceful naivety can certainly work in a beautiful way when you need it, because you don't really understand what's going on."

"That's very true, Michael. You acted with compassion through instinct, because it seemed that there was something going on that you didn't understand. Because of beautiful graceful naivety, you couldn't know the real truth. I have learned through history that man will occasionally stumble over the truth, but most of the time he will pick himself up and continue on."

"Stumbling over the truth seems to be at the essence of all the tasks I'm assigned to in order to earn my stars."

"I am certain that the pursuit of truth should never be cursed, belittled or abandoned."

"I'll remember that."

He paused, as if he was giving me time to think about what he had said.

"So, once again, my friend, armed only with graceful naivety, you arrive in a strange place not knowing what is going on, and all you do know is that in some way you will need to help."

"I suppose that's why I've been sent here."

"Yes, it is! And you will need this." he said, passing me a tiny little clear glass jar with a twisty bright metal cap with the letter 'M' embossed in the top.

"That's the moonbeam jar that Gabriel gave me."

"Use it wisely, my friend, and remember everyone has his day and some days last longer than others."

He puffed on his cigar again. The hut filled with smoke. I put the jar in the pocket of my donkey jacket. Winston Churchill was gone. I pulled my yellow NCB helmet more tightly onto my head and walked back down the black slope to where the tipping gang were working.

The tipping gang on tip number 7 were hard at work, moving the unwanted bi-products of coal mining this way and that. They all wore dark blue overalls and black jackets, strong black boots and the regulation yellow NCB helmet. Many wore thick gloves, to avoid the occupational hazard of multiple cuts and grazes from the spoil. I couldn't help but think, that their labours drew a parallel with insects crawling over a termite mound; industrious, certainly, but in this case very possibly pointless.

"Good morning, Boyo. You must be the new man.", was the greeting from a broad shouldered man, with a yellow foreman's band around his right upper arm. His coal blackened face illustrated a yellow toothed smile, while he rested briefly on the handle of a shovel.

"I'm Michael." I replied, holding out my hand to be shaken.

There was no handshaking response, but he did say, "We've already got a Mick over there. Nevertheless, Boyo, I'm glad you could join us."

He pointed with his shovel to an area where loose shale and rocks looked as if they would tumble over the edge any second, and said, "Get yourself a spade, and start work over there."

I went to work immediately, surrounded by a gaggle of men all diligently going about their arduous endeavours.

"You've brought a bit of sunshine with you then," said a thin tall man, with coal dust ingrained into his face and beard.

"What?"

"That'll be your nickname, then. We'll call you Sunshine, as we can't call you Mick."

"It's sunny up here, but still foggy down in the valley, though." I answered.

"The air's cooler down there. Should warm up later."

Another gang member, older than the thin man, who had a very pronounced limp, came over and joined the conversation, as all our shovels scratched at the surface slag.

"Don't talk to me about the weather," he said, "Makes my bloody leg hurt like it's on fire when it's cold and rainy. At least it's a bit brighter today, Dafyd."

"Be grateful for that small mercy then, Owen. For most of the last week it's been rain, rain, lots of rain, and more bloody rain."

Hundreds of feet below us, in the shadow of the manmade mountain, village life went on as it had for decades. A postman's van drove through the village, a large lorry crawled along Moy Road, heading south for Cardiff, the village baker and butcher dressed their shop windows and children were making their way to Pantglas Junior School in Aberfan village.

My new comrades and I scratched and scraped as we talked.

"Have you worked here for long?" I asked my termite mound, gammy legged, comrade.

"No, I used to work down the pit at Merthyr. But 5 years ago, they put me up here to shovel this black, spiky, shit around, after I had my leg crushed at the coalface. I suppose I should be very grateful to still have a job, after spending 30 years underground."

"How old are you, Owen?"

"I'll be 50 next year. I started down the pit working alongside my dad when I was 14."

"It's a dirty and dangerous job. Why do you do it?"

He looked at me as if I was a mental retard, shook his head in disbelief and rolled his eyes.

"You're not very bright are you, Sunshine? There's bugger all other work round here. If you live in the valleys, there's no choice. It's work in the pit, or on the tip, or nothing."

Another man, called Dylan, joined the conversation. "It's been like that since before the turn of the century," he said, "South Wales has good quality coal and they want it out of the ground yesterday."

"But surely, they can't keep dumping this rubbish on this hillside?" I asked.

Dylan smiled, "For 50 years Merthyr Vale Colliery been piling up muck on the side of Mynydd Merthyr. Look around you. This is just one of the massive tips. There are millions of cubic metres of excavated mining debris everywhere. They haven't got any other solution to the problem."

The slowest and oldest member of the tipping team was Evan. He puffed and wheezed his way through the work, a permanent cigarette between his blackened lips. His eyes were deep yellowish hollows in the grime of his face. He stopped and stooped for a moment to catch his breath, and said, "My grandfather was a sheep farmer, and he used to walk in these mountains when they were green."

"Oh my God, He's going to talk about the good old days again." said Dafyd.

Evan ignored him, and spoke again, "My grandad told me, that there are natural springs below the surface of this hillside."

"Where does all the water from those springs go now?" I asked.

"Ha! Nobody knows." laughed Dafyd.

"It's not a laughing matter, laddie." declared Evan.

"Be grateful for your job, you old windbag. Without the NCB we'd all be penniless."

"I know that we work for the NCB, but they don't care about us."

"They pay our wages, don't they?"

"Yes, laddie, they do indeed, but the NCB and the private mine owners before them, are cruel heartless men, who only care about their profits."

Evan lit another cigarette in disgust, shook his head and shuffled away.

It was Owen's opportunity to put a sarcastic tuppence into the discussion.

"My grandad spent 40 years down the pit and died of black lung. But that's OK, because they give it a posh name nowadays. It's called silicosis. But whatever they call it, it still kills you."

"My brother worked at Gresford Colliery, near Wrexham, in North Wales. He was killed in a mining accident in1934." said Dylan, "It was an explosion."

Dafyd scoffed, "They never established the cause."

Dylan was adamant, "You know and I know it was a cover up. The cause was failures in safety procedures and poor mine management."

The faintest smudge of tears came to Dylan's eyes, as he added; "Only eleven bodies were ever recovered. The remains of the other victims, over 260 men and boys, were left entombed. My brother was one of them."

"So many people killed, that's terrible." I said.

"Dylan's right about the boss men not giving a monkey's," said Owen, "My brother-in-law's father was killed in an explosion at the Universal Colliery in Senghenydd, near Caerphilly. I will always remember it, because it happened on my birthday, 14th October 1913."

"That day, over 400 miners lost their lives."

"How did that happen?" I asked.

"Well, some of the coal seams contained high quantities of firedamp."

"What's that?"

"It's a highly explosive gas; a mixture of methane and hydrogen."

"They should have had canaries there to warn them?" said Dafyd.

"It all happened so quickly. Canaries can give a warning, but even then some of our brave boys suffocated from gas in the mine, because they didn't hear that the canaries had stopped chirping."

The conversation dried up, but the termite imitating toil continued.

After a few minutes, Dylan leaned on his spade and added, "It's not just down the pit though lad. This work isn't pleasant and our lads get injured on the tips as well. We can moan about it all and blame the National Coal Board, but nobody knows what the solution is."

"Come on lads, enough chattering." said the Boss man, "We've got work to do."

"OK, Boss," Dylan replied, "But you know that every word we have said is true."

Boss man sighed, "Yes, I know just as well as you do. My oldest brother, Llewelyn is a clerk at Merthyr Council. He told me that the council have been writing letters to the NCB for years, saying how worried they were about the tips towering above the Pantglas area, and pointing out that if they were to move, a very serious situation would occur."

I'd never realised that coalmining could be so very dangerous, but I'd had a baptism of fire as an introduction to the perils of working for the NCB. There seemed to a quiet desperation mingled into the conversation and camaraderie of the tipping gang; a realisation that their livelihoods were largely dependent upon turning a blind eye to the inherent, but all too obvious risks of working for the NCB. Victims they certainly were, of a traditional system that valued profits more than lives. Quiet dissenters they were, with families dependent upon their sweat and toil. Only Dafyd stood out, as someone, who for reasons known only to himself and unfathomable to others, belittled their concerns.

A feeble sun glanced intermittently through the grey cloud ceiling, that delighted in threatening still more rain. Through the swirls of mist, down in the valley, the children had reached their safe haven in the Hall of Pantglas Junior School. Hundreds of feet above the village, precariously perched on the side of Mynydd Merthyr, tipping and piling, scratching and scraping, continued, as it had done for decades, at colliery waste tip number 7.

We had been at work for about 2 hours, when the other Michael came scampering down across the loose rock and shale on the upper flank of the waste tip about 30 feet above us to the right.

He was waving his spade in the air, and shouting. "Boss! Boss! Quick! Come and have a look!"

"What's up, Mick?" the head man shouted back.

"I think we've got problems. The tip has gone all fluid, and I think it's about to slide away."

"Shit! Quickly! Get on the telephone and issue a warning."

"I can't! As I told you earlier, Boss, the cables been stolen again overnight."

"Oh, my God! Oh, my God! We can't do anything other than pray."

After over a week of heavy rainfall, the inevitable and also unthinkable, was about to happen. The yellow October sun suddenly faded. The dim light played hide and seek behind the grey clouds. A cold chill cut the air like a sharp knife stabbing at my face. The atmosphere was still, with impending doom and dark foreboding.

I watched with my new comrades, helpless, as a small subsidence swelled and grew into an enormous fluid landslide, and began to slip down the mountainside. It started slowly and quietly and in seconds had gathered speed and an ominous rumbling noise. The build-up of water in the accumulated rock and shale began to flow downhill in the form of a black monstrous slurry. An unstoppable wave of slimy coal waste was sliding down towards the Aberfan Valley.

The working men on tip 7 were frozen in terror, lips quivering in silent prayer, as the front part of the mass became liquefied and moved down the slope at high speed in a series of viscous surges. They could only hope, with hearts filled with dread that the landslip would peter out on the lower slopes of the mountain. But the hope appeared to be in vain. The first obstacle in the path of the surge was a farm cottage. This was engulfed by liquefied debris and disappeared in seconds. Then, the full horror of what was happening tore at the heavy hearts and tortured minds of my comrades, when they realised that the ugly black serpent was curling its path down the mountain, directly towards the Aberfan village; across Moy Road, into the mist that obscured the village. Moments after the farm had been wiped off the face of the Earth, the serpent devoured a row of terraced houses along Moy Road, and was heading for an impact with the northern side of Pantglas Junior School.

I watched and wished that I had been able to do something, anything at all, to prevent this happening. Tears filled my eyes. My heart was filled with lead. Everything, anything in the path of the slip from tip number 7 would be smothered, engulfed, swamped in coaly slime. Everything that breathed, anything that lived, would be drowned in a tidal wave of muck, victim to a crime; the crime of manslaughter by the NCB. I closed my eyes, and my knees buckled underneath me and in an instant I was somewhere else.

The school hall clock clicked a stuttering big hand to ten past nine. A thin swirling mist had filled the valley bottom since dawn's weak sun had broken the morning. A diffused eerie light penetrated the windows of the Pantglas Junior School. In the dimly lit assembly hall, the children of Aberfan were singing "All Things Bright and Beautiful". Their happy smiling faces illustrated the joy of the day; the last day before the half term holiday. A week lay ahead in which the children could truly be themselves; play games, meet friends, and have fun.

I was standing in a row, flanked by the staff; headmaster and teachers, looking forward to sending their pupils off at the end of the school day, back to their neat terraced house homes.

The singing was truly beautiful; words expressed in innocence and faith, as only children could express them. Faces radiated joy. Hearts leapt with expectation.

"All things bright and beautiful,
All creatures great and small,
All things wise and wonderful:
The Lord God made them all."

When the song finished, the children filed quietly away towards their classrooms. Somehow, I knew where I had to go and followed a group of kids into a room on the northern side of the school. For some reason, the words of one of the verses of "All things bright and beautiful" stuck in my thoughts and hammered at my fears. I didn't have any inkling of why that was.

"The purple-headed mountains,
The river running by,
The sunset and the morning
That brightens up the sky...."

The first lesson of the last day was just about to begin. A clock on the classroom wall showed 9.15. Everybody was sat at their desks; children attentively waiting for the teacher to begin. Mr Davis wrote out the maths class work on the blackboard. He was about to speak. The lesson was seconds old, when I heard a tremendous rumbling sound. No words left Mr Davis' lips.

The classroom fell into a silent dread. Mr Davis was the favourite teacher of many of the children. They looked to him for something, anything, any possible indication of what to do, how to react. He had no answers. He was helpless. It sounded like a jet plane was about to land on the village. Some children froze in their seats, others ducked, or covered their faces or heads with their hands. They were all petrified as the ominous sound grew louder and louder, growing to a thunderous roar. Light in the classroom became progressively dimmer. Closer and closer came the terrifying noise. I covered my ears and cowered. Then, with a cacophony of crashing of breaking masonry and glass, a black angry mass burst through the windows, and demolished the wall, growling like a venomous monster intent on devouring everything in its path. In seconds, everyone in the classroom was gone, swallowed by the blackness, crushed and suffocated. Then, again there was silence. Silence so intense, that you couldn't hear a bird singing or a child crying. I had the strange feeling that I had been in the same situation before. Then it came to me.

Being engulfed by the landslide was like the sensation of dying, that I had experienced on my way to Heaven. There it was again!

Night fell so heavily. It fell for me like it had fallen once before. One second I was standing in a classroom full of children and the next all there was around me was darkness. There was a complete nothingness; for a moment my mind was totally blank. So black and impenetrable was the darkness, that all I could feel was its claustrophobic intensity all around me, gripping me tight like I was floating in treacle. Black, black and more black tumbled over me in undulating waves, squeezing and scrambling all my senses into one; just a pure sense of being. But I was not afraid.

I had no choice in the matter, but my being told me that I must submit myself willingly to the dark, surrender to the unknown. My surrender was rewarded.

All attempts at movement in the dirty, heavy mass of debris required Herculean strength, but I fumbled for my moonbeam jar in my pocket, twisted the top off and placed an index finger inside the jar. I held my finger upwards and twirled it around in the abject blackness. Nothing!

Again, I placed my finger inside the jar, and twirled it upwards again. Nothing!

I tipped the jar up on my hand and shook it, until it felt like it was empty. Then, I rubbed my hands together around the jar, creating a little warmth. There was the faintest glow. I rubbed harder and faster, until the light opened my eyelids fully. I brought my finger up to my face and found my mouth in the slimy muck of the landslide and prised my mouth open with my fingers. There was no possibility of breathing, and pulling the moonbeam jar up to my mouth in the suffocating darkness, required gargantuan strength. From somewhere deep in my being, I found a puff of air and blew it into the jar, then another and another. Slowly, pinpricks of light appeared around me, growing in intensity and with each one more breath came to me, until I was blowing again and again into the jar. Tiny dots of light joined together, building bit by bit into a creamy white arc of crisscrossing moonbeams over my head and forming into the shape that resembled a large fishing net.

I was still rooted to the spot, with my feet trapped in the weight of the black muck, but I began to spin the net of moonbeams over my head with both my arms. Somehow, this made space around me, air to breathe, more and more light to see better. Once my feet were free, I knew exactly what I had to do. To move through the classroom, searching, trawling with my moonbeam net, to find every one of the children and lead them away. It didn't take too long to find the first child, a little girl called Myfanwy. She smiled. I held her hand. Together we found Nerys, then Rhys, and Megan, and Blodwyn. Soon the light of the moonbeams had grown bright enough and the net large enough for the children to search one by one, for their friends and classmates, on their own. Holding hands, we searched every inch of the classroom, under desks, in corners, in the very depths of the rubble and mud. Myfanwy found Carys, Nerys found Gareth, Rhys found Emlyn, Megan found Lewys, and Blodwyn found Tomos. Our circle grew and grew, and as we joined together in a long chain, we began singing again. At first, it was a low stuttering, an unsure muttering of the chorus.

"All things bright and beautiful,
All creatures great and small,
All things wise and wonderful:
The Lord God made them all."

Together, we took the moonbeam net through the whole school and found all the children and all their teachers, whose lives had been so tragically terminated in a few seconds, by the ugly violent and indiscriminate black monster that had left it's lair on the side of tip number 7 and roared down the mountain to swallow up everything in its path. As our congregation rose in numbers, the joy and exuberance of our singing expanded, swelled and became louder.

"All things bright and beautiful,
All creatures great and small,
All things wise and wonderful:
The Lord God made them all."

When we were sure that we had found everyone, I asked the children and teachers to hold hands into a tight circle and look upwards in silence. I placed my little moonbeam jar on ground in the middle of their midst and stood outside the circle, and watched as the moonbeam net went round and round above them and then fell on to the group in a blinding flash of light. They were gone. But this time they had gone to Heaven.

Suddenly, I was back where the tipping gang on tip number 7 had been working only 15 minutes before. The men had all gone; abandoned their work and rushed down the hillside as soon as they realised what was happening down in the valley. A raw and eerie silence filled the autumn skies. I sat there alone.

I could clearly see where a great black splurge of coal waste slime had carved a tortuous path, from just below my feet, and spread its tentacles, intent on delivering its murderous load down into the misty valley of Aberfan.

I watched, as emergency vehicles began to arrive, as lorries loaded with miners came from the Merthyr Colliery to assist with rescue efforts, as men dug with spades and with their bare hands to scrape away the clinging, cloying mess, as women huddled in groups fearful, tearful, anxious, dreading that their children had been stolen from them. I watched, as villagers cried, when the bodies were wrapped in white sheets and carried away to the temporary mortuary at the Bethania Chapel.

It was Friday 21st October 1966. It was the saddest day in the history of the Borough of Merthyr Tydfil and the village of Aberfan. I don't know how long I sat there and watched.

When I returned to Heaven, Gabriel was waiting for me. He embraced me with open arms.

"That was difficult!" I said.

"I know, Michael, but once again you have come through with shining colours. What you were able to do was excellent."

"But why did it have to happen? Why couldn't I have stopped the landslide, and saved everybody's life?"

"I think you know by now, that in some situations we are powerless to prevent a disaster. We cannot change what is destined to occur because of man's ignorance or intolerance or neglect."

"But I was working with the tipping gang, when the debris began to shift downhill. I was there when it started. I saw it happening. Nobody stood a cat in Hell's chance in the face of that awful landslip. But when I found myself in the school, I couldn't do anything about it. Why didn't I know what was happening when I got there?"

"I know it's difficult to understand for you, Michael, but once again it's a matter of time and of beautiful graceful naivety. Effectively, you were transported back in time by about 5 minutes when you arrived in the school. That means that the slip had not started to happen."

"I see! But I had been there. Why didn't I remember that it was going to happen?"

"That's where beautiful graceful naivety comes in again."

"That was something much less than beautiful."

"I'm sorry, but that's the way these things work."

Gabriel could see how troubled I was. He let me brood about it for a while, then he added, "I want you to know something else."

"What's that?"

"The disaster happened so quickly that a telephone warning would not have saved any lives. But, be grateful that all the children and their teachers are now safe up here in Heaven with us, and every one of them has a star in his or her pocket."

"Why couldn't it have happened on the next day?"

"I know that it's very distressing to face up to, but it's once again all to do with the way that time works."

"I thought that what you told me only applied here in Heaven?"

"No, I explained that time is different here, but you must understand that time in the Earthly Realm is linear, constant and unalterable."

"What does that mean?"

"Well, think about it, Michael. Had the children left the assembly for their classrooms a few minutes later, the loss of life would have been significantly reduced. They would not have reached their classrooms when the landslide hit. The classrooms were on the side of the building nearest the landslide."

"That's really cruel!"

"Yes! I agree. You should also know, that if the landslide had struck a few minutes earlier, then the children would not have been in their classrooms, and if it had struck a few hours later, the school would have already broken up for half-term."

"That is even more cruel!"

"I can't disagree, but once again we are powerless to stop things happening when they do. All we can do is make sure that we do our best to bring victims up to Heaven with a star in their pocket. The rest is destiny and history, and is written in the stars."

Gabriel could easily sense the distress my latest task was causing me. This time it was mainly children who had been killed. He allowed me to contemplate what he had just told me.

"Life will go on in the Earthly Realm, Michael, and up here in Heaven our time is eternal. The inquests and enquiries will go on down below."

"What will the verdict be?"

"Well, the landslip engulfed a farm, the Pantglas Junior School, and about 20 houses along Moy Road in the village, before coming to rest. In a few minutes, 144 men, women and children lost their lives. The majority of casualties died within the primary school walls. About half of the children at the school, and 5 of their teachers, were killed. All together 116 of the victims were children, most of them between the ages of 7 and 10.

"And where will the blame lie?"

"They held a tribunal, and it concluded that blame for the disaster rests upon the National Coal Board, that they were guilty of extreme negligence and that the Chairman, Lord Robens, was culpable for making misleading statements."

"Did they learn any lessons from it?"

"Yes! Within a few years, all mining tips that threatened the safety of pit villages were removed from the landscape, and the mountains and hillsides became green again."

"I'm so glad about that."

"But the biggest lesson for angels, Michael, must be that sometimes we just need a miracle."

Gabriel was just about to leave when he said, "Look out for a man called Lloyd George. He will come along soon, and present you with your green star."

Chapter 6

Blue Star - 10th April, 1912

So my rainbow was building nicely and I now had my red, orange and yellow stars carefully folded away in my purple pouch and was looking out for Lloyd George to appear at sometime and present me with my green star. I'd already learned a lot of lessons along the way, not least of all, about how each of my tasks would be very different. Sometimes I would only be "gone" for a few hours, and have one big incident to deal with, like at Hillsborough. At other times I'd be "away" for several days, and have lots of seemingly minor crises to deal with, like when I was in the Ukraine. The things that seemed to be consistent were that, in the places I had suddenly been transported back to in the Earthly Realm, I would always be in a state of beautiful graceful naivety upon arrival. I would always be able to help, even if I didn't understand what the significance of my being there was at the time. People would always be saved from danger or disaster.

It was a fantastic education to have my stars presented to me by wonderful inspirational people, like Bill Shankly, Mikhail Gorbachev and Winston Churchill; people I could have a one to one chat with, learning from their words of wisdom.

Back in Heaven, there were also many things to learn and routine tasks to carry out. My latest duty was in the frozen zone, where I was learning how to make hailstones of different sizes from very small to golf ball sized. Then, I progressed on to making snowflakes from single or multiple ice crystals. It was necessary to process them through differing temperature and humidity conditions, so that every snowflake was completely unique. If they were made properly, they would allow the tiny crystal facets to reflect the whole spectrum of light, and were pure white.

Hail and snowflake structures were extremely delicate and needed to be stored carefully in massive secret ice warehouses. As an apprentice angel, I didn't feel the cold like humans would. Sometimes we had snowball fights; only for fun, nothing serious, and we never damaged the products of our labours.

It was during one of those fun times that Lloyd George suddenly appeared from behind a vast army of jolly singing snowmen. He looked very out of place in his thick woolly suit and waistcoat with a wing collar shirt and blue tie. The snowmen all stood at ease and stopped singing "Jingle Bells", and then he spoke in a broad soft Welsh accent.

"Hello, young man, I'm very pleased to meet with you." he said.

"Hello! I've been expecting you." I replied.

"Little old me? I do hope you're not disappointed, my boy."

"No, I'm honoured to meet you."

"The feeling is mutual. You did what you could at Aberfan, and you have my heartfelt thanks."

"I did what very little I could and I hope it was enough."

"Aberfan was an awful, tragic accident and leaves the worst possible legacy for that small mining community. A village without children has lost its hopes and dreams and cannot look to the future with any confidence."

"I am filled with sadness for what happened. No amount of grieving will bring the children back. But Gabriel assures me that every child died with a star in his pocket."

"And I must thank you for that, young man. Here is your green star. Keep it safe and be proud to receive it."

"Thank you, Sir."

"I believe you have a few more difficult tasks to do yet before you earn the Angel's Rainbow. So I have some advice for you."

As I tucked the green star carefully in my purple pouch, Mr George cleared his throat and said, "Don't be afraid to take a big step if one is indicated. You can't cross a chasm in two small jumps."

"That is good advice indeed, Sir, thank you."

"You will find yourself transported to tragic circumstances to earn your stars, and armed only with common sense, a good heart, and beautiful graceful naivety, you will be unaware of the dangers you face. But you must never be afraid and you must always be strong."

"I will try to be, Sir."

"I have made some good friends since I've been here, and one of them is a man called Dylan Thomas. My friend Dylan expresses it wonderfully."

"What does he say?"

"Do not go gentle into that good night...

but rage, rage against the dying of the light."

"Wow! Those are fantastic words."

"Better still, he also wrote:-

'And death shall have no dominion.

Dead men naked they shall be one

With the man in the wind and the west moon;

When their bones are picked clean and the clean bones gone,

They shall have stars at elbow and foot;

Though they go mad they shall be sane,

Though they sink through the sea they shall rise again

Though lovers be lost love shall not;

And death shall have no dominion.'

And as you go about your tasks, you must work on your tasks as if you have that tattooed on your heart, my friend."

I felt very humbled by this man and thought to say something to compliment him. So I said, "You are most certainly very eloquent, Sir."

He smiled at me and replied, "The finest eloquence is that which gets things done; the worst is that which delays them."

Then he disappeared back behind the rows of jolly snowmen.

Soon after, I'd finished my ice warehouse duties and decided to find my way back to my cloud. As I walked across the last blindingly bright sheet of the freshly made snowfields, I tripped up and plummeted into a very deep crevasse. It seemed that I was falling for a very long time, and then suddenly I found myself back in the Earthly Realm. I was in Southampton docks, walking up a gangplank, onto an enormous brand new ocean liner at 8.30 am on a bright and clear morning.

The dockside at Southampton was a huge, bustling, noisy theatre of activity. People milled around in all directions, waiting to board the ship. Some gentlemen were smartly dressed, in their best suits and waistcoats, with tall top hats. They were standing together with beautiful ladies, in their expensive finery, wearing floral bonnets and long flowing lacy dresses. There were whole families of scruffy citizens; men in crumpled corduroy trousers and grubby overcoats, women simply clothed, in brown or grey smocks, and children, with hand-me-down, jumble sale outfits, snotty noses and no shoes. Stewards and seamen from the ship marshalled people into their places, and tall cranes lifted huge piles of luggage and ship's supplies aboard. Excited chatter filled the expectant air. Billows of cigarette and cigar smoke curled upwards into the coolness of the morning skies. Some very important people arrived in a blaze of their own pride and joy, as their new automobiles clanked their way onto the quay and puffed dark fumes into the faces of the waiting throng.

I stopped halfway up the gangplank and stood there amazed at the size of the ship. The red plumb line was a dizzying depth below me, where the salt water sloshed gently at the colossal bulk. The black, shiny hull curved majestically to my left and right, but so long was the vessel, that I couldn't see the bow or the stern. The upper deck levels were all pure white, with so many windows it would have taken hours to count them all. Above the decks, four huge gold and black funnels towered high into the heaven, belching black smoke.

"Hurry along there, son." instructed a smartly dressed steward, "We've all got work to do. There's no time for hanging about and admiring the beastie."

He looked down at me from the top of the plank, "Muster in the crew's mess hall. Quickly now lad!"

I climbed the rest of the way up and soon I was assembled in the mess hall with hundreds of others.

A smart man, with a neatly trimmed beard and an immaculately pressed dark blue naval uniform, banged a gavel on a large mahogany desk and the room fell silent.

"Welcome aboard the Titanic, the pride of the White Star Line, and the largest ship ever built. Let me just tell you a little bit about our lovely ship, before we assign you to your duties."

We all stood in silence and waited while he explained with great pride.

"The Titanic is an Olympic-class ocean liner, and was built in Belfast by Harland and Wolff. Our ship weighs over 46,000 tons, and is nearly 900 feet long and nearly 100 feet wide, and stands 175 feet tall from keel to funnel. We have the best engines that money can buy, with 24 boilers, that allow the ship to skim us across the ocean at 24 knots. There are 20 lifeboats; enough for nearly 1,200 passengers."

The silence grew, with mouths agape at the statistics.

"Titanic has 9 decks, and can accommodate nearly 2,500 passengers, separated into 3 classes; more than 800 first class, 600 second class and 1,000 third class. The passenger facilities on board are designed to maintain the highest standards of luxury. The interior design doesn't follow traditional criteria. Here, we don't have that typical heavy style of a manor house or an English country house.

If you get any spare time, you might get the chance to see what I mean."

The speaker smiled a derisory smile, followed by a quiet stifled laugh.

"Let me warn you, that some areas of the ship are out of bounds to the staff. Beware! We don't take kindly to stewards breaking the regulations."

The warmth of the introduction seemed to be disappearing rapidly and the atmosphere of welcome had changed in an instant.

"Now, the important bit for you." he continued, "This is our maiden voyage to New York, via Cherbourg and Queenstown, and I am absolutely adamant that everything about this little flit across the Atlantic will be excellent and exceptional. There are 900 crew aboard and every one of you will be working to the highest standards or you won't be working for White Star ever again. Do I make myself clear?"

There were mumbles of agreement, but our orator wasn't interested in any reaction and was confident that he required no form of agreement.

"You will now be assigned to your duties." he said, and then he turned towards the officer's quarters and strode militarily away.

After a little wait, I reached the front of a long queue, and reported to the man who would be my boss.

Charlie Armstrong was a stockily built ex-boxer with missing incisors and small ears. His smart dark blue suit, light blue shirt, black tie and highly polished black shoes said "Do as you are told!"

It didn't take long to discover that he believed in an economy of words, issued with an attitude that was gruff and short tempered. He didn't look up as he spoke to me.

"Name?"

"Michael Hartson."

"Michael Hartson, Sir!" he replied, looking at me sternly, under his lowered eyebrows.

"Michael Hartson, Sir!" I replied quickly.

"Experience?"

"No, Sir!"

"Where you from?"

"Southampton, Sir."

"Really?"

He said it as if he didn't believe me.

"We'll start you as a glory-hole steward, then."

"Yes, Sir."

"Off you go then, laddie. Follow Albert. He'll show you what to do. Remember we only want excellent workers here."

I followed an elderly gentleman in a brown uniform, wondering what a glory-hole steward was expected to do and how I could make it excellent. Soon I was kitted out in a brown uniform and ready for work.

"What do I have to do then?" I asked.

"It's easy!" Albert replied, "All we have to do is spend 14 hours a day up to our ankles in shit and piss. Your eyes will sting, your nose will itch, and you won't be able to get the flavours out of the back of your throat. It's a crap job, but we do get paid, and fed, and get some sleep. If you don't like the work you can think about jumping ship when we get to New York."

"I'm sorry?"

"You really are a greenhorn, aren't you, sunshine. A glory-hole steward's function is to clean and maintain the common toilets in First, Second and Third Class, and in the crew areas."

My heart sank to the bottom of my boots.

Passengers of all classes began boarding the vessel, and filling it with activity and excitement. There was so much excitement that glory-hole duties were very quickly required.

"Don't despair, lad," said Albert, noticing my rather hangdog expression, as we mopped yet another floor swimming in urine, and transformed it with the odour of strong disinfectant, "The ship has to float on whatever flows into the sea."

He grinned at me, and slapped my shoulder, "We'll all be able to say to our grandchildren that we sailed on the maiden voyage of the biggest ship ever made. I've worked for White Star for donkey's years, and it's a real privilege to be here today on the Titanic."

"I never thought of it like that." I replied.

"They say it's unsinkable, you know, and it glides through the waves like a duck on a millpond. We might even get a few glimpses of New York when we dock there."

For nearly 3 hours, there was no let-up in our tedious and unpleasant work, but at 12 noon we managed to steal a few minutes off duty, as the ship cast off amid great pomp and circumstance. We could hear the ship's band playing jolly tunes above us, as above them the sirens repeatedly played their low 'A' note. Then, the enormous engines started up and with a low rumble we moved gracefully away from our Southampton berth, out into the Solent, and across the English Channel towards Cherbourg.

We spent most of our time on the lower decks, with only occasional quick peeks through port holes, but Albert was right. We glided across the placid ocean with a calm and confident ease and had very little sense of movement.

I learned very quickly that the 1st class toilets were 10 times more disgusting than even the crew's quarters toilets. Albert explained.

"Well, lad, it's what they eat and drink you see. The 3rd class lot in steerage bring their own food; simple stuff, no frills; the sort of grub that you and I would eat every day. The toffs in the 1st class have fancy gourmet meals concocted by the ship's French chefs, and they wash it all down with loads of expensive red wine. Did you know that all them top knobs like to eat stuff that's half rotten? They hang up their game birds till they've got maggots, and most of their meat has been hanging around for weeks. It's no bloody wonder that they all end up shitting through the eye of a needle."

Albert's acerbic overview continued, "Then you've got your 2nd class, many of whom walk around like they have a nasty smell under their noses. They try the fancy dishes, but they ain't got used to 'em yet, and most of the time that leads to toilet disasters. I'll tell you, lad, there's a great education to be had in studying the toilet habits of the different classes."

So, the Titanic left Southampton at noon in a blaze of glory, and at 7.30 on a fine bright evening, it smoothed a majestic way into the dockside at Cherbourg in France. Only 90 minutes later, the ship set sail again, on its way to Queenstown in Ireland.

My shift finished sometime close to midnight, and I spent the night tossing and turning, exhausted, in a narrow bunk in a dormitory deep in the bowels of the vessel, with the low hum of the engines burning in my ears. It was difficult to sleep in strange and uncomfortable conditions, being continually interrupted throughout the night by the noisy comings and goings of what seemed like hundreds of other stewards, coming from or going to their duties.

Albert woke me up, with a very welcome cup of strong tea and some toast and marmalade. He looked refreshed and ready for another day's onslaught. I felt like I'd slept for at least 5 minutes, and thought I smelled like the Elephant's compound at London Zoo. The condition of the toilets had not improved overnight and I set about my never ending cleaning duties with as much enthusiasm as I could muster.

The cyclical nature of the arduous work was only broken up by Albert's wit and sarcasm in the face of his lifetime's duties. At the middle of my 2nd day of my glory-hole drudgery, we docked at Queenstown at 12.30 pm. We would be there for only one hour.

Before the ship began heading west across the Atlantic to New York, Albert told me that I had been summoned to see Charlie Armstrong.

As I climbed the 5 flights of steep stairs to his tiny office, I wondered if he was going to dismiss me or clap me in irons for not going about my work with enough diligence. Even worse thoughts occurred to me, like what would be the fate of stewards who got the sack. Were they made to walk the plank, or just dumped overboard with the other flotsam and jetsam?

I knocked nervously on Mr Armstrong's door, and he beckoned me in. I stood at his small desk as he studied some papers.

"Michael, I wanted to see how you're getting on."

"Yes, Sir?"

"Albert tells me you're doing good work."

"Yes, Sir."

He leaned back and his face changed. He looked friendly. He wasn't the stern, man of few words, any more. There was a thin smile.

"Do you know boy?" he said, "I like hard workers."

"I've done my best, Sir."

He sighed and then puffed out his cheeks, and paused, looking me straight in the eyes. Then he spoke the longest collection of words I'd heard him say up to that point."

"There are 322 stewards on board the Titanic. There are waiters, waitresses, maids and attendants who perform over 57 different functions in each class's dining saloon, public rooms, cabins and recreational facilities. I've heard good reports about you, and I like people who work hard and want to improve themselves."

"Thank you, Sir."

"You're a good old Southampton lad and I look after me own. I'm going to promote you, young man."

I was relieved. One day of being a glory-hole steward was enough for anybody.

"Here's a note. Find Joey Jenkins. I'm reassigning you as a boot boy."

"What will my duties be, Sir?"

"Boots are shoe shiners; stewards who are responsible for cleaning and shining the passenger's boots and shoes."

"Thank you, Sir."

"You'll find the work less taxing, and as a little reward, you can take an hour off, and go have a good butcher's around this beautiful ship."

"Thank you, Sir."

"OK! Now get out of here, I've got work to do."

Joey Jenkins was a bit of a Jack-the-lad. Tall and slim, with a dark pencil moustache and well-oiled dark hair with greying sideburns, he wore a grey waistcoat and trousers and carried a wooden box with all the shoe cleaning paraphernalia tucked into neat compartments. I could see a reflection of my face in his coal black shoes.

"Promoted from shovelling shit after just one day, you must be a genius, Mick."

"I'm not sure about that."

"Did old Charlie give you an hour off to take a little walkabout?"

"Yes, Sir."

"No need to elevate me, Mick, I ain't no toff. Call me Joey."

"Charlie's alright once you get to know him. He comes across as a hard man at first, but if you work hard he looks after you. So you've had a good look at this massive tub then?"

"Yes, Joey,"

"Bloody magnificent, ain't it? First Class cabins finished in the Empire style, and as you walk around you find styles ranging from the Renaissance to Victorian in the cabins and public rooms in 1st and 2nd Class. I've worked in some swanky hotels when I was a lad and the Titanic is just like a floating hotel that glides from one place to another like it was on rails."

"I loved it outside on deck as we cast off from Queenstown and headed smoothly out into the vast open spaces of the Atlantic. It felt like we were going to the end of the world. I walked the whole length of the ship, from one end to the other, tasted the salt spraying in the air, and best of all got the taste of the glory-holes out of my lungs."

Joey giggled, "Well, Mick, my mate, it won't be long before the aromas of shit and piss from yesterday are replaced by the lingering odour of boot polish today. This is a great little job, and there ain't a lot to it."

"You'll tell me what to do?"

"Well, the 3rd class folk don't clean their scruffy shoes. So we don't have to mix with them in a professional capacity. Time off's fun with 'em though. They know how to have a good time; music, singin', dancin' and the odd bottle of potcheen passed around."

"What's potcheen?"

"An experience waiting for you, Mick. It's illegal whiskey and it's bloody hot stuff."

I looked confused, but Joey ignored it.

"Anyways," he continued, "It's the toffs who want their shoes kept shiny and bright. I cleaned Bruce Ismay's shoes yesterday."

"Who is Bruce Ismay?"

"He's the bloke who built the ship, and he's the top knob in the White Star Line. He's so far up his own arse he can't see his stuck-in-the-air nose."

"Are they all like that, then? The gentry, I mean."

"No, some of them are worse. They don't want their little feet tainted by treading the same boards as the rabble below their toffee noses. So be 'umble with 'em, shine their leather boots 'til they dazzle, and you'll get good tips. I made 3 shillings in tips yesterday."

"Sure sounds better than being a glory-hole steward."

"It is! But it's not all good, 'cause then there's the 2nd classers; tight sods a lot of 'em are, and their shoes might stink. Sometimes you get tips, and sometimes you get sod all."

"Still better than the glory-hole."

"Too right, mate. OK, let's get to work."

My first day as a shoe shine boy passed very quickly. After I was armed with one of Joey's boxes of polish, dusters and brushes and re-kitted into the grey suit and waistcoat with highly polished black shoes, a bit too small, I was quickly into my stride. The toff's tips totted up nicely, and at the end of the busy time before dinner for the 1st class passengers, I had eleven pence farthing in tips.

Before I went back to my bunk in bedlam, I took another stroll around the ship. Leaning over the rail on the boat deck, I breathed in great lungfulls of clean Atlantic Ocean air. It was a crisp clear night with not a cloud in the vast sky and every star in heaven putting on a wonderful lightshow, as the RMS Titanic skimmed across the black enormousness of the waves with steady and purposeful whoosh.

Perhaps, I had already got used to trying to sleep in a claustrophobic madhouse, or maybe I was just tired and elated at being free of glory-hole drudgery, but I slept extremely well. There was only one big interruption, when a loud discussion among crew members woke me up. Apparently, there had been a fire in the coal bunkers, but they were told it had been safely extinguished.

Over the next two days, I fell into a happy routine, as we sailed ever westward in calm and clear weather. The work was easy and increasingly rewarding as I accumulated my tips. Joey Jenkins persisted as a jolly Jack-the-lad, and was pleased that I had settled in so quickly.

"You're a good worker, Mick, and the punters seem to like you."

"I like the work, Joey. Thanks for looking out for me."

"Nah! You don't need me, mate. You can stand on your own feet."

"I love the Titanic; it's truly magnificent."

"Yeah, it ain't bad, but it's been an easy crossing. The sea's been very calm. It ain't always like that. Sometimes, even on these big White Star ships, you get a raging storm lasting for days and then were chucked around in massive waves like you're in never ending whirlpool and everybody's puking up."

"I'm glad it's not like that."

"It's not all bad, though. Guess what, mate? They puke up on their shoes, and then they queue up to get 'em cleaned again as soon as we get a bit of calm sea."

"Do you think we'll get there without any storms?"

"You never can tell, but what I do know, is that it's getting a lot colder outside. It's raw and icy out on deck, and they'll have somebody in the crow's nest looking out for icebergs."

"Why do they need to do that?"

"I dunno! Seems a bit pointless with the Titanic."

"Because it's supposed to be unsinkable?"

"Yeah! The icebergs take one look and swim away."

On Sunday morning, I took another little stroll on the boat deck before starting work, but I wasn't out there for long. It was bitter cold and I quickly returned to the cosy warmth of my shoe shine pitch near the 1st class cabins. The ship's constant motion and the reassuring low hum of the engines became a comforting backdrop to the rising excitement of the passengers on board, as the floating hotel closed in inexorably on our destination in New York.

The midnight hour was almost upon us and me and Joey were about to make our way back to the bunkroom. The smooth certainty of the ship's passage across the water, which had been the foundation stone for the voyage over 4 days, was abruptly interrupted by a sudden inexplicable shudder. Lights flickered on and off intermittently throughout the ship. Passengers stopped talking in mid-sentence. For a few moments, there was silence, as the world stopped and gasped a sudden shallow breath. That was quickly broken by a strange scraping vibration, as the ship lurched and leaned slightly over from the starboard to the portside, and then quickly uprighted itself, bobbing up and down. Then all activity, chatter and festivity carried on just as before as if nothing had happened.

Joey looked at me with a worried smile." There's something very wrong!" he said.

Questions flashed through my brain, I gibbered, "Why? What? How do you know?"

"I've been on these White Star ships for over 10 years, and I ain't felt nothin' like that before."

"Like what? What do you mean?"

"That juddering! This ship's bloody enormous, and it goes at 28 knots top speed. Only a football team of giant squid or a navy of blue whales could stop it going like that."

"Those are seaman's superstitions, aren't they? Things like that don't really happen."

"Perhaps not, mate. It's got to be bigger than that. Maybe the only thing that can stop the Titanic is the Hand of God."

"What do you think we should do now?"

Joey shrugged his shoulders, "We're about 400 miles from the nearest landfall. There's very little we can do. Could be something and nothing. We have to wait for instructions. I've got some potcheen hidden under my bunk. Let's go and have a drink."

I'd never tried potcheen before. The little mouthful I swallowed burned my tongue like sulphuric acid and scraped at my throat like I'd eaten a lighted candle, but it did warm my insides nicely. Down below decks, we all sensed the ship slowing down. The engines still droned on below us and the lights in the bunkroom still illuminated us in a constant low level gloom.

Twenty minutes passed in hushed conversation. Crewmates around us slept and snored. After 4 days at sea, the atmosphere was full of expectation and bonhomie, even though the air was distinctly saturated with the smell of good honest toil and sweat. A second slug of potcheen started to make me feel sleepy.

"Nothin' to worry about, Mick." Joey smiled, "I think we can turn in. Should be another good day tomorrow. The toffs will want to go ashore in New York with shiny shoes. Last day before arrival is always the best one for tips."

Suddenly, the quiet calm was broken by an almighty commotion. Albert came running down the stairs as fast as his old legs would carry him. He shouted, "Wake up! Wake up! They're uncovering the lifeboats. One of the officers told me that the ship has hit an iceberg."

Many crewmen groaned in their bunks and rolled over.

A stocky chap who slept in his flat cap, shouted back, "Albert, that ain't funny! We're all tired. Cut it out!"

"No, it's true," he said, "I'd swear it on a stack of Bibles."

"Fuck off or I'll knock your teeth out, you old shit shoveller."

Joey added, "There's always some joker thinks it's funny to disturb the peace."

"It's probably just a safety drill," said Mr Flatcap, "I'm going back to sleep."

From my short experience of working with Albert, he didn't strike me as the sort of bloke who would joke about something like that. Something began to nag at the back of my mind about the lifeboats situation.

"Suit yourself!" said Albert, "I'm not kidding. Stay where you are if you want to drown in your beds, but I'm going up on deck to see what's really happening."

"I think we should go and have a look for ourselves and see what's going on." I said to Joey.

"Yeah, OK!" he said, "But if we are goin' to be nosy, let's take the polishing equipment with us. It gives us an excuse to be out of bounds."

We climbed quickly back up to the boat deck and came out on the starboard side. There were a few couples out there taking a stroll, arm in arm, braced against each other to keep out the chill air. The ship's rails were cold and icy, but as far as the business of the ship moving on through the night went, it just looked like business as usual.

"Let's walk all the way round, and I'll have a smoke. Do you want a fag?" said my boot boy friend.

"Er! No thanks."

My companion's Jack-the-lad attitude meant we could walk anywhere on the vessel with confidence or bluster and bravado. As a result, we flitted through doors, inside and outside, 1st class, 2nd class, 3rd class, and even walked down the grand staircase, rubbing shoulders with some very elegantly dressed people, who seemed a little confused by our presence. We were challenged once or twice, but because we had taken the precaution of keeping out polishing boxes with us, Joey just claimed he'd been summoned to a cabin to clean Monsieur du Pont's family's shoes and that he'd got a bit lost. Some lifeboats had been uncovered on the port side, but there was no evidence of a safety drill going on. Everywhere inside appeared to be business as normal. After 20 minutes wandering around, we were just about to return to our bunks.

"Let's get some shuteye, mate. Like I told you, it'll be a busy day tomorrow."

"Yes, I'm a bit tired now."

All of a sudden, there was a flash of light in the skies. Joey looked up, and then looked worried.

"Change of plan, Mick." he said, "There is something wrong! That's a distress signal."

In an instant, it was like a plague of ants scurrying towards a spoon of sugar, as people started appearing on the boat deck from every door. Huge crowds began assembling, a rowdy mob, whatever class they portrayed with their fine or their ragged clothes, all jostling and cajoling each other as the realisation spread quickly through the ship that the lifeboats were being launched.

"Was it possible?" I thought, "No! It's a dream, a nightmare; I'll wake up in a minute. It's unthinkable."

Joey might have been reading my mind, echoing my thoughts, "So the Titanic is unsinkable, is it? Unsinkable, my arse! Why are they launching the lifeboats then?"

I shook myself. It wasn't a dream, it was a waking nightmare. The worst imaginable thing was happening.

"Quick, mate, let's get below decks and warn our mates. Albert wasn't kidding, and our comrades don't deserve to drown."

We rushed back down to the bunkroom, against the flow of human traffic. It was like a giant unfairly balanced rugby scrum; the two of us against all humanity. All humanity, in a desperate panic. We reached the bunkroom and banged walls, plates, anything that came to hand, to create as much noise as possible and shouted at the top of our voices until we were hoarse.

"Get out! Get up! The Titanic is sinking! It's not a joke! The Titanic is sinking! Get up! Get out!"

Our crewmates stirred in their bunks, rubbed eyes, yawned, asked questions expressing utter disbelief, but we did our utmost to convince them that they needed to understand the serious nature of the situation.

"We've done our best," said the bravest shoe shine boy, "Let's quickly get back on deck."

At least we were heading in the same direction as everybody else now. In a few minutes we had climbed to the top of a stairwell which connected to an area of 3rd class cabins. Charlie Armstrong was standing there with a bunch of keys in his hand. He'd just locked a scissor gate where some stairs came up from 3rd class. Almost as soon as he locked it, people began to appear running up the stairs and shaking the gate, screaming to be allowed through.

"Oy! You two!" he indicated in our direction, "Where do you think you are going?"

"No shoes to shine now, Charlie," Joey smiled," We're making for the lifeboats like everybody else."

"No, you're not. Stay here, and stop that rabble breaking out." he instructed, pointing to the mass of sad souls pressed up against the gate. Then, he pulled a small revolver out of his pocket, and waved it menacingly in our direction.

"You have got to be kidding, Charlie, I'm a boot boy, not a bleedin' hero. Right now, it's every man for himself, and these people deserve as much chance to get into the lifeboats as them toffs in their fancy overcoats. Open the gate, and let 'em through."

"No! Definitely not!"

"Alright, if you don't give me the keys, I'll break the gate down."

"I'd like to see you try."

"Charlie, give me the keys!" Joey insisted moving closer to the boss.

"No, stand back or I'll shoot."

The bravest boot boy leapt on the ex-boxer and tangled with him to get the keys. Fists flew and feet kicked out. There was spit and feathers, cursing and swearing, and sweat and toil, as each of them attempted to better the other.

Then with a dull thud, they fell onto the wooden floor with Charlie held in a head lock by Joey. They rolled from side to side, puffing and panting, faces reddened with the strain of the battle. The ship's lights began to flicker off and on, and off again in a regular pattern and displaying the struggle as a weird stroboscopic scenario. The two men rolled across the floor, this way and that; a frantic entanglement of two bodies, fighting to get hold of the keys. Charlie threw punches and Joey kicked out and then he head butted his opponent and stood up with the keys clenched in his fist. With a final killer blow, he kicked the vanquished boxer in the testicles and moved quickly towards the gate to open it. Charlie groaned and for a moment was paralysed and motionless.

Joey was a yard away from the gate when a shot rang out and his body slumped headfirst and lifeless to the ground, with blood gushing from his back just below the left side of his ribcage. He was dead. The coward had shot him in the back. I recoiled in horror and curled up in ball on the ground, thinking I would be the next victim.

"Get up, you squirming coward and do as you are told." the sweat stained and ruffled boss man shouted at me, "Or I'll shoot you as well."

I got up slowly, tears of fright filling my eyes, raising my hands, palms outward, in a totally useless gesture of defence. I stayed silent, shaking in fear.

"Pull yourself together man. Stand up straight."

"Yes, Sir" I whispered.

"I looked after you, boy. So now you can do something for me. Take this gun, and stop these useless urchins from escaping. If they manage to break the gate shoot them."

He handed the warm revolver into my limp grip. I'd never handled a gun before.

"Right now boy, it's every man for himself. Stay here until I come and get you."

He quickly scrambled through a door on the starboard side. Somehow I knew he wasn't coming back.

I thought about making a run for it to the opposite side of the ship, but in the dim flickering light I could see the pleading faces of the men, women and children trapped behind the scissor gate. Outside, I could hear voices shouting and the metallic clangs as lifeboats were lowered and launched from their davits. Intermittently, distress flares lit up the skies.

A stout, dark haired man with a rough woollen coat, a battered black Homburg hat and dark brown trousers, beckoned me over to him, his arms stretching through the metal frame of the gate. I feared to go too close, in case he grabbed the gun and attempted to shoot me, but his face told me that wouldn't be in his nature. He spoke in a quiet and measured voice.

"What's your name, young man?" he asked.

"Michael, Michael Hartson."

"Well, Michael Hartson, I can't say that I'm pleased to meet you in these trying circumstances, but my name is Brendan O'Flanagan."

He held his hand out to shake mine and I accepted it.

"May I talk to you, Sir?"

He spoke slowly and chose his words carefully. I was immediately convinced that he was a passionate and honest man, who despite his ragged clothes, swarthy growth of beard and unkempt appearance had immense quality to offer the world. I nodded agreement.

"There are women and children here. My family and friends are depending on you to help us survive this awful mess. You see, in a few minutes, the water will be creeping up the stairs behind us. If you can't help us, then we'll all be crushed against the gate as the water rises, and then you can watch us all scream and holler before we drown. Have a heart, Sir. Think! Are any of the women and children trapped here less valuable than all those fancily dressed toffs in their warm coats and top hats upstairs, using their wealth to earn their places in the lifeboats?"

Brendan looked deep into my eyes. His soft Irish brogue, delivered quietly in the panic of the situation, told me volumes about the quality of the man and his outlook on life and death. I didn't have the keys to open the cage in which these people were imprisoned. Charlie had run off with them. I shivered at the thought of having to use the gun.

The Irishman spoke again, "Didn't I see you cleaning the toilets a day or two ago. Sir? You're one of us; you being just a humble boot boy yourself. Don't wrong your own kind."

The impassioned plea pulled at my heartstrings and tears came quickly to my eyes. This time, they were tears of compassion, not fear.

"Sir, we are on this ship to find ourselves a new life in America. There's a great man, who was recently the president of the Promised Land we seek. His name is Theodore Roosevelt."

I wondered where the thread of the discussion was going, and replied, "Yes!"

Brendan fixed a stare on me and said, "Nobody cares how much you know, until they know how much you care."

Then he grinned and added, "Theodore Roosevelt said that!"

I couldn't think of anything to say in reply.

"Will you show us how much you care, Michael? Please!"

The ship lurched and swayed erratically from side to side, and the lights were finally extinguished. In the darkness, I heard screams and a sloshing and swirling of seawater, chasing my prisoners up the stairs.

A second's further thought told me what I had to do.

"OK, I'm going to shoot the lock off the gate. I'm not familiar with guns, so make some space, and turn your faces away, because I think there'll be a blast."

Just before I fired the gun, I emptied the contents of my rainbow bag holding a collection of falling stars, on the deck ahead of the stairwell. My hand shook as I took aim, and in the moment's silence, there was a loud echoing bang, as I shot the lock off the gate. Brendan prised the gate open, just as the grey angry waters swirled and surged violently up the stairs behind the prisoners. I stood back, waiting for an onrush to barge me out of the way, and saw a bright blue sparkling brilliant passageway of stars forming and leading up to the boat deck. As the passengers streamed past me, they ran without hesitation along the star path. I hoped that their destiny wasn't to be like lemmings heading for the edge of a cliff. Only Brendan stopped to shake my hand again and smile the broadest smile I'd seen that day. He spoke again and the words came to me as if they had told me what to do in this situation. These words seemed to embed themselves in my being.

"Theodore Roosevelt also said, 'Keep your eyes on the stars and your feet on the ground', and you have given us all a chance to do that."

"Thank you," I said, "I've learned a lesson in humanity from you."

"No, thank you, Sir" he replied, "At least now we all have a slim chance of being saved."

"Why do you say that your chances are only slim?"

"Have you done the mathematics, lad? There are near on 3,400 including the crew on board this ship and in their infinite wisdom, Mr Big Knob Ismay and his scumbag builders have only provided enough lifeboats for 1,200."

Suddenly, the full horror came to me, like I'd been run over by a steamroller. That's what didn't add up. That was what had been eating away at me since the little talk on the first day of the trip in Southampton docks.

"Best of luck, my friend." said Brendan, "See you in New York or in Heaven.", and then he was gone.

I threw the gun into the sea as soon as I reached the starboard boat deck, and then I stood back and watched the struggles, the panic, the distress, the weeping and wailing, as all classes fought and squabbled for places in the lifeboats. There was shouting and fighting and occasionally shots rang out.

The bow end of Titanic sank steadily further into the water, until the nameplate was obscured by water and gave a tragic maritime anonymity to the greatest vessel ever to skim the waves.

Over the next hour, all the lifeboats including 3 large inflatables were launched, many prematurely, before they'd reached full capacity. A few more distress rockets lit the sky, but there was no sign of any rescue vessels. In most cases, a "women and children first" protocol was followed by the officers loading the lifeboats.

I was helpless. I could do nothing further. All I could do was watch, but I saw Brendan O'Flanagan, loading children and their mothers into a lifeboat, before he jumped into the ocean.

Out on deck, the ship's band were still playing. As the Titanic plummeted into its death throes, they played on.

The tune was "Nearer, My God, To Thee". I sang the words under my breath, as the cold of the night air began to bite at my lungs.

"Nearer, my God to Thee, nearer to Thee
E'en though it be a cross that raiseth me

Still all my song shall be nearer, my God to thee
Nearer, my God, to Thee, nearer to Thee

Though like the wanderer, the sun gone down
Darkness be over me, my rest a stone

Yet in my dreams I'll be, nearer my God to Thee
Nearer, my God, to Thee, nearer to Thee

Or if on joyful wing, cleaving the sky
Sun, moon, and stars forgot, upward I fly

Still all my song shall be, nearer, my God, to Thee
Nearer, my God, to Thee, nearer to Thee
Nearer, my God, to Thee, nearer to Thee."

I remembered that the hymn was loosely based on Jacob's dream in Genesis 28: verses11-19.

Soon, the ship's bow was fully sunk and the stern began to rise straight up in the air. The remainder of the lights blinked and then went out forever. With a sound like distress call of a thousand dying whales, the forward funnel snapped off, and crashed onto the deck. Shortly after, the enormous metal bulk of the ship broke into 2 pieces and the bow section quickly sank. Then, within a few minutes, the stern section dipped forward and plunged under the waves. It had taken 2 hours and 40 minutes for the unsinkable Titanic to sink. It was obvious that more than a thousand people were still on board when the ship sunk.

I hung on 'til the very last moment, until I was plunged into the coldest water I had ever experienced. Angels didn't ordinarily feel the cold, but in these circumstances I surely did. Angels are not good swimmers, but a lifejacket kept me afloat and I bobbed up and down surrounded by the bodies of shivering or dead people, until I finally passed out.

Then, I found myself back in Heaven sitting on my favourite cloud. The experience had been so distressing that I found it difficult to feel in any way pleased with myself. What had I done to help? My part in saving people had been so small and thousands of people had died. I began to wonder whether I was capable of achieving stars in all the colours of the rainbow to earn my wings. The task in itself had not been any less difficult than previous ones, but the outcome bore very heavily on my conscience. I needed some explanation to reassure me. After what seemed to be a long time brooding about it alone, Gabriel finally turned up.

"Michael, I know this has been different and that you have been troubled by the experience of earning your blue star."

"Yes, I have, Gabriel, and I'm not sure that I can continue with this apprenticeship."

"Let me explain," he said, "Hopefully this will clarify and ease your mind."

"Please!"

"You remember how there is a big difference in how time works in the Earthly and Heavenly Realms?"

"Yes."

"The events that you are transported to in order to help are in a timeframe governed by the Earthly Realm. They are all in the past. They have already happened. We send you there to do what you can, with common sense and beautiful graceful naivety, and what you manage to do is worthwhile, and significant. We can no more stop some of these people dying than we could stop you dying before you came to us. That is not how it works. It cannot be that way. You might say it is written in the stars."

"Will they all be saved and will they all go to Heaven?"

"That isn't determined immediately. What I can say is that those that died will leave with a star in their pocket."

"What about those that survived?"

"They will have longer lives in the Earthly Realm and will all have a chance to die with a star in their pocket, but we have no jurisdiction over that. That depends on the way they live the rest of their lives and what is in their hearts. Do not be sad that you couldn't do more. Be glad that you were able to do something."

"What happened to the people I was able to help?"

"Some of the 3rd class passengers in steerage owe the fact that they were saved entirely to you. Despite instructions, you refused to shoot them when they panicked on the stairs and then you used your heavenly powers to open the scissor gates for them, releasing them from certain death by drowning on board."

"But I opened the gate by shooting off the lock."

"No, Michael, there were no bullets in the gun. Joey was killed by Charlie with the last bullet."

"Did he die with a star in his pocket?"

"Yes, and so did Albert."

That brought a smile to my face.

"What's more," continued Gabriel, "Is that you lit the way with stars from your bag to the best place for the people trapped behind the scissor gate. They made a path towards a lifeboat that could accommodate them all. They all survived."

"What about Brendan O'Flanagan?"

"Ah yes, Brendan jumped into the sea a few minutes before the ship sank and he swam to the nearest lifeboat. He survived."

"I'm so glad."

"Well, Michael you went down with the ship and theoretically you died of hypothermia in the freezing water. But because you are an apprentice angel you are now back here and we are very pleased with you."

"Thank you, Gabriel."

"The biggest lesson here is that, although the Titanic was the largest and best vessel ever built up to that date, the sinking was a result of a catalogue of human errors; flawed construction, inadequate lifeboats, hubris, bad decisions by senior officers, lack of regard for people other than 1st class passengers and a belief, with no basis in fact, that the ship was unsinkable. Humans have self-determination. God is powerless to intervene if they make a mistake or a miscalculation. But humans are never infallible. Do you understand?"

"Yes, I think so."

"Good! Your blue Star will be presented by someone that Brendan told you about,"

"Who will that be?"

"Theodore Roosevelt."

Chapter 7

Indigo Star - 24th December, 1914

"Hello, Michael. It's good to meet you." he said, as he tweaked his bushy moustache between the fingers of his right hand. I recognised him immediately. It was Theodore Roosevelt.

"I wondered when you might turn up." I replied.

"I've got your blue star for you and I had the privilege of watching you earn it. America has changed a great deal since I was the president, but I think it's basically heading in the right direction. What you did for those people on the Titanic was highly commendable, my friend. Those families who were saved have helped to change America into the great nation it has become in the meantime."

"I only did what I felt I had to do at the time and to be honest, it wasn't much."

"It was, however, just enough, Michael. Here is your blue star. You have earned it."

"Thank you, Sir. Does it come with wise words?"

"Why, of course, my boy. I have some pearls of wisdom for you. But tell me, do you have any questions?"

There was the same question burning that had bothered me throughout my apprenticeship as an angel.

"Flitting from Heaven to Earth and back again and experiencing two different concepts of time can be very confusing. Do you have any advice?"

"Yes! Think about this. Nine-tenths of wisdom is being wise in time."

"That will take a lot of thinking about. Wherever I find myself in time, I worry about whether I can always do what's expected of me."

"OK, I understand that, but all you have to do is believe you can and you're halfway there."

"But I don't want to make any mistakes when I find myself in the Earthly Realm."

Theodore laughed, and put his hand on my shoulder. Then he looked straight at me and said, "The only man who never makes a mistake is the man who never does anything."

"Perhaps I can think about all the things you say and try to live up to them."

He turned to walk away, saying, "Of course you can, Michael."

Somehow that Christmas was always destined to be different. Just like every other Christmas, we had spent weeks before enjoying our time helping Santa and the elves getting all the children's presents ready, streamlining Santa's sleigh and polishing Rudolph and the other reindeers noses. We had the usual deadline to meet and everything had to be ready on Christmas Eve.

I think I've said before now, that I've spent a very long, time training to be an angel and enjoying every minute of it. I remember long ago, starting with simple things, like sewing crystals made from raindrops on the edges of clouds, so that they would all have a silver lining. Then I spent some time knitting sunbeams together in the right order to make rainbows and making sure that they were positioned not to touch the ground, so that there was no need to hide a pot of gold at each end. Eventually, I progressed to making clouds; every possible kind, from great big towering cumulonimbus to delicate feather-like cirrus and big dramatic storm clouds with their frightening thunder and lightning. I'd often be sitting with my angel friends on a favourite cloud playing my golden harp and winding harp strings from angel hair and we sometimes invented new colour shades for our skies to help us paint precious gold sunsets blazing day's glorious end. As always, some of my very favourite nights were spent catching falling stars and putting them in my pocket and saving them for a rainy day. Gabriel had given me a special rainbow bag to put my falling stars in, so that they would never fade away. They were very special, because when I needed them I could use them to perform magical deeds.

That Christmas Eve, as I was taking a little rest idly swinging on a star after a hard day's work, I was asked to go and see Gabriel again. He told me that he was continually delighted with my progress and that very soon I would go with my friend Sebastian on a special mission. He said that he knew how rewarding I found guardian angel duty and gently reminded me that it was all about looking after people who needed a bit of help, maybe sitting over someone's shoulder and whispering to them to save them from harm or danger. He said that when I'd gone on my last angel's holiday and so skilfully used that crashing aeroplane as a timely distraction to work my magic deeds; it had brought a tear to his eye and a lump to his throat.

"What is this special mission?" I asked Gabriel, "And what will I be doing?"

He just smiled at me and said it was a great honour to be selected and I'd have to wait and see, because special missions always needed at least two experienced angels to work out what to do for the best. He couldn't tell me where I would be going; just that it would be very soon. I went back to my duties.

I was carrying some moonbeams home in a jar, wondering what my special mission would be, when I bumped into my old friend Sebastian and he told me how excited he was to be going with me.

He knew, that unlike a holiday, a special mission would be much more difficult and that it was a big test only allocated to experienced angels. But he also advised me, that we had to be very, very careful because there were always consequences. Then he said with a broad smile "We'll be fine my friend, if we do the right thing!"

Just like before when I'd gone on my holiday, I found when I tried to sleep that night I was nervous and excited. I kept waking up with very loud and disturbing noises ringing in my ears and each time my eyes were blinded by flashes of the brightest light. The noises and flashes of light were louder, brighter and more violent and insistent than the thunder and lightning of the biggest thunderstorm I'd ever helped to roll together.

The next morning when I woke up, I wasn't on my beautiful cloud with a silver lining, sewn by my own fair hand. I was in a very different place; a trench with a lot of very cold and distressed men, wearing mud splattered khaki uniforms. They were eating cold food out of tins and smoking endless cigarettes. I was wearing the same uniform and my feet were ankle-deep in squelching mud. Every now and then, the leader, who carried a stick and wore a slightly different uniform with a leather flat hat, blew a whistle and then there would be a lot of shouting and the noises and flashes I'd heard and seen earlier would start again from another trench about 200 yards away. The ground shook with every explosion, the noises were ringing in my ears, and smoke billowed up and filled my lungs with choking, acrid, dirty air. Some men climbed out of the top of the trench and ran towards the noises firing their rifles and throwing grenades. There were screams and shouts and lots of very bad language. Most of the men were never seen again, but those who managed to crawl back terrified to the comparative safety of the trench, were covered in mud and blood. Sometimes they dragged back badly injured comrades with fingers, hands, feet or even arms and legs missing.

It was very cold; snow was falling all the time. There were only three colours to be seen in this hellhole; shades of khaki and brown for uniforms and mud, white snow in the skies and collecting in holes in the ground, and red blood running in rivulets in every groove of the ground and often in the wrinkles of the men's faces. There was an awful burnt, charred, sickly smell.

As suddenly as the commotion had begun, it stopped. The whole world seemed to breathe a sigh of relief. But big, tough looking men were crying like babies, injured men were screaming in agony, dying men were stuttering their last prayers. There was very little anyone could do to help. I was very afraid.

A man next to me leaned against the back of the trench, lit a cigarette and turned to look at me. He had fear in his bloodshot weary eyes and his face was contorted as he cried and issued some despairing words.

"They told us it would be over by Christmas and all us brave boys would be going home as heroes. We're fighting for king and country, they said. What do they know?"

We sat there for a while in the despair and desolation, only waiting for the next whistle to spring us into another futile action. The snow began to pile up in the hollows in the ground and there was a rush of icy chill which cut right through me and then the leader in the leather hat hit me with his stick and shouted at me, "Oy! New boy! Go with the work detail to collect the dead bodies. Hold up this Red Cross flag and if you're lucky the bastards over there might not shoot you."

My companion, who had told me about the Christmas promise, was assigned to lead the work detail. He reluctantly finished smoking his cigarette, looked at me and said, "I'm Ernie Williams from Whitechapel. Where'd you come from, Sonny?"

Before I could answer, the leader snarled as us, "Nobody gives a flying fuck what your names are. Just do as you are told. Now! Or you will be target practice for tomorrow morning's firing squad."

Ernie, myself and 3 others got to our feet ready to go as lambs to the slaughter.

Leather hat put on his sternest grimmest face and ushered me and the others over the top of the trench, into the cold unrelenting wind of no-man's land and pointed us towards the opposite trench. As I climbed nervously over the top, something very strange happened. All the men started singing.

"God save our gracious king, long live our noble king, God save our king..."

It sounded very out of place in this hell on Earth.

We all stumbled forward in a daze, edging our way through the freezing mud and depressions filled with snow, barbed wire, discarded weapons and hats, and bits of bodies, peering through the snow, with smoke and the stench of death in our nostrils. As I negotiated my way, expecting to be felled by machine gun fire any moment, I thought I saw another man with a Red Cross flag moving towards me from the enemy trench. He was wearing a different uniform. It was a funny shade of darkish green, with a thin red band around his hat. Then another strange thing happened. From the trench in front of me I heard more singing, almost like a protesting chant of the singing behind me.

"Deutschland, Deutschland uber alles, uber alles in der Weldt....."

As the other man with the flag drew closer, I thought I recognised him. No! My eyes were playing tricks with me. Surely not! It can't be! We were only a few steps away from each other. A familiar smile, a hand offered in friendship. I clasped the hand and shook it with all my compassion.

"Sebastian! Sebastian! My dear friend, I am so glad to see you." I spluttered.

"Hello, Michael. I'm so pleased you are here. We have work to do. Are you ready?" my fellow angel replied.

Instinctively we pulled our rainbow bags from our pockets.

"You know what to do, don't you?" Sebastian said. I nodded, and we set off in opposite directions, scattering handfuls of our collected falling stars from our rainbow bags into the air, up and down the unholy area of no-man's land. They floated in the misty, snow filled atmosphere, twinkling in gentle flickering snowflakes and slowly glided down to the mud beneath our feet. After a while, when our pouches had been emptied, the ground was aglow with a strange translucent indigo light, which seemed to swirl like a ghostly whirlpool. The singing from either side had stopped and we could see candles being lit and the eyes of men peering over the tops of the trenches in curiosity.

Suddenly, there was singing again, but not the patriotic, divisive words of earlier. Behind me they sang, "Silent night, holy night, all is calm, all is bright..."

In front of me they sang, "Stille Nacht, heilige Nacht, Alles schläft; einsam wacht..."

But they sang together, in harmony, beautifully, the same tune, but different words.

Sebastian and I just stood there smiling at each other. Over and over again, the song echoed out across the field we had been preparing. And then, just before dawn, the song ended with a collective triumphant chorus.

From one side they concluded with, "Jesus, Lord, at Thy birth, Jesus, Lord, at Thy birth."

And from the other, "Christ, in deiner Geburt! Christ, in deiner Geburt!"

There was a pause, like the whole world was standing still for a moment, and then a stream of a million blindingly bright twinkling stars, began falling like a glorious continuous rain shower, making their way in a magnificent triumphant drizzling blanket, out of the fast fading blackness of the heavens, and down to cover the ground .

We spontaneously hugged each other and as we did this, men began climbing out of the opposite trenches running towards us, shouting "Merry Christmas!" and " Fröhliche Weihnachten!"

Soon we were surrounded by men from both sides, shaking hands, smiling, laughing and swapping cigarettes and sweets. The bright twinkling stars swirled all around all of us, seeming to wrap us in a huge sense of relief and joy. Then the men formed a circle around Sebastian and me, and each man took a snow ball out of his pocket and with a tumultuous shout of," Hurrah! Hurrah! Hurrah!" threw the snowballs in the air above our heads. We ducked, both expecting to be hit by an avalanche of wet snow. Then there was another long silence, as if the whole Universe was taking a deep breath, followed by a huge flash of blinding light. Everybody flattened themselves quickly on the ground, thinking the hostilities had begun again, but when they dared to look up; out of the new dawn light a football fell to the ground. Sebastian got to his feet and kicked the football in the air and that signalled the start of a kick about.

Some men threw down their coats for makeshift goals and soon Tommies United were playing Hermann Athletic, with one hundred men a side, and nobody counting the goals scored. In a strange ironic twist, the Tommies' goalkeeper was Werner Karlsblatt, a butcher from Wiesbaden, and the

Hermann's top scorer was Sidney Whitehouse, a blacksmith from Redditch, and nobody was in the least bit worried about that.

"We've done a good job here, Sebastian." I smiled at my angel comrade, as the game continued around us.

"Indeed we have, Michael, my friend." he replied.

We stood in what would have been the centre circle of the makeshift football pitch, very pleased with ourselves, as the ball came flying through the air towards us. We both jumped up to head the ball, cracked heads and fell to the floor knocked out.

When I opened my eyes, I was back on my favourite cloud, and Sebastian was sitting next to me.

"We did the right thing, my friend." he smiled," Or we wouldn't be back here now."

And with that, we carried on catching falling stars and putting them in our pockets and saving them for a rainy day. A few days later, we were back on the cloud, talking about our special mission, when Gabriel turned up.

"I am so pleased with you, Michael and Sebastian," he said, "Christmas was different for those men this year, but you do need to know that sadly the next day the fighting resumed."

"So what was the point then?" I asked, feeling a little confused.

"Ah, well," Gabriel explained, "You see, it's a fact that sooner or later all the men there that day will die, if not in battle, then after the war is over. That's just the way life is."

"Yes, I know that," I said, "But that doesn't explain why we went."

Gabriel sighed, "My friend, you still have much to learn."

He paused, and his face broke into gentle smile, "Michael!" he said, "Because of the work that you and Sebastian did on that Christmas day, every man there will benefit. Whether they died as enemies on the battlefield or carried their awful memories of the conflict into old age, when they reach Heaven, they will all be friends."

Then he passed me a piece of parchment, with a beautiful golden handwritten poem called "Armistice" written on it, and said, "Read this, my friend. It might help you to understand."

"My boy's years behind me, once eager and bold,
For King and for Country, for freedom I'm told,

Kitchener wants me, with courage inspired,
To beat down the Kaiser, and save the Empire.

We marched off to war, patriotic and proud,
Girls cheered and threw flowers, bands played long and loud,
But excitement soon done, the ugly truth dawned;
For battle in Flanders, unlearned and unwarned.

In waterlogged trenches, all barbed wire and mud,
Machines guns and mustard gas, wasted our blood,
Deafened and deadened, and shellshocked and spent,
As four year's of comrades in arms came and went.

In safety remote great Generals planned,
Sacrifices relentless for acres of land,
At Ypres and Verdun and along the Somme,
In savage abandon, shells, bullets and bombs.

Then orders came down, "Attack! Boys Attack!"
As dark stench of death hung heavy and black,
And choking back tears, with no chance for Goodbyes,
I watched helpless as brave men were blown to the skies.

All the King's horses and all the King's men,
Couldn't patch Charlie together again,
In my pocket his diary to give to his wife,
Not much to show for such a young life.

Today there's a strange eerie sense in the air,
There's rumours an armistice has been declared,
Have the Germans surrendered? Have we won victory?
Is it over for good, or just temporary?

So they've worked out a truce timed precise to the minute,
A ceasefire dreamed up by a war-monger cynic,
In some mad numbers game eleven was chosen,
Fate marched to that standstill. The instant was frozen.

Though sadder and wiser we came home as men,
A land fit for heroes they promised us then,
A fast fading band who fought a lost cause,
now remembers the War an end to all wars."

"Keep that," he said, "And read it, over and over. It tells you all you need to know."

Then, before he left, Gabriel looked at me and added, "Michael, you have earned your indigo star, and it will be presented to you by a man called Benjamin Disraeli."

Chapter 8

Violet Star - 11th September, 2001

One of the most difficult tasks that all angels were trained to do in Heaven, was to spend their time painting rainbows. To do this, I was issued with a small handheld device called a rainbow wand. Pure white light was not difficult to find in Heaven, but harnessing it to produce rainbows wasn't easy. First thing was to get the rainbow wand to collect water droplets. Then, you had to aim it very precisely in the section of sky directly opposite the Sun. Finally, and after much practice, I managed to get the colour bands in the right order and consistency from red on the outer side to violet on the inner side. The fun bit was to fly quickly through the heavens in a perfect semi-circular arc, releasing the rainbow into the sky. Imperfect rainbows disappeared in a split second, but once you got it right, you could sit back and admire your rainbow with the other angels until it dissipated naturally. I had just painted a wonderful bright rainbow across the Yorkshire Dales, when Gabriel popped in to talk to me.

"Michael, you have done very well so far," he praised, "But your tasks will now become far more difficult. You already have some understanding of the way time may behave differently when there are connections between the Earthly and Heavenly Realms, but there is much more to learn."

"What do I need to do to prepare?"

"That is just the thing, Michael. You cannot prepare. You must go armed only with your beautiful graceful naivety and your common sense and just do what seems to be right. Your previous experiences on the tasks you have been successful in so far will be useful, but there is much more to learn and the only way to learn it is on the job."

"OK! I think I understand." I replied.

"I believe you are beginning to." Gabriel smiled, "Just do your best."

Suddenly, I was sitting on a bench in Blenheim Circus Park, alongside the terracotta coloured tarmac path, fringed by the early summer flowerbeds blooming luxuriously with peonies, primula and clematis in neatly arranged bursts of a myriad of colours. When I looked around me, I saw a splendid display of huge blue and pink blooms on the azalea and rhododendron shrubs.

I noticed that I was dressed light and casually, in t-shirt and jeans adorned by what had been my favourite designer labels, and my Dolce and Gabbana trainers. Courtney was sitting beside me. Her hair was shorter and she looked a little older and plumper. On her lap was a toddler, a baby boy, dressed very smartly in light blue designer babywear. He looked somehow familiar. It quickly occurred to me that Courtney couldn't see me. I desperately wanted to speak to her, and to tell her how much I loved and missed her, but it was impossible because to her I was invisible. That was immensely frustrating. I was there, but I wasn't there. How could that be possible?

I could hear and see a band was playing over on the bandstand. I recognised the sounds. It was Redberryash. The song was they were singing was "Clear September Sky - Question".

"Action and reaction in line forever stand,
Jump from the bridge Oblivion,
Into a blood-stained hand,
Whilst Empathy and Apathy,
Stare on in disbelief,
And streams of tears cascade,
Over waterfalls of grief.

Pandora's Box falls open, and we step back in awe,
And wonder what in Heaven's Name,
Is all this fighting for?
And building in his wilderness, great monuments to sin,
The heathen shakes God's golden gates,
And pleads to be let in.

Young heroes die together, old villains live apart,
We speak of love thy neighbour,
But hate still fills our hearts,
Forgotten or forgiven, dark tyranny endures,

Long memory 'n' swift vengeance,
Are they mine, or are they yours?

It's only one small step, just another grain of sand,
From Once upon a Time, to Never-Never Land,
All the castles in the air, all the fallout from the blast,
All the secrets that we keep, all the stones that we may cast,
Still mean nothing in the end, have no reason and no rhyme,
Falling out of Never-Never Land to Once upon a Time,
Falling out of Never-Never Land to Once upon a Time."

I was so engrossed in listening to the words of the song, that I didn't see when Courtney and the toddler disappeared. I was sat on the park bench alone at the end of the song. Something very strange happened. I saw myself jogging by, dressed exactly as I had been on that early summer evening in May; the same evening that the Captain's Table terrorist attack occurred. There were 2 Michael Hartsons; one on the bench and one jogging along the terracotta path?

Words rattled around my head; words I'd heard before, spoken by a soft and gentle voice.

"Take a deep breath.
Look around you.
It's a beautiful world if you let it be.
Enjoy the warm sunshine.
Drink in the blue sky.
Smell the flowers.
Delight in their colours.
See the happiness of people together.
Listen to the birds singing and the ducks quacking.
Hear the music.
Feel the satisfaction in the blend of music and words.
Take your time.
Live your life at a stroll not a sprint."

There he was; the tramp that I had known as George O'Donnell was sat at the other end of the bench. He was still and silent. A black light shone through him. He turned and smiled at me and suddenly "Whoosh!"

I found myself falling, falling out of Never-Never Land to Once upon a Time. In a flash, I was somewhere else. I was in the departure lounge of a busy airport in North America. It was just before 7.30 am on a beautiful blue bright September morning. Logan International Airport in Boston was just another airport on just another working day. People were moving to and fro in every direction, some carrying bags or cases, going about their business, just as on any Tuesday morning.

I ordered a coffee at the refreshment desk and sat down to read "Time" magazine. Half a page and 3 slurps later, the airport public address system requested passengers for American Airlines flight number 11, bound for Los Angeles International Airport, California, to proceed to the boarding gate B32. I shuffled forwards with my fellow passengers and boarded the plane. I was greeted by two cheerful, smiling flight attendants called Betty and Amy.

There were plenty of empty seats on board and I decided to sit somewhere near the back of the plane, and concentrate on my magazine. The Boeing 767 moved to the runway and took off at 07.59 am; 14 minutes late.

Opposite me on the other side of the aisle was a tall, well-built man in a smart grey business suit and an open-necked light blue shirt. I noticed he was reading the same issue of "Time" magazine as me.

"Good article on page 34, my friend." said the man in the opposite aisle.

I turned to acknowledge his advice and then he added, "Forgive me. Good morning. I'm Jack, Jack Connolly-Travers."

I returned his greeting, "Michael Hartson, pleased to meet you."

"What's your purpose in flying to L.A. today, Mike?" he asked.

I improvised with, "Always wanted to go there; doing a bit of California dreaming."

"Good a reason as any." he replied, "I live there. Got a big house on the Westside. I've been in the cinematic business for 20 years. I've been in New York negotiating a big deal for a major movie network. Now I'm going home to see my wife and kids."

He took a few photographs of his nearest and dearest from his jacket pocket and flashed them to me quickly. I examined them politely, and then was distracted by a nearby flight attendant, hoping that she could soon ply me with a fresh coffee.

"Is this flight usually this empty?" I asked a flight attendant

"It varies a lot; depends on what day of the week it is. Friday's are busy though." she replied with a smile, and then added, "We only have 81 passengers today, so you're going to get great service from the cabin crew."

"That's good! Keep the coffee coming then."

"No problem, Sir. Have you been to L.A. before?"

"No, it's my first visit there."

"It's a great, bustling city. Hollywood is where imagination becomes reality and dreams come true. You'll love it."

"I hope so. How long is the flight?"

"Maybe 5 hours. Are you in the movie industry or entertainment business, Sir?"

"No!" I laughed.

"What do you do?"

I had to think quickly. "I'm a trouble shooter for a very well-known company." She winked at me and moved to the next coffee guzzler.

About 15 minutes into the flight, there was a commotion at the front of the plane. When I looked up, I could see two Middle Eastern men near the front, with knives in their hands. Passengers were screaming and shouting. There was a short scuffle. Two flight attendants were stabbed.

"What the fuck's going on up there?" Jack asked looking at me.

"I don't know, but let's quietly move forwards." I replied.

Getting up out of our seats unnoticed, we moved forward until we were sitting in row 10. As we moved, three more men walked forward towards the cockpit. It was clear that the plane was being hijacked.

"Shit!" said Jack, "I don't like the look of this. These guys are terrorists. We're in trouble."

I didn't think it was a good idea to draw attention to ourselves, so I put my finger across my mouth indicating him to "Shush!"

We both sat and listened to the small items of activity around us. Some women nearby began to cry quietly. Some men sat on the edge of their seats, looking as if they might spring into action if the opportunity arose to overpower the gang of hijackers. I could hear Betty on the airphone, reporting back to the authorities at American Airlines.

Quietly and calmly she said, "The cockpit is not answering, somebody's stabbed in business class—and I think there's Mace—that we can't breathe—I don't know, I think we're getting hijacked. Two cabin crew have been stabbed."

Shortly afterwards, Amy reported, "There are five hijackers, all Middle Eastern. They've come from first-class seats: 2A, 2B, 9A, 9C and 9B."

Most passengers were by now frozen in fear. Sitting in row 10, and not wishing to draw attention to myself, I buried my face in my magazine, occasionally peeping out from behind it. When I focussed back and turned to page 34, the words swirled round and round as if my eyes were stirring up a whirlpool. After a few seconds the page had reformed into an image of names and faces:

"Mohamed Atta, Abdulaziz al-Omari, Wail al-Shehri, Waleed al-Shehri, and Satam al-Suqami"

"What was the reason for that?" I asked myself, "What could I do?"

Perhaps we were all helpless? The hijack had happened so quickly and viciously with passengers being stabbed. I feared that Jack would do something stupid, when he stood up, moved forward and asked to speak to one of the terrorists. There was a short interchange of angry words and a brief scuffle in which he dropped to the floor. Then he crawled back to his seat with a bloody mouth, 2 teeth missing and a large lump developing on his cheek, where he had been kicked in the head. An agitated voice broke over the air intercom speaking in short staccato sentences.

"We have some planes. Just stay quiet and you'll be okay. We are returning to the airport."

Was it a wave of relief or an air of utter disbelief that fell over the frightened passengers?

A few seconds later, there was another message, "Nobody move. Everything will be okay. If you try to make any moves, you'll endanger yourself and the airplane. Just stay quiet."

Confusion reigned in troubled minds, as this brought no new information or reassurance.

Shortly after that transmission, the engine note changed dramatically, as the plane made a rapid change of direction, banking steeply to more terrified shouting and screaming.

Then the voice on the air intercom repeated, "Nobody move please. We are going back to the airport. Don't try to make any stupid moves."

Jack looked at me, and whispered through a blood stained handkerchief, "We're heading south towards New York. I don't know what these mad bastards are playing at, but my gut feeling is that maybe they don't know themselves."

One of the terrorists looked over in our direction and I quickly gestured for my cinematic friend to remain quiet. He ignored me and continued to whisper,

"The boys from NORAD will be on the case soon. They're the military defence force. They'll give these no-hopers something to think about. If they want some serious kick-arse, just stick around and see what you get."

I began to imagine what would happen if we became surrounded by military planes. How would the hijackers react? What could possibly be done to retrieve the situation? In the wrong circumstances, I feared that perhaps the military authorities would have no hesitation in shooting our 767 out of the skies.

About 10 minutes after the course change, I heard Amy speaking on the airphone. "Something is wrong. We are in a rapid descent... we are all over the place."

After a brief silence she spoke again, "I see the water. I see the buildings. I see buildings..."

I peeped out of the window. Jack realised far too loudly, "New York. Shit! They're going to crash onto New York City."

There was another pause, and then Amy reported, "We are flying low. We are flying very, very low. We are flying way too low."

Seconds later she said, "Oh my God, we are way too low."

Jack shouted again, "We're headed straight for the World Trade Center."

The twin engines of the 767 created a deafening roar towards a maximum speed. Passengers cowered low in their seats, uttering silent prayers; their faces tear stained and contorted. The claustrophobic confines of the plane were drenched heavily, in a trembling, tumultuous tsunami of fear.

I sensed that it was time to take action and ran to the front of the plane. My body was riddled with bullets from two of the hijacker's pistols. The bullets went right through me, as if I was made of fresh air. I felt no impact or pain. Once at the front of the plane, I removed my rainbow wand from my pocket and walked slowly towards the back of plane, circling the wand around and around, enveloping the interior of the fuselage in a swirl of magnificent protective rainbow colours. The terrorists stood transfixed and confused as to why I had not gone down in their short hail of bullets.

A split second before flight 11 ploughed into the North Tower of the World Trade Centre, I found myself in an infinitely small place at the back of the aircraft. I looked back towards the cockpit. My rainbow wand had spun a perfect soft and welcoming circle over the inside of the fuselage of the aircraft, enclosing the inside of the doomed plane in a brilliant light filled swirling cocoon of the brightest rainbow shades. I called out softly, "Come this way! Follow me!"

All the passengers and then the aircrew rose from their seats and with beaming smiles on their faces, walked slowly through the embracing rainbow tunnel towards me. Everyone on the plane, except for the terrorists, escaped into the rainbow swirl, and went instantly up to Heaven, each of them with a star in their pocket. Before we left, I saw Jack talking to the terrorists. He was the last man and he shook my hand vigorously as we escaped. I never knew why I had the names and faces of the hijackers imprinted in my memory, but I was certain that somehow they had been prevented from joining their captives.

My work was done, but for a while I was in some kind of suspended animation. It seemed that I was trapped inside a never ending time tunnel. The linear time that I was used to in the Earthly Realm did not happen here. Here, time twisted and turned and undulated and tumbled. I fell tumbling and turning into another place and time.

But strangely, I found I was boarding a plane, a Boeing 767, at Logan International Airport in Boston, exactly as I had done about an hour before. I wondered whether time had in some bizarre way distorted, to transport me back to when I had boarded flight number 11.

I thought to myself, "This is some weird kind of déjà vu!"

I noticed that I had a watch on my wrist, and that had never been the case with any other of my tasks. When I looked at the watch, it looked strangely familiar. My TAG Heuer Aquaracer indicated that it was 07.30 am. Only about 60 passengers boarded the plane, and just as on flight 11, there were loads of empty seats. Once again I decided to sit at the back.

Within a few minutes, all was quickly clarified, when a member of the cabin staff announced the imminent departure of United Airlines flight number 175, for Los Angeles International Airport, California. So, I told myself, I was on a similar plane, at the same airport, but a different flight, on the same day, to the same destination, at slightly different time. The plane took off a little late, at 08.14 am.

We were 5 minutes in the air, when I picked up my copy of "Time" magazine, and it fell open at the page 34. When I focussed on the page, it happened again. The words swirled round and round, as if my eyes were stirring up a whirlpool. When the page reformed, it revealed an image of names and faces:

"Marwan al-Shehhi, Fayez Banihammad, Mohand al-Shehri, Hamza al-Ghamdi, and Ahmed al-Ghamdi"

Was my mind playing tricks with me? These were different names and different, if not dissimilar faces. There were just too many coincidences. I knew what had happened earlier in my time frame, while I had been on flight 11, but why did events on flight 175 seem to be a repeat with minor variations?

It was time for me to be on full alert. I decided to watch anything and everything very carefully from that moment on. I scanned the seats for further clues and nearly jumped out of my skin when I noticed a tall, well-built man in a smart grey business suit and an open-necked light blue shirt on the other side of the aisle. It was Jack Connolly-Travers. He was reading "Time" magazine. He turned and winked at me. Soon we reached our cruising height and the plane levelled off. I took the opportunity to visit the toilet, carefully scanning the passengers as I moved forwards. I noticed a dispersed group of five Middle Eastern passengers ahead of me; the faces that had appeared on page 34. When I returned to my seat, I looked out of the window at the clear blue skies and saw the silver flash of another plane somewhere south of our position.

Suddenly I heard shouting and screaming, coming from the front of the plane. The group of Middle Eastern men had risen from their seats in row 2 and a little further back in rows 6 and 9 with knives in hands. It was difficult to determine exactly what was happening, but clearly this plane was also being hijacked.

One of the passengers in a seat quite close to me, made a phone call. He said, quietly, "I think they've taken over the cockpit—an attendant has been stabbed—and someone else up front may have been killed. The plane is making strange moves. Call United Airlines—tell them it's Flight 175, Boston to LA."

Then I heard one of the flight attendants, reporting that the flight had been hijacked. She added that both pilots had been killed, a flight attendant had been stabbed and that the hijackers were probably flying the plane. Shortly after that the plane changed direction. Nearby, my new friend Jack whispered, "Son of a bitch! They're heading for New York City."

The man who had made the previous call, phoned again, "It's getting bad, Dad. A stewardess was stabbed. They seem to have knives and Mace. They said they have a bomb. It's getting very bad on the plane. Passengers are throwing up and getting sick. The plane is making jerky movements. I don't think the pilot is flying the plane. I think we are going down. I think they intend to go to Chicago or someplace and fly into a building. Don't worry, Dad. If it happens, it'll be very fast. My God! My God!"

The call ended abruptly. A woman screamed as the plane banked steeply to the left. Engines were screeching wildly up to a maximum speed. A split second before flight 175 scythed its left wing into the South Tower of the World Trade Centre, I saw Jack standing at the emergency exit over the right hand wing. He took a small velvet bag out of his pocket, and spread its contents over the floor of the plane. A million bright twinkling stars lit a narrow path out through the fuselage, and all the way along to the wingtip. Time stood still.

"Everybody! Quickly! Come this way!" he shouted.

The passengers and aircrew rose from their seats. All their pent up trepidation and stark fear immediately dispersed. Every man, woman and child, without hesitation, and with beaming smiles on their faces, walked slowly towards where Jack was standing and turned along the star strewn path to safety. Everyone on the plane escaped into the starlight, and went instantly up to Heaven, each of them with a star in their pocket. I knew what I had to do!

I stood alongside Jack and the five terrorists came towards me one at a time, all young men in their twenties. I recognised each one from my fuzzed page in "Time" magazine, Marwan al-Shehhi, Fayez Banihammad, Mohand al-Shehri, Hamza al-Ghamdi, and Ahmed al-Ghamdi. With tears in my eyes, I held my hand up, and denied them access to the sanctuary of the star trail. Their smiles vanished, before their faces dissolved, as they disappeared into a horrific void of blackness. It seemed cruel, but Jack reassured me, "Remember, my friend, these young impressionable men have already made their choice. They are going to their own heaven, where they can spend the whole of Eternity searching aimlessly for the 21 virgins each of them has been promised in their indoctrinations."

We shook hands and arm in arm, made our way out along the right wing of the plane.

Once again, my work was done, and once again I found myself in some kind of suspended animation, another never ending time tunnel. Linear time didn't prevail here. Again time twisted and turned, and undulated and tumbled. Once again, I fell, tumbling and turning into yet another place and time.

Suddenly, I was back in place I knew very well. Sitting on a bench in Blenheim Circus Park, I could see Heidi-Maria, Melissa and Courtney sitting beside me. Courtney looked absolutely beautiful in a floral patterned smock style dress and was clearly very pregnant. The smell of springtime freshness was in the air. The flowerbeds of the garden were filled with daffodils in all shades of yellow and amazingly vibrant red tulips. The warmth of early season sunshine shone on the faces of the procession of people moving through the park along the terracotta path. Again, a band was playing. It was Redberryash, and the song was "Clear September Sky - Answer"

"Just another Trader's day
In a clear September sky,
Where the tallest stone and steel trees proudly grow.
Deadly arrow's suicide aim,
For some heathen God-less name,
Sends trees crashing to the streets far below.

The Sand Angel's evil hand,
Hurled a curse upon this Land,
Swirling shadows dark to hide the Devil's breath.
At ground zero's great impasse,
Wise eyes through the looking glass
Spied the Angel's new name, became "Death".

And as long as Freedom lives;
Must we forget? Must we forgive?
Stone-hearted men who bend the lens of time,
For they stand on shifting sands;
May forever they be damned,
For our Lord assured, "Vengeance is mine!"

It's only one small step, just another grain of sand
From Once upon a Time, to Never-Never Land.
All the castles in the air, all the fallout from the blast,
All the secrets that we keep, all the stones that we may cast,
Still mean nothing in the end, have no reason and no rhyme,
Falling out of Never-Never Land to Once upon a Time,
Falling out of Never-Never Land to Once upon a Time."

When the song finished, Courtney and the girls had vanished. George O'Donnell was sat at the other end of the bench. A black light shone through him. He smiled at me, and Whoosh!

In a flash, I was somewhere else.

I found myself falling again. Was I falling out of Never-Never Land to Once upon a Time?

Skies above me were damp and hazy and I could see sunshine glinting through raindrops, as they fell quietly on to the green undulating pastures of Wensleydale. I surfed slowly downwards, along the soft curve of a magnificent rainbow; not one of mine. No! This rainbow had been fashioned by the expert hand of someone much more experienced.

"One of my best, I think." said a voice, adding, "What do you think?"

"Certainly, it's one of the most wonderful and vibrant rainbows I've ever seen." I replied.

There was no pot of gold at the end, but there was a dandily dressed man, wearing his hair in Shirley Temple ringlets, and sporting a canary yellow velvet waistcoat over his lace-and-brocade flamboyance.

He extended a limp wrist in my direction, as if to lift me foppishly off the end of the rainbow. I grasped his hand, noticing the lacy cuffs of his silk shirt and he said quietly, "I've been expecting you Michael. You are becoming quite a legend here in Heaven. I'm going to present you with your indigo star. My name is Benjamin Disraeli."

"I'm very pleased to meet you, Sir."

"No need to be formal, young man. We are all cut from the same fine cloth here."

"OK! How shall I refer to you in your finery?" I asked, tuning into his ambience.

"Call me anything you like; Benjy, Dizzi. But all of this is no matter. You have been on a difficult journey earning your indigo star. How do you feel?"

"Well Benjy I'm not sure! I've been whooshing here and there, from place to place and time to time. Some very confusing things have been happening."

"Even in the mixture of Realms in which we dwell, it is often true to say that what we anticipate seldom occurs: but what we least expect generally happens."

"Sometimes, I have wondered if I am sufficiently well equipped to deal with the situations before me and the last task is a great example. This beautiful graceful naivety business can be both a benefit and a burden."

"You have learned well if you believe that to be the case. I have often determined that to be conscious that you are ignorant of the facts is a great step to knowledge."

"I might need to think about that for a while before it becomes clear. After each task, I am most concerned about whether my actions are good enough, are timely and whether I have done everything possible?"

"What do you mean by that, Michael?"

"Well, people still die, and I'd be happier if that could be prevented."

"You know it can't Michael. Our good friend Gabriel has already explained that to you. You must remember that action may not always bring happiness; but there is no happiness without action."

With that my new pal, Benjy took the indigo star from his pocket, and wearing a cheeky grin, he pressed the star into my palm. You've earned this, truly, and now you are at the end of your rainbow, you have shown that you can live up to the assertion that man is only great when he acts from passion."

"And I've always done that, have I?"

"You have always tried to do that, and that's all you need to do. I saw the way you yearned to talk to Courtney in the park and I felt your pain when you realised she couldn't see you."

"I didn't understand why I was suddenly back in the park."

"I know! But you will, Michael, you will."

He smiled at me as if to say, "Lessons learned!", and then he said, "I must be going. We will meet again, I am sure."

When I realised that I was alone once again, the rainbow over the Yorkshire Dales had vanished. In a split second I was back on my favourite cloud and in Heaven making new rainbows.

Chapter 9

White Star - 6th August, 1945

There were a lot of loose threads and unanswered questions, generated by the task I had just completed. It was certainly true that the situations I had experienced to earn my rainbow of stars had become progressively more complicated, sometimes confusing, and often distressing in terms of the little I was able to do to help. But, I thought carefully about when, where and how I had been able to intervene to make sure that the victims of the many disasters found their way quickly up to Heaven; each of them with a star in their pocket. I felt that I had earned my violet star and completed all my assignments to achieve the rainbow, and along the way I had learned many valuable lessons, both from the tasks themselves, and also from the wonderful people that had presented me with my collection of stars. Now it seemed that I was in the old routines, back to the simple things that we do up in Heaven; making clouds, snow, hail and rainbows. Enjoyable and therapeutic though these tasks were, I was impatient, and began to ask myself a lot of difficult questions.

"Had I done something wrong along the way and failed to earn the Angel's Rainbow?"

"Where was Gabriel? He hadn't appeared at the end of the last task to tell me who was going to present me with my violet star."

"Was Gabriel displeased with me?"

"Why was there a delay?"

"Was there a delay or was this the way that things were supposed to happen?"

"Was this just another demonstration of how time worked differently in Heaven?"

That night, I fell into a fitful sleep and heard disturbing and alarming words, repeated over and over again.

"Oh, fatal day - oh, day of sorrow,
It was no trouble she could borrow;
But in the future she could see
The clouds of infelicity."

After a short pause, the words continued:

"He is the bird of ill omen.
How harsh his midnight cry!
It seems to shriek, in mournful sounds,
Death! Death!"

I didn't understand why these words kept coming back to me to haunt my thoughts again and again. The next day continued the same as the last, and then the day after, and still there was no sign of Gabriel, and no hint of recognition that my apprenticeship was complete.

Then the next night continued the same as the last, and the night after, and every night the same words were repeated.

"Oh, fatal day - oh, day of sorrow,
It was no trouble she could borrow;
But in the future she could see
The clouds of infelicity.
He is the bird of ill omen.
How harsh his midnight cry!
It seems to shriek, in mournful sounds,
Death! Death!"

After many days and nights of worrying and tossing and turning, at last something happened to break the chain. I was sitting on my cloud watching a beautiful red sunset, when a handsome man came walking towards me, with a slow and relaxed confident stride. He stopped and sat down beside me. I couldn't help but notice, that he wore a perfectly pressed light grey suit, a dazzling white shirt and a skinny blue and dark grey striped tie. His coal black shoes were pointed and highly polished.

"Hi Michael! I'm John Fitzgerald Kennedy." he smiled.

I shook his outstretched hand, as he added, "I've heard such a lot of good things about you."

"I've been expecting you. Well, I've been expecting somebody." I said.

"Sorry, but there's been so much work to do and I've spent a long time talking to Gabriel about your final task."

"I thought I was finished and that I'd earned all my stars."

"Not yet, Michael. But let's get everything in the right order. First of all, I'm here to say well done and to present you with your violet star. Your last task was so difficult, dangerous and different to anything you have experienced before. The 911 terrorist events were the worst, most underhand, dirty and low down attacks on my beloved country in its long and bloody history and I'm so glad you were sent there to help by diverting some people away from the carnage. It was worse in many ways than the Japanese attack on Pearl Harbour in December 1941. But as usual, Michael, you came through with flying colours."

That made me feel very humble, and I think he noticed.

Then he giggled, "Whoops! That's a bit ironic, isn't it? The task was all about flying and then earning colours."

He took the violet star out of his suit pocket and shook my hand again, and wearing the widest toothy smile said, "So this is the final star of your rainbow, Michael. Congratulations!"

I took the star from him, glad at last to know that I had been worthy of it.

"Now," he said, "There is one more mission that we have to send you on. The reason for this is obvious, if you think about it. You obviously know how rainbows are produced from pure white light, so you'll figure where all the colours that you've earned so far have come from."

"So are you telling me now, that I have to go back to perform another task in the Earthly Realm?"

"Precisely, and this time it will be a task that will entitle you to a white star."

"Oh, I get it! A white star of course."

We sat and smiled at each other for a while.

Then he said, "You've been troubled for a while, haven't you?"

"Yes!" I replied, "Had voices repeating things to me night after night, again and again. It has set me right on edge."

"Those voices are relevant to your final mission. Do not be too concerned, but do be alert and aware. All will become clear. When you need me, I will be there to help you, my friend."

I felt reassured, knowing that whatever I still had to do, this great man was going to help me.

"Let me start by giving you a few pieces of advice right now." he said.

I'd been through this process of gathering pearls of wisdom from other great men after my previous tasks. I set myself to listen and learn.

"Did you know that when written in Chinese, the word 'crisis' is composed of two characters?"

"No, I didn't, but why is that relevant?"

"Because, the first character represents danger, and the other represents opportunity. What you need to do is reflect on all your tasks completed and understand how each of them was a crisis which generated danger, and thereby created opportunity."

I quickly thought through my excursions back to the Earthly Realm and realised the significance of what my companion was saying.

We stared at the last dying rays of the magnificent sunset, and when he knew I was ready, he added, "It is important, Michael, that you understand that whether we are in the Earthly or Heavenly Realm, we must ensure that we use time as a tool, not as a couch."

That seemed to be a salutary lesson, especially bearing in mind the usual difficulties and confusions in trying to understand how time behaved differently in each Realm. Then the former President waved casually, and said, "See you around, Michael."

He was gone. I was glad I had been given the opportunity to meet him.

It wasn't much more than a few seconds later when Gabriel arrived on my cloud.

"So, Michael," he said, "You have now earned all the stars in the colours of the rainbow, and now you know that there is still more to do."

"Yes, President Kennedy told me about the white star."

Gabriel looked deep into my eyes and said, "This will be the most difficult task you have ever encountered. You will be in several different places at the same time, you will not be visible, and however hard you may try, you will apparently not be able to provide any help."

That sounded absolutely pointless, so I asked, "What will be the point then?"

He replied, "To teach you the final lesson."

"I don't understand!" I said, "What is the final lesson?"

Gabriel was very patient with me as he explained, "There will be times when you can do nothing to help. What will be, will be. Remember all the places you have been sent back to, are in the past, they are history. We cannot change history. History is the foundation stone for the future. Terrible things will happen, and many people's lives may be affected, or shortened, or terminated by them. That is something that we can't change. But throughout history, there have been angels who have done what they could to help a few, while understanding that they cannot save the many. You could say that Jesus Christ was the first angel to show the way with his miracles; small miracles that saved a few, but affected many. Two thousand years after he visited the Earthly Realm, people still read about his life and his miracles. He lives on in their lives, and his miracles still affect people today."

This seemed to be a perfectly reasonable explanation, but I had the impression that perhaps there was something more, that Gabriel couldn't tell me at the moment. Perhaps, it was something that I would have to learn on the task.

Then came what I thought was the crunch, when he repeated, "This time, Michael you will not be visible. You will observe what is happening and maybe feel that you are helpless to intervene. In all previous locations, you have looked for your rainbow bag of falling stars, the jar of moonbeams, the rainbow wand, or a star in your pocket. But this time, there will be no magic solutions."

"But how am I going to be able to help?" I asked, confused and concerned.

"Good luck, my friend," was the reply, with a wry smile, "Just remember all the lessons you have learned so far and I am sure you will come through again with shining colours."

The Wakahisa family's large apartment near to the Aioi Bridge was very neat and tidy; bare wooden floors, swept daily, sparse furniture made from local timber and bamboo and all the amenities that you'd expect for the family of a senior government official. I had been there about a week, an unseen spirit being, invisible to the residents, walking a soft edge, lost in dark shadows, streaming in on moonbeams, riding in sunlight, just watching and waiting.

Takuma Wakahisa was the head of the family, a proud and diligent man, who had worked for the Prefecture since he had been a young man. He had no chance to enjoy the warm August sunshine and came home late as usual. Because of his status in the city administration, his petite wife, Nosomi was able to stay at home and look after the children. Other wives had been conscripted into a number of auxiliary employments in the city, and in particular into the munitions factories. The Wakahisa family always ate their evening meal together, sitting on the floor around a large low table. Hikaru was nearly 14 years of age, and the oldest of the three sons. He had maturity beyond his age and was always glad when his father came home. He needed a more adult kind of conversation than he got from his 2 brothers, Sora, aged 12, and Hiromitsu, 8.

"How was your day, Father?" he asked.

Takuma answered his number one son with what sounded like a new resignation.

"I have been very busy. Our workload increases every time the Americans bomb another of our cities. We have been at war with China since 1937 and with America since 1941. Supplies are always running short. Many men have given their lives for the Emperor and many women make great sacrifices, but I do not know if we will ever gain victory over our enemies."

"You must not say that, Father! Emperor Hirohito assures us of a great victory. It is written in the scriptures."

"Do not be so sure, my son. I am worried. You will be conscripted into the cadet army soon and I do not want you or your brothers to either die in battle, or be forced to commit hara-kiri in humiliation of defeat."

"Father, we must all live and die for the honour of our great nation and Emperor. That is our way, and it was you who told me so when I was a little boy."

Nosomi was walking in and out of the room from the kitchen, carrying the food she had prepared for the meal, with help from the 2 girls, Nariko and Yoko. They all sat down together.

"I don't want to die in battle." said Sora.

"And neither do I, Father." added Hiromitsu.

"You boys are always talking about the war. Give it a rest now, please." instructed Nosomi.

"Why must we have a war, Daddy?" asked Nariko, "It does seem like a terrible thing to do, to send all our young men off to fight and die."

"It's because the Emperor says we have to." said Hikaru, with some annoyance at what he thought was his 10 year old sister's stupidity.

"He is a very important man and he sits next to God, or maybe he is one himself. We learned that in school." added Nariko.

"That's enough now, let's talk about something else." said Nosomi, "You kids are all too young to understand."

"I'm not!" insisted Hikaru.

"Enough, I said!" declared his mother.

Takuma was pleased that he wouldn't get any more difficult questions. Hikaru frowned, and looked hard at his father. There was a lull in conversation until Nosomi brought up the subject of the fine weather, and preparations for Yoko's 8th birthday on 6th August.

I had watched the way the whole family behaved and interacted for a few days, and despite the many years that their nation had been at war, first with China and other countries in South East Asia and then with the United States of America, they appeared to be a happy and relatively prosperous family. Their values were solid and consistent, as they practiced the Shinto religion, which was heavily entrenched in traditional and ritualistic practices and superstition, and focused on sincerity, honesty and purity.

Later in the evening, when the children had all gone to bed, Takuma and Nosomi were alone.

"You look worried and very tired, husband. Is there something wrong?"

"I don't know. I have a bad feeling. I haven't slept well these last few days."

Nosomi knew that Takuma lived up to his name, which meant "true".

"Tell me what's troubling you, please." she pleaded.

He smiled. "But you don't want me to talk about the war, my little one."

Don't tease!" she replied, "Just say what's on your mind."

"OK! I am worried, because we have reports at the government office, that the Americans have fire bombed every major city except ours. The bigwigs think that they're saving us for something special."

"What does something special mean?"

"I don't know, but I have a recurring nightmare, that it is something truly awful, something nobody has ever experienced before, that will be world shatteringly terrible."

"Do you have any idea what that is?"

No, I don't, and there's another thing."

"What?"

"This apartment has become uncomfortable and disturbing to return to the last few evenings."

"Why do you that? Is it me or the children?"

"No, of course not! You're going to think I've been working too hard, and I'm going off my mind. I keep hearing whispers. It's like the walls, the floor and the roof; everything in the apartment, is trying to tell me something."

"Whispers? What do they say?"

"It's like a warning, telling me to take you and the children and run away, run away to somewhere safe."

Nosomi went to the kitchen and made jasmine tea. When she returned, her husband was propped up against the wall with tears in his eyes, staring blankly into space.

"We must leave, tomorrow morning early." he whined.

"We can't! It will be Yoko's birthday tomorrow. Don't be silly. Here, have some tea and tell me more about your worries."

"Yoko's birthday will still happen wherever we are. We must leave. The whispers are telling me to get out of the city before it is too late."

"Too late for what? I don't understand."

"Just too late, that is all."

"But what about your job? They'll sack you, or worse still shoot you, if you don't turn up. What will happen to me and the children then?"

"Nosi, my sweet woman, I have a government pass. I can do what I want and go where I want. Sure, I will be challenged at roadblocks and sentry points, but all the soldiers, of all ranks, will honour my credentials."

"Where will we go?"

"I've made up my mind. Tomorrow morning, we will walk out of the city to the west and go up to Mount Ohmine, to my brother, Yuri's house in the forest. Prepare some food and water for tomorrow. We will wake the children up early and say we are going out for a picnic."

I am a shadow in the wind; a warm wind on a flat island. It feels like I have been here before. What I have seen, is that in a few weeks, this little island of Tinian in North Marianas, has been transformed from a blood soaked battleground, into the biggest air base in the world.

As I scan the island, I can count six wide, smooth-surfaced runways stretching for miles in every direction, towards the surrounding ocean. Hundreds, perhaps as many as three hundred, massive silver birds line the airfield, all emblazoned with a huge B29 badge on their tailfins. It is a good job that I am just a spirit being. A spirit being, an invisible nothingness that can go where he wants and see everything. Without this protection, I would surely be stopped, arrested, imprisoned and possibly shot. There are thousands of lightly dressed military men here; most of them busy looking after the airplanes, but some acting as guards, carrying automatic weapons. Around me, there is a small city of metal hangars and a village of tents and canopies, with jeeps, trucks and vehicles of all shapes and sizes, moving purposefully between them. Through it all, the noises of airplanes and their gigantic engines, firing up, taking off, landing, taxiing are everywhere.

Suddenly, the ground shakes and a terrifying roar, like an angry flock of dragons with a toothache, thunders in the air. A B29 sweeps along beside me; four enormous propellers swirling like a tornado, on wings so long they slice the air like forked lightning. Even as a spirit being, I cower at the magnificent awesome power of this beast of the skies. The discordant note of the screaming engines rises in pitch, as the airplane forces its way along the runway and up into the sky. Ten seconds after leaving the ground, with the noise at last abating, there is an ear-splitting explosion as the over-laden craft crashes on take-off. Flames engulf the stricken plane, igniting the fuel, and repeated explosions echo across the flat field, as black acrid smoke fills the warm air. In seconds, men stream out from the hangars, like worker ants on a food pilgrimage, as sirens vibrate to summon emergency action. They board fire trucks and head quickly for the end of the runway.

I float into a long metal hut, guarded by 2 soldiers with machine guns at the ready. There is a crude sign on the door saying, "Silverplate - 509th - Top Secret!" Inside it's hot, and there are about 30 men sitting on the floor, being briefed by a bigwig in a smart uniform.

"Men, you all know we have a difficult job to do. The Japs don't give up a square inch of land without a fearsome battle. They are a relentless and fanatical enemy and whilst we respect that, we all know that too much American blood has already been spilt in this terrible war. Our boys have done a great job busting Hitler's arse in Germany. Now we have to finish this war and send our men home to their families, back to the land of the free and the home of the brave."

There was a muffled cheer and all eyes and ears were 100% focussed on the speaker.

"Today, we will be loading 'Little Boy' into place, ready for what may in history be one day heralded, as the most important mission of the Pacific war. What you have seen outside a few minutes ago, with another crew and another plane lost on take off, can't happen when we take 'Little Boy' home tomorrow.

We cannot fail."

He paused for effect.

"Our single weapon for the mission is a simple 'gun-type' uranium bomb. But do not underestimate it. It has terrifyingly awesome power. On July 16th this year, at just before 5.30 am, we detonated a nuclear bomb in the desert in New Mexico. I was at the Trinity testing site for the Manhattan project and saw what this son of a bitch can do. Here's short film clip of what happened."

Everyone in the room held their breath, as a silent film lasting less than a minute was shown.

Afterwards there was a stunned silence.

"Questions!" asked the speaker.

One man raised his hand.

"If this bomb is so powerful, what happens if we crash on take-off? The whole island will be blown into the ocean."

"We are aware of that problem. The bomb won't be armed, and will not detonate if there is a crash on take-off. Nevertheless, that must not happen. It's a 3,000 mile round trip to the intended target, and the plane will be fully fuelled. It's a risk we have to take, because we can't afford any delay in this mission. There are expectations from the men at the top. They reckon that the Japs will guess they're on a hiding to nothing when we drop this beast on their fat yellow heads. Then they'll surrender quickly and the war will be at an end."

A ripple of angst fluttered in the room, as the crew of the B29 contemplated the worst. It dissipated quickly, with the collective thought that without risks, nothing would be achieved to end the war.

"Right, men, let's go and watch 'Little Boy' being loaded into the plane."

I followed the men out of the hut, as they climbed into a convoy of jeeps and made for a corner of the airfield. 'Little Boy' was recumbent on a cradle in a bomb loading pit. Asleep and impotent, about 10 feet long and 3 feet wide, shaped like a fat sausage, coloured charcoal black, the bomb was loaded with painstaking care, slowly and patiently, into the modified bomb bay of the Silverplate B29 aircraft. The eleven man crew then climbed aboard their plane, which had been named "Enola Gay" by the commander and pilot, and then taxied to Runway Able at North Field.

It was 7 am, and a beautiful, bright, sunny day, a great day for a picnic on 5th August. The children had been rounded up and fed their breakfast and then

Takuma Wakahisa called the family together and explained.

"Today and tomorrow we are on holiday," he said with a smile, "Your mother and I have decided that we should go out of the city, up to Mount Ohmine for a picnic, and to visit your uncle Yori. It's going to be a long walk, but it will be worthwhile."

Hikaru frowned and was quick to protest, "I don't want to go; I have cadet school this evening and I really don't want to miss that."

"That's not important, my son. You can catch up with your friends next time you see them. Next week, probably."

"But, Father, it's not fair; I will be letting myself, my friends and the Emperor Hirohito down if I don't attend."

"Don't worry, I will be able to sort all that out for you. I'm a government official, remember, and it won't be a problem, I promise you."

Hikaru shrugged his shoulders, even filled with teenage know-it-all-ness and bravado, he knew that there was no point in arguing with his father.

I watched, as the family made their preparations to leave the apartment. The adults carried food and water in their rucksacks, and the children dressed in their best walking shoes and summer clothes.

Yoko held her favourite doll, Michiko under her arm. She wasn't going anywhere without her best friend.

"Bring something warmer to wear later," instructed Nosomi to each of her children separately, "It will be colder when we get up into the mountains and forests."

"How far away does Uncle Yori live?" asked Sora?

"It's a long way, and will take us all day to get there." his father replied.

"How far, Father?"

"It's about 15 miles." said Hikaru.

Takuma was annoyed, "Schhh!" he insisted, "You didn't need to tell him that!"

"I can't walk 15 miles." said Hiromitsu, as Sora nodded in agreement.

"Neither can I." agreed Nariko.

"Will you carry me if I get tired, Daddy?" Yoko pleaded.

"Of course, my child."

Then the head of the family took a deep breath and raised his voice a little; just that little that indicated to everybody that there would be no further argument or discussion.

"That's enough fussing and worrying. Right, if we are all ready, let's go."

The apartment door was locked and the party headed for the Aioi Bridge, crossing over the longest part of the bridge over the Ota River, just to the north of the island containing the district of Nakajima-cho. There wasn't much military activity in this district, but the river was busy with barges, loaded with timber and coal and boxes of foodstuffs. I floated along with the Wakahisa family. It was a quiet and sunny day. To the south, the river flowed placidly under the bridge, on its way out towards the Seto Inland Sea.

"It seems a bit silly to walk 15 miles to have a picnic," said Sora to his big brother, as they strode along, "Surely we could walk for a few miles, have a picnic, and then stroll back home."

"You are right, Sora, but Dad is insistent on going all the way up to Mount Ohmine, to see Uncle Yori. I would rather be back home in time for my cadet school, but you know what he is like when he makes his mind up about something."

"Be quiet, boys, and just do as you are told. You must do as your father says." said their mother, "Let's have no more argument, please!"

Takuma knew the route he would take very well. As a boy, he had walked all around the Hiroshima Prefecture, and particularly along the trails that led up into the forests around Mount Ohmine. I noticed he walked with a fixed gaze and purpose. It was almost as if he was quietly but steadily running away from something sinister and frightening. After about 90 minutes walking, the group stopped, sat down on a grassy bank by a small stream and drank some water.

There were a few military convoys and columns of marching soldiers, but the family party had been largely ignored. They'd covered maybe 3 miles, and had only been challenged once by soldiers manning a checkpoint. Takuma had shown his government pass, and barked harshly at the head man, who had eventually cowered down and allowed the family to pass. Position, status, pride and honour were everything in this world.

Yoko had begun to cry, "Mummy! I'm frightened!" she said, "I don't like all these men with noisy lorries and big guns shouting at everybody. I want to go home. Michiko is sad that we have left our home today. Look! She is crying too."

Nosomi answered softly, "Your daddy is a very important and clever man. He will make sure that we all stay safe, especially you and Michiko. Don't worry!"

I wished that somehow I could pick up this littlest member of the family, and hug her and stop her being scared, but all I could do was look on in my hopeless and helpless invisibility.

"Surely, Father, as an important man in the government, you could have borrowed a car or small truck to take us up to the mountains. Why didn't you do that?" asked Hikaru.

"That's a nice idea son, but we have to walk because everything has been commandeered for the war effort by the 20,000 troops that are stationed in our city."

Soon the dust and dazzle of the city faded into the distance, as the spaces between houses became larger, and the houses started to give way to crude shacks and summer dwellings. The land became greener and the air more bracing, as they began to climb up into the hillsides, away from the heat and humidity. By the time the sun was at its highest point in the blue and cloudless sky, they had been walking for 4 hours. It was time for a long break in the shade, and the promised picnic. They stopped in a clearing in the forest and quite close to a sawmill. The fresh air had made them all hungry, but their rations were meagre. Nosomi knew that there was still a long way to go before they would reach their destination. She saved some food for later in the trek. The children played and ran around in the forest for a while playing hide and seek. Father and Mother were alone and welcomed the opportunity to talk for a few minutes.

"Will we get there today, do you think?" asked Nosomi.

"Yes, if we keep going. It may be late afternoon or early evening, but we will get there." Takuma assured her.

"Do you feel any better now, or can you still hear the voices; the whispering?"

"I still hear them and they tell me what I must do?"

"And what is that?"

"To be strong and take my family to safety."

"Do you know what is going to happen then?"

"I have no idea, but the voices are insistent that we must not stay in the city any longer. It is possible that we may never go back."

"That would be horrible. I love our home and what about the children and their education. They have all grown up in Hiroshima. They know no other life."

"That's as may be, but nevertheless we must continue on to Mount Ohmine whatever happens. My brother will look after us as long as we need to stay with him."

"So this is not just a two day adventure. You have tricked us all into leaving, possibly for ever."

"Woman, I want no more argument about this. Call the kids together. We are leaving. Now!"

The mountain road fizzled out into a rough track and the going became harder and sometimes steeper, but I noticed the strain that had contorted Takuma's face earlier disappeared, as he saw the city fade into a miniature image in the increasing distance below the hills the family were climbing. They saw no one; they encountered no resistance, no checkpoints, no soldiers; no hindrance to their purpose. Yoko was exhausted and the older children took it in turns with their father to give her a piggyback. Everybody had aching legs and sore feet. There were some blisters which occasionally required cooling in the many mountain streams which flowed swiftly down the mountainsides, but as the day wore on their collective purpose never faltered. As they neared their destination, they began to sing together. They shared happiness in long and joy filled songs. Father waved his hand to indicate a stop.

"We have climbed as high as we need to now." Takuma asserted, "We will have a few minutes rest, and then it is downhill all the way along that little path there to Yori's house."

I had been with the family all the way and now as the sun began to sink lower in the evening sky and the air became cooler, I was so glad for them that their trial for the day was over. Hikaru looked at his father and saw how tired he was. He decided to take charge.

"Right, come on then, let's hold hands and keep singing. We will be at Uncle Yori's lovely house in a few minutes."

The father looked at his eldest son with some pride and he looked back with a knowing, caring smile. Twenty minutes later, they found a cool and fragrant clearing in the woods and a large wooden cabin with piles of freshly cut timber stacked at one side. Uncle Yori was busy, stripped to the waist, washing himself at the pump. The widest grin split his face, as he realised that he was being invaded by the Wakahisa family; his family, who he had not seen in many months.

That night, they all slept contented together in one big room, like sardines stretched alongside each other. They ached in their bones, their muscles were heavy, but their bellies were full from several large helpings of the huge, tasty wild boar stew that Auntie Hanako had made for them.

That day's adventure was over. Tomorrow would be another different day.

It was a few hours after midnight and it was quiet at the side of Runway Able, North Field. The spirit being, that I now existed as, was waiting deep in the bowels of a B29 Silverplate Super Fortress. Earlier on the previous day, the airplane had been named, "Enola Gay" and had that moniker emblazoned on the nose cone. The low hum of distant activity suddenly turned into a tornado of action around the airplane, as several jeeps pulled up and eleven airmen climbed noisily into their mission craft. Then four huge, boisterously loud engines were fired up, splitting the cool night air with an incessant cacophony, before the over-fuelled cumbersome metal avenger taxied along to the end of the runway ready for take off. Tense minutes followed, as the engines roared up to maximum velocity, before the plane rolled forward, and then with speed gradually increasing, strained and struggled to meet the freedom of the skies. Two miles of runway were just enough. There was a collective sigh of relief from all the members of the crew.

I looked at the man sitting in the pilot's seat. Somehow, I knew his name. He was Colonel Paul Warfield Tibbets Junior. He had a quiet, confident air. The responsibility of piloting the massive plane fell easily on his shoulders.

"So, Skipper, why did you call our ship "Enola Gay"?" asked one of the crew, as we climbed steadily through the dark morning skies to the north of the Marianas.

"I named it after my mother, Enola Gay Tibbets. She acquired the name from the heroine of a novel written by Mary Young Ridenbaugh. Enola Gay is the title character of that book"

"Why not your dad? This war is a man thing."

"Well, maybe, but my mother was always a courageous red-haired woman and her quiet confidence has always been a source of strength to me since my boyhood."

"And your dad?"

"Well, he wanted me to pursue a medical career and when I decided to become a pilot, he thought I'd lost my marbles. I did a great deal of soul searching about the change and my mother stuck by me."

We were flying over vast tracts of empty ocean, heading north, north-west and the crew settled back into a long flight, sometimes grabbing forty winks in between bursts of activity, monitoring the aircraft and preparing for their mission. I didn't understand why I was incarcerated in this aircraft and what, if anything, I was expected to do.

I ghosted my way towards the back of the plane. It was more out of curiosity and for something to do rather than just sit and watch.

I noticed that some way into the flight, we were joined by two other planes. They flew pretty close alongside us and as we gained height and lifted over the eastern horizon, in the early rays of morning sunlight, I could see a name painted on the nose cone of the one of them called "The Great Artiste". Strangely, the other plane had no name on the nose cone.

I could hardly believe my eyes, when a familiar figure came floating towards me.

"Are you invisible, too?" I asked, "Or am I seeing things?"

"No, Michael, I'm invisible here, just like you." he replied.

We shook ghostly hands.

"You may remember, that I told you that I would help you with this mission."

"Yes, I'm very confused as to why I am here."

"I understand. You do not know where you are going. So I will tell you. You are in a plane flying to Hiroshima. Hiroshima is the capital of Hiroshima Prefecture and it's the largest city in the Chūgoku region of western Honshu, the largest island of Japan."

"And why am I going there?"

"Why, it's obvious. Isn't it? To accomplish the task that earns you your white star, the final star, so that you have completed the Angel's Rainbow."

As quickly as JFK had appeared he vanished again and I was left feeling none the wiser.

Then I sensed someone moving towards me and saw one of the airmen attaching devices inside the casing of a large black cylinder labelled 'Little Boy'. Sometime later, another different airman removed a series of safety devices from the casing. I found this very confusing. The crew seemed to be lavishing a great deal of attention on this contraption. It was becoming obvious to me that whatever 'Little Boy' was, that what it was intended to do, and the mission to deliver it to Hiroshima, were of prime importance. Then I remembered the film clip I'd seen the previous day, and had witnessed the enormous destructive power of an atomic bomb. It came to me in a flash. 'Little Boy' was a nuclear weapon which was going to be dropped on

Hiroshima. I asked myself a lot of questions.

"Was I supposed to try and stop the mission?"

"How could I possibly even attempt that as an invisible being, a ghost, a spirit?"

I couldn't touch or alter anything. I had no rainbow bag of falling stars, no jar of moonbeams, no rainbow wand, no star in my pocket, and no magic solutions. I was helpless and now I felt hopeless.

"Was it merely my task to watch and do nothing?"

"How was that supposed to be of any help?"

Distressed, I floated back to the front of the plane. I studied the instrumentation. The airplane was at 32,333 feet above sea level, and the time was 8.15 am. The bombardier did his work, and 'Little Boy' was released into the clear skies over the city of Hiroshima. Immediately after that 'Enola Gay' made a steep banking manoeuvre, away from the target area. Then, nothing happened. I sensed that every member of the crew was holding their breath.

The Wakahisa family had woken early, to another lovely bright sunny August day, but now away from the noisy buzz of the city, and peacefully at ease in the forest clearing that was home to Uncle Yori and Auntie Hanako. I watched, happily invisible, in the lower branches of a tall red cedar, as the children played happily. The three boys ran around in the nearby trees, hiding, jumping out to surprise each other, careering around like a mad posse, shouting and jeering, full of big smiles and laughter. Little Yoko sat quietly on a swing in the garden with Michiko on her lap, singing softly to herself. It was her 8th birthday. Nariko was busy gathering wild flowers from a sunny slope at the back of Uncle Yori's log cabin. Takuma and Nosomi had been for a short stroll in the forest, holding hands and smiling at each other. The couple who lived on Mount Ohmine, were employed in their daily chores; Yori was chopping firewood and Hanako was preparing some food for breakfast. The warm blue skies above them were filled with late summer promise. The clearing was surrounded by a diverse collection of mature oak, maple, chestnut and beech trees, standing proudly, honouring the Earth beneath and the heavens above.

This was a small paradise in a turbulent war torn world.

Suddenly, time stood still; and the leaves ceased to rustle on the welcome breeze that drifted lazily from the greenness of the tall trees surrounding the homestead. The forest held its breath, as flocks of birds took flight in panic and flew swiftly out of the trees and headed westward. There was a dead stifling silence. In seconds, Takuma had gathered his family around him as they watched and trembled in utter disbelief. Something strange and fearsome was happening in the distance over the city that they had walked away from the previous day. The most brilliant and intense white light, like a thousand suns shining all at once, filled the skies, obliterating the perfect blue horizon. They all shielded their eyes, and cowered down towards the sanctuary of the ground. Uncle Yori beckoned the whole family towards him, and as quick as gazelles being chased by a lion, they followed him through a narrow ditch that led to a small cave underneath the log cabin. Then, a loud boom like a mountain crashing on to the Earth filled their ears and made Mount Ohmine tremble and shake like the most terrifying earthquake. It seemed that every molecule of the atmosphere was being sucked together and shrunk, and then being hurtled violently outwards again in a reverberating wave, and this was happening a million times in a split second. Then the whole forest swayed westwards in a gigantic arboreal tidal wave, accompanied by the sound of air rushing across the mountain in an eccentric hurricane. Every member of the family lay flat and belly down on the cold rock, hands over their ears, eyes closed, not daring to breathe, dry mouthed and wet eyed, until the noise of a booming that broke the skies and the rushing that drove the wind, was spent. My ghostly presence waited with them, tucked into a crevice in the rock wall.

A short time that felt like millennia passed.

Uncle Yori was the first to move. Slowly, he crept outside, and I floated behind, following him up the incline of the narrow ditch. He still needed to shield his eyes from the light, and the air felt strangely warm in a very uncomfortable way, as if an alien, crushing, choking wind was blowing across the landscape. The rest of the family followed, until they were all outside again, looking down the mountain in terrified silence. When it became possible to focus out to the distance, an incredible, unbelievable sight confronted the family. The City of Hiroshima had disappeared from the face of the Earth, and had been replaced by a raging fire, burning with all the violence and intensity of an erupting volcano. And above the place where the city had been, a massive billowing mushroom cloud was surging its way 10 miles up into the sky.

Takuma began to cry, partly because the home that he had lived in for his whole life had been wiped off the planet and partly because he finally understood why the voices and whispers had been telling him to leave. Nosomi eyes were filled with tears, as she gathered the children around her and quietly explained that they could never go back to their home.

"I don't mind, Mummy," Yoko smiled, "Me and Michiko like it here at Uncle Yori's house."

Then I found myself in another place. Again I was in a plane, a very similar aircraft to "Enola Gay", but all the faces on board were different. I looked around me, trying to work out what was going on. One of the crew was busily occupied wielding a large camera apparatus, as another man was reading out loud in a deadpan voice while writing on a clipboard.

"Warm day, blue skies,
perfect visibility,
8.15 am Japanese time,
"Little Boy" released,
at 31,000 feet.
District Nakajima-cho,
t-shaped Aioi bridge,
target on the River Ota,
over Hiroshima.
Wait 45 seconds until,
detonation successful,
2,000 feet above ground level.
Intense white light,
very loud explosion,
estimated spread 3 miles wide,
mushroom cloud,
10 miles high.
12 miles clear before
shock wave hits,
no damage sustained to our ship.
Fire visible over wide area,
mission accomplished!
Let's head home, boys. "

"I've never seen anything like that before and I don't want to see it ever again." exclaimed one crewman; white faced and shaking.

Another crewman added, "What we have unleashed here today, has wreaked a terrible vengeance on our enemies. I've flown on incendiary bomb missions all around Japan and what this weapon can do makes them look like fly swatting."

He paused, and then added, "Here there has been tremendous destruction and immense damage, a terrifying shockwave, and a wave of intense heat that frazzled everything that it touched. We have created a wasteland. Nobody survived that. History will bear witness to this day having released a terrible irreversible curse on all the citizens of our world."

A third man spoke, "This has been nothing short of a necessary evil. We have been forced to inflict this on the enemy in order to bring a quick end to the war. I sure hope it works and we never have to do that again."

Captain George Marquardt, the aircraft commander, cut in, "Boys, we in Crew B-10 are the 'Up An' Atom' team. We had a job to do. It's killing people before they kill us. That is all! No more talking; it's over."

There was silence for a long time, as the crew settled back into the long flight home, and back to Tinian Island. One hour later, I looked back towards Japan, and could see a spiralling pall of smoke, blackening the skies to the North. Hiroshima, now a totally flattened city, continued to burn furiously. It sickened me, and I floated back into the rear of the plane to contemplate what I had been a witness to. I tried to sleep, but was troubled by the same disturbing and alarming words, that had been repeated over and over again back in Heaven, before this task had begun.

"Oh, fatal day - oh, day of sorrow,
It was no trouble she could borrow;
But in the future she could see
The clouds of infelicity."
He is the bird of ill omen.
How harsh his midnight cry!
It seems to shriek, in mournful sounds,
Death! Death!"

Now at last the words made sense. I had been issued with a stark warning of things to come. Exhausted, I fell into a fitful and shallow sleep. Several hours into the flight, I was awoken by familiar spirit being.

"There are more clues in the book, Michael." said my companion.

"What book?" I asked.

"You know; the novel about Enola Gay."

"What clues?"

"There are many."

"Deliver us from the Prince of Darkness. Deliver us from his fiery embraces. Rather fear Him that is able to destroy both soul and body."

"That is awful!"

"It gets worse, Michael."

"The funnel-shaped cloud deals death and destruction to all that come within its whirling, deadly grasp."

"That's an omen." I gasped in disbelief.

"There's more!"

"The vital question at issue now, is how to remedy the great evil that is about to engulf our moral law and prosperous government. I feel that something should be speedily done to stem the tide of extravagance threatening to ruin every civilized country on the face of the globe."

"Those are truly prophetic words."

"Yes, and Michael, they are spoken by the title character of the novel. Today, another Enola Gay has spoken in no uncertain terms and in the same doom laden context."

"I imagine that there are many lessons to learn from this most difficult of tasks."

"And I am sure, Michael, that you will have quickly learned enough to deserve your white star."

"Possibly! But I don't really know why did this terrible thing have to happen?"

"Michael, Please! Things do not happen. Things are made to happen."

"But wasn't this an awful thing to do; to kill so many people with one bomb?"

"Perhaps, you are right, but don't forget that there are risks and costs to action. But they are far less than the long range risks of comfortable inaction."

"I suppose, in a historical context it will be justified if it brings an early end to the war."

"That is so, my friend, and in the end, we must be assured that victory has a thousand fathers, but defeat is an orphan."

JFK smiled as if to say, "Lesson over!" for the second time in a few days, and then his ghostly countenance fizzled slowly away into the ether.

"Necessary Evil" touched down on Tinian Island at about 3 pm, together with 'The Great Artiste' and 'Enola Gay'. The mission was over, and so was mine.

I returned to the Heavenly Realm with the certainty that I would never look at clouds in quite the same way again. Throughout my trials to earn the Angel's Rainbow, there had been a common theme. Again and again, I was suddenly thrust into a situation in the Earthly Realm, armed only with my beautiful graceful naivety, where something awful was happening or about to happen. Then, I had played a small part in making things better for some people, usually by intervening with stars or moonbeams. But for this task, whilst I certainly had the beautiful graceful naivety, I felt that, because I had been invisible and flitted between many different places, I had been completely unable to do anything to help. That troubled me greatly, but I also felt that perhaps, I had felt some of this confusion before, particularly immediately before I had been sent on this white star mission. Anyway, my expectation was that Gabriel would make all clear to me, like he had done many times before. Sure enough, after a while Gabriel sat down next to me on my favourite cloud, beaming a smile from wing to wing, and just said, "Hello, Michael. I know you have been troubled; so let's talk about it."

"I must admit to being confused, as to why I was sent on this mission. Most of all I am not sure that I achieved anything to earn my white star and complete the Angel's Rainbow." I said

Gabriel explained.

"Perhaps, because you found yourself in different places throughout the mission, it never occurred to you what influence you were having on events. As I have outlined before, we cannot stop something which has already occurred in the past. But we can help people to avoid them being killed or injured. Sometimes, all we do is make sure that anyone who dies does so with a star in their pocket."

"That's all very well, but it still doesn't clarify what I did to help on this task."

"My friend, your presence in the Wakahisa household was the cause of Takuma's unrest. The voices he heard; the whispers that troubled him, both of these things, occurred simply because you were there in the household. You were his guardian angel. Without knowing that you were doing it, you warned him of a coming threat to his family and as a result of those voices and whispers, he and his family survived the atom bomb blast."

"But why the Wakahisa family? Why not everyone in Hiroshima?"

"As I have said before, that is not in the Realms of possibility."

"All the people who perished, died with stars in their pockets?"

"Of course!"

I was beginning to understand and to feel better about what part I had played in the disaster.

"Michael, you could not have been aware of it, but Takuma had some essence of his family's destiny written into his DNA."

"What do you mean?"

"It's in the names, Michael. Takuma means true or truth. Wakahisa means forever young, Nosomi means hope, and the children all have names which illustrate a portent; a sign of things to come."

My confusion began to return. Gabriel explained further.

"Gather all these things together and work it out. Then tell me. Was it a happy accident or some sort of prophetic knowledge on the part of Takuma and Nosomi?"

"OK! What are you saying?"

"Here goes! Hikaru means shining brilliance, and Sora means sky. Hiromitsu means large light. Therefore the 3 sons have names which connect in the context of what happened in Hiroshima."

"That's spine chilling!"

"Yes, and the two daughters also fit the prophecy, with Nariko meaning thunder child, and Yoko translates as child of the sun."

I thought about what was said for a while and things began to slip into place. Gabriel was very patient. He waited, smiling, for me to speak again. He knew there would be more questions.

"OK! So what about my ghostly appearances on Tinian Island, and then alongside the crewmen in the planes?"

"Well, it amounts to the same thing really, Michael. Let's start from the understanding that these men on the atomic bomb mission had a job to do, but they weren't totally aware of the immense destructive power that they were unleashing or the full range of consequences. Then, examine the clues. 'Enola Gay', the words that came from the novel that echoed in your thoughts before the mission, the names of the planes. Do you see the connection?"

"Yes, but again, what part did I play?"

"Michael, you did the same thing. Your presence in those places placed the crewmen in a reflective mood and JFK helped you with that. They would think very carefully about what they had done and what small but extremely significant part they had played in the history of planet Earth. Because of their actions, the planet now forever exists under the threat of a nuclear war and mutual annihilation. In the widest context, mankind fiddled with things beyond his full understanding, but used them for the purpose of saving lives. This was a case of using an extremely wicked method in the cause of saving lives. But unfortunately the action unloaded a dangerous and irreversible legacy for future generations."

Gabriel had clarified and I felt a lot better about what had happened and how, despite my worries, it was now clear that I had been able to help in a small way.

"So, Michael," he said, "You've done it! You have completed all your tasks, earned all your stars for the colours of the rainbow and been successful in completing the white star mission. You have generated pure white light with your dedication and diligence. We are very proud of you and very pleased for you. Your white star will be presented by someone very, very special at a Heavenly celebration, where you will be awarded your wings for completing the Angel's Rainbow."

Book Three

The Heavenly Realm

Never and Forever

Chapter 1 - Heavenly Celebration - No time and all time

Chapter 1

Heavenly Celebration

(Time without end and no time at all)

Michael was sitting next to his angel friend Sebastian and feeling very pleased with himself. He opened his purple pouch and took out the star that had somehow been sneaked into his wallet in Blenheim Circus Gardens. Then he laid his complete collection of coloured stars out in front of him on the fluffy surface of the cumulus cloud where he was sitting. Sebastian smiled at Michael.

Something told Michael that he should start to examine each one of his stars very carefully and closely.

He picked up the purple velvet star that he had been given when he was still living in the Earthly Realm and pressed it into the palm of his left hand. As if by some instantaneous magic, an old tramp appeared out of the sky and sat down next to him. His all-knowing brown eyes were set deep in a worn and wrinkled face, beneath a weather stained cap. Michael recognised him immediately as George O'Donnell.

"Hello, my friend," said George, smiling, "It's good to see you once again, especially now that you're a fully-fledged angel."

The two of them shook hands. George looked deep into Michael's eyes, and said, "I want you to remember always what it says on your first star."

Michael examined the star, and read out the inscription, "Look! Listen! Learn!"

"Do you understand, my friend, just how important this has been to you? You have successfully completed your journey so far, but it is by no means over. For there is always more to see, more to hear, and most important of all, more to learn."

Michael replied, "Thank you, George; I will always do my best to live up to the lessons you have taught me."

At once, he experienced a warm comforting glow about him and felt that he fully appreciated the significance of the message.

George continued, "Do you remember, when you first came to Heaven you were told about the Begin, and what the 5 letters represented?"

"Yes, sometimes that was difficult to understand, but hopefully you'd agree that I got it in the end."

"Of course, you did! We all knew that you would. So tell me, what do you think it means."

"Well, first of all, a beginner is just starting to learn how to do something. That was me when I started out to earn my rainbow stars."

"Yes, OK. And what else?"

"Well, Gabriel called it beautiful graceful naivety, but the full description is beautiful enlightened graceful intelligent naivety. That's all I was equipped with to carry out each of my tasks back in the Earthly Realm."

"Well done. Now! I want you to look through your stars in rainbow order."

As the new angel picked up the red star, he could hear what sounded like a very large crowd of people behind him singing a familiar song, and in front of him he saw two figures come walking across the clouds towards him arm in arm. One man was dressed in a smart grey suit, and the other was a 30 something gentleman, dressed from head to foot in red. As they approached the sounds of singing swelled and grew into an inspirational anthem.

"When you walk through a storm hold your head up high and don't be afraid of the dark..."

There they were; Liverpool supporter, Will McCluskey, and the great man himself, Bill Shankly.

A stream of red stars circled around them.

"Thanks for looking after me that day at Hillsborough. I was supposed to look after you, but it didn't turn out that way, did it?" said Will.

"I was only too pleased to be able to help in some small way." Michael replied.

"We all had a lucky escape, my friend. Unfortunately 96 of our loyal fans weren't so lucky."

"People dying at a football match because of the stupidity and arrogance of the authorities; it's surely a wicked and terrible thing." added Mr Shankly.

"At least justice was done in the end, even if it took 25 years to get it." said Will.

The three of us contemplated together for a moment or two.

"Anyway; to happier matters," Bill smiled, "We are both very pleased that you completed your angel tasks and earned your red star that day."

"Thank you, both." said Michael.

"And I hope that I helped you along your way with what I told you." said Bill.

"Yes you did, and do you know the wise words I remember best?"

Will looked at me and grinned, as if he knew something important. "Believe, and your half way there?"

He said it in such a way, that it came as a question with a smile

"Precisely!" the new angel replied, "Believe, and your half way there!"

The Liverpool friends sat down beside Michael.

Moments later, all the remaining stars that formed the Angel's Rainbow floated up off the cloud and began to dance to the choir's song slowly in the atmosphere above Michael's head.

"At the end of the storm, there's a golden sky and the sweet, silver song of a lark."

As Michael looked up, beams of brilliant white light shot sideways through each star and gradually formed seven perfect magnificent coloured arches above him, each of them a vibrant and intensely bright colour of the rainbow. The new rainbow stretched from one side of the heavens to the other, in the most beautiful full circle Michael had ever seen. Light of all the colours of the Universe enveloped him, and began surrounding him in a glowing golden luminous ball.

The singing continued to swell and grow, louder and sweeter.

"Walk on through the wind, walk on through the rain,
though your dreams be tossed and blown."

Michael turned around towards the choir and couldn't believe his ears and eyes. There were hundreds, maybe thousands of people, all singing in perfect harmony.

"Walk on, walk on with hope in your heart, and you'll never walk alone."

As he began to examine faces, he spotted a man he had encountered very briefly. The man was blessed with a flat nose, huge jug ears, piggy eyes, and all his upper front teeth were missing. A series of wavy parallel lines on his forehead combined so well with his warts and other big red blobs, that it looked like a stave with two bars of a Rachmaninov symphony written across it. The top of his head sported not a single hair, but delighted in oozing a continuous stream of sweat which he frequently wiped with a large grey green handkerchief. Michael recognised him as the Chernobyl survivor, Leonid Kedziersky from Prypyat. Standing by his side, was a distinguished looking man with a prominent port wine stain on his forehead; Mikhail Gorbachev.

A stream of orange stars circled around them.

As if it was possible, the singing continued to swell and grow, even louder and even sweeter.

"Walk on, walk on, with hope in your heart, and you'll never walk alone
You'll never walk alone."

Mikhail Gorbachev's wise words came into Michael's head.

"If what you have done yesterday still looks big to you, you haven't done much today."

Next to the two Russians was a large group of men, women and children of all ages, and in their midst stood an old grey haired man in a tattered black three piece suit, holding hands with an old woman also dressed in black. All the survivors from Auschwitz that Michael had saved were standing there. In the middle of them were Jacob and Magda Bettelheim from Bratislava. Standing shoulder to shoulder with them, was a large man in a thick dark blue suit and a bowler hat. He had puffed out cheeks, and was smoking a large cigar. It was Winston Churchill.

A stream of yellow stars circled around them.

Could it be possible, that the singing continued to swell and grow even louder still, and even sweeter still?

"Walk on, walk on, with hope in your heart, and you'll never walk alone
You'll never walk alone."

More words came into Michael's head; the words of Winston Churchill.
"Everyone has his day and some days last longer than others."

The gathering crowd began to move forwards and to form into a large circle around Michael. The singing reached a massive, overwhelming crescendo and then died away to silence.

"Walk on, walk on, with hope in your heart, and you'll never walk alone
You'll never walk alone."

It was an exquisite, hanging silence; a moment of perfect and wonderful suspense. Then, quietly at first, but moving upwards in volume a new song began. It began with the sweet sound of children singing. All the children who died at Aberfan were there singing "All things bright and beautiful".

"All things bright and beautiful,
All creatures great and small,
All things wise and wonderful:
The Lord God made them all."

In front of them, stood a man in a thick woolly suit and waistcoat, with a wing collar shirt and blue tie. Michael recognised him immediately, and as he did he was reminded of the wise words of Lloyd George.

"Don't be afraid to take a big step if one is indicated. You can't cross a chasm in two small jumps."

A stream of green stars circled around them, as the song continued and the gathering throng joined in.

"All things bright and beautiful,
All creatures great and small,
All things wise and wonderful:
The Lord God made them all."

The song reached a quiet conclusion with only the children singing, and then faded away. Once again there was an exquisite, hanging silence; another moment of perfect and wonderful suspense. Then, Michael heard a violin playing a sad and haunting tune, accompanied by the sounds of waves crashing on a shore.

A stout, dark haired man with a rough woollen coat, a battered black Homburg hat and dark brown trousers, started to walk towards him. Alongside him was another man of impressive charisma, who was tweaking his bushy moustache between the fingers of his right hand. Brendan O'Flanagan and Theodore Roosevelt greeted him with handshakes and backslaps, as a stream of blue stars circled around them.

Brendan was first to speak, but not before the assembled masses had begun to sing again. They sang truly poignant words, as a violin played and spines tingled.

"Nearer, my God to Thee, nearer to Thee
E'en though it be a cross that raiseth me

Still all my song shall be nearer, my God to thee
Nearer, my God, to Thee, nearer to Thee."

Brendan's words reminded Michael of what he had done on that fateful day on board the Titanic.

"Nobody cares how much you know, until they know how much you care."

When he repeated the words, he enfolded Michael in an affectionate bear hug and kissed him on both cheeks. It made the new angel think carefully about the many tasks he had performed when back in the Earthly Realm to earn his rainbow of stars.

"Though like the wanderer, the sun gone down
Darkness be over me, my rest a stone

Yet in my dreams I'll be, nearer my God to Thee
Nearer, my God, to Thee, nearer to Thee."

Then Theodore Roosevelt spoke softly to Michael. "You did very well, my friend. You have achieved the Angel's Rainbow, because you responded exactly to the words I gave to you."

Michael remembered the words, "Keep your eyes on the stars, and your feet on the ground?"

"Precisely! And you certainly did that."

"I had many wise words to guide me, even through the many complications of time."

"No doubt you also remembered then that I told you that nine-tenths of wisdom is being wise in time."

"That helped me a great deal to understand."

"Or if on joyful wing, cleaving the sky
Sun, moon, and stars forgot, upward I fly."

The two men joined the throng, leaving the new angel to listen to the conclusion of the song.

"Still all my song shall be, nearer, my God, to Thee
Nearer, my God, to Thee, nearer to Thee
Nearer, my God, to Thee, nearer to Thee."

Again, the singing stopped. Again, there was an exquisite, hanging silence. Again, there was another moment of perfect and wonderful suspense. The growing choir had gathered in a vast circle of faces around Michael and began to sing a Christmas song. Sebastian placed an arm over Michael's shoulder and remembered an experience they had shared.

Behind the two angels the choir sang.

"Silent night, holy night, all is calm, all is bright..."

In front of the two angels the choir sang.

"Stille Nacht, heilige Nacht, Alles schläft; einsam wacht..."

But all around him, they sang together, in harmony, beautifully, the same tune, but different words. Soon, emerging from the choir, Michael spotted a man in an army uniform; Ernie Williams from Whitechapel and another dandily dressed man wearing his hair in Shirley Temple ringlets and sporting a canary yellow velvet waistcoat over his lace-and-brocade flamboyance. A stream of indigo stars circled around them.

Ernie Williams said, "Thank you and well done, Mick. I enjoyed that football match and made many German friends. We may have been enemies back there in that hellhole, but we are all mates now."

Then Benjamin Disraeli approached him, and said, "Congratulations, my friend, on your triumphant achievement. I am sure that you can recall my words."

"Yes, I did," Michael replied, "Man is only great when he acts from passion?"

"Well done! Those words have served you well."

The song concluded as it had begun, with words from two languages sung in harmony.

"Jesus, Lord, at Thy birth, Jesus, Lord, at Thy birth."

"Christ, in deiner Geburt! Christ, in deiner Geburt!"

Michael's heart was filled to bursting. Yet he knew there was more to come. He knew that his heavenly celebration would not be complete, until all the colours of the rainbow had been represented. The crowd around him had swelled enormously, as the red, orange, yellow, green, blue and indigo stars and the experiences they represented had passed before him. Here were all happy smiling faces, joyous in their tribute to someone who had helped them, perhaps in small ways, but certainly in significant ways. Tears of joy welled in Michael's eyes, as he examined the assembled masses for the next event. The silence, that had so beautifully preceded the arrival of others, was now replaced with something resembling a Gregorian chant.

It began quietly and solemnly, almost sombre. But soon, it grew into a loud and compelling rejoicing, continually rising to a crescendo, and then falling again, before the start of the next round of chanting.

Michael was so wrapped up in the triumphant atmosphere of the singing, while his face beamed at the massive collection of people and angels, that for a while he didn't notice two men sidling up to him.

At last, he noticed their presence, as a swirl of violet stars circled above them. Their faces were instantly recognised. There was Jack Connolly-Travers, a passenger travelling to Los Angeles on both the planes that had been hijacked to fly into the twin towers of the World trade Centre. Michael remembered how Jack had been very friendly and had helped the escape on Flight 11. Next to Jack was the iconic figure of a great man; John Fitzgerald Kennedy, an easily recognisable statesmen of great historic significance, and an invisible friend on "Enola Gay".

The intensity and volume of the surrounding throng's chant began to rise and rise, as JFK looked at Michael and said, "Today is a momentous day for you, my friend. You have proved your qualities and demonstrated the true feelings of your heart. Yours is a victory for the good. Victory has a thousand fathers, but defeat is an orphan."

Almost as soon as he said it, a stream of white stars began to circle around them and two people appeared out of the crowd. Michael knew who they were. Takuma Wakahisa from Hiroshima, who had taken his family up to Mount Ohmine, and the bombardier on "Enola Gaye", Captain James W. Strudwick. They walked towards him smiling, hand in hand, clearly now the best of friends.

For a while, the stream of white stars circled around and above the five men, and then the chant fell to a low rumble, as if to give time to reflect. Jack and John, and Takuma and James merged into the crowd, and there was silence. It was a haunting, pregnant silence. It was a silence deep and impenetrable. The rainbow that had circled and enveloped the celebration in a vast colour filled protective panorama began to disintegrate as if it was formed of icicles melting in the skies. And, as each band of colour dropped away and disappeared, the heavens above gradually and inexorably became darker and darker. Darker and darker, until the whole Universe was barren and starless, was the way. Then it was total darkness; no light, no sound, nothing, nothing but nothingness.

Michael could see no faces, hear no singing; and all he sensed was a familiar feeling, a feeling that he had experienced only once before.

So black and impenetrable was the darkness, that all he could feel was its claustrophobic intensity all around him, gripping him tight like he was floating in treacle. Black, black and more black tumbled over him in undulating waves, squeezing and scrambling all his senses into one; just a pure sense of being.

He was not afraid.

In the blackness, he felt as if he was being pulled and persuaded very gently towards something exciting and new and wonderful, without actually knowing what that thing was. There was no fear or hesitancy or reluctance to go along. He had no choice in the matter, but his being told him that he must submit himself willingly to the dark, surrender to the unknown.

The darkness swirled and he began to fall, spinning faster and faster. He was falling, plummeting and spinning, tumbling forever.

And then he heard a sound, he felt a sound, he smelled a sound, he tasted a sound, he touched a sound; a beautiful sound. The most beautiful sound he had ever heard.

It was like a whisper, "Michael! You are home!"

But he felt the sound - like warm waves in the ocean washing over him; like a cool, refreshing breeze on a warm day blowing through him.

"Michael, Michael! You are home, you are home!"

The sound filled his nostrils with the homely smell of new baked bread; with the essence of vanilla; with the heady perfume of jasmine and patchouli; with the bouquet of Ramey 2008 Chardonnay.

"Michael, Michael, Michael! You are home, you are home, you are home!"

The sound made his taste buds explode with the luscious tang of the sweetest flower dew honey; with the flavour of fresh fish and chips with lashings of malt vinegar eaten by hand from a newspaper; with the taste of freshly ground Blue Mountain Arabica coffee beans.

"Michael, Michael, Michael! You are home, you are home, you are home!"

The sound was smoothing, wrapping his being in the softest velvet cushioned blanket; caressing him in a universe of cotton wool; anointing him in an ocean of the most precious aromatic oil.

Then he saw it. There was the merest pinprick of light and he was being drawn towards it. Ever so slowly it came, like a billion of the brightest stars in the Universe cascading into his being one at a time through the tiniest of tiny holes in the blackness. He didn't see it with his eyes. He saw it with all of his being. A sense of being overwhelmed filled him. All of his experience pulled him towards this growing, glowing and bright fantastic light that permeated his being as if he was melting ever so slowly into it.

And all the time, he was not afraid.

Billions of stars, billions of planets, billions of moons circled his being in a gigantic swirling lightshow. All the galaxies of the Universe surrounded him in a warm protective glow. He was suspended for a moment at the centre of all creation.

When the light had totally enveloped him, he began to sense colours, every colour imaginable. With a whoosh, the colours separated and a huge vibrant exceeding beautiful rainbow spanned the skies. Then he found himself standing at one end of the rainbow. He could touch the colours, and they responded with the sounds of all positive emotions; love, hope, faith, peace, longing, belonging, being; with wonderful smells and tastes, with soft and gentle caresses. His being rose steadily through the space below the rainbow, until he was standing on the highest point of its arch.

He glided through the air like an albatross and saw a vast ocean below him, where placid blue waters were moving quiet and lazy. The ocean rose up into a mountainous swell and he plunged into the depths like a cormorant and swam underwater. He gyrated and tumbled with massive shoals of small fishes. He danced and sang with pods of playful dolphins. He waltzed in the depths of the ocean with families of blue whales.

Then, he fluttered like a butterfly high over rugged red deserts, where the heat of the midday sun painted mirages, shimmering rude and remote, on distant horizons. Then he flew above lush, warm, green forests which spread far past his gaze into infinity. He soared through perfect blue skies among a flock of birds migrating south for the winter, under sleek silver clouds that were floating high and aloof. In the distance, he touched the summits of gigantic white mountains, as they stood like formidable giants, guarding treasures undreamed of. And all the time, he knew he was making his way homewards towards sunsets that were setting the skies fire red and then turning to precious gold, blazing day's glorious end.

He landed at the opposite end of the rainbow and looked back to see the magnificent arch of colours stretching forever high and brilliant across the skies. All at once he knew that he had made a journey to somewhere new and exciting.

All the bands of colours of the rainbow simultaneously disintegrated in a massive blinding flash. All at once, and for one brief moment, the skies grew dark and then billions of stars of all the colours of the rainbow, lit up the skies again, falling slowly in a continuous stream from the heavens, like a giant firework display. A firework display that despite its immensely colourful brilliance, was totally silent. It was almost an eerie and unnatural silence, like the quiet continuous pattern of snowflakes, falling and settling slowly on the ground. And as each tiny star flake landed on the cloud where Michael was standing, it turned pure white. The settling stars gathered under him, until his feet were surrounded by a pure white circular blanket, and from this platform there began to stretch out ahead of him, the form of a pure white pathway. His eyes were blinded by the brilliance, until he could no longer keep them open. Then he heard a soft and gentle voice say to him, "Open your eyes, my son, and you will see a new light."

Without hesitation, he obeyed the instruction.

When he opened his eyes, the pure white path and circle had turned to gold; a gold so intense and gorgeously luminescent, that it seemed to envelope him in something omniscient and all powerful. A man stood beside him in a radiant white robe. The man smiled and embraced him with both arms in a warm and friendly hug. He looked at Michael with steely blue eyes and said, "There is no need to tell you who I am, because you are no longer an apprentice angel. This is the end of the beginning. Now you will become an angel with wings. Welcome to the fulfilment of Heaven."

Michael's heart filled with an immense and overwhelming joy. He said nothing as the man presented him with his final star, a pure white star that would complete the Angel's Rainbow.

Then Jesus looked at Michael, and said, "I don't have any wise sayings for you to remember. There is no need. You have learned very well. What I do have is some wonderful surprises just for you."

He waved his right hand in the air and out of the huge crowd familiar faces began to appear, and one by one they approached Michael to smile and shake hands.

First, there was Eric McClintock, the man also known as Maverick Mack, looking very comfortable in his own skin and smartly attired in his standard light grey Jasper Littman, Saville Row business suit, a made to measure Egyptian light blue cotton shirt and a handmade Berg and Berg dark blue wool tie. His shoes were black Burberry leather. Alongside Eric was Michael's oldest and closest friend Brandon Taylor. He looked like a younger version of his expensively attired boss. The only differences were his pink silk tie and his Jeffery West brown shoes.

Then all the other terrorist victims from the Captain's Table massacre who had been colleagues at, or rivals of, Connor, Hartson and Bromberger Futures began to appear. Andrew McPherson, the right hand man to Bradley Connor was there with David Northcote-Green, the posh kid from Cambridge who had been recruited by Max Bromberger, and finally Michael's bright young Essex boy protégé, Wayne Chandler.

The friends assembled in a joyous group hug, happy to be reunited. As they did so, another older man stood outside the clinch waiting patiently with a huge beaming smile on his face. The group broke up and Michael burst into tears as he saw his father, Edward Hartson stretching out a hand. Edward looked exactly the same as when Michael had last seen him, in the ambulance on the way to hospital after his fatal heart attack. He had fallen out of an apple tree in his back garden and was dressed in grey green dungarees and a pair of green wellies. Michael ignored the offered handshake, and with tears flowing down his cheeks, threw himself into an embrace.

"Well done, son," said Edward, "I am so proud of you. You are everything I always wanted you to become."

Jesus had been watching. He had seen the affection, the friendship, and the tears.

"I must be going now," he said, "There is always more work to be done. But Michael, please do not be afraid to ask me for help whenever you need it. I will always be there for you. My good friends Gabriel and Sebastian will look after you for now."

Gabriel then appeared at Sebastian and Michael's side, and said, "We have two more gifts for you, to celebrate your Angel's Rainbow. Come with us, please."

They beckoned the newly fledged angel away. Then the three of them took flight across the heavens and descended into a blinding red sunset over a placid blue sea. For many moments, the immense brightness did not allow for any possibility to see at all. Michael whispered to Gabriel, "Where are we going?"

Gabriel answered, "We have another surprise for you, Michael. We will allow you a peep back into the Earthly Realm."

"To see what exactly?"

There was no reply, but when he opened his eyes, Michael was standing at the gates outside a primary school in Chelsea. He saw a little boy in a very smart brand new school uniform, skipping down the path towards the gate, where a gaggle of young mums stood waiting. Michael recognised one of the mums.

"I recognise my Courtney," he said, "But who is the little boy?"

"You are correct," Gabriel replied, "The woman you see is your Courtney. She is collecting her son, after his first day at school. The little boy is your son, and his name is Ryan. You did not know when you came to us in Heaven, that Courtney was pregnant with your child."

Now, the emotion of the day suddenly overwhelmed the new angel. There had been so many wonderful and heart touching experiences, but this one had reached a new summit. He knelt down and cried, and cried, and cried. They were tears of complete and absolute joy. Gabriel put a hand on his shoulder and waited.

After a while he spoke softly, "When you left the Earthly Realm, Courtney was pregnant with your child. She had worried about how the baby and herself would manage, but because you had provided for her in your will, she has coped extremely well and little Ryan has been well provided for."

Eventually, Michael regained his composure. Gabriel and Sebastian had waited patiently while he did so.

"There's more, my friend. We have another nice surprise for you." said Gabriel.

Again, the three angels took flight across the heavens, and this time they plunged into darkness; a darkness so deep and vast and impenetrable that Michael felt afraid and began to wonder if something had gone very badly wrong.

"Do not be afraid." he heard Gabriel say. And as he said it, the darkness was broken by a spectacular milky white moonbeam, which the angels began to glide along. For what seemed like ages, they glided all the way to a full moon, shining bright and welcoming in the night sky.

Michael closed his eyes and whispered, "Where are we going now?"

Gabriel answered, "To see and hear some very good friends of yours. We are giving you a unique opportunity to be there, when something new and exciting first comes together."

When Michael opened his eyes, he was sitting in a recording studio. He looked around the room and instantly recognised his old school friend, Neville Waterford. Then, Michael heard the recording engineer say, "OK, boys, let's try it again. All ready? And the band played on, take 4."

Redberryash began to play an unfamiliar song.

"When Charlie's war was over, and the medals were awarded,
Brave boys all heading homeward, in straight lines going forward,

In celebration of victory, or humiliation of defeat,
The incessant drum was echoing, all along the street.

Then Chloe's last show closed down, in the theatre at the end of the pier,
Washed away like the sands on the beach, gone, no longer here,
There's just the stench of cigarettes, and sickly lukewarm beer,
And the drum will not be silenced, by the cruel, cold atmosphere.

Each life is just another song,
A rhythm and a melody, some words you sing in harmony,
And even if the tune is wrong,
If you're singing in a different key, still in the end it's clear to see,
Whether the ride was short or long,
The band still played on.

When the lovers danced their last waltz, and the party was all done,
All the balloons had been deflated, burst and broken just for fun,
All the battles for true love were lost, only greed and lust had won,
Through the triumph and the tragedy, the drumbeat still went on.

When Charlie's heart stopped beating, and so he breathed no more,
Chloe cast her eyes straight downwards, staring blankly at the floor,
She cried with pain so deep inside, as she stood behind the door,
Charlie was trapped on the outside now, just another pebble on the shore.

Each life is just another song,
A rhythm and a melody, some words you sing in harmony,
And even if the tune is wrong,
If you're singing in a different key, still in the end it's clear to see,
Whether the ride was short or long,
The band still played on.

Then Chloe's world was broken, and she lived inside her head,
Not another word was spoken; there was nothing to be said,
She drifted through a wilderness, till her lifeblood dripped no more,
Charlie welcomed her with open arms, when they met on Heaven's shore.

This band has been playing in time since the dawn of creation,
Your ticket for the show lets you go to one destination,
You take chances; make choices, for distractions and for excursions,
You get kicked in the teeth with detours, delays and diversions,
One day you find your time is up, and there's nowhere else to go,
There's no more succour in your cup, there's nothing more to know.

And when the fateful day arrives, for totting up your score,
Maybe you'll be wondering, what was all the struggle for,
But the scenes were written just for you, and you played them from the heart,
And the band will go on playing now, long after you depart.
And the band played on,
And the band played on,
And the band played on."

When the song finished, all the wonderful experiences of the heavenly celebration flashed quickly before the new angel's eyes. He found himself sitting back on the cumulus cloud, next to Sebastian and Gabriel. Michael had a wonderful, fulfilled sensation. He felt different. He noticed that a black light radiated from him, just like it had from George O'Donnell when they had first met. There were still some important questions that he sought answers to.

"Gabriel, thank you so much for your help, but can you spare me another heavenly moment?" he asked.

"Of course, Michael, we have endless time to talk. Fire away!"

"Now that my tasks are all completed and I have earned my Angel's Rainbow, I keep thinking back to when I arrived here with a star in my pocket which was given to me by the tramp in the Blenheim Circus Park. But the big question that remains with me, is why me?"

"Haven't you guessed by now, Michael? We selected you because of what entered your heart after meeting George. We recognised your potential as an angel. You changed for the better. The remainder of your life took a different and more compassionate course. In short, your heart was in the right place."

"But I'm not unique. There are lots of other angels here; millions of them."

Yes, and everybody who leaves the Earthly Realm with a star in their pocket, can become an angel, if they can complete their tasks to earn the Angel's Rainbow."

"So, when I was in the Earthly Realm I was flesh and bones, but what am I now?"

"Why isn't it obvious, Michael? You are stardust, the essence of the Universe that fills the void and gives meaning to all life."

"That makes me feel very proud, but very humble at the same time. Can you tell me what happens now that I have qualified as an angel?"

"There is still much work to do and you are now fully equipped to do it."

"But where does it all end?"

"It ends as it began, Michael. As I have explained in many previous discussions with you, time does not work in the same way here in Heaven as it does in the Earthly Realm. In the Earthly Realm time is a simple linear process that persists only from any person's birth to their death. Here in Heaven we have time without end and we have no time at all. Because of that there are no concepts of past, present and future in a strict linear order. Eventually, however, there will be a Universal Spiritual Impasse, when there will be nothing further we can do."

"What will happen to us all then?"

Gabriel beamed at me with an all knowing smile.

"Let us fly to the heart of the stars,

and be lost in the dust of endless time.

For we are but moments in the fullness of ages;

a fleeting brush with sweet echoes,

sweet, sweet echoes of love."

Appendices

Poems and Songs

Going in search of Angels

Written 24th November, 2000 (adapted 16th September, 2016)
Recorded at Highfield Studios - 23rd May, 2017

One day you may stand alone upon a tightrope line;
along which trod no men of God to leave a guiding sign,
as pages of your history are vividly recalled,
Will you balance there and wonder where all heroes have to fall?

If confusion clouds your fevered quest for any shadowed door
that directs you safely from far wilderness before,
If there were faces in the mirror, you'd know if one of them was yours,
before you tread the endless stair the devil's children scorned.

In the meantime try going in search of angels.
Biding out your time; try going in search of angels.
Hoping to find a lifeline? Try going in search of angels.
Riding blind, try going in search of angels.

Surrounded by the ancient mists that haunt the plains of time;
saved or marooned, blessed or doomed; a captive for no crime,
And if at once headlong you fell before the gates of Heaven or Hell;
until you land will you be damned? Could you be falling still!

That day when you must stand alone and gamble for the prize,
will healing hands in soft caress offer up some compromise?
Will cooling touch of whisper winds calm, soothe or hypnotise?
Will your choice be sacrifice, or home in paradise?

In the meantime try going in search of angels.
Biding out your time; try going in search of angels.
Hoping to find a lifeline? Try going in search of angels.
Riding blind, try going in search of angels.

Promises and Regrets

Written by Michael Haley, between 21st December, 2011 and 8th February, 2012 (Chorus added 5th June, 2015)
Recorded at Highfield Studios - 23rd May, 2017

I was naked on arrival, with nothing to bring,
But hell-bent on survival, with new songs to sing,
Growing into someone with hopes, and plans, and dreams,
When I was so very young, and the world was my pearl,
With my heart on my sleeve; my mind in a swirl,
Impatient and impetuous, but time was not what it seemed.

Now most of my experience is in the rear view mirror,
Reflections and memories as my hair grows grey and thinner.
Now wonder's turned to wisdom and emptiness into space.
Can I content myself with how I spent my days?
Did I grow happy with my lot or just set in my ways?
As time became etched in every precious line of my face.

Sometimes I wish I'd stopped to take a longer look
at some of the good times along your way.
As years and years went rushing by so fast before my eyes -
And the promise of tomorrow turned into the regrets of yesterday.

Did I do it all for love; did I do it for art?
Did I lead with my head or follow my heart?
Can I put it all down to providence or fate?
Will I fall as a saint or stand tall as a sinner?
Can I live long as a loser or die young as a winner?
Am I a fool rushing in or an angel who hesitates?

I remember when my life was still way ahead in view,
And I had so many things to look forward to,
And I held no fear for the mountains I needed to climb,
Then all my days and years went flashing by,
And some of those I love had to say goodbye,
Then I found my mind was playing tricks with time.

Sometimes I wish I'd stopped to take a longer look
at some of the good times along your way.
As years and years went rushing by
so fast before my eyes -
And the promise of tomorrow turned
into the regrets of yesterday.

Separate Heavens

Written 21st April, 2004
Recorded at Amber Studios - 16th November, 2005

Someone opens up the book, and our pages slowly turn,
and as we take a closer look, there's so much more to learn.
Sometimes we follow dead-end trails in the shadows of our fears;
knowing that co-incidence can't be what it appears.

Yesterday's a place that we now think we understand,
and it's no good regretting or forgetting where we stand,
for when it's gone it's history, and can't be re-arranged,
what's done is done, the sun's set on it, and the past cannot be changed.

If life is just a lazy stroll around a crazy maze,
If time is just an instrument for counting out our days;
perhaps you're lost among the mist of possibilities,
or peeping round the corner into vast infinities.

So let's just walk a way together while we can,
and not head off to our separate heavens never holding hands.
Only a fool would bend the rules to return from whence they came;
today's the only way to play at winning in the game.
So let's just talk a while together and be glad;
thank our lucky stars for all the good times that we have.
Let no man steal the song you sing,
let no hand re-write your lines;
you'll never get to your own heaven,
if you ever change your mind.

Only Turning Over Stones (Meet the Spirit)

Written in July, 1998
Recorded at Amber Studios - September 2000

We're lonely when we turn our heads,
Not hearing where our memories echo from,
And then we wonder at times of solitude,
Where all our good time friends have gone.
One day your heart stops singin';
It seems that time stands still,
Now you can stop and look back upon your life
as if watching from a distant hill.
Then it's time to meet the spirit in the sky,
To be gone,
No chance to turn around and say goodbye to anyone.
Why do we try to find the reason why?
There's not one,
There's not one.

When lowly souls just dream away,
Awake too late just howling at the moon,
And sadness waits for cruel fate;
All because our winter comes too soon.
When loves last brown leaf falls from the tree,
And away inside the wind she sweeps,
New snow will fill this window sill,
And deep upon the hill still sleeps.
Then it's time to meet the spirit in the sky,
To be gone,
No chance to turn around and say goodbye to anyone.
Why do we try to find the reason why?
There's not one,
There's not one

Careworn and windblown; it's only mem'ries we own,
Turning over stones,
We all travel alone; destination unknown,
Turning over stones,
Foolish devil-may-care; rising up to the dare,
Turning over stones,
On a wing and a prayer; searching here, searching there,
Turning over, turning over, only turning over stones.

Dangerous Curves

Written 5th to10th April, 2012
Recorded at Highfield Studios - 1st June 2015

I'm driving in my Porsche in the dead of night,
Roaring through the countryside, blazing headlights,
Pedal to the metal, squealing tyres and burning rubber,
Shifting through my gears beyond a hundred miles an hour,
I'm your tail-gater and I'm bringing up your rear,
I don't want no motorways, no straight roads, or low gears,
Want to feel the G-force, the horsepower, and the swerve,
Man I'm just a petrolhead on dangerous curves,
Dangerous curves, dangerous curves,
Man I'm just a petrolhead on dangerous curves,
Running my wheels over dangerous curves,
Showing my skills on dangerous curves,
Moving in for the kill on dangerous curves,
Man I'm just a petrolhead on dangerous curves.

Dressed up in my finery for nightlife on the pull,
Wallet stuffed with ready cash, attitude full of bull (shit),
Not looking for that special someone, no just a one night stand,
No long term commitment babes, no-one ties my hands,
I'm God's gift to women; you know I'm the man,
Got the looks, got the dosh, ain't no also-ran,
No computer dating, can't get what I deserve,
Looking for a lady with dangerous curves,
Dangerous curves, dangerous curves,
Looking for a lady with dangerous curves,
Kissing and caressing those dangerous curves,
Counting my blessings for dangerous curves,

Ain't doing no confessing on dangerous curves.
Looking for a lady with dangerous curves.

I went to see the doctor; I was feeling below par,
Drove there at breakneck speed in my turbo charged car,
He fixed monitor wires to my body and my head,
He umm'd and ah'd, and took some notes, and this is what he said,
I've been looking at your test results, so let's not pretend,
Someone here's been burning the candle at both ends,
You'd better slow down my friend, you been living on your nerves,
There's overwhelming evidence for dangerous curves,
Dangerous curves, dangerous curves,
There's overwhelming evidence for dangerous curves,
Live fast, die young, on dangerous curves,
Won't last too long on dangerous curves,
One day you'll die on dangerous curves.
There's overwhelming evidence for dangerous curves.

Don't you wonder?

Written 2nd August, 2002 & 11th August, 2003
Recorded at Amber Studios - 18th/24th September, 2003

So your mind wanders empty, there's ice in your veins,
Staring eyes cold and angry, see your spirit in chains;
But your heart is on fire crying out to be heard,
Just the way that you play and fine words that you say in your songs;
And you've stood on the edge for so long, just tryin' to be strong -
Don't you wonder? Don't you wonder?
Don't you wonder? What went wrong?

A small voice in your head just won't go away,
You've a choice to take chances, ev'ry dog has its day,
But you choose not to gamble, win or lose, it's OK;
At the point of no return, the return of no point is so strong;
And you've stood on the edge for too long, to be rushing headlong -
Don't you wonder? Don't you wonder?
Don't you wonder? What went wrong?

And so every day I tear out my soul and display it for you to review.
I keep hearin' you say you think it's OK, but not what you're looking for;
So what's new? So what's new?

We all pray for the circle remaining unbroken;
And so may the broken stay unchained and encircled;
If the game's worth the candle, we'd just better play on,
Or put out the fire, shake the bird off the wire and be gone;
'Cause we've lived on the edge for too long and we've gotta stay strong -
Don't you wonder? Don't you wonder?
Don't you wonder? What went wrong?

You know there's only one way that you're gonna pay
the fare that you owe for the ride.
When you've been there before, your heart dropped to the floor
And your spirit's all broken inside.
Outside on your own, Where have you been?
Outsider alone; Still lookin' in;
Cut down to the bone; head in a spin,
Face turned to stone, you never can win,
Just a voice on the phone, not listenin',
For reasons unknown, still wonderin',
Outside on your own, still wonderin'.

Horizon (for Rosalind)

Written 12th September, 1999
Recorded at Highfield Studios - 23rd May, 2017

The horizon is not at the end of your nose,
Or the tips of your fingers, or tips of your toes,
The horizon is set at the end of a rainbow.

In placid blue waters moving quiet and lazy,
In rugged red deserts shimmering rude and remote,
In lush, warm, green forests spreading far past your gaze,
In sleek silver clouds floating high and aloof,
In distant white mountains guarding treasures undreamed of,
In precious gold sunsets blazing day's glorious end.

The horizon's as far as your mind's eye perceives,
It's as wide as the truths, in which you believe,
It's as high as the ideals you seek to achieve,
It's as deep as the sorrow you feel when you grieve,
It's as big as the love that you give and receive.

The horizon is always just out of reach,
It's as bitter as vinegar, sweet as a peach,
An elusive illusion beyond pure extremes,
To bring into focus our hopes and our dreams.

All you can become

Written 20th August, 2002
Recorded at Amber Studios 18th/24th September, 2003

And in the end my friend all you can become
is the sum of all the words you've said,
and all the deeds you've done,
of everyone you've ever met,
and ev'rything you've seen,
the depths of your experience,
and the places you have been.

Your value is in who you are and how you became that way,
and one day you may understand why it has to be that way.

And in the end my friend all you can become
is the sum of all the words you've said,
and all the deeds you've done,
of every blade that cut you,
and every word that soothed,
of all the times your heart stood still,
and the times your spirit moved.

Your value is in who you are and how you became that way,
and one day you may understand why it has to be that way.

And in the end my friend all you can become
is the sum of all the words you've said,
of all the love that you poured out,
and gathered in together,
of ev'ry breath you ever breathed,
and ev'ry trial endeavoured.

And in the end you know my friend what you'll become is not
the sum of all your treasures and the riches you have got.

Your value is in who you are and how you became that way,
and when you understand my friend I've nothing more to say.

Everlasting Light

Written 1st October, 2000
Recorded at Amber Studios - May 2001

Found a fairy circle in the meadow,
Fresh and wet, with new morning dew,
So I stepped inside this magic little spotlight,
Made a wish, and then I thought of you,
Then turned around, one, and two, and three,
Warmed in watery, summer's-gone sunshine,
Sealed the wish into my achin' heart,
And now it's just a matter of time.

Beside a secret garden's wishing well,
Almost hidden by a tangled leafy hue,
We kissed, and then I risked a lucky penny,
Made a wish, and then I thought of you,
We held our breath while waiting for the splash,
Of my penny falling far below,
Until the rippling echoes of the water,
Told me now it's time for you to go.

You left a howling hollow in my heart,
An empty vacant space, so icy blue,
I wandered lonely underneath the tall skies,
Whispered a prayer, and then I thought of you,
Then shivered in the green tree shade,
My broken heart was pounding fit to burst,
I saw a chequered road stretching out afar,
And disappearing into distant dust.

Now a holy beacon shines my way,
A bright guiding light there to see me through,
And as sure as sunset follows sunrise everyday,
I say a prayer, and then I think of you,
Amongst the busy turmoil of my days,
Against the darkest forces in my nights,
Leaving pale and faded shadows to the past,
Towards the everlasting light.

Armistice

Written November 1998
Recorded at Amber Studios - January 2000

My boy's years behind me, once eager and bold,
For King and for Country, for freedom I'm told,
Kitchener wants me, with courage inspired,
To beat down the Kaiser, and save the Empire.

We marched off to war, patriotic and proud,
Girls cheered and threw flowers, bands played long and loud,
But excitement soon done, the ugly truth dawned,
For battle in Flanders, unlearned and unwarned.

In waterlogged trenches, all barbed wire and mud,
Machines guns and mustard gas, wasted our blood,
Deafened and deadened, and shell-shocked and spent,
As four year's of comrades in arms came and went.

In safety remote great Generals planned,
Sacrifices relentless for acres of land,
At Ypres and Verdun and along the Somme,
In savage abandon, shells, bullets and bombs.

Then orders came down, Attack! Boys Attack!
As dark stench of death hung heavy and black,
And choking back tears, with no chance for Goodbyes,
I watched helpless as brave men were blown to the skies.

All the King's horses and all the King's men,
Couldn't patch Charlie together again,

In my pocket his diary to give to his wife,
Not much to show for such a young life.

Today there's a strange eerie sense in the air,
There's rumours an armistice has been declared,
Have the Germans surrendered? Have we won victory?
Is it over for good, or just temporary?

So they've worked out a truce timed precise to the minute,
A ceasefire dreamed up by a war-monger cynic,
In some mad numbers game eleven was chosen,
Fate marched to that standstill. The instant was frozen.

Though sadder and wiser we came home as men,
A land fit for heroes they promised us then,
A fast fading band who fought a lost cause,
Now remembers the War an end to all wars.

Clear September Sky - part 2 - the Answer

Written 29th October, 2002 & 4th December, 2002
Recorded at Amber Studios - 18th/24th September, 2003

Just another Trader's day,
In a clear September sky,
Where the tallest stone and steel trees proudly grow,
Deadly arrow's suicide aim,
For some heathen God-less name,
Sends trees crashing to the streets far below.

The Sand Angel's evil hand,
Hurled a curse upon this Land,
Swirling shadows dark to hide the Devil's breath,
At ground zero's great impasse,
Wise eyes through the looking glass,
Spied the Angel's new name, became Death.

And as long as Freedom lives,
Must we forget? Must we forgive?
Stone-hearted men who bend the lens of time,
For they stand on shifting sands,
May forever they be damned!
For our Lord assured, "Vengeance is mine!"

It's only one small step, just another grain of sand,
From Once upon a Time, to Never-Never Land,
All the castles in the air, all the fallout from the blast,
All the secrets that we keep, all the stones that we may cast,
Still mean nothing in the end, have no reason and no rhyme,
Falling out of Never-Never Land to Once upon a Time,
Falling out of Never-Never Land to Once upon a Time.

Clear September Sky - part 1 - Question

Written 4th December, 2002 & 7th August, 2003
Recorded at Amber Studios - 18th/24th September, 2003

Action and reaction in line forever stand,
Jump from the bridge Oblivion,
Into a blood-stained hand,
Whilst Empathy and Apathy,
Stare on in disbelief,
And streams of tears cascade,
Over waterfalls of grief.

Pandora's Box falls open, and we step back in awe,
And wonder what in Heaven's Name,
Is all this fighting for?
And building in his wilderness, great monuments to sin,
The heathen shakes God's golden gates,
And pleads to be let in.

Young heroes die together, old villains live apart,
We speak of love thy neighbour,
But hate still fills our hearts,
Forgotten or forgiven, dark tyranny endures,
Long memory and swift vengeance,
Are they mine, or are they yours?

It's only one small step, just another grain of sand,
From Once upon a Time, to Never-Never Land,
All those castles in the air, all the fallout from the blast,
All the secrets that we keep, all the stones that we may cast,
Still mean nothing in the end, have no reason and no rhyme,
Falling out of Never-Never Land to Once upon a Time,
Falling out of Never-Never Land to Once upon a Time.

And the band played on

Written 16th to 28th March, 2014
Recorded at Highfield Studios - November 2015

When Charlie's war was over, and the medals were awarded,
Brave boys all heading homeward, in straight lines going forward,
In celebration of victory, or humiliation of defeat,
The incessant drum was echoing, all along the street.

Then Chloe's last show closed down, in the theatre at the end of the pier,
Washed away like the sands on the beach, gone, no longer here,
There's just the stench of cigarettes, and sickly lukewarm beer,
And the drums will not be silenced, in the cruel, cold atmosphere.

Each life is just another song,
A rhythm and a melody, some words you sing in harmony,
And even if the tune is wrong,
If you're singing in a different key, still in the end it's clear to see,
Whether the ride was short or long,
The band still played on.

When the lovers danced their last waltz, and the party was all done,
All the balloons had been deflated, burst and broken just for fun,
All the battles for true love were lost, only greed and lust had won,
Through the triumph and the tragedy, the drumbeat still went on.

When Charlie's heart stopped beating, and so he breathed no more,
Chloe cast her eyes straight downwards, staring blankly at the floor,
She cried with pain so deep inside, as she stood behind the door,
Charlie was trapped on the outside now, just another pebble on the shore.

Each life is just another song,
A rhythm and a melody, some words you sing in harmony,
And even if the tune is wrong,
If you're singing in a different key, still in the end it's clear to see,
Whether the ride was short or long,
The band still played on.

Then Chloe's world was broken, and she lived inside her head,
Not another word was spoken; there was nothing to be said,
She drifted through a wilderness, till her lifeblood dripped no more,
Charlie welcomed her with open arms, when they met on Heaven's shore.

This band has been playing in time since the dawn of creation,
Your ticket for the show lets you go to one destination,
You take chances; make choices, for distractions and for excursions,
You get kicked in the teeth by detours, delays and diversions,
One day you find your time is up, and there's nowhere else to go,
There's no more succour in your cup, there's nothing more to know.

And when the fateful day arrives, for totting up your score,
Well, maybe you'll be wondering, what was all the struggle for?
But the scenes were written just for you, and you played them from the heart,
And the band will go on playing now, long after you depart.
And the band played on,
And the band played on,
And the band played on.

Stardust (Nicole's Song)

Written between 27th October, 2016 and 17th November, 2016
Recorded at Highfield Studios - 23rd May, 2017

Let us fly to the heart of the stars
and be lost in the dust of endless time,
for we are but moments in the fullness of ages,
a fleeting brush with sweet echoes of love.

We've tip-toed lonely shores of an ocean of sweet dreams,
and been found in the sounds of crashing waves,
We are lost like a smile in the trail of the stars,
a stolen kiss from the lips of our Earth.

We've heard music in the mountains singing songs to the heavens,
in the glacier and volcano we've seen ice and seen fire,
but we become humbled in the smallness of our being,
and can only stand and wonder at awesome power.

Let us fly to the heart of the stars
and be lost in the dust of endless time,
for we are but moments in the fullness of ages,
a fleeting brush with sweet echoes of love.

In the cold eye of a storm we have heard whispering winds
We've counted every grain of sand on our small beach,
But we're silenced in amazement at how many stars fill the Universe,
And far too many answers are still out of reach.

Let us fly to the heart of the stars
and be lost in the dust of endless time,
for we are but moments in the fullness of ages,
a fleeting brush with sweet echoes of love.

Mike Haley

Mike Haley was born and raised in Essex, and considers himself to be a true Essex man. He has lived in the County Town, and then the City of Chelmsford, for more than 35 years. His working life was spent in computers and telecommunications.

He bought his first "proper" guitar, a 12-string acoustic, in 1968. He taught himself to play, and intends to carry on doing so until he gets it right.

He has been writing poems, songs and short stories since he was about 16.

Mike is a divorcee who lives alone, and has a daughter Michelle, and two grandsons Callum and Connor. He is an ardent fan of Chelmsford City Football Club, and a regular attendee at many local writing and poetry reading groups. His favourite poets are the songwriters Bob Dylan and Roy Harper.

Between 2000 and 2008, he recorded 12 demo albums of original songs.

He performs mostly solo; one man, one guitar, and sometimes in bands, the last of which was called Redberryash.

Most of his creative emphasis up until 2012 had been in writing songs and poems.

Since then he has written 2 novels, compiled 2 poetry books, and recorded 2 new albums.

"Angel's Rainbow" is Mike Haley's 3rd novel.

Find out more, by looking at Mike's website, which is called "redberryash.co.uk"

You can contact Mike at his official email address: info@redberryash.co.uk

Chelmsford 2012 - Many Hearts - One Mind

A novel by Michael Haley

ISBN 978-1-910104-76-7

Chelmsford 2012 - Many Hearts - One Mind
is the 1st novel in a 2 part series

In 2012 the Olympics came to London.
After 2 dry winter's the government declared a drought.
Soon after, it started raining and didn't stop for 4 months.
The Queen celebrated her Diamond Jubilee.
Chelmsford was granted city status.
And became the First City of Essex.

Tiny was running a small computer games company.
He planned to transform his baby into a global player.
Work colleague, Hugh, was Tiny's oldest, funniest and fattest friend.
He was eating, drinking, and joking himself into oblivion.
Norman was the company's young computer games genius.
He had been totting up notches on the bedpost.
Gordon was the company accountant.
He was a gay activist with his own agenda.

The story up to July 2012 changed all their lives.

First City of Essex - Many Diversions One Destination

Written by Michael Haley

ISBN 978-1-910530-04-7

First City of Essex - Many Diversions, One Destination
Is the 2nd novel in a 2 part series

2012 was a momentous year for Britain, and for Chelmsford.
The year began with a drought, and then it didn't stop raining for 4 months.
Chelmsford was granted city status
and became the First City of Essex.
The Queen celebrated her Diamond Jubilee.
Then there was the Olympics, and the Paralympics.

Will Tiny's grandiose plans for 1stCitySoft succeed?
Will Hugh live to enjoy the fruits of his labours?
Will Norman and Clarisa stay together?
What will happen to Gordon, the crooked accountant?
Will the Vicarage Road gay clique survive?
Is there a future for Duncan and Caroline?
Will 2012 be a special year for the mighty Clarets?
Will the World come to an end on 21st December?

The story up to December 2012 changed all their lives.

An Idea Appeared

A collection of Poems and Songs by Michael Haley

ISBN 978-1-910330-64-1

I'd been writing poems and songs since I was a spotty teenager, and stories perhaps since I was a wrinkly pensioner. Therefore I decided to attempt to compile and edit all of my writings of any quality from the very beginning up to the present day.

Like many of my writing projects, this seemed to grow exponentially, until it occurred to me that the editing and compiling into an acceptable format, was going to take many months of hard work. So in the interim I put together this little collection of poems and songs, illustrating the full range of my creations.

That is how the little poetry compilation "An Idea Appeared" came about.

Perhaps the little collection could be regarded as an aperitif, or an hors d'oeuvres, or even an amuse bouche, but then again it's none of them because there aren't any French songs or poems included. Whatever the classification, I hope you enjoy this little sampler, and come back for more.

An idea appeared

Written 13th September, 1999

When pen came to paper an idea appeared;
at first just a verse, or a phrase that endeared;
Some words in a row that sounded quite clever,
Complementing each other by standing together;
Some lines once refined and a rhyme neatly timed;
a discreet little meter, a sing-song like chime,
Then an idea that swelled, blossomed, evolved,
until all the loose ends were tried, tied, and solved,
and every fine detail was tested and cleared;
When pen came to paper, an idea appeared.

Turning Over Stones

A compilation of poems, songs, stories and recording history of Michael Haley covering the period 1949 to 1998

ISBN: 978-1-911044-46-8

I have been assembling a complete collection of my writings over a long period of time, and when the project seemed to grow exponentially I decided to convert the project into 3 separate undertakings.

This is Volume 1 - a collection titled "Turning Over Stones" covering the period 1949 to 1998.

The title comes from a song which I wrote the lyric for in July, 1998. But it also serves to illustrate the process I have been going through to uncover (hopefully) all my gems.

Volumes 2 and 3 will follow in the future.

All 3 volumes bring together a collection of written work including biographical extracts, poems, song lyrics a recording history, and other pieces of writing. The items are assembled in a chronological order to illustrate the life and times of the author working with words from the beginning in 1949 and finishing in 1998. Each individual creation is preceded by a short descriptive text adding further to the understanding of moods, feelings and attitudes at the time of writing.

It is a fascinating and highly personal insight into one man's life.

Volume 2 will be "Tall Words on a Wall" 1998 to 2004, to be published sometime in the near future.

This title derives from the final song lyric of this compilation which was written on 6th June, 2004.

Volume 3 will be "Walls Come Tumbling Down" 2004 to the present day. This will also be published in the future.

The title just seems at this moment in time to be an appropriate one for what happened in the world and in my life since 2004.

Maybe this collection is a biography or maybe it's a chronology.

Maybe it's a bit of both?

There is a lot more to come in the other 2 volumes covering poems, songs, stories and recording history up to the present time.

Lightning Source UK Ltd.
Milton Keynes UK
UKOW04f2300290817
308194UK00001B/31/P

9 781912 192441